# DON'T STEP INTO MY OFFICE

# DON'T STEP INTO MY OFFICE

### A NOVEL

## DAVID FISHKIND

Arcade Publishing • New York

Copyright © 2026 by David Fishkind

All rights reserved. No part of this book may be reproduced in any manner without the express written consent of the publisher, except in the case of brief excerpts in critical reviews or articles. All inquiries should be addressed to Arcade Publishing, 307 West 36th Street, 11th Floor, New York, NY 10018.

Arcade Publishing books may be purchased in bulk at special discounts for sales promotion, corporate gifts, fund-raising, or educational purposes. Special editions can also be created to specifications. For details, contact the Special Sales Department, Arcade Publishing, 307 West 36th Street, 11th Floor, New York, NY 10018 or arcade@skyhorsepublishing.com.

First Edition

Arcade Publishing® is a registered trademark of Skyhorse Publishing, Inc.®, a Delaware corporation.

Visit our website at www.arcadepub.com.

10 9 8 7 6 5 4 3 2 1

Library of Congress Cataloging-in-Publication Data is available on file.

Cover painting: by *The Monk by the Sea* (1808–1810) by Caspar David Friedrich
Jacket design by David Ter-Avanesyan

Print ISBN: 978-1-64821-149-2
Ebook ISBN: 978-1-64821-150-8

Printed in the United States of America

*for my family*

This is a valley of ashes—a fantastic farm where ashes grow like wheat into ridges and hills and grotesque gardens; where ashes take the forms of houses and chimneys and rising smoke and, finally, with a transcendent effort, of men who move dimly and already crumbling through the powdery air.
—F. Scott Fitzgerald, *The Great Gatsby*

# IN A DREAM

On my twenty-sixth birthday, I wanted to disappear. Instead, I pulled myself together and rode the subway an hour and a half north to the Metropolitan Museum of Art.

I thought I could see something different. Something that would snap me out of the inane, sorry loop I'd been living in. And over the course of my journey, I scrutinized the museum's holdings on my phone, rejecting exhibition after exhibition out of hand until finally I resolved to take a look at the musical instruments collection, which, for some reason I was embarrassed to admit even to my internal monologue, I hadn't before that moment known existed.

I climbed the grand granite steps, paid my usual one-cent entry donation, and weaved through turns and corridors to the allotted dreary alcove, where a wall panel informed me the gallery was closed for repairs.

Immediately I became dubious. When I inquired, however, a security guard was all too eager to relay the story.

—Some fucking guy came through a few months back. I don't know how we missed him. He struck those pretty priceless relics with a hammer. One by one. Systematical. We got it all on surveillance.

—Why though, I asked.

—Some people are just nuts.

—You think?

It seemed as if he might say something else, but the guard stiffly shrugged, then drifted out of sight.

I was nonplussed. Still, my phone verified his report. According to an article, this vandal had yet to be caught, and law enforcement remained at odds in determining a motive.

I cringed, scrolling through photos of rare fortepianos. It really was too bad. I didn't know how to play instruments, and I wasn't particularly fond of music. I'd only wanted a novel aesthetic experience, and I became nauseated and bitter, roaming the hallways full of self-pity.

I glanced over my shoulder. I withdrew a homemade weed edible from my wallet and unwrapped it in the shadow of the *Reliquary Arm of St. Valentine*. Flecks of baked sativa sprinkled to the floor. I tried to catch them unsuccessfully, and I swallowed the rest whole.

Next, I had to decide if I was going to make good on meeting my friends at a bar in the Lower East Side. Alexander, Matthew, and Miriam. I could already see their cheerless faces, and I rambled all the way downtown without making up my mind.

But I felt relaxed. I was getting stoned. I cupped my hands on the establishment's window and thought I discerned their faithful silhouettes. Upon further inspection, it was merely Christmas lights. Everything a bit smoke-damaged. I deferred to my phone.

My mother had texted, *Happy birthday baby*, under a decades-old photo of us. Followed by, *Hard to believe you were ever so easy to tuck under an arm and just waltz away with. Your father and I saw that movie about LA last night. Not really my style. Please give us a call when you can, we miss your voice*

That was ten hours ago, though, and they'd be preparing for bed.

Meanwhile, I hadn't eaten anything but the edible since the previous evening. I touched my lower abdomen. I'd developed a firm, wandering lump. It often settled there. It was worse when I ate, and when I didn't eat. I pushed it toward my rib cage. A low squeal of air moved inside me, and the lump seemed to temporarily dissolve.

—Everyone is gay, someone wailed.

I pivoted, and the bar's bouncer saluted me.

—Kurt Cobain, she continued.

I edged off and sat on a stoop.

*sup*, I texted Miriam.

I hunched my jacket. I blew on my fists. Music trickled from the bar, its door swinging with temptation.

*sup*, I texted Matthew.

I checked my email to confirm our tentative engagement, but my phone said I couldn't refresh my email because I was using too much storage for other things, then it proceeded to die.

I didn't want to text Alexander anyway. He probably would've responded with a non sequitur that was meant to impose some kind of dominance over me. Because I wasn't worth a straight answer. Because I was such a weak, vacant person.

I bought two tallboys of Budweiser from a bodega around the corner, sucked one down, and punted the can. I cracked the other and lurched along the sidewalk, down a flight of stairs to the safety of my solitude, to the subway platform.

It had been forty-one days since the election was called. And there were thirty-one left before the inaugural address.

## DON'T STEP INTO MY OFFICE

These were nasty numbers, prime ones, and I did not relish them. Rather, I stood jiggling my leg amid sticky, dripping, stalactite-like formations deep within the city's bowels, willing the train to arrive. I fondled a hole in my shirt. Like most of my favorite clothes, it had begun to disintegrate, succumbing to time. I sipped my beer. I too was unraveling, and soon the train jerked to my side.

I boarded and sat across from a youthful, angry-looking blond man in a suit. He was throwing back his head, laughing, wrenching his neck to squint behind him at the dark messes of tunnel.

I wore earbuds. The cord extended to my phone, which had died, and with my eyes closed, I listened to the man's damp cackle. His throat chattered like a cat's. I blinked, and he had moved. Now he was sitting adjacent me, though on another bench, separated by aisle and sliding doors.

As light flooded into the streaked windows, he stood up, got off at the stop, marched to the next car over, staggered in, and when the train started churning again, came through the doors marked, RIDING OR MOVING BETWEEN CARS IS PROHIBITED.

We made eye contact. He opened his mouth, but I couldn't understand if he was saying anything. He sat down beside me, leaned in, gnashed his teeth. I removed an earbud.

—What?

He laughed until he was crying and slid away, massaging his temples with his fingertips, cradling his diaphragm.

—Chill out, I said.

—Okay, he relented. —I'm . . .

He wiped his eyes.

—I'm almost done, he said. —I'm sorry.

He got off at the following stop and changed cars.

Sometime after that I was awoken by an MTA employee at the end of the line. Empty beer can clenched in my fist. An overhead display panel said, *9:29*.

For an instant I worried the blond man would be waiting for me on the platform, but, besides the few stragglers already making their way down an exit ramp, it was desolate. I stretched and touched my toes. I accidentally nodded to a couple of cops loitering by the bathrooms. They nodded back like we were cool, and a lady pushed a shopping cart down a flight of stairs.

My back hurt, from being eccentric all week, I thought. I'd been being very eccentric. I was on holiday break, which was a small part of the semipermanent break I was taking from work, life, women, and so forth.

I didn't like stuff. I had nine thousand dollars in my checking account, and I was going to not work until I didn't have it anymore. Then, if a certain production company for doing fashion shoots hadn't folded, I was going to ask my former boss if I could return to it as the person who rented, transported, and inventoried camera and lighting equipment.

The plan was airtight, in that, if I didn't get the job, I'd find another one, or I wouldn't, and fate would proceed from there.

Outside, the wind blew off my hat. It was a beanie with the letter H on it, and I jogged to retrieve it, making my way under a shining black sky toward the beach.

I'd moved to the beach two months earlier, because my friend Sam, who'd lived by the beach, was moving upstate to have a child with his second wife. I hadn't given it much consideration. I didn't like having roommates. Sam's apartment couldn't accommodate roommates, and I could afford it, so I'd taken over as tenant.

I watched a raccoon roll a trash can across the sand. I watched roller coasters do nothing in the ashen glow. Something was burning, and every now and then the soft roar of an airplane sparked overhead.

Birthdays are all right, I thought. But I wanted everything to be different.

My mother had labored three calendar dates, among the shortest of the year, with barely a sunrise to kindle her. And still she'd managed to guide me through those smallest breaks of darkness.

Ostensibly, I figured, I existed. Birthnights seldom got their due. And for those of us delivered in the flickering shrieks of the witching hour, I thought, this Bud's for you. I was fresh out of beer, though, so I toasted my new lease on life by spitting at the ocean.

I was famished. A second elapsed when I thought I might be sick. I grabbed the boardwalk railing to steady me. I needed to see the tide, the jetties, the gleam of minerals.

I darted over the strand and climbed an inky rock, enticed by the sound of the bay. Moss and algae came away and settled beneath my nails. A barnacle tore the ass of my jeans.

—I'm smart, I said.

Clouds parted. The moon showed its waning gibbous. It had been a week since full illumination, and my mania was receding in tandem.

I extracted a pale glob of mucus from my sinus and imagined the ensuing several days, curled in on myself. Glints across screens. Flecks of indica. I owned more than six heavy blankets. Maybe I'd sleep right through to the new year.

And this glad prospect diminished my hunger, but not enough. I had popcorn and coffee at home. I was ready to surrender. I slid down the rock and let the barnacles express themselves.

Streetlights sprang like buoys, where the water lacked them. I dragged my feet in their direction.

I was halfway to the boardwalk when I heard the scream.
—Oh fucking god, it howled.
Shadows twisted down the shoreline toward my building.
—Just stop, it choked.
I was stoned, plausibly a tad drunk, and this type of thing takes moments to react to. And moments are precious.
Then the sounds got atypical. I couldn't distinguish them from machine, music, or animal, but I found myself sprinting closer. Throbbing racked between my ears. My chest pierced with icy shards. I was out of shape, and though the action, some slamming or gouging of a sharp or blunt object in downward repetition, was less than a hundred yards away, by the time I approached, it was done. The assailant departed so rapidly. In glaring obscurity. Refracted by light. Just a flash of recognition, and a ravenous slavering.
Actually beholding the body required something else. At first I didn't understand it was a person. In the moonlight, it looked like a pile of potatoes, putrid and sprouting pell-mell.
There was blood on its face. Its arms looked like its face. It had been badly beaten, and slashes were swelling in the frozen air. They were clotting, black and gray and green and brown and black. The mouth sputtered.
—Are you okay, I said.
The mouth frothed. Liquid and gruff. The eyes were swollen shut. The eyelids had yellow fluid on them. One of the ears was severely enlarged. The nose was sideways, pulped into the face. The stomach spasmed. The body sloughed blood.
—What's your name, I said.

The sounds were awful.
—Should I call the cops?
It sort of coughed.
—How many fingers am I holding up?
Convulsions of some type.
—I'm going to call the cops, I said.

My hand went in my pocket. It dropped my phone in the sand and picked it up and punched buttons. I clawed at the screen.

I tried to turn my phone on for a while before I remembered it had died outside the bar. I tried to turn it on for a while after that too.

—Fucking A, I said.
The body was, like, dying.
—Are you going to be okay, I asked.
—*Arrjgghchuuuluu*, it replied.
—Um, I said.

I started to cry. I looked at the boardwalk, the lights. Nothing happened. A plane sparked overhead.

—What should I do, I said.
—*Bsssdduhh*, echoed back.
The wheels of expiration were in motion.
—Oh god, what's your name?
I kicked the sand. I jumped a couple times.
—Fucking goddamn it, I cried.
I ran toward the boardwalk. Then I ran back to the body.
—How do I make sure you don't die?
It was silent.

I don't remember a lot between then and getting home except that I kept dropping my keys.

I know it would've been about an eight-minute walk, which means, running, I could've done it in three. But I can't remember if I ran or not.

There were gutters on the block between the beach and my apartment. At some point, I was on my knees, vomiting into one. My keys fell out of my jacket pocket and balanced on the grate. I thought about how lucky I was.

I picked them up and dropped them on the grate, and they balanced again. I picked them up and dropped them under a parked car. I picked them up and dropped them in a puddle.

With snot running down my chin, weeping, I allowed myself to entertain the possibility that this key situation would go on forever. I dropped them a lot of times outside the door to the courtyard surrounding my building.

There was an amorphous tree that one of the residents had decorated, and feral cats huddled under it, eyes glittering. I never looked behind me.

Five lunges later, and I was inside, instinctively checking my mailbox. There, I discovered some greeting cards, as well as the power to change my mind about what had happened entirely.

I ascended the stairs, let myself into my unit, stripped naked, and lay on a rug by the radiator.

My apartment consisted of three rooms: the one I was in, the bathroom, and the kitchen. There were books on the shelves and tchotchkes on the books and a few boxes I hadn't bothered unpacking. I kept a portable radio in the kitchen. And I could see all of this, everything that belonged to me in the world, from where I'd plunged.

I rolled onto my back. Above the front door hung a gold plaque, which I'd discovered mostly buried in sand the week prior. I'd been taking a walk, not so unlike the one I'd lately returned from, when its gilded corner caught my eye.

It had shimmered in the dying sunlight. It had winked at me. And I'd seized the opportunity, abducted it and pounded a nail through the flimsy metal and crown molding.

It was about the size of an envelope, the kind of nameplate you might find affixed to an assistant professor's cubicle. But instead of a title or denomination, it said simply, MY OFFICE.

I admired the sign. It dangled above my domain. But I hadn't decided if it belonged to me yet.

My cat, Turmeric, strutted in from the kitchen and moved against my body, alternating cloying purrs and mews of hunger. I smelled vomit in my nose and on my face and through the sodden clothes next to me.

—Hello yellow, I said.

Turmeric let out a pathetic whine and sauntered off. I put my face in the rug.

Still, time renders all will-less, and sooner or later I found my bones limping to the kitchen, depositing a pat of wet food in Turmeric's bowl.

—I say, I said, pitching over her, modifying my tone into that of an exaggerated pass for a Cockney accent. —Better'n a paddling on the fanny, you bloody ingrate . . . in'it?

While Turmeric devoured the slop, I poured myself a glass of kombucha mixed with gin from a carafe in the fridge, escorted my cocktail to the tub, and drew a scalding bath.

I washed my face, brushed my teeth. I picked spew from my nostrils. I needed to think. If I plugged in my phone, there'd be more options. While it stayed dead, I could do only so much.

I lit a candle and flicked off the ceiling light. I propped my highball on the rim of the basin and slithered in, submerged to my neck. I felt my abdomen. The lump was there, but less prominent. I pushed at it. Bubbles broke on the bathwater's surface. I laughed, then stopped.

What should I do, I thought. And how long had passed since the murder?

Then I interrupted this thought with another: if that's even what it really was!

Because maybe what I'd witnessed had not indeed been a murder. Maybe it was a basic case of desecrating a dead body! Maybe the slavering figure hadn't even killed it but unwittingly stumbled across it! Maybe the person had done that stuff to him or her or themself! Or maybe it wasn't a person! But a dummy! Maybe I'd hallucinated it all! Though I didn't think so.

So I entertained the dummy explanation, why not? It could've been a dummy with a tape recorder. Or special effects, the remnants of a low-budget horror film. An imitation. A trick! Maybe some sicko had been gunning to entrap a person like me into thinking they'd happened upon some vestige of genuine violence! Surly true crime havoc! A social experiment! Maybe I had been chosen! Pursued! Documented! The whole experience! My reaction surveilled, transposed to a sliver of data! My vulnerable status, my utter traumatic beguilement only piecework in an unprecedented and inconceivably convoluted investigation! A classified black ops program! A dissertation on gore itself! My grim dread may have been but a brick in the bona fide terror matrix! Maybe I was the dummy! Maybe I was being targeted! This very moment! Right now!

But that didn't seem right either. So what about desecration? What if the body had been kidnapped from a cemetery or morgue? Or the product of your garden-variety waterfront suicide? And the slavering figure was, like, only some pervert who'd wanted to take a stab at a dead corpse? Wouldn't I just be adding to the perplexity by reporting it? Would I really be making stuff more lucid for the cops, whom I already detested on principle, by presenting them with my interpretation of an event I'd hardly beheld in the first place? Perceived under the influence of alcohol, and an illegal substance to boot? And if this were the case of some deviant indulging his or her or their own kinks with a previously deceased vessel, did I even really care? Wasn't I, self-proclaimed eccentric, somewhat as debauched in my own tastes and fancies as any other freak? More or less? And, given the pretense of the question, then, should it really fall on my shoulders? This burden of passing judgment? Had the world ever been fair or clear-cut?

I ran my fingers through the water. I took a sip of kombucha and gin.

How much time had passed was irrelevant to my verdict. Grasping authorities would tell themselves their own stories. Perhaps they already were. So why should they be rewarded with intelligence for which I could scarcely account? In fact, as logic followed, should they not be exactly the last party privy to it, cloaked in bias, proven time and again to be the least impartial of critics, considering there was nothing they could do short of inciting hysteria and squandering tax dollars? How many cases like this ran a risk of eventual designation within the sphere of quote-unquote repeat offenses anyhow? Were they not almost always the one-off results of hot-blooded disagreements between people who'd known and, probably, at least at one point, loved one another? Was the inevitable guilt of the perpetrator who'd spend the rest of his or her or their life hobbled by the weight of transgression not enough? Unless, of course, they were a psychopath and ergo free of guilt. At any rate, was it as though the supposed murder would retroactively find itself prevented by way of a handful of NYPD personnel knowing about it?

—No, I said.

And wasn't it nice to have landed on an unambiguous answer?

So even if it were a murder. And really, I had no way to be sure. No way to know at all. What was done was done. It would've been totally inconvenient to go about involving myself. I'd involved myself enough.

I drained the tub, stepped into long underwear and wool socks, and plugged in my phone. I brought the greeting cards to my bed, where Turmeric was balled up waiting for me.

I opened one from my paternal grandma, unsigned, and who would die five months later. A fifty-dollar bill fell on the sheets. I opened another from my parents, who, in spite of my mother's appeal that I reach out to them, had gone ahead and called me anyway while I'd wallowed through the Met, and whose ring I'd blithely ignored. I opened a card from New York University, where I'd expended four enchanting years. They hoped I'd find it in my heart to contribute a gift that giving season.

This flat stack of well wishes warming my lap, I fell into an ancient, sarcophagal sleep.

I was so hungry. Someone was knocking at the door, and I hadn't eaten anything other than the weed edible in more than forty hours.

The lump sizzled. It fermented inside me. My phone said, *12:13*, and I folded blankets off one at a time.

I'd been dreaming of an enormous matte black magazine with legs and that you could walk on. It kept arching its back.

You needed a bunch of people to flip a page, but I was too demure to ask for help.

—Just a second, I heard myself declare, tinny and feeble among cresting caffeine withdrawal.

Turmeric was digging in her litter. I scooted across the room and tripped the lever on the aluminum box enclosing the front door's peephole.

Through its fisheye lens, I saw two cops in thick blue coats and earmuffs. One was turned to the other.

—Banana fritter, he said.

The other stared at the glass. I wondered if the lever system was ascertainable on his end. I turned the dead bolt and swung the door open an inch before it caught on the chain.

—Sorry, I said.

I closed the door, unhooked the lock, and opened it again.

—Sorry, I repeated.

—Mr. Garlicker, the one who hadn't said banana fritter said. He said it as a question.

—Yes?

—Mr. Jacob Garlicker?

—That's right, I said. —What's up?

—May we come inside?

The banana fritter one was quiet. He took his phone out, started scrolling.

—Um . . . Sorry, like, but can I ask why?

—Well, to be frank, we've got some sensitive business we'd like to discuss with you . . . and we'd prefer to discuss it with discretion.

—Uh, I said.

I looked over my shoulder. The sour mound of vomit clothes was under my antique love seat.

—Well, actually . . . if it's all right with you, I'd rather talk in the hall. If that's okay.

Neither said anything.

—Unless, like . . . Unless you have the right to come into my apartment without me inviting you in.

—We don't, the banana fritter one averred.

—Terrific, I said. —Can you hold on a second?

The door closed. I went momentarily blind. I held on to something. I waited to pass out or not.

I was having thoughts. The kinds of thoughts anyone might have in this situation. Some of them became mine. And I donned a ratty sweater and my beanie with the letter H on it.

I felt bad, remembering my father. The hat was because of him, and I shuffled into flip-flops, grabbed my keys, and stepped into the hallway, where the banana fritter cop was showing the other his phone.

—Gourmet, he said.

—Mr. Garlicker, the non-fritter cop asked again.

—Yeah.

—I'm Detective Powell, he said. —Homicide division.

He offered his hand, and I shook it.

—This is Detective Winston.

Winston clasped my hand with the one he was holding his phone in. I wanted to deliquesce.

—You're not in trouble, Powell said.

—Oh, I swallowed. —Good.

—Everything okay?

—Sorry, I said. —Sorry, like . . . I don't know?

—You nervous, Winston asked.

—I think, like, anyone would be.

—Not if you haven't done anything wrong.

—Actually, I said. —I feel, like, because of the sociopolitical us-versus-them climate that's been established over the past several decades, beginning with the expansion of a more militarized and ubiquitous visibility since the Giuliani administration and erection of the Department of Homeland Security, it's fairly typical for people to feel uneasy around, uh, like . . .

I panted.

—Not if you haven't done anything wrong, Winston said.

—Um . . .

—You on anything, Mr. Garlic?

—Listen, Powell said. —I don't care if he's riding a crack moose. We're here because . . .

He breathed and rubbed his forehead theatrically.

—Can we see some ID, Winston said.

—You don't have to show us ID, Powell said.

—How do we even know this is Garlicker?

—He's in his apartment. He says he is. That's not what we're here . . .

—ID, Winston insisted. —Let's see the ID, pal.

—Mr. Garlicker, Powell said.

—It's okay, I said, wheezing a little. —No, like, if it makes it easier, I don't care. Hold on, will you guys hang tight out here?

I didn't wait for an answer and unlocked the door. Turmeric wanted to put her head in the hallway. I had to use my shin to guide her elsewhere. I had to be careful to look like I wasn't abusing her maybe.

The latch caught. I was desperate. I got on my knees, pulled my jeans from under the love seat. The love seat had animal paws for feet. I reached in my back pocket, retrieved my wallet, removed my driver's license.

My entire body twitched, handing the cops the ID. And a beat happened, where it didn't seem like they knew the protocol of who should preside over this. Then Powell took it, and he did something with it with his phone. He handed it to Winston, who did the same, then handed it back to Powell, who handed it back to me.

—Thank you, Winston said.

—No problem, I answered.

They were typing, scrolling. I tried to take my phone out to check my email, but it was on my bed. Someone in one of the other units was listening to classical music.

—All right, Powell said. —Thank you, Mr. Garlicker.

—You're welcome.

—Happy birthday, Winston said.

—Oh, I smiled. —Thanks.

—What kind of a name is that, anyway?

My eyebrows started working of their own volition.

—Just . . . a . . . normal one.

—You sure you wouldn't feel more comfortable talking inside, Powell asked.

—Uh . . . yeah, I said. —I think this is fine.

—Because, he trailed off. —Discretion . . .

—It's okay.

—Well, then, Powell sighed. —We're here to investigate a murder.

I tried to sense if my face had crumpled.

—Are you familiar with a Lauren Smith?

—Uh, I said. —I don't think so?

—She's your downstairs neighbor, Powell said.

—She *was*, Winston interrupted.

—Jesus, I said. —I'm . . . no . . . I don't know . . . I wouldn't know her by name.

A pigeon landed on the ledge of the hallway window. I wanted it on my team.

—There are, like, eight apartments in this building, and . . .

Powell retrieved a small, professionally done headshot of a generic-looking girl. I sort of recognized her, though I probably wouldn't have under better circumstances.

—This is her, he said.

—Okay.

—This isn't her only place. She appears to have maintained a lease at at least one other address.

I nodded.

—This is more of a getaway type spot, it would seem. Most of the unit had been converted to an art workshop.

—Damn, I said. —That's cool. I didn't know there were any artists in this building.

—Are you an artist, Winston asked.

—Um . . .

—What do you do for a living?

—Well, technically I'm unemployed right now.

Both cops typed on their phones.

—But my first novel manuscript is being considered by an important agent . . .

I waited.

—Sofia Cutler, I said. —A literary agent.

Powell showed me the photo again.

—Have you at all, in any way, been acquainted with this woman?

I took a moment before answering. I thought about the words, pictured them in my head.

—I do recognize her, I said. —But only from living here.

—How long have you lived here?

—About two months.

—Have you, in those two months, had any one-on-one encounters with the victim?

Winston plugged a pair of earbuds in his phone. He put one of the nodes to his skull.

—I don't think so.

They didn't say anything.

—I mean, she didn't live directly below me. The guy who does told me to stop clomping around so much a few weeks after I moved in . . . so I know him better.

—Who is he, Winston pried.

—He's, like . . . I don't know his name.

—Have you witnessed any events you might view as out of the ordinary, Powell asked.

I pretended to think.

—No.

—What about noises? Arguments, objects breaking? Residents leaving at weird hours?

—I really don't know. I try to keep to myself. I don't, like, like to involve myself in other people's . . . stuff.

—Noted, Winston said.

—Well, all right, Powell hemmed. —Is there anything else you'd like to tell us? Anything at all that might help us better understand what happened or lead us in the direction of who may be responsible for this?

—What exactly did happen?

—That's on a strictly need-to-know basis, Powell rejoined.

—Do I . . . need to know?

—It does not appear that you do.

—Is there a, like . . . killer on the loose?

—Why would you ask that, Winston said.

—Out of... concern... for myself?

—These things are usually pretty isolated, Powell stated. —Almost exclusively.

—Was, she, like... Was she killed in this building?

—Now, Winston interrupted Powell before he could respond. —Don't you think you would've been a little more aware of the situation had that been the case?

—I don't know, I said. —I guess it depends.

—Depends on if you were on anything?

—What, I stammered.

I looked at the ground. I was maybe by definition starving at that point, burning calories my body couldn't afford.

—Here, Powell said.

He handed me a piece of paper.

—My card.

—Here, Winston said.

He handed me an identical piece of paper. Both cards had Powell's name and contact info on them. I didn't want to say anything.

—Thanks, I said.

—Give us a call if you think of something, Powell said. —Whatever you believe might be relevant or helpful... would be relevant and helpful.

—Thanks, I hesitated. —I'll do that.

—Have a wonderful day, Mr. Garlic, Winston said. —And happy Chanukah.

He showed a flurry of squat, bisque teeth and put a Yankees cap over his earmuffs. They went down the stairs without talking, not stopping at anyone else's apartment. I listened for the door to the courtyard to click.

How rapt a body can get in anticipating sound. This one proved to be as underwhelming as that of a stranger in a restaurant hawking up a hunk of meat, and I stood in front of my unit, propping it open with my flip-flop.

I stuck my arm around the door and pawed blindly for the aluminum box. I wanted to see if an outside observer could ascertain the peephole lever system.

I tripped it. The shade retracted against an ache of hissing metal. Light flashed into the lens. Clearly, anyone paying attention would have no problem at all. This demonstrated a distinct flaw in the very nature of a peephole.

What was the world even for, I thought.

The words rebounded about my echo chamber as I disrobed, step-by-step, through the four it took me to get back into bed.

# THURSDAY

The sky was smudged blue and ash. The sun tried to set behind lavender clouds and orange dust and it kept changing perspective as our ferry plummeted southwest, as though it, the old star, felt confused.

We'd barely undocked when the boat started to rattle. I looked up from my frayed, heavily annotated copy of *The Great Gatsby* I was not really reading and rolled it into a cone. Black belches of smoke were escaping some hatch pipe on the upper deck.

I'd ridden this route, perhaps this very vessel, dozens of times. I sat alfresco when weather permitted, and it had never shaken like this. The wrought iron pole of a tower viewer with its binoculars detached shivered in its foundation. Car alarms exploded from below. Buoys tossed in the harbor. Water surged white-green furrows.

But no one was reacting. They were looking at phones, taking photos, wresting dogs by their necks, leisurely talking, so I decided not to worry.

In the wake, I watched the little city in which both my parents had been born and raised shrink away. I saw the churches and rail yard, the parking lots and prison and electric and nuclear power plants, the scorched trees and wastewater facility fade in the atmosphere.

I kept my eye on the free-floating red brick lighthouse that marked the end of the river and the beginning of the sound. I watched it get bigger until it was precisely in front of me. It was one hundred and thirteen years old. It bobbed through time. Lights flickered within.

When it too was out of sight, I realized the rattling had stopped. No more smoke spewed from the ferry. The sky appeared muddier.

My wife was inside, by now hopefully finished being frustrated that we hadn't had time to stop and get her an Italian ice, her heels propped on the cat carrier, forearm snarled by a rope harnessed around our dog's torso.

Her parents and their house and their topiary and their reactions and memories and their colleagues and nemeses and friends awaited us across the inlet. Darkness fell. I couldn't see.

I closed my eyes and thought about the island. Despite the hoops one was required to jump through to get there, it was so quiet, sumptuous and jammed with natural-seeming beauty, clean-smelling air, dense foliage.

It was worth the drama. And I didn't belong. No matter how much I relished it, that easternmost county of the Empire State had a way of imposing my alienness. The shy shaded eyes of the ladies on the shoreline. They reclined, buffed and rebuffed, oblivious to it all, the terror world, and its missing pieces, the increasingly hostile status quo of the lesser nine months.

Skin changed with the sun and the sand. It protected them. Everyone was vulnerable, but some people had better defense mechanisms. Or it was something like that.

In the middle of my thirty-third year, I tugged at my collar. I burped. I itched. All my clothes were different. And everything that had happened in every person's life skidded behind me as the wind blew off my hat.

It was a canvas bucket hat with the letter H on it. It had belonged to my father. I'd grabbed it off a pegboard in the basement of my parents' abandoned Rhode Island condominium hardly an hour earlier, and already it was tumbling away.

I feigned an attempt to go after it, but was really only acting as a witness, resigned to all futility. Resigned and filled with fervor, permitting whatever the world needed to happen to take place.

I watched, vision adjusting to the dimness, as it toppled over itself through a gust and came to rest against the scaled liver spots of a varicose-veined shin. An ancient hag, seated along a blue bench, leaned deeper in her irrevocable hunch, grasping the brim between gnarled fingers adorned with heavy rings.

She examined the H with approval. I moved toward her, nodding. My lips pulled back.

—Very impressive, she croaked.

—Thanks.

—You wouldn't know it, but I'm one of the world's leading experts on the Protestant establishment.

—You don't say, I said.

She managed some kind of flourish, transporting the upper half of her body against the bench back, my hat pummeling in the salty breeze.

—Life is full of surprises.

—Don't I know it, I agreed.

She appeared to consider something.

—To where are you destined?

Her tone was wily. The faint rumble of car alarms.

—The Hamptons, I answered.

—It's far less gauche to call it Long Island. Or even better, out east.

—But we're . . . traveling south.

—Don't get fresh, she snapped.

The woman handed me my hat, looking away into the opaque wall of murk, which became little spots of light as we began to approach the coast.

—Thank you, I said.

She took out a handkerchief like she was inspecting it for flaws.

—The natives called it *Paumanok*. The island that pays tribute. But it's not the island that pays, now is it?

I paused.

—I don't know.

The loudspeaker made an announcement, and I straightened.

—Well, I said. —Be seeing you.

The crone scattered particles into her pocket square. She waved me aside. Her hand cratered with divots, and I knew my wife would be putting everything into her tremendous tote bag, craning, helpless, waiting for me to come take the weight of Turmeric from under her Prada-shod feet.

And we were twisting away from each other, this ancient hag and me. Our lives parting forever. At some point I'd committed an error. Soon I would mean nothing.

Yet for the first time in the better part of the past seven years, I felt present: open, undissembled, resilient.

I found Emma exactly where I'd left her eighty minutes prior, inside the pet-friendly picnic table zone, poised forsakenly, upper body canting to one side under the heft of her tote, wearing dark Matsuda sunglasses amid the blackness of the night.

Houdini, our three-and-a-half-year-old Bedlington terrier, was panting compulsively, pink and gray tongue billowing from his jaw like a damaged web.

When he'd arrived in one of a grid of kennels in the back of a Sprinter van, making the journey from Little Egypt, Illinois, to Greenwich Village during the early months of the pandemic, he'd been panting. And as lockdown turned to protests, and placid side streets filled with flash-bangs and firetrucks, the skies with helicopters and long-range acoustic devices, he'd persisted. For a month, I'd assumed the organ was too big for his snout.

Eventually, though, he'd stopped. Only to unfurl the wet muscle at the first sign of distress. Being on a boat, I'd learned, was one of Houdini's many triggers. I bent to ruffle his head. The dog ducked and attempted to slide between my wife's legs.

—My family, I cried.

—Can you please take the cat?

—Of course, my love.

I cradled the carrier in my armpit. Battered plastic perforated with holes. Turmeric's eyes shone from them.

—Mrow, I said.

Turmeric puled. An intercom crackled. I disencumbered the great bag from Emma's shoulder. It was heavier than I'd expected, and I canted to one side as we made our way down the narrow stairwell to the vehicle deck.

Our 2003 Camry was parked in such a manner that I couldn't imagine how we'd gotten out of it to begin with. The driver's side door held flush against a solid rampart. Trunk obstructed by a Rivian R1T's front bumper burrowing into our sun-bleached BERNIE BEATS TRUMP sticker.

The ferry was roiling, docking. Houdini veered, his nose spraying bits of moisture, gulping fumes, one alarm still choking its warning, and the passenger side door gave just enough for me to unlock the car and thrust everyone in.

I clambered over wife and dog. The emergency brake sticking up like a dare.

—You know they used one of those to power a lobotomy last winter?

I swiveled toward Emma. She was blonde, petite, creamy-skinned, wrenched in her seat regarding the luxury electric pickup, all smooth and no clearance, through the rear windshield.

—Where did you read that, I asked.

—Twitter.

—The forces of the universe are so mysterious, I said.

—I'm exhausted, Emma exhaled.

—And hungry, I added.

She made a noise, and a gate opened at the end of the boat. Horns honked, and when I engaged the ignition, we were greeted with a familiar blast of canned air, the stereo blaring mid-song, —But hear that witch wind whinin' . . .

I killed the volume and grinned.

—Sorry, I said.

Minutes passed before I realized it was the song Emma had chosen to begin the moment we'd kissed, ten months earlier, and pranced up the aisle we'd only just descended, our marriage conducted, and our futures brand new.

I wasn't particularly fond of music, and I turned the volume back up at a snail's pace, but the ballad must have concluded. The speakers emitted a soft hum like waiting. We filed behind a Tesla, a Land Rover, an Alfa Romeo. The pale light of the moon, which had been full three nights before, dipped between sheets of haze.

The dog was trying to stand on the cat carrier in the back seat. I kept glancing at the rearview mirror, breathing through my nose, relaxing.

I couldn't think of what to say. Inanity, which had proven so innate to my solitude, lately came to afflict and undermine my self-assurance. Ever since I'd elected to share my life with other creatures.

I shot a quick look at Emma, barely registering her reaction, and turned to face the road as soon as I sensed her acknowledgement of my sightline.

What worlds existed within my wife? What secrets?

I should try to express that I'm relaxing, I thought. Then we can be more connected. Perhaps her reserve was just deference to my cold exterior. I only needed to let her in.

Shadows of tree limbs reached through the windshield, graved our faces with crisscrossing lines.

—I'm stressed out, I said.

—Really, Emma asked. —Why?

Before I could think of an answer, she was slapping the dashboard. Houdini vaulted over the center console onto her lap.

—Look, look, she was saying. —Stop here! Go! Go! Turn left!

She squeezed my thigh, and I swerved into the parking lot. The quaint red CANDY MAN sign kindled by headlights. Oyster shells crunched under tires. The Camry bucked. The cat carrier bounced. Turmeric howled. Houdini clawed at the window glass.

—Everyone okay?

Emma splayed across the upholstery, digging through her tote bag. She flung back golden tresses, felt wallet in hand.

—I'll just be a second, she jumped out of the car.

A bell tinkled as the door swung behind her, and Emma disappeared into the store. I rolled down the window, cut the engine. The scent of brackish humidity. Sedate cricket murmurs.

I could see the slender outline of my wife's body pulling boxes off shelves, weighing plastic baggies in upturned palms like the scales of justice.

Emma dumped a heap on the countertop. She was wearing a heather charcoal pleated skirt and cotton panties I glimpsed among the frenzy. A wan figure materialized, metallic calculator in hand, and she and Emma embraced.

—Thank you, my wife called, package-loaded to her neck, jostling push bar with rear end. —And happy Fourth!

The figure bowed, a gesture between reverence and burlesque, tip jar burnished with dust, as Emma lashed her head in my direction, bell clanging.

—Come on now, she urged, slipping into her imitation of my own Cockney parody. —Get the door for your gentle consort, I does be requiring my victuals.

Twenty minutes later, she balled a small mountain of cellophane wrappers in the glove compartment and suspired. I stared into the windshield, smiling.

—I was so hungry, Emma giggled.

—I know, my love.

I listened to the tires whir.

—Anything in there for me?

We were winding around the island, heading back in the direction we'd come from, but on the southern fork, enclosing the bay. Houdini had stopped panting.

Emma dug through the bag of dark pecan turtles, white chocolate pretzel bark, hand-dipped yogurt-covered coconut drops, ring jells, marzipan, and candy-coated animal crackers.

—Licorice, she asked. —Is licorice gluten-free?

—Anise is a flavor all about being an alcoholic.

She scrutinized the label.

—It isn't, she said. —I'm sorry.

My wife leaned over the center console. She planted a kiss on my forehead. She took my chin in her hand and tilted it to hers. My eyes strained, then briefly closed.

Our tongues explored each other's surfaces. I tasted sugar and milk. I imagined the trace remnants of wheat varnishing the failures of my intestinal folds.

Lip suction released an audible pop. I returned my gaze to the road. A family of deer, the rats of Suffolk County, lined up at a crosswalk.

Emma rolled a fat joint on her skirt. She licked the paper, sparked up, cracked a window, took a deep hit, and held it. Two slivers of smoke escaped her nostrils. Then she dragged harder until half the paper was consumed in her dilating lungs.

We passed a gigantic ferrocement duck with a door embedded in its breast. Emma let out the cloud like it was going to rain, leaned her cheek on the window, and relinquished the smoldering roach.

—I'm going to rest my eyes.

Her hair curled. I touched it, barely. Then I finished the joint, jettisoning the cardboard filter through the slit in the glass.

—Good night, I said.

I listened to their breath, my three alive companions, bound by devotion, kindness, intent, food, and excrement.

Turmeric had lost a front fang and about half her lives since we'd fled the city and she'd discovered the great outdoors. Her nose was crushed in, and she whistled like a garden gnome, ticking the seconds off our journey.

Houdini had settled back into my wife's lap. He was too big for it, though, and one paw rested on the dash. His tail wafted over a titian-tinted buttonhole of a rectum.

And Emma sank into the passenger window. Her calves rising involuntarily, skirt gathering at the crotch, revealing her perfect white ass.

I'd handled three out of four of our carpool's ordure, including my own, in the past month at best. My firm, wandering lump having taken on a dictatorial role, delivering me to humility when I needed it most, or didn't.

Poop was reality. We were dispatched to a world among shit. Part of the deal of getting married was Emma wanted kids. Like most men of my generation, of all generations, I remained reluctant. I could only hope, after prolonged investment in hygienic instruction, that new guard would respectively pay the gift forward. Or rather, back. In the meantime, we ministered to our pets. Life found a way of inclining one toward fecal maintenance, which was fine, if you could afford to come to terms with it.

And suddenly, I knew exactly where I was. The ivory manor, paint peeling, picket-fenced, and red geraniums in its window boxes, overlooking the traffic light. I turned left, passed the windmill, the pond, the library, the bagel-cum-pizza parlor, the Michelin-starred fried chicken deli, the pop-up galleries, and the Balenciaga store.

I weaved by farm stands. A marquee buzzed with insects outside the live music bar. Weathervanes and cupolas cropped up behind hedgerows. The perfume of the fish market, and my alien return to the cedar-shingled cottage just north of the two-lane highway was complete.

An American flag quivered. And as I pulled in the driveway, I scarcely recognized the neighbor's towering A-frame beside us. Since the previous summer, it had been slathered a glossy black. The porch raised, affixed with perplexing wrought iron ornaments. The column of oaks separating this monstrosity from my in-laws' modest Cape Cod–style house was badly pruned. A pickleball court had been poured, and a yard sign sagged in the scrubby crabgrass, broadcasting MARABELLE MINNOWITTER AGENCY's claim on the eyesore.

I shuddered. Houdini lunged to the window. It appeared as though every light inside my wife's parents' property burned.

I negotiated a sharp U-turn and parked on the pine needle–strewn dirt. The passenger door creaked open. The dog collapsed in the brush. Turmeric bayed. Emma yawned. Less than an hour now remained before her father's birthday would start.

While my wife hung out the trunk looking for something, I righted Turmeric's carrier and unfastened it. I cradled her in my arms.

—Little grimble, I cooed.

I kissed her nose. She was covered in delicate camouflaging motifs, and once free, she'd vanish for days at a time, scandalous and aloof. If she could shrug, I think it's all my cat would do, carcass of a decapitated chipmunk languishing from her jowls. She swiped my arm, and I dropped her, and she darted past a shrub clipped into the likeness of a hedgehog through a hole in the fence to the backyard and a tall growth of pines.

—Consarn you, I called, shaking my fist. —Your name is yellow!

Houdini elongated, performing a splendid yoga flow. Emma had bags on each shoulder, plus a rolling suitcase, and she reeled away. The dog looked longingly after her, then at me. I patted my thigh, and we followed her to the light.

—We're here, my wife cried.

The screen door banged between us. I held it open for Houdini, who lifted his leg and urinated on the side of the garage before scurrying under my outstretched arm. A vintage celadon Fiat and pristine white M3 groveled below an exposed bulb.

I basked in the whine of the door's hinge, the twinkle of fireflies, the distant crash of the ocean, watched the Camry's headlights blink out automatically.

Inside, I found my father-in-law lying on a towel on the kitchen floor, head propped up by pillows, Eames chair moored under his slippers, feet elevated in an anti-inflammatory pose.

A juice glass rested next to his ear filled with red wine. On the counter overlooking him, a CRT Panasonic with built-in VCR flaunted images from one of the various foreign wars our country was funding.

—Michael, I said.

—Hey Jacob.

I crouched, extending a convoluted sort of hug over his body.

—Happy almost birthday.

—Oh man, Michael said. —Get a look at what they're doing to our boys!

I leaned back and sat on my hands. The TV showed night-vision images of tanks driving over mud.

—That's . . . awful.

—It's the absolute pits!

—I hope . . . the war ends, I said.

—Well everyone hopes the war ends. But no one should even be thinking about peace talks until all territory has been reclaimed with just action.

—I, um . . . yeah. Territory is so important.

The screen flared. It showed all white for a second, then the armored vehicles resumed driving.

—Holy hell, Michael griped.

—Oh cheer up, Jane scolded.

Her voice was warm like pie, but my mother-in-law was actually holding a Danish over her husband's hoary head.

I stood up. Assessing him from above, I could see Michael's glasses had fallen off. His hair was tied back. It had been braided at some point and come stringily undone.

—Take this away from me, she pleaded, foisting the pastry in my direction.

I faltered.

—Would that I could, but...

—How many times do I have to tell you, Emma screamed from some unseen corner. —Jacob's gluten-free!

—Oh that's right, Jane rebuked herself. —Foolish, forgetful, and flabby! Oh, but it's so nice to see you!

We hugged, and she kissed my cheek, flakes of Danish coming off on the back of my shirt and raining down to Michael's face.

—I can help you with that, Janey.

He arched, reaching.

—Open up, mister seventy, she said and deposited the crumbs between his coffee-, wine-, and cigar–stained teeth.

—I'm not seventy yet!

My father-in-law ejected dough morsels.

—No, and you might not make it if you don't chew your dessert.

—Are you excited for your party, I asked.

—I'm trying to look on the bright side. But I never thought I'd see the day they'd pay such desecration to our honorable troops.

He pawed for the juice glass. Jane moved it to his hand, and Emma appeared, changed out of her skirt and sunglasses into baggy linen pants and an oversized hoodie that said WIT'S END.

—You were arrested twice protesting Vietnam, she said, feeding herself from a saucer of licorice pellets.

—That was different, Emmeline. I could've been drafted.

—I'm not talking about this.

—Are we supposed to stand idly by while evil totalitarians erode the world's democracy?

—Yes, Emma said. —And take down that grotesque, fascist flag you've got hanging out front.

—It was Independence Day, Jane butted in.

—Have a little pride in your homeland.

—We would've stuck out like sore thumbs.

—Better than reveling in the blood of innocents.

—Who's innocent, Michael rasped.

—Who are we talking about, I asked.

—This is ridiculous, Emma moaned. —I'm going to bed!

My wife swallowed the rest of her licorice whole, marched out of view, slammed a door.

—She's had a long evening, I said.

Jane nodded, her eyes gracious and flashing behind some impenetrable cognizance.

—And with her new job starting Monday . . .

—Oh, we're so excited for her! We're so excited you're here, my mother-in-law effused. —Can I get you a drink?

—So are we, I said, ignoring her question. —We really are. Only twenty minutes till the big day. I'm going to get in a position like you.

I regarded Michael. He was attempting to tip the juice glass toward his mouth.

—You gotta treat your body like a temple, he said.

In the bedroom, my wife was squatted over her unzipped suitcase, reassembling a bong. From photos, I knew the room had been decorated the same since Emma's childhood.

Stuffed pigs hovered from high shelves, encircled by Polaroids of a picnic on a volcano, a commencement ceremony, swimming with dolphins in some tropical locale. There were consolation ribbons discolored by time. Something about horses, though I knew Emma had never, not even as a preadolescent, enjoyed riding. An early format plasma television was mounted above a vanity and dresser, hand-painted with Matisse cutout-style silhouettes, and dappled with picked-at band stickers. The perimeter of the room papered in an off-pink, floral whorl.

Emma filled the bong's reservoir from a liter of Smartwater. She cocked the pipe, eyes crossed looking down as the chamber purled and the glass brimmed with vapor.

I took the tube from her clutches and a good rip and stared into the wall. Grim, carnival faces appeared in the repeating arrangement of rosebuds and vines. I shook my head.

—Nice, I coughed.

Emma unpacked. She hung two Lacoste tennis dresses in the closet. She piled books under the bedside lamp. She stacked shoes in dresser drawers and slid them away.

I lay down on the Turkish zoo animal rug. Houdini, sandwiched beneath the box spring, blinked at me. I blinked back.

Emma took another hit, tucked her legs under her knees in a diamond pose, and covered her face with her hands.

—What's up, baby?

—I'm stressed out, she mumbled.

—Are you sure? Remember when I said that earlier? I was really feeling relaxed.

—No, she said.

—No, you're not stressed out, or no . . . something else?

—When did my dad get so old?

—He's not old for another . . .

I padded around for my phone, couldn't find it.

—Probably ten minutes.

—He loves war.

—Sixty-nine is fine, I said.

—And my mom doesn't even seem to notice.

—Seventy is heavenly.

—And I don't want to start my new job.

—Oho, I intoned. —So that's it.

—No, Emma said.

—Don't you want . . . health insurance?

—No.

—And a . . . 401(k)?

—No.

—What about . . . disposable income?

—That's better.

She did a backward somersault, rose to stand, and suckled the bong. I did too. We lay on the quilt, covered in patches, flayed, falling apart. I put my hand in my wife's pants.

—Are you excited for your dad's birthday party?

—Gah, Emma grumbled and laughed. Then her tone became stilted. —I'm actually not.

—Well I am, I said. —I'm married to a woman with a job.

—And I'm married to . . .

—A slob.

—A starving artist.

—I'm doing my best to gain the weight back.

My hand sought deeper crevices, danker pastures. It moved faster, investigating.

—But it's true, I insinuated. —I'm your fruitless nobody. Such a neurotic, slovenly boor.

—You're no bore.

Emma folded her lips in my neck.

—Such a loutish, draggletailed slob, I insisted.

She ran her tongue over my jugular, sampling, savoring. She nibbled.

—Not a slob, Emma said. —You're getting the whole thing mixed up. It's your knob . . . that's . . . in need of . . .

She slithered, limbs multiplying, each digit a tentacle, gliding and glazing across me.

—My slobber, she gurgled, undoing my trousers, easing them down in sinuous embrace.

—God, that's right, I took over the narration, as her throat filled with me. —I was mistaken. It's my . . . knob . . . that's in need of a . . . sloberous . . . cure . . . It's all . . .

I forgot the thread.

And we stopped talking for seven minutes or so, yielding ourselves to each other, blissful and stoned and loosed from the minutiae of the world.

When we came back to earth, Houdini had resurfaced and was rumpled by the door, facing away from us.

—Mm, Emma sighed. —That was nice.

—Yes, it was. The dog's pissed.

—That's how you know.

My wife was right.

—We should do that more often.

—How often are married couples supposed to?

—Hm, Emma pretended to think. —At least once every five or six weeks.

I tried to remember the last time.

—Five weeks sounds about right.

—Something wrong?

—No.

—You don't think we're supposed to be making love more frequently?

—I think . . .

I wanted another hit. But for it to be opium or something. Something stronger than what weed could contact.

—I think we're supposed to do it as frequently as we want. Anyway, it's like . . . I don't know. I think the only thing wrong with lovemaking in general is its regimented depiction in media. Desire doesn't need a schedule. It waxes and wanes. It's tidal. So what if conditions haven't exactly been fuckfestive the past few months.

—Fuckfestive, Emma echoed.

I was staring at the stuccoed ceiling. There should've been a fan.

—I just mean . . . Sorry, I said. —Maybe you're trying to say you want to make love more. I'm sorry. I get confused. It's been hard for me to be in the moment lately. All this stuff about parents, and . . . I mean, you know. Never mind. It's just been hard for me to feel carefree.

A hot breeze grinded the old clapboard shutters against the cottage.

—But I felt present tonight? I felt relaxed? I love you vigorously, Emma, no matter how often.

—Prove it, bub.
—How?
—Meet me back here in a week.
—I'll see what I can do. What day is it again?
—I want you to put a baby in me, Emma said.
—Loud and clear.
—I'm teasing. Or . . . I'm not.
—That's why you got a job.
—You know what I mean.
—Health insurance.
—That's why women ever get jobs. But listen. Jacob. It was perfect. Everything is going to be okay. Everything will be normal again. Or . . . that's the wrong word. Not normal, but . . .
—It's okay, I interrupted.

I sat and clamped on boxers and cracked the door for the dog. He squeaked out, nails clicking, as Emma reached for the bong.

I glanced at the window, trying to remember the moon. It was washed out by the bedside lamp though, and I only saw shades of myself. The faint mole on my lover's left hip.

There were things I should do, like brush my teeth or pee or stretch, probe vital unknowns. But I took another hit and lay back down and started counting instead, asleep with the room entirely lit up before I got to double digits.

# FRIDAY

The weed, however, wasn't strong enough. I dreamed straight through the night.

I dreamed of a slanted corner café where blind arachnids pulsed through sand beneath the sidewalk. I sat at a wobbly table under a warped flight of stairs, outside, and yet amid what I intuited could only be my in-laws' cottage basement. The lid of the washing machine pulled back, gaping and wounded next to a locked chalky cabinet, not able to get comfortable, and waiting impatiently for my mother and father to show up and whisk me away in their Chrysler Pacifica.

I'd shared a middling eighteen years with those mist-obscured, misplaced parents, the only child of a research chemist turned biotech salesman and a physical therapist for developmentally disabled youth, reined in by the predictability of suburban central Massachusetts.

As a boy, I'd been agitated at the mere whisper of sleep. That I must submit each sunset to paralytic captivity seemed unconscionable. A kind of death. And bit by bit, bolt-upright self-imposed insomnia chipped away at my soul, resulting in bloodshot melancholy, malnourishment, and malaise, instilling a chronic estrangement I was too weary to get across.

Rather, I cultivated neuroses. I withdrew and grew erratic in uncertain cycles. My mother did her utmost to brush off nervy guidance counselors, bitter Hebrew school instructors. She was inured to her own clients' more extreme jejune loops, toiling on behalf of an underfunded public school district, not my own, which, in truth, maintained all the qualities of a New England prep academy, save for its deadened architecture and total omission of the arts. My mother's patience was her heart. But taut eyes betrayed disquiet. And I waded through those years a haunted drone.

Later, in college, alone in downtown Manhattan, I caught glimpses of what real life might involve. Endless feats of responsibility and apprehension, but the laziest shortcuts to oblivion too, a slew of drugs at my fingertips, steps beyond my dorm room, enabling a push off the edge as often as I desired without an iota to extract or uphold. Likewise, I latched onto literature. Nebulous to its core. I'd hoped it would make me a better communicator, but it turned me into a writer, publishing navel-gazing poetry and stories, trying to describe my ambiguous pain all too late.

It wasn't my terror world anyway. The whole thing was. And the day my parents picked up and moved to Rhode Island, swept our history under the rug, I was inspired. Long-drawn depression had stripped me clean. All I needed was a stable, humdrum pattern in which to lose myself, be it writing fiction or getting high or nurturing a monogamous relationship. I didn't know how to achieve that, and I didn't try to learn, but it came to me anyway: fate.

I drowned the roar of my dreams under alcohol, and, when that was no longer an option, weed. Sometimes, however, the weed wasn't strong enough. And that morning I awoke bristling.

The sky was gray with first light. I turned off the lamp and kissed Emma's forehead.

—It's imperative, she murmured.

—So true, I said.

A soft scratching emanated from the kitchen. Everything was veiled. The tiles cold underfoot. My stomach ached. My lump twinged. I got as far as the neon green glare of the stove's digital timepiece, it was five o'clock, then beelined to the bathroom.

The scratching carried on as I flushed, washed my hands, and scrambled back to the kitchen, too afflicted by my dream to guess what I was expecting.

Still, I should've known. Turmeric's tail flicked beneath the sink, her head and front paws immersed in a trash can. I yanked her out, turned her around, holding her up by the armpits.

—Why are you causing trouble?

She squirmed.

—You're supposed to stay outside. Don't you remember? Emma's mom is allergic to cats.

Turmeric's eyes rolled as I attempted to keep their mazelike contours in focus. I opened the sliding glass door, rocked back, and heaved her clear over the brick patio into the backyard.

A dust devil whirled from the soil, and I made my way to the Camry, gunned it to a Starbucks in the village, ordered the biggest, coldest coffee they sold, and no one cared I was barefoot in my T-shirt and boxers, because if you were buying something, not working, everyone on the island just assumed you were too rich to hassle, chugged it, and cruised to the beach, which required a permit to park, but the policy wasn't supposed to be enforced for another hour.

Surf skated. Foam blinkered the shore. I kicked around wistfully. The sun crept over the dunes. Dorsal fins crested maybe forty feet out, and I wept.

I wasn't especially sad, just haphazard and weepy, mourning a mystery I could neither explain nor elude, half-jogging, partway in the water, letting the ebb and flow splash my midsection through the plum dusky morning, as I shoved past two elderly freaks.

—Did you hear about the shark at Jones, one asked.

—That is very far away, the other said.

Eventually I tore off my shirt and collapsed in the swell, diving headfirst between an inch of break, and emerged flustered to the limit of sanity, a crescendo of sand and salt water and particulate matter worming into my ear canal.

I gagged, hopping on one foot, smacking my skull, vying to dislodge the foreign bodies. By contrast, they settled more soundly, grating into a deeper cavity of my sinus. I went to my knees, pinky prodding my eardrum, berserk and forlorn, off the deep end with this abrupt departure from equilibrium. I pounded my fists and divulged a blubbering sob so acute that it brought me back to the present.

I looked around. No one seemed to have witnessed the escapade.

—It's okay, I said.

I slung my T-shirt over my shoulder. I fondled the lymph nodes punctuating my neck. The obstruction would come out on its own. I didn't believe that though. I just needed to chill, maybe run around a bit more, bodysurf, lie on my side, not think about it. I didn't want to though. And I hobbled histrionically toward the parking lot, convulsing like a lunatic and catching my toenail on some gilded corner.

The sun had fully risen. I whimpered and fell to my ass in its radiance. My underwear filthy, genitals prickling with gritty sweat. My toe leaked a trail of blood, and I buried it in the sand.

I clawed at the corner and came back with a handful of gold plaque. It was a rectangle. A nameplate, like the one I'd nailed above the front door of my apartment in Coney Island so many years earlier, and it said simply, MY OFFICE.

It shimmered. It winked in the sunlight. I held the thing limp, staring down at its surface. And I was transported, flinching through flashbacks of that gore-soaked Brooklyn coastline, those cops clogging my doorway, pathetic and violated, as though I didn't have a choice.

—Jacob, someone inquired.

I reeled, trembling, cowering under the all-too-familiar voice.

In my freewheeling twenties, I hadn't exactly made a habit of lying to police. As a rule, I'd avoided them at all costs. But that early winter afternoon following my twenty-sixth birthday, I'd lied to Powell and Winston with alacritous indifference.

For one thing, I had witnessed an event I viewed as out of the ordinary. For another, my first novel manuscript, a thinly veiled autofictional brooding, had not been being considered by an *important* agent per se, but by an anonymous hireling at a once-prestigious outfit, which had, in the preceding years, cut its staff down to two personnel: the literary agency's eponymous founder, who'd formerly represented a few major players in the game, and whom I'd never met, and the menial junior agent I'd reached out to after scrolling her photos on Twitter.

They were dreadfully alluring. And from some cursory sleuthing, I'd learned she was only a year older than I, and that we shared the same birthday. It felt like a sign.

On the third Monday of the new year, four days before Trump's inauguration, I'd received her response:

*Dear Jacob,*

*I've read a significant portion of your novel and am very intrigued. I think your tone, construction, and sensibility are well-honed and unique. That said, I believe the text will need a lot of editorial work. If you're interested in embarking on this journey with me, I'd love to collaborate.*

*Sincerely yours,*
*Sofia Cutler*

*A. Martha Philips, Ltd.*
*433 Lafayette St. #5C*
*New York, NY 10003*

I'd been in no position to propose otherwise. I'd shaved, dressed in a falling-apart brown tweed suit, and met my emissary among the clash of Astor Place for coffee.

Sofia was enthusiastic and shrewd. She assured me we had a real gem on our hands, something that could bypass the slog of small press distribution and speed me along toward the moon.

We talked advance figures. We discussed the complex breakdown of rights and royalties and translation. I signed a contract and we shook hands, then hugged.

—I feel like we understand each other, Sofia said.

And I'd concurred, leaving the meeting in a driving sleet, forehead down, buried against my lapel, filled with the potentiality that I could walk away from the trauma, the remorse, sin, and disgust. That what I'd wanted from the beginning, to be a better communicator, had actually, maybe unwittingly, been accomplished, and that I was traversing the sidewalks of destiny.

What I hadn't known was myriad. And that morning on the beach in Long Island was the first time I'd heard Sofia's prurient cadence in almost six years.

—Jacob, she repeated, but it was no longer a question.

She loomed over me, exposed and defenseless in my seminude crouch, digit bleeding into the strand, her aquiline features blocking out the low sun. Through the mire of my ear, my ex-agent sounded ragged and asunder.

Then I stood, wrestled into my T-shirt wrists-first, and, perspectives shifting, stared down at Sofia, who smirked, lusciously insouciant, striking as earnest a pose as someone who gives herself to a career in the arts could.

—Jacob, she said a third time, unfolding toned, olive arms, holding out a hand, which I regarded, and made no move to engage. —Is everything all right?

—Yes, I wheezed. —Why?

Sofia laughed. Her body relaxed. She was in control now, and she knew it.

—God, she giggled. —You're exactly the same.

—I'm really not.

I dug at my ear, turned to the green frothing waves. The tide was coming in.

—You *really* are, Sofia said.

She was wearing a sports bra and low-rise bike shorts that squeezed into her crotch. The years appeared to have ripened her, and instead of eroded, Sofia seemed younger, suppler, more bewitching, and I found myself incessantly forcing my eyes from her magnetic anatomy.

—What are you . . .

I was dizzy.

—Doing here, I managed.

—I live here, Sofia replied, pulling a phone from the ass of her shorts, bending suggestively and restoring it against a firm cheek.

—You live *here*?

—Sure, she said. —I do. Now. I couldn't stand being in the city anymore. Not through all that . . .

She lifted a hand, and I understood what she meant.

—And an opportunity arose, so I took it.

—With your husband?

Sofia studied me. Haltingly, she shook her head.

—But you're still married.

—Well, we never got divorced, she admitted.

—I am too. Married, I mean.

—I know, she tittered. —I saw on Instagram. Your wife's dress was pretty amazing. Alexander McQueen, spring/summer '04. If I'm not mistaken?

I tilted my head, squinting, incredulous.

—I don't know.

—No, that was it. She has great taste! Congratulations!

—Thank you.

Seagull sounds. Seaweed seething over itself.

—You *live* here, I said.

—Yeah! You say it like it's a bad thing. You're here, aren't you?

—The literary agency industry must be booming.

—Well, we did get lucky enough to acquire some choice volumes.

—Oh right, I said. —The one about the heroin guy who doesn't think the military is so bad after all. And the, um, don't tell me . . . you know, the white guy who writes like he's black?

—That's one perspective.

—Not novels of male ennui, though. Those are too plentiful, right?

Sofia raised an eyebrow, mock-attempting to determine the authenticity of the remark.

—Jacob! Are you seriously still . . .

And the editors' rejections of years earlier came flooding back. All of them praising my writing as *cool*, *poised*, even *stylish*, and, though for its *palpable sangfroid*, as one Scribner heavyweight put it, they just couldn't imagine their marketing teams being able to wrangle the necessary readership for publishing terms to make sense, they were certain my agent would find a great home for it.

But Sofia hadn't.

And could I blame her? Sometimes, yes, I had no trouble at all. Stomping around, deriding her under my breath, half-finished abuses itching the tip of my tongue, vainglorious malice, sworn vengeance, smug contempt. At others, well, she hadn't written the novel.

—Yes, I said, and shook my sand-laden head. —I mean no. No, I'm . . . over it. I've moved on.

—Whatever, Sofia tossed back her hair. —Don't take it out on me, though. In 2017, masculine apathy *was* passé. Now it's *en vogue encore une fois*. I don't control the trends.

—Don't you though?

—I guess, she relented. —If you think books have anything to do with that. All the same, I wouldn't have expected you to be so indignant! It's been seven years since you spun that yarn. Aren't your cells supposed to have been replaced with new, fresh, optimistic ones by now? Aren't we supposed to be optimists? Astrologically? The archers? Fanning into the unknown fury to seek exotic pleasures?

—They have, I said. —My cells. I am. Optimistic, I mean.

—What about your spiteful ones?

—They must've regenerated too. I'm between jobs again. Anyway, you're the one who coerced me into believing in myself, then left me high and dry.

Sofia snickered.

—I still believe in you! And you left yourself out there. Which, by the way, I'd hardly classify as *dry* . . .

—I quit drinking.

—High, on the other hand, she continued, trailed off. —This is weird. I saw you flipping out from, like, a hundred yards away? I can still spot your maudlin throes. So, what, you don't live here? Why are you thrashing around Two Mile Hollow at six in the morning?

—It's my father-in-law's birthday. They're having a party this weekend.

—I thought you couldn't stand the elites? I thought it was fundamental to your *Weltanschauung* that you renounce material amenities and the exploitative wealth they rode in on . . .

—I got sand in my ear, I monotoned.

—Aw, Jakey. Of course you don't think money is vile anymore. Not if you married into it.

—Emma isn't . . .

—Your secret's safe with me, Sofia interrupted. —I forgive you. Even though you never responded to my emails. Or my texts. You know you're still contracted with me. Published anything lately? I'm entitled to fifteen percent.

—No, I said.

—Well, I can tell I caught you at an inopportune juncture . . . But it's great to see you! It really is. There's no reason to stay hung up on the past. I did what I could for you when I could. And you did too . . . for me . . .

I wanted to object, but she kept going.

—We were . . . still learning . . . But hey, you're unemployed, all your cells are different. Maybe we can figure something out! Maybe there's a new angle for that old manuscript of yours.

—I don't think so, I muttered.

—Or something else! God, you know how to push my buttons. You *are* a man of letters. But now my heart rate is down, and I need to get in my steps before my eight-thirty Zoom. It's a workday, after all. So listen, are you still at the same number?

I nodded.

—Excellent. Can I text you? Maybe we can meet up? Get a drink? Very professional, strictly professional. I want to see if there's a chance to get your prose out there. We're so young. Relatively. That has to, like, count for something?

—I told you, I'm teetotal now.

—Yeah, yeah . . . Well, if you aren't too busy, maybe I'll see you tonight? At the Talkhouse? At, say, ten?

—I'm pretty busy.

—I know you are!

Sofia laughed, bit her lip, touched her hip, touched my forearm.

—I'll see you later, she chirped and sprinted off.

The bulge of her phone pirouetting with her adroit, measured gait. The imprint pulsing on my eyelids. As they shut. And I crumpled. Out of breath.

Naturally there'd been an affair.

The thinly veiled autofiction that had brought us together told the story of a bris, a tryst, a breakup, an abortion, included a treatise explicating the differences between the *shiksa* and JAP, and closed with a more-protracted romance through which the narrator realizes he's too unreconciled, too enamored and revolted by his own image and affect, to offer anything to a woman.

And almost as predictably as my lothario protagonist inveigled a very particular type of damaged coquette, while Sofia was still preparing her edits, among the rainy, gelid spring, she'd shown up outside my apartment, disheveled and fulsome with a lust she contended I'd provoked.

With the help of my manuscript, she'd come to know me too well. She'd learned how to push my buttons, and she moved in so quickly, telling me precisely what I wanted her to. I was a fabulist, a narcissist, on the brink of my own ego's climax. I was easy to convince.

So we drank to the future. I mixed dry Botanist martinis, and a couple weeks later Sofia dragged me to Atlantic City, where she asked me to take her on the beach in the moonlight.

The next morning she'd wanted to get hitched, but as we drew up to the courthouse, she became hysterical, shrieking that I took advantage of her unmitigated ardor at every hazard.

She'd clobbered her fists on my shoulders the whole bus ride back to the city, and I'd nudged her into a bar. It was a historical landmark, where they put sawdust on the floor and perpetuated a myth that Abraham Lincoln had gotten drunk there.

The check came, and she slid it over to her side of the table. She stared into my eyes. Her voice balanced, breath hot.

—How are you, she asked.

I balked.

—What do you mean?

—You seem . . . a little strained.

My ducts stinging with lewd, livid tears, I pried the bill from her fingertips.

—Don't forget, I said. —You work for me.

I didn't find out for a couple more months that she was already married. She had confessed to me the week before she submitted my novel, along with some other pathological crap. Like when she'd said she'd gone to Swarthmore, I guess she'd meant Farmingdale State. And how she'd told me she was a twin, next she was claiming to actually be a triplet. She'd thought I would resent her because her mother had been in vitro fertilized and I'd read an essay by Joy Williams decrying the practice.

To an extent, she was right, but I'd read the essay after she'd told me she was a twin, so I decided to stop sifting for truth and just resent her anyway.

In the meantime, we insufflated ungodly amounts of ketamine. We took baths with iced glasses of gin filled with tea leaves until our skin puckered and screwed. And when it was all over, my novel shelved, unsold, Sofia woke me to say goodbye in the still black hours of torpor. I'd looked at my phone. It said, *4:21 Wednesday, December 20.*

—Don't go, I'd moaned.

—It's over, she whispered.

—But it's my birthday.

I sniffled.

—It's my birthday too, my agent had said.

And that Friday morning, five and a half years hence, when Sofia had transformed into a scant blip of atmospheric reflection along the sea, I took a deep breath, counting to four, holding for seven, and released, slackening from my hunched shoulders down, until my fists unballed.

I realized I was still clenching the MY OFFICE plaque. It left pink, razor-thin indentations across my palm. It looked identical to the one I'd flung into the Coney Island Bay before abandoning the city. But the tides couldn't have pushed it just this far. And if they had, the salt, the sheer motion of time would've surely chewed its superficial engravings. In fact, this one looked newer, cleaner, more emphatic and intimidating.

I lobbed the thing up. It cut the air, glimmering, singing a fine metal twang, and stabbed my hand when I caught it again.

I limped to the Camry. An orange envelope slumped on its windshield held by a wiper blade. I peeled it open with a corner of the plaque. The ticket said, *$270*, among other things.

I rotated. There were two cars in the lot affixed with beach permit stickers. The attendant booth was empty. I returned the ticket to its envelope and punted it half the span of a parking spot. Then I picked it up and drove to my in-laws' house.

Emma was already changed into one of her Lacoste dresses by the time I arrived, a white one, and bent over, lacing white tennis shoes, displaying the crest of her perfect white ass. Still stirred from my run-in on the beach, I was overcome with a salacity only more coffee could stifle.

I poured some from a pot heating on the chrome Moccamaster and leaned back against the counter, sweating. Houdini caromed around his bowl, mostly allowing kibble to fall from the gaps in his triangular mouth.

—Hi, I said.

—Good morning, Emma exclaimed, not looking up from her feet, which she sprained in different positions. —Where were you?

—I just . . . went for a walk on the beach.

—Did you pick up the paper?

—No, I stiffened. —I'm sorry.

—It's at the end of the driveway. And don't forget to wish my father a happy birthday!

—I did twice last night.

—But it wasn't his birthday last night.

—You're right, I said. —And when you're right, you're right.

—You should bring him the paper. It'll make his day.

—Yes ma'am.

—And remember to put down the toilet seat!

In the driveway, Turmeric was sitting on the plastic bag containing the *New York Times*.

—TGIF, yellow.

I reached down and tugged at the plastic. The cat wouldn't budge.

—You ate garbage, I said.

She stuck her tail up, and I poked at it, and she curled around and nipped my bloody toe and slunk off. The bag was slimy. I carried it dangling from my pinky and rapped on my in-laws' bedroom door.

—What's that, a voice croaked.

—Happy birthday, I called. —I brought the paper.

—Oh, Jacob, you're too kind. Don't come in now, though . . .

The sounds of breathing, little objects being knocked off of sideboards.

—Just leave it, we'll be out in a sec.

I extracted the Arts section, placing the rest on the ground, and moved outside to the brick patio, where I sat at a hammered glass table and perused the crossword. I didn't get far. A buck ambled through the backyard and caught its antlers on a birdfeeder, violently jerking its haunches and neck, taking most of a beech limb with it, and galloped into the pines.

I turned around. Emma was standing over my shoulders wearing her sunglasses.

—Are you going to play tennis?

—Yeah. Do you want to?

—Who are you playing with?

—I don't know yet, she replied. —I called the club first thing and they had an open slot for an hour of doubles. I'm sure you can sit in as an alternate. Did you pack whites?

I couldn't imagine I had, but I was unacquainted with my post-matrimonial wardrobe. I dropped the MY OFFICE plaque on the unmade bed and, within my duffel bag, discovered mesh shorts and a polo.

I slipped into a pair of Michael's cushioned Asics lying by the door.

—How do I look?

—Like a billion dollars, Emma massaged my kidneys. —Or the son-in-law of them.

—Thanks, I said.

I picked up my keys. Emma seized them and hurled the jumble at an enormous Baccarat ashtray.

—We're married now. We can drive the BMW.

I grinned.

—But I'm driving, she said.

Like any proper Manhattanite, my wife had only gotten her license after several attempts the year before, at the age of twenty-eight, and we lurched through the serpentine sleepy streets lined with tall hedges, elms, willows, and chestnuts, Emma struggling with the gearshift and clutch, the white M3 bucking and stalling and sputtering back to life amid the island's fertile, saline aromas.

The morning lingered deceivingly gloomy under the cover of verdure. Then we turned off Hither Lane and the sky opened, horizon sprawling in every direction. Wispy clouds swept across azure blue. The sun dazzled. And lush hillocks puffed up, quaint paddock fencing delineating the sandy road from the golf course, the beach grass, the shingle-sided mansions, their widow walks, and the pinnacle of it all: the country club, its rambling gables and chimneys and turrets, its four flags beating in the ocean breeze.

Emma wrenched the wheel, bumping up around the dunes to the back parking lot, where we throttled to a stop. I exhaled. My knuckles were standing up shiny on the grab handle over my head. I extended and cracked them and stepped out of the car.

The past three summers, when I'd been lucky enough to discover the island in all its balmy glory, had nonetheless been tenuous ones. Scarred by the leaden notes of the pandemic, people remained distanced, masked, services limited and polite, or at worst sympathetic.

We'd smiled with our eyes, apologized for the collective confusion. Things moved along languidly, with deliberation. No one wanting to appear fed up or put out by the state of affairs.

All that was over.

At the country club, Suffolk County's most affluent denizens were flaunting their finest, renewed by survival, bedecked in thousand-dollar straw hats, tanned and treated skin stretched over bionically improved joints, sipping matcha and signature cocktails in the splendor of dawn.

Emma left the keys on the dashboard and waltzed off. Automatically, my mouth opened to admonish her, but I checked myself. Looking around, it was probably the clunkiest sedan in the lot.

She took a few phantom backswings, grabbed her racket from the trunk, and twirled it.

—You ready?

—Sure, I said. —I forgot my racket, though. I think it's still in Rhode Island.

—You can borrow one from the club. Or use mine, she was saying, drifting toward the grass courts, habituated. —You're an alternate. They probably won't even realize you're here.

There was no way her racket was sized for my handling, but I also didn't care. I was busy smelling the water, forgetting Sofia and my life before summer, and everything else.

It was my wife's final weekend of our early retirement, our three-and-a-half-year reprieve from material reality, courtesy of two preposterous executive administrations, a litany of lies and aberrations with regard to health and human safety, the free market, and the very machinations of civilization. This was Emma's homecoming, before she reentered professional life and everything changed again. And yet, for me, I suspected, things would remain oddly fixed.

A gate swung behind us, and Emma announced herself, and they recognized her. I nodded, and they nodded, the eighteen karats on my left hand accounting for my presence.

Until the last quarter of the previous century, and the country club had been open for a century before that, Jews had been permitted on the grounds only under special circumstances. Mel Blanc, for instance, had been allowed to play golf as a guest. Th-Th-Tha, Th-Th-That's all, folks! Gatsbys might've snuck in, but Gatzes would surely have been turned away, and that was all right by me. I'd googled the membership fees. The figure made no lasting impact as a number. As a concept, though, I got the picture, and I wasn't in it.

Emma was addressing people. They inquired about her father, her mother, her career, and acknowledged me through glazed twitches. I was an alternate. Should Emma decide a better husband existed, I was swappable, as far as it concerned this contingent.

I wore my canvas bucket hat with the letter H. I hadn't remembered putting it on, and I trailed the bobbing piqué weave of my wife's skirt to an overlong bench, where she and her cadre converged to generously apply sunscreen.

Soon my wife was calling first service. The felty green balls throbbed like tolls from a bell tower. Life happened and ran out millions of times a day. I listened to the accents of nylon strings, grunting blows. So much better than music, I thought, wafting off into vacant meditation.

Then jolted up. My eyes must have closed. Someone was sitting next to me, and sidling closer, a spoor of bodily excretions and effluvium making it known. Emma appeared on the other end of the net, and to my left perched the ancient hag from the ferry, her bony, vein-drawn physique tilting into my personal space.

—Is that your only hat then?

Sand in my ear plummeted, making a shattering sound only I could detect, and I had to churn my neck in an arc to ward off the dull anguish before I could comprehend the question.

—What, I said.

—You must be awfully fond of it.

My wife hurtled to baseline. She sliced a winner to the opposite corner. The old lady's mouth parted. The odor grew worse. Like she was rotting inside. I scooted away. She scooted in turn. I tried something else.

—Are you here to play tennis?

—Do I look like I'm here to play tennis?

She was wearing a cream dress with sleeves, white cable knit socks, HOKA sneakers, and gargantuan Celine sunglasses. I hesitated.

—Yes?

She reached into a bag at her feet, withdrew a phone the size of a dinner plate, scrolled, and typed a message in hugely magnified text, then glared at me as though I were eavesdropping.

—I hear you're having a little trouble acclimating to the environment, she said.

I looked around. Emma and her partner were high-fiving.

—What are you talking about?

I took off my hat and ran my fingers through my hair.

—We have some mutual associates, she mused.

It hung in the air. The morning humidity had thickened, and it was getting harder to breathe. She plucked the hat from my grip and examined it closely, as she had the evening prior.

—It's less impressive if you flaunt it, she said.

I snatched it back, my ear panging. I didn't want to indulge her. I wanted to relax.

—So, she went on. —What year did you graduate?

—I didn't, I said. —It's just a hat.

Emma was loping in our direction, and the crone put on a cool mien. She pulled a handkerchief out of her breast and dabbed her face, waving.

—Emma, she crooned.

—Hello Alice!

My wife greeted the old bag with an air kiss near her cheek.

—I see you've met my charming husband.

—As a matter of fact, my dear, we met on the ferry last night. Emma fake-hit me in the chest.

—You met Alice and didn't even mention it!

—We weren't formally introduced, I said. —I didn't know you two were friends.

—I've known Emma since she was the size of a pea, Alice asserted.

I turned to my wife. She was gleaming.

—It's true, the biddy persisted. —I hired Michael to oversee the design of my pool house the very summer before you were born. And when I discovered your mother was with child, I took a categorical affinity to the woman, and we had a ball of a time. I just adore your whole family.

—Will you be here tomorrow for my father's party?

—I wouldn't miss it, dear.

Alice hacked into her handkerchief.

—But that reminds me. I must be running along.

—Bye, Alice!

Emma lifted a bottle of Voss as the battle-ax marched off. She nuzzled her forehead against my neck.

—You didn't say goodbye to Alice, my wife said.

The old lady was shifting, darting, accosting everyone worth knowing, and flagrantly snubbing those who weren't.

—Bye, I mumbled under the din of tennis bonks.

—Do you want to play for a bit?

My wife had risen. Artesian water dappled her chest. She glowed in the sunlight.

—No, no, I said. —It's okay. You should finish. I was just . . . relaxing . . . I'm just happy to be here . . . with you . . . Thanks.

—Okay weirdo, Emma intoned.

My wife and her partner won the match, six-to-one and six-to-love, and after I'd showered and redressed and was sitting on the patio with Emma, Michael, and Jane, who were picking at fresh pastries, surrounded by ikebana arrangements and discarded gift bags, as I half-consciously leafed through my *The Great Gatsby* paperback, Emma brought up our bewildering exchange.

—Jacob met Alice on the ferry last night, she said. —And this morning she sat right down next to him on a tennis bench.

—Ripping, Michael said, distracted.

He'd overturned one of his gift bags and was shaking it steadily, hoping to wrest something more from its depths.

—She must really like you, Jane added.

I winced.

—I don't know. She mostly seemed interested in my hat.

—She probably just didn't want you to get a sunburn, Emma teased.

—I don't burn, I said.

—Consider yourself lucky, Jane put her hand on my arm. —Speaking of . . . Sweetie, would you mind grabbing the Neutrogena from the powder room?

—Jacob?

Emma smirked in my direction. I stood up. Jane held my arm.

—I asked *you*, Emma. If *you* would be so kind as to . . .

—Okay, okay, my wife snarled.

She was gone before I could offer a look of condolence.

—What are you reading, dear?

The sand was wrapped around my medulla oblongata. And my mother-in-law's *dear*, so soon after Alice's, sent a shiver through it, crunching like snow in a dusty, evil desert.

—Just *Gatsby* again.

I handed it over the end table separating our chaise lounges.

—Oh, I love that, Jane said.

She flipped to the title page, ran a French-manicured tip across its withering epigraph.

—Then wear the gold hat, if that will move her; If you can bounce high, bounce for her too, Till she cry "Lover, gold-hatted, high-bouncing lover, I must have you!"

Jane broke into a spasm of laughter. Birds shot about, and she handed the dog-eared, broken-spined coil back, ticking her nail on the wicker table between us.

—I'll tell you a family secret, she said, simpering, lowering her sunglasses half an inch. —It's about the butler's nose.

And Jane touched her nose. And I nodded, playing along, hoping Emma would return from her errand soon.

Michael was snoring from another of the chaises. Jane inspected me an instant more, then slid the glasses back up her face so as to ensure its inscrutability, and I stared into the sun until alerting splotches of purple and red forced me to shut my eyes, and I got up, skidded indoors.

The afternoon lolled, and I slouched from room to room. Emma looked glossy, kind of lustrous and polished, lying on her bed peering into her laptop. Jane made phone calls. Michael grazed from the fridge. He was doing his best to keep it low-key, his official party pushed back one more day to delay gratification, though a backyard get-together was still planned for that evening.

—We're so excited to see you, Jane insisted to the other end of the line. —Oh, that would be wonderful!

And so forth. Houdini wandered up from the basement looking guilty. Thunder crashed, and six minutes of downpour licked the abode clean. Then the sun came out hotter than before.

—Emmeline, Jane hollered.

I tiptoed to her room. My wife was crawling under the bed. I backed out, closed the door.

—Hi Jane, I said.

—Have you seen my daughter? She was supposed to go to the fish market to pick up lemons for dinner. And she never brought my sunblock.

—Allow me. You just need lemons?

Jane looked over her shoulder.

—And Newports, she spoke swiftly. —Menthols.

She handed me a platinum American Express. And as I walked to the market, it thundered again. A sheet of dry lightning strobed across the sky, but this time it didn't rain

Lemons cost six dollars each. I hoped ten would be enough. And as I tapped her card, Jane texted, *Can you pick up an xtra large order of fried chicken from Brent's? Xo xo*

There, I asked a guy in a grisly apron if the deli made anything gluten-free. He shook his head and tossed me a disintegrating sack filled with grease. I held it suspended between thumb and forefinger, and was about to buy the cigarettes when my phone vibrated again.

*Would you mind terribly grabbing a few bags of ice while you're at it?*

Through some miracle of virtue, I delivered this multitude across the kitchen island. Then I dashed to the bathroom to scour gluten drippings off my skin. Voices emanated from the patio. I threw my shirt at a hamper, changed into one so similar I barely registered the act, and made my way out the sliding glass door.

A small buffet table with catering trays had been arrayed, in addition to a full wet bar, stocked with the most mouthwatering spirits. I could almost hear their screams. I turned on a heel, skirted to Emma's bedroom, and smoked the rest of the previous night's bong to ash.

Outside, I found my wife in a white poplin dress with puffed sleeves and a headband, sipping a champagne kir. She wasn't wearing sunglasses, and her crystal blue eyes were not focused on the architect monopolizing her. They were set deep in her psyche, discrete and untold.

I poured myself a seltzer and squeezed a lemon wedge into it. I noticed Jane sneaking off around the fence, fiddling with the pocket of her Marimekko sundress. A moment later, a tuft of smoke twisted between the boxwoods.

Michael was back on his chaise lounge, gnawing a stubby cigar, a tumbler of red liquor and a crispy brown drumstick competing for his lips. He wore Top-Siders and a hat with a feather in it. Allies encircled his roost.

I sauntered over to Emma and caught the tail end of her father's colleague's gin slur:

—You've just got to come down for the seminar. We're doing it up total communist style.

He shook a cane toward the sky and hobbled off.

—I didn't know there were communists here.

—Jeremiah is *not* a communist, Emma sipped from her flute.

—Your drink looks . . . refreshing.

I pushed my nose toward it. My wife swirled it away, wiggling an index finger.

—Care*ful*, she needled.

—I was just kidding.

But my tongue was slick with saliva.

—Is there anything gluten-free on the menu?

—Goddamn my mother, Emma fumed. —I warned her.

—It's all right, I said.

I shuffled to the buffet and pondered a small plate of squid.

—I planned this whole trip, a ruddy old man garbled, dapper in seersucker, angled around an emaciated, blue made-up lady, a townie I guessed, one who didn't belong to the retinue, tweaking slightly, eyes bulged, silver rayon dress, maybe four decades his junior. —A grand tour. And when I arrived, what did I discover but Madagascar isn't Africa at all! More like South Asia. I wanted awe. Hot dank fire. Heart of darkness. Steaming *black*. Not some ecotourist zoo!

—Last time I took a vacay, the lady cracked up before she could get to the point. —I left the dog for three days. Came home, and she'd ate all my shrooms. Goofed out of her gourd!

I sucked a lemon wedge. The sun set. A distant train played its whistle. Everyone seemed to be floating. Angelic, free of angst, drunk. My phone vibrated, and I stood at the patio's edge.

*We still on for the Talkhouse?*

It vibrated again.

*See you in an hour* was affixed with the paw prints emoji.

I could always ignore it, but when my gaze landed on Emma, I saw her nibbling a Jordan almond, cornered by the dapper gent and his escort. He adjusted my wife's sleeve, groped inside.

—Dr. Masterson, Emma chided. —I'm a married woman.

—And I'm a devout academic. I mustn't stop learning. Now how *does* that sleeve work?

—As I was saying, she brushed him off. —Jacob's father gave the most touching speech.

—Where's he now, the townie asked.

I skulked off through the cottage and kneeled on my wife's bed, smoking resin from the tarry pipe, trying to decide what to do. My phone vibrated a third time. I powered it down without looking and stashed it in the closet in the pocket of my gray suit, the one in which I'd been married.

I checked myself out in a floor-to-ceiling mirror. I wore my bucket hat and found a navy-blue blazer among Michael's wardrobe, stuffed the tattered Fitzgerald book in its front flap pocket.

I could hear someone tickling the keys of an electric Yamaha, as the group burst into a muffled, tipsy rendition of "For He's a Jolly Good Fellow." I went out the front door, caught it before it could slam, and eased off the latch. Houdini panted from my wife's bedroom window. His eyes glistened. I met them and waved.

The bar was a mile from my in-laws' house. Past the fish market, the deli, the final Jitney debarkation of the evening. Riders wrinkled under streetlamps, aluminum luggage trunks battered by moths, and blue light thrummed off screens, graining masks on the travel-worn faces.

I showed a bouncer my ID. And inside, a jazz ensemble was either setting up tuning or in the middle of some fantastic set. I could never tell. I scanned the room for Sofia without luck and plopped in a sticky, pleather barstool and ordered a bitters and soda.

I slurped the tincture, knocking my wedding band against the edge of buffed wood. The bartop was wet. I smelled a ghostly whiff of beer, and my heart palpitated at the threat of gluten contamination. I was abrading my palm on the underside of the stool when a lithe outline sprung behind me and pinched my scapula.

My ex-agent was wearing a too-short, too-formfitting black strapless dress, which might have suited her better had I not written such a detailed account of my most profound, deep-seated vices and foibles, which she'd exclusively had the privilege of poring over countless instances and could exploit to her advantage at will. She pulled up a stool, crossed and recrossed her legs.

—Is everything okay?

—I thought we covered that this morning.

Sofia sighed.

—I mean here. The club?

I shrugged, and she cast over the bar, fine elbows and reedy frame. The bartender nodded.

—I'll have an extra dry martini, Sofia purred. —With Botanist gin . . . and an olive.

I swiveled on my stool.

—This place is nice, right?

—Sure. I just don't understand . . .

The ensemble was doing something.

—What is music anyway?

Sofia rolled her eyes.

—No, I'm serious. What *is* it?

—It's . . . cosmic . . . It's a part of the human condition . . . Everyone likes music.

—Sure.

—What's wrong?

—I just don't understand what I'm supposed to be enjoying!

—It's like . . . our bodies . . . represented through sound.

—Like coughs and burps?

—Like waves and vibrations, Sofia's patience was infuriating. —Our heartbeats. The flow of blood and digestion, gestation and time. The circadian rhythm.

—Rhythm . . . Two syllables, zero vowels. Graphemically maniacal. It's like a prime number. The whole thing is made up. *Time* is made up! And our digestive systems are deranged.

The bartender slid over Sofia's martini. It sparkled and sweated. She tasted the drink.

—Are you done?

I dropped my head in my arm. I lifted it, leered.

—When did you move to Long Island?

—Last fall, Sofia answered.

—Why, though?

—Why not? My boss was spending more time out here. She acquired a few investment properties by the beach and offered to rent me one so we didn't have to keep meeting on Zoom. What would you have done? Twelve hundred a month for your own house in East Hampton?

She let that sink in.

—Anyway, it's just a bungalow. It doesn't even have basement access. Or . . . Anyway, I met with her today. You know, Martha Philips?

—Of A. Martha Philips, Limited, I presume?

Sofia exhaled and drew back, foisting her puny chest at me, killing most of the drink.

—Okay, well. We're willing to revisit your manuscript. There might be an opportunity with this new indie press. But mostly I want to know if you've been working on anything else.

—Yay, I said.

—*All* right, Sofia tapped the bar for another martini, rearranging the bust of her dress. —I thought you'd at least act grateful.

—I'm just . . . God . . .

I drank my flavored water.

—I need a second to take this in. I'm pretty much over that entire experience.

—Yeah, you seem totally well-adjusted.

—It's just like . . . for the longest time, it felt like my novel was cursed.

The bartender replaced Sofia's glass with a fresh one, nacreous and teetering at the brim.

—Don't be so romantic, she said after a swig.

—No, I'm serious. Someone was killed on the beach, like, right outside my apartment, just a few weeks after I sent it to you. I never told you about that. It was on my birthday.

—*Our* birthday.

—Whatever, I said. —It's not going to make sense to you, but that murder, that whole . . . horrific . . . thing . . . It felt tied to me. To how I was living. And my novel . . . The casual, dismissive tone I took toward abasement and decadence, toward women, toward violence, and my entitlement, my assurance that it would be published and transform my layabout lifestyle.

My voice quavered. My mouth was dry, and I swallowed.

—Someone *died*. And then . . . more people . . . My . . . friends . . . And I fell to pieces. Only the promise of that novel, and . . . and your presence . . . That was all that was holding me together. When you left, I really went through it. And somehow, I managed to get it all back together. I have all this good stuff in my life now. I'm married, I've got this cute little family, and then just when it starts to seem stable . . . Then this . . . this shit with my . . . my par . . .

I grabbed my hair, pushing the word away before I could fully pronounce it, pushing the deluge of invasive thoughts from my consciousness, and ran a palm over my clammy face.

—Sometimes it feels like I unleashed a reaper. Years ago. Conjured to punish myself for trying to profit off stuff that didn't belong to me . . . The interiorities and intimacies of people who'd been in my life . . . And it was telling me I was wrong, taking them away . . . because of . . . what I'd witnessed . . . Or my lack of integrity as a witness . . . Or . . . I don't know.

My sinuses burned. The trapped sand gnashed into me, and I bit the inside of my cheek.

—Well, that's terrible.

Sofia put her hand on my knee. I twitched it off.

—Yeah. So you'll have to forgive me if I'm not more enthused. Because even if the better part of me knows better, I still believe that novel is cursed.

I closed my eyes. Strange chords jabbed at my conscience. After a while, I regained composure. I lapped my drink, then looked to Sofia. She wore an expression of bogus concern.

—Maybe, she uttered finally, placing a hand over mine, which I didn't immediately move. —Maybe it's you.

I moved it.

—Oh, I said. —Very reassuring. So I'm cursed?

—No, Jacob. Just . . . maybe you're still neurotic, and a little paranoid because of that. And maybe, ma-y-be, she drew it out in three syllables. —Just a bit . . . self-involved?

—I completed two years of therapy, I said.

—You do have a habit of putting stuff together that didn't really happen the way it might have seemed . . . to you.

—Well it's easy to say that when you were the one pathologically lying. Your husband, your college, your family. Stringing me along so you could make a . . . a . . . humiliate me, I guess.

—See! This is exactly what I mean! What motive would I have had to humiliate you? Jacob, have you ever considered the way things played out between us from *my* perspective? Has it ever occurred to you that I was also unstable, also naive and young and selfish? I never wanted to hurt you. I was going through my own shit. My marriage was *failing*. After so many years, you've got to be able to empathize in some way? You must be able to understand my intentions were not in opposition to you? We were feeding off each other's insecurities.

—You really shouldn't talk neutrally on this. Not after what you put me through.

—Obviously I liked your writing, Sofia said. —And *obviously* I wanted to sell your novel. That was my commission at stake, and I never got paid a cent!

I scoffed.

—And obviously I liked you, Jacob. The timing was just all wrong.

I twirled my glass on the bar. The bartender grabbed it mid-spin.

—I'm *not* saying you're crazy. I'm not saying anything. I'm just saying you may have created a narrative to preserve your . . . self. Like Didion. We tell ourselves stories in order to live?

—Men can't have babies, I said. —Telling stories is the closest we'll ever get.

—I don't want children, Sofia said.

I closed my eyes. Rubbed my temples with my fingers and felt unexpectedly bored.

—What's your point?

—That the timing isn't wrong now! We can still help each other. I want that. Don't you?

—I've got a lot going on, I growled.

But when I met Sofia's eyes, they looked sincere.

—So . . . Have you been working on anything new?

—Yes.

—Well what is it?

—I've been taking notes on *The Great Gatsby*'s relationship to antisemitism. I think it's all but explicitly stated by Fitzgerald that Jay Gatsby, né Gatz, *Gatz*, is actually a Jew, hiding his history and identity to finagle a way into high society and win back Daisy, and the whole book is about race, eugenics, and scapegoating in the wake of World War I.

Sofia was beaming. I whipped the book out of my pocket and flung it open on the bar.

—I'm serious, I said. —Look, right here. From the very first chapter, the first real dialogue of the novel at all, you've got Tom Buchanan talking about *The Rise of the Colored Empires* by *this man Goddard*. Well that's a direct allusion to a real book: *The Rising Tide of Color Against White World-Supremacy* by Lothrop Stoddard, a confirmed member of the KKK, mind you. And Tom says here, look...

I pressed my index finger into a quote I'd read hundreds, maybe thousands, of times.

—*The idea is if we don't look out the white race will be utterly submerged*... And here: *It's up to us, who are the dominant race, to watch out or these other races will have control of things*. Blah blah blah... Basically, his preoccupation with non-Nordics swooping in and usurping the master race's rightful inheritance is realized when conman gangster Gatsby, who is actually *Jewish*, weasels into his circle and steals his wife, so of course he has to die. The fixation on noses throughout the text is damning enough...

Sofia grabbed my wrist.

—I believe you! I've never heard that take before! You could write an essay. Or work it into a hilarious study of paranoia and neuroses. This is exactly what I'm talking about!

—It's all on my Twitter, *gatsbyjewish*, one word, no underscore. And I'm not paranoid. Fitzgerald wrote his editor that he'd had a particular man in mind when modeling Gatsby. Top scholarly conjectures single out Herbert Bayard Swope, Max

Gerlach, and J. G. Robin, né *Rabinovitch*. Tycoons, bootleggers, revelers, embezzlers, and not a goy among them. The hints are everywhere. The modernists expected more of their readers. They expected us to dig and infer, to draw essential conclusions.

—I agree. And I think you're really onto something!

I could feel my stomach settle, my heart rate pitching from drumroll to trudge.

—Jacob, Sofia entreated. —Can we be friends?

—How does that work?

—You get another drink. We make a little toast, touch glasses, and set an appointment to follow up. I want to include Martha too, see what she thinks. Maybe bring that indie publisher in on this theory of yours. How's next Friday? In the city? The agency office?

—That sounds . . .

I breathed.

—Fine . . . That sounds good.

Sofia smiled. With her eyes first, then her lips. She leaned over the bar, glanced back.

—Bitters and soda, I said.

# IN A DAZE

So goes the eternal return.

As much as I'd convinced myself by the first anniversary of that ominous twenty-sixth birthnight, deluded and jilted, alone in my apartment, without prospects, and at long last penniless, that I was done with literary agents for good, this too would prove a misjudgment.

But in the interim, shambling toward the limit of those fateful 2010s, I found comfort in reciting like a mantra that the circumstances of my existence had nothing to do with me. Things simply happened. Trump was never supposed to be president. The Weinstein scandal only broke when it did to cover up holes and inconsistencies in the Vegas shooting narrative.

My manuscript just wasn't marketable. As an FSG editor had sagely pointed out, *Novels of male ennui are perhaps a little plentiful at the moment.*

And the Jewish slant of my fiction couldn't have helped its case either. It was a matter of tradition. Semitic men had been paying penance on behalf of the atrocities their whiter, weightier counterparts carried out for millennia, and would continue perpetrating after the dust had cleared.

Before Weinstein, there'd been Madoff. Soon, they'd be coming for Franken, Epstein, Bankman-Fried. Behind Trump there was Kushner, Mnuchin, Weisselberg, Cohen, Cohn. Or take the century of carnage waged at the behest of Lord Balfour. No shortage of meeker, swarthier, more menacing shmucks to take the heat.

It was so painfully blatant. But I lived in an echo chamber, where solely I heard the truth's ricochets.

Meanwhile, the lump in my lower abdomen had grown firmer and more mad. At times it seemed to be trying to claw its way out, nodes erupting and gusting against the sluggish flow of my viscera.

It rained on Christmas. A fog rolled in from the bay, and I couldn't see out my windows. I ordered weed delivery and whiskey delivery, then, suspicious the color of the liquor was responsible for my gastric distress, switched to vodka, but it didn't make any difference.

I ordered ketamine delivery and fell through chasms of dimness, striving to see around corners, which softened and braided the closer I encroached on their margins. I gobbled Xanax and Vicodin, came to squinting back at Turmeric's slit pupils, and I'd forge a hasty weed edible, and we'd sleep until the earth swung the light of the sun or the moon into novel positions.

I opened old cans of olives. I turned on the radio, tried to listen to music, but I just didn't get it. I stayed inside, stoned, documentaries streaming on mute. *The Civil War*, *The Vietnam War*, *Bitter Lake*, *Shoah*. I'll admit, I was exasperated.

On my parents' forty-second anniversary, the day before New Year's Eve, I texted my former boss and asked for my job renting, transporting, and inventorying camera and lighting equipment back. And I got it, with a pay reduction on a probationary basis. Some people were too nice.

Six days later, at the end of my first reenlisted shift, I dumped the last of the fixtures on a warehouse loading dock. My gut was swollen, distended from flexing butt cheeks in the cab of a box truck, gulping air, counting to ten, counting backward from one thousand by sevens.

I looked at my phone. Five notifications cascaded, texts from my friend Miriam, who earlier that day had invited me to an opening at her friend's art gallery in Bushwick.

*Hey!*
*Happy New Year bitch asszs come out!!!/*
*We durkn*
*We meaning me and everyone*
*come!*

I regarded each word, contemplating the years of joy and supplication that had led Miriam to this language, abruptly thrust upon me. My fingers were cool, practically feline.

*no*, they typed.

I reached for the steering wheel. My phone glowed.

Miriam had texted, *Booooooooooooo*

Yeah, I thought. Boo. I rolled down the window, listened to the ring of white noise, watching shadows like they were an after school special.

I parked the truck in the depot lot, sat at a bar, and scratched out Keno cards with a nubby pencil, crumbling potato chips from the free bowl the bartender brought me into powder.

I played my birthday, Sofia's birthday, over and over, losing, then my mother's birthday, but that time the numbers came back blinking two-digit installments reconstructing my ex-agent's birth date and year, for what would've been a hundred and twenty bucks. I spun a glass on its base until it fell over, and I was ushered to the door nape-first.

Outside, a guy held his dick, emptying it to the heavens. When he was done, I gave him ten dollars.

—Family is everything, he said.

I nodded and ordered a car. Upon its arrival, a half dozen cats swarmed out to greet it. The driver swerved, cursing in preternaturally pacifying, I guessed, Arabic. I got in the back seat.

—Jacob, he asked.

—Thanks. Can you hurry?

—I'm sorry?

—Sorry, I said. —I didn't mean it like that.

—Do we know each other, the driver asked.

I met his eyes in the rearview mirror. He turned around.

—Jal, he said.

He stuck out his hand, and I took it. He'd been a creative writing instructor of mine, a onetime NYU MFA candidate, and now Jal was driving a Yaris for a ridesharing app.

—Damn, I said. —I'm . . . How have you been? I'm sorry for not recognizing you.

—It's okay! Hey, this is wild, right? I don't think this has ever happened to me!

—Me either.

I didn't know what else to say. He'd taught me Introduction to Fiction when I was nineteen. His thesis, a collection of loosely interconnected stories about two friendless men in Brooklyn who ran a failing laundromat, had sold at auction to a Big Six publisher, before it became Five. I tried to remember which, tried to imagine what had become of that promise and momentum, while he did stuff on his phone, put on music, and started toward the gallery.

—I'm sorry, I said. —Can you not play any music?

—No music?

—Yeah . . . I . . . I just don't . . . Never mind. It's fine.

—No music, Jal repeated. —Do you need water? Gum?

—No.

I felt keenly ashamed and watched red and yellow lights bleed along the windshield. The roads streaked with salt. I rested my head on the window.

—Jacob, Jal said.

—Yeah?

I couldn't tell if I'd been asleep.

—Do you like working for free?

—Uh . . . no, I said.

—Because by the time you get the car, the registration, the license, signed up with all the apps, they've got you. They suck you in. I work twelve hours. I make nothing. What is that?

—Uh, I said.

—It's okay!

Jal laughed.

—Hey, I said.

—Hey.

—So, like . . . You know storyboarding. So how come on *Law & Order* cops are always going to people's apartments and the people are always there? Like how often are people in New York really at their apartments at any given time?

—I don't know, Jal said. —Seems unrealistic.

—Anyway . . . Have you been working on anything?

But the car jerked to a halt. Jal leaned back over the center console and handed me a card.

—We're here, man, he itched his nose. —It was great seeing you. Hit me up sometime.

At the gallery, Miriam took my arm and led me past whatever was on the walls, as well as a petite, sexy blonde woman in a green tube top and leather pants with dark drawn-on eyebrows, up a narrow flight of stairs to an unheated room, a woodshop.

Half a boat hung from the rafters, and Matthew was already there. A dropout, dumbfuck painter, who couldn't manage to stop getting arrested for petty offenses, and who I couldn't stop admiring for his dearth of self-awareness, lying on the cold pancake-colored concrete.

We cracked beers and Matthew cut lines of a legal powder I'd never heard of, and which was only legal because no one in government had either, assuming they hadn't clandestinely produced and distributed it for their own nefarious purposes, and we snorted and stretched out, resting our backs against an industrial table saw.

—Day-ay-ay-ay-ay-ay-ay, Miriam said.

Matthew crawled away and lay prone. He let out a tiny, frog-like hiccup.

—My life is a brick, I stated. —A world suck.

—That's crazy.

—I know.

—What's going on with your novel?

—Nothing, I said. —It's scrapped.

—That's crazy.

The powder quickly had me nodding. The beer tasted like bread. My stomach hated it.

—Hey, I said. —Were you guys at 169 Bar on my birthday?

—On your birthday, Matthew clucked.

I shook my head.

—Yeah. But I mean last year. I'm sorry. I meant last year.

—Last year?

—He means 2016, Miriam said.

—That's so long ago.

—Never mind, I sniffed.

—I . . . cannot remember, Miriam guffawed. —I don't think so, though . . . Since I . . . was in *Roma* . . . *Italia* . . . for *Natale* . . . *La Festa delle Luci* . . . I think . . . I can't remember.

She was lovely and tall with gray hostile eyes, wearing a pink Polo under a shredded striped Comme des Garçons shirt buttoned up to the neck, shrouding her glamorous torso in patterns that assaulted my vision, which was getting more kaleidoscopic and hard to deal with.

—I'm sorry, I said. —I'm . . . weird.

—Why weird?

—I couldn't make you out through the window.

—Where, Matthew asked.

—But didn't you realize, Miriam said. —When you got closer, that it wasn't . . . us?

—I never got any closer.

—I don't know what you mean, dude.

—Yeah, I said. —Don't worry about it.

—Cool. How's Sofia?

—We broke up. I've been thinking about calling a therapist.

Matthew rolled over on his back. Miriam discreetly extracted her phone.

—I'm very sensitive, I said.

—Okay, Miriam replied.

And then after a beat:

—Sorry. I'm not ignoring you, I'm reading an article about all the pesticides in Cheerios.

She held up the screen. I couldn't focus my eyes.

Absently, I arose and floundered down the stairs. I grabbed another beer from a trash can filled with ice, stooped through blurred art-world characters out-of-doors to the sidewalk, where I attempted a one-armed push-up, and landed on my chin.

By the time I made it to my favorite bar around the block, Matthew was already there, swaying on the dancefloor under a sordid disco ball. Miriam was squeezed in a booth, nuzzled against our friend Alexander.

—Sup dildo, he mouthed.

—I'm a dildo, I said.

I sat down. Someone pushed me a glass filled with sparkling mead, and I put my arms on the table and my face in my arms with my hand out clutching the stem. Every few seconds, I craned my neck, dropped the glass to my lips.

—What happened to your face, Miriam asked.

I touched my jaw. The skin was raw and bumpy where I'd fallen. It had a pulse.

—What was that powder, I said.

—Yeah, what was that powder, Alexander repeated.

I couldn't tell if he was mocking me. This was a man who'd mastered expressionlessness. He held his phone and his glass and a piece of rope in his hand.

—Research chemical, Matthew squawked, scooting into the booth.

—Pow-ow-ow-ow-ow-ow-ow, Miriam said.

Alexander put his hand over her mouth, and she wrenched, laughing, biting at him. He drew the hand back and appeared to consider something far away. Then he slapped her playfully, but it sounded more complex. People at the table next to us turned. Miriam continued to guffaw.

I shivered, my body negotiating a circle on my side of the booth.

—Should I leave?

—Yeah, Alexander said.

—Nooooooo, Miriam hooted. —Jacob, no. It's Friday. We're having fun. Have a drink.

She took a bottle and proceeded to pour mead into my mostly full glass. Fermented honey dribbled down the sides and over my hand. Miriam held my hand and pushed it toward my face.

—You gotta licky it up.

—Baby, Alexander said. —Pay attention to me.

I licked my hand and stood doubtfully, fumbling for a bathroom, and when I reemerged, Miriam and Alexander and Matthew had abdicated their booth.

I could make them out at the other end of the establishment, hamming it up with a guy in military fatigues and stilettos. I strained, seeking their gaze, but instead locked on the eyebrows of the blonde from the gallery. I made my way to the unoccupied place by her side.

—I'm Jacob.

I sat down.

She laughed.

The world turned.

—I'm Emma, she said.

And soon I was grilling her on what she did, where she'd gone to school, how she'd gotten here, and if she wanted to dance. I drank her Negroni. Our frames nested like wafers.

—What do *you* do, she asked, pupils dilating, lips plumped up and mottled with bright lusty spit.

—Well, I was going to be the voice of my generation. But now I'm just your friend.

Emma grinned. I finished her drink and ordered another round.

—You should quit your job, I said.

—I want to, she paused. —I've been wanting to.

—I can't recommend it enough. I just went back to work today after a year off. It's bad.

—Uh oh, Emma teased. —What are you going to do?

—I don't know.

—How were you going to be the voice of your generation?

—I wrote a novel.

—There must be better ways than that. What's it called?

—*Your Opinion of Jacob Garlicker.*

She looked away, unamused.

—But it's not going to be published, I said. —So don't worry.

—Is that your name?

—Would it be hard to believe?

—I'm . . . just making sure.

My cold hand up her thigh.

—Do you want to hear a joke?

—Yes, I said.

—On a hot summer day, a traveling salesman strolls down a long country road without a soul in sight. Sooner or later, he happens upon an old homestead, where he meets Farmer Joe, who seems genuinely interested in making a purchase. After some idle barter, Joe excuses himself. I'll be back, he promises. Just need to feed my pig. The salesman thinks he's got this rube on the hook. He says he'll be happy to wait. So Farmer Joe departs and the salesman hangs by the door. Well, twenty minutes pass, and he starts feeling impatient. He could really use the business, though. He's got all these Japanese knives, and he resolves to wait a bit longer. So a bit becomes an hour, and an hour becomes two. The salesman decides to go and find Farmer Joe. He walks around the barn to an empty pig pen. The man is nowhere in sight. Now the salesman is capital-F fed up, more determined than ever to sell a knife. He tramps into the pasture, over creeks, valleys, and hills, eventually to an orchard, where he finds Farmer Joe beneath a peach tree, hog hoisted in his arms supping on fruit from the branches one bite at a time. Irate, the salesman yells, What on earth are you doing? That will take hours! Farmer Joe, somewhat startled, replies, Sure. But what's time to a pig?

I ran a hand down my face.

—That's it, Emma said.

—It's good.

—You were supposed to laugh.

—I'm laughing, I said.

—I can tell.

—How come I haven't met you before?

She shrugged.

—I guess you weren't ready.

As the night wore on, we got clumsy, fell into each other's arms and hard, hungry kisses. Emma lost a buckle on her shoe, and when I came back from the bathroom, I realized most of the crowd had dispersed. She was perched in a corner booth, fussing with her severed strap, wound into a crapulous and, from my vantage, incoherent tête-à-tête with Miriam.

—You mean upside down, Emma was asking. —Or inside out?

Miriam used her spindly arms to demonstrate whatever as I approached.

—We aren't talking about you, she snapped and stormed away.

Emma smelled like vetiver. Bass hummed from a subwoofer. Pre-ejaculate wet my leg.

—So, Emma said.
—Where do you live, I asked.
—Manhattan . . . What about you?
I hesitated.
—Coney Island.
Emma laughed.
—Really? Why?
—I love the beach. Don't you?
—As a matter of fact . . .
—Where in Manhattan?
It was Emma's turn to hesitate.
—Greenwich Village.
—Well la-di-da.
—I live with my parents.
—That settles that, I guess. Did you find your buckle?
Emma flinched, shook her head. We sank to the tacky floor under the table and got back up.
—Give me your number, I choked, already flagging under the encounter, the imminent blitz of hangover, and passed Emma my phone. —So I can text if I find it.
She typed and handed it back. She'd sent herself a message. *jacob garlic*, it said.
—You know, Emma wavered. —There's this place in Bed-Stuy . . .
—If only it were ten minutes ago, I wouldn't have had the strength to say good night.
We lingered a few feet apart.
—Let me know when your novel sees print, she said.
—I will, I smiled. —But it won't.
She blew me a kiss.

The next morning Emma texted to tell me she'd found the buckle in the pocket of her plastered-on leather pants. And we made plans to hang out the following week, but I canceled them.

I had unfinished business to attend to before I could entangle my life in hers. I had to bottom out.

And by the end of that summer I had, trying to drive a box truck over the Belt Parkway median at five o'clock on a Sunday morning while under the influence of ketamine and alcohol.

Since I'd said goodbye to my agent, and my novel was shelved, the haunted feeling that so consumed my solitude had returned, not only for me, but seemingly anyone I kept close.

First to go was my creative writing instructor. Within a month of my calling the number on his card, Jal fell victim to a fentanyl overdose. I'd caught up with him after dropping my truck off and flaking on Emma, and we started hanging out, getting drunker and more out of control.

One night we snorted heroin in a bar's tight bathroom stall and took a long walk through Ridgewood, where he came out to me as trans, despite having no interest in transitioning.

—Which pronouns should I use then, I asked. —I mean, going forward?

—Whatever makes you second-guess your good intentions.

She invited me back to her studio, and I said no.

In any case, Jal was saved by a passerby's Narcan spray that same night, slumped against her stoop, and we barely spoke again. Maybe she was embarrassed. I didn't find out about the initial OD until her funeral. All I knew was she properly died a week later by a hotter opioid hit.

It pushed me over. An almost friend. A real person I'd known and even begun to care for. And she had really died.

Jal was gone. And the way I was living, I didn't have many friends left.

Sometime that spring, Matthew joined her. This time the fentanyl compressed into a tablet cleverly disguised as Klonopin. He took his final sips of oxygen splayed in the foyer of a derelict residential building a block from Woodhull Hospital, and was pronounced dead there, just as my bygone pedagogue had been months earlier.

It felt like a bad joke. The guilt rose from the bottom of my stomach, and my pain soared.

With the loss of these companions, on top of everything else, I didn't want to know anyone. I couldn't stand to entrust or devote. Fear fed my anguish, the yearnings of writing, my evermore-abstruse attempts at communication, and I began to lose sight of what was truly there.

At which point, my mother invited me to celebrate her sixty-first birthday. She'd rented a cabin on the coast of Maine, none the wiser to my darkening condition. It was easier to thrash on the rug in front of the radiator, chuck viscous liquor handles out the window, lose my phone under rocks in the jetties for days. But I couldn't say no.

I transferred from train to bus to bus with a debilitating, apoplectic cold coming on. My nose turgid with mucus, yet somehow I crammed ketamine and bad cocaine in there too, smoking heroic joints inside to my parents' disdain, and killed a bottle of rosé to myself every evening.

I gave my mother a necklace adorned with a miniscule sapphire. I could hazily summon the browned-out flash of my hand digging through someone's purse, propped on a barstool while she'd stretched on tiptoe, trying to read a cocktail list. It still reeked of this stranger's perfume.

—Is there anything, my mother faltered. —Anything we can do to help tide you over?

Her model of pediatric physical therapy required the clinician to foster endemic empathy, which in turn I'd learned to aloofly deflect.

—It was daunting when I changed careers, my father said. —You've got to search inward for nuggets of light. Do you still have that LSAT prep book? Or what about a coding boot camp?

—*Yom huledet*, I said, and stutter-stepped to the bathroom.

I littered bits of me all over. I saw bugs in the sheets, up the walls. I picked holes in my skin. My T-shirt disintegrated. My flip-flops fell apart while I walked.

One afternoon, sitting on a sweep of crags by the shore, glowering into the vacancy that ruled me, I detected a stifled whimper coming from the shallow pool that formed in the ebb.

My heart leapt. My intestines convulsed. I tore to the basin, where a seal pup sniveled in the overcast. Its eyes were misty and innocent. Its fin mangled, ensnared under a rock.

I had to tell someone. But did I have time? Should I call animal control? What would they do, though? The seal was a child. It was separated from its parents, its family and comrades. Maybe the seal had pets. And wasn't animal control just cops for fauna? Would the pup be permitted to paddle out on its own, or promptly abducted without heed for its eccentricities or interior will? Even if these tyrants ultimately restored the creature to its habitat, would the seal be able to locate its kinfolk again? And if it did, would it find itself ostracized, traumatized, denigrated? Would it ever recover from the terror of being controlled? And how polluted was the tide pool? How long could a wounded seal survive exposed to the indifferent world?

The pup made a sound. I turned in circles, stoned and half-drunk in the glittering buzz.

Catching sight of a log of driftwood, I wielded the timber and pushed at the rock pinning its fin. The beast bared razor teeth, mouth red, ululating. I pushed again. It flailed.

—Shh, I said.

I managed to roll the rock then. And liberated, the seal regarded me with a look of such disorientation, I knew I'd done the wrong thing.

I watched it plop, onerous, dizzily tumbling toward the sea. It swam in circular jags, favoring its uninjured fin, bobbing in the surf, confused, alone, singing a song of rare agony.

I watched until its head descended underwater and didn't surface again. And when I returned to the city the following evening, alternating between toots of K and gin in the jolting back seat of a Megabus chilled to my bones, I beelined to the depot lot, plunged a key into a box truck's ignition, and let the Belt Parkway elect my next move.

In the aftermath of the wreck, my mother rushed out to my beach. I gave her the bed and lay on a mat on the floor, fuzzy episodes of *The Office* blinking over me whenever I dared open my eyes.

I called a sliding-scale counseling center and got set up with a therapist, who bore my sob-garbled nonsense and explained it right back. She vied to parse just why I didn't actually want to kill myself, though I was considering suicide more all the time.

Suicide as a thing. An essence, an emanation. Like a Wikipedia page. Like the very one suicide had. And I referred to it, its origins and chronicles and rites. Not that I wanted to think about how, but I did. Each second to myself assailed with visions of hanging, falling, wrists slit, piling on drugs in the bath and drowning again and again.

I lost thirty pounds, and when I casually brought up the lump filling my bloated gut to my therapist, she made it out to be dire. Appointments were scheduled, wherein specialists guided cameras up my rectum and down my throat, finding nothing treatable, and ordering more tests with which to bill my insurance until they ran out.

Among this thready opacity, I was encouraged by every authority, though their tones invariably verged on threats, to quit drinking, lest I show up sloshed to some consultation and be tethered to an inpatient bed. I couldn't tell how seriously to take this, but I feared, stripped of physical freedom, I'd discover a lot worse than death. So suddenly, I kicked the habit. Much more easily than I expected. And thus most drugs went by that wayside too, save for weed, for which ironically they advocated, for my appetite's sake. The only official medical directive I received, after months of inconclusive testing, was technically a guess: avoid gluten, and I had ever since.

Gradually I became stable, talking my way into an administrative assistant position coordinating schedules and spreadsheets for the production company for doing fashion shoots, suckling THC lollipops, speaking in exaggerated accents to Turmeric, preparing ginger-dense probiotic meals, and pacing the perimeter of my apartment, attempting to calculate exactly how and when my life would have to change, or if it would have to, before total global collapse set in.

Even as I harbored an aspiration to fashion one of the thick orange extension cords Sam had left behind in the apartment years before into a noose and string myself up in the closet, I started to accept the soft futility of everything. Life would always be at least a little terrible, and I should try to adopt a receptive attitude about it.

I hadn't reached out to a peer in eight months when I decided to badger Emma by text. A dry *hi*, an offhand flirt, just to see if I still knew how to interact. And she was so gentle and amenable, I ran over with giddiness. I sent her pictures of Turmeric. She screenshotted poems and memes. We initiated a book club and read *Middlemarch* and *Bob the Gambler* and *Dark Money*. Whenever it came time to meet and discuss, though, an excuse flew from my fingertips.

Likewise, I made increasingly regular visits to Rhode Island at my father's spurring on:

—It's not complicated. We're accessible. Mom misses you, go get a train.

For the first time since young childhood, I felt my relationship with my parents bloom. They were people, I realized. They had internal lives.

My mother signed over her old Camry so I could make the trip more efficiently. Her pen hovering above the title. Her skin lax, yet resilient.

And as the final equinox of that doleful decade crept up, I impulsively drove to the Adirondacks, trunk replete with a colossal dose of LSD. Once and for all, I'd resigned that I would succumb to hypothermia while I tripped. The temperature, however, never dropped below fifty degrees. I can't tell what I saw, because it was fractalized in every respect, but I returned without even meager desire to take my own life, or much desire at all.

That week, Emma invited me to an opening at Miriam's friend's gallery.

All the walls were painted black. A hallway had been fashioned, and I traversed it to its terminus. Through an enclosed glass partition, a ringing rotary phone came into view, hanging above an enormous wax baby bird, shriveled and featherless, strapped to an operating table. And there Emma tarried, gawking at the loud mess.

—This sucks, she confirmed.
—Do you want a ride home?
—Yes, she said.

And in the town house on Tenth Street, her parents away for the weekend, preserved by the asylum of the island, Emma and I consummated our fate.

For the next glorious half a year, we saw each other every week, cooked dinner, went on windy cathartic walks. Each time we'd pass the site of that tenebrous horror from my twenty-sixth birthday, I was impelled to divulge to Emma what I'd seen. But I never knew how to begin, and more often, I wondered if I'd been wholly mistaken, drugged out and desperate for narrative. Though deep down I knew the transgression had been all too real, over time, whether deliberate or inadvertent, I'd forget to notice it completely, only recalling we'd trampled over that unhallowed ground hours or days later, certain I had nothing to confess but my own inanity.

Better we save money, pretend Bernie Sanders could be president, make love and plans.

—This summer, Emma yawned. —I really do want to quit my job.
—You should, I said.
—And get a dog.
—Okay.

—Named Houdini.

—It all sounds fine to me.

Two months later, alternate-side parking rules were suspended for an unspecified period. The subways stopped running routinely. The city went on lockdown.

First, I lost my job, then Emma hers. Three weeks after it temporarily closed its doors to visitors, the museum where she worked laid off or furloughed ninety-five employees.

My therapist scheduled phone sessions, which we neglected to keep. Emma and I jogged on the boardwalk. We walked on the beach. Graphics cropped up with two arrows, displaying a hollow spectrum of six feet. Signs on the BQE said, STAY INSIDE, and we acquiesced.

Houdini arrived panting and tongue to the sidewalk the week the flash-bangs began.

Someone flung an old copy of *The Great Gatsby* at my window, and I went downstairs and picked it up with a plastic bag. I smothered it in hand sanitizer, which smelled like cheap tequila and was produced in a prison upstate, and in the dead center of the book, I found a single line highlighted in red ink:

*The rich get richer and the poor get—children.*

Emma and I protested the cops until people started sleeping outside City Hall. We took the Camry to Long Island to cool off, then Rhode Island, and sprawled on the wall-to-wall carpet of the condo's upstairs loft space.

When my annual lease renewal appeared in the mail, myriad roads and storefronts were still shuttered throughout the five boroughs. People scrunched under masks. Everyone looked sorrowful and more gorgeous, eyes being uncanny reverent portals to the soul, chins being iffy at best.

The document contained a rent hike, so I crumpled it up, and we cleaned out the apartment, transporting my possessions to my parents' basement.

I discarded a lot of things. I donated whatever clothes hadn't been reduced to rags. I sold my antique love seat with animal paws for feet. I shuffled to the shoreline and stared at the water. I cast the nameplate that said *MY OFFICE* into the bay.

Houdini edged toward the surf. He scampered away from the flow.

My car groaned low on its chassis, weighed down by epochs of accretion. We forced Turmeric into her carrier, and Emma and I held hands as we drove away from the city, sweltering, dustified, blaring with grief.

The following winter, the world volatile, our bank accounts brimming from unemployment benefits, I got down on one knee and presented her a gold ring set with a diamond my paternal grandma had given my mother at some time immemorial and obliterated.

—Yes, Emma said.

# SATURDAY

Bats kept swooping overhead as I walked from the bar back to my in-laws' house.

I expected to find the party still in full swing, but all was silent. The windows clouded. Back patio empty. Braids of foil from broken bottle seals flitting along the bricks.

Turmeric materialized, her eyes flashing through the vapor. She purred and performed figure eights between my shins.

—Yellow, I grunted.

I stooped to pet her, but my cat loped off to the vacant A-frame next door, and I slipped in the cottage, guiding my way through by touch. Warily, I eased the knob to Emma's bedroom.

Houdini perked up. He was splayed across my side of the mattress and let out a whine like air leaving a balloon. My wife slept soundly. Ashes from a smoked bowl dusted her cheek. I blew on it, gently cleaved the pipe from her grip. I tried to spark the remains, but there was nothing to catch.

I undressed and slithered up against Emma's back. I attempted to spoon, but my wife's limbs were static. Rigid and laden with unconsciousness. And oddly chilled.

Yet I sensed the supple bob of her breathing. I endeavored to rearrange her skeleton with mine to no avail. I lay supine and stared at the stucco. I couldn't see anything.

In the morning, my ear hurt bad. And I was alone, rent from sleep by the throbbing. Loud stabs down my spine. A sallow glare through the window. It didn't feel as though I had REMed.

And worse still, as I hobbled into the kitchen, delirious for caffeine and on the threshold of tears, I discovered Emma was ignoring me.

—Hi, I whispered.

I batted at the Moccamaster, not yet attempting eye contact. My wife didn't answer, and after I'd downed a tall serving of lukewarm mud, I turned to smile at her, but she was gone.

Turmeric caressed the back of my legs with her tail, then nibbled my Achilles tendon, and I yelped. My head was weighed down. Like my ear had become the durable leather casing of a bludgeoning sap filled with powdered lead, and I lurched to the glass sliding door. I threw my whole body into it, a cacophony ringing through my brainpan as the oppressive ingress met me, and lurched out to the patio, where the sun blazed midday heat.

Emma reclined on a chaise lounge snapping the paper, eyes concealed by sunglasses.

—Hi, I whispered a bit louder.

She dipped the newsprint.

—Good morning, I tried to soften.

Emma opened and closed her mouth.

—What, I said.

She folded the paper, tapped it against a milky thigh. My muscles tensed, anticipating the worst. Instead, she was mellow.

—It's hardly morning, she uttered, moving toward the sliding glass door.

—What time is it?

—Why don't you check your phone?

Emma bolted inside. I racked my doughy mind for what my phone had to do with things. Then I remembered where it was.

Emma was not in the kitchen. She wasn't in her bedroom either. Or the closet, where I dug through the pockets of my suit.

The device took a while to turn on. Its screen blinked and went black, glitching, then prompted for a passcode. I keyed it in wearily.

My phone said, *1:13*, and issued a series of vibrations and notifications from the previous night. I had a half dozen missed calls, and Emma had texted plenty more times than that.

*Where did you sneak off to?*

*I'm getting worried . . .*

*Would you please just give me some indication you're ok and not in trouble? This is weird*

*I'm going to bed*

*Are you all right?????????*

I didn't read through them all, but I got the gist and sagged to the floor, scrolling Twitter abstractedly.

I hadn't told Emma about running into Sofia the morning prior for any number of reasons. I hadn't lied. She'd asked where I'd been, and I was forthright: I'd gone for a walk on the beach.

Perhaps I couldn't profess to have been entirely truthful. And if I wanted to fix things, I could always come clean, explain what had transpired, why it had drawn me away in the night. But I didn't want to. The way I'd felt crouched in the sand, and again at the backyard party, the way I'd felt for the past almost year, I only longed to forget, get drunk like a normal eccentric, desolate and adrift, disaffected to all, because I knew how things worked even if I appeared to be little more than an appendage propping up Michael's daughter amid a frothing birthday romp.

And anyway, if I did let her in on my interiorities, my most distorted adumbrations of headlong reality, Emma still wouldn't understand. If I emboldened myself to admit the narrow ambitions and misgivings at the root of these recent run-ins with Sofia, my wife would merely remind me that we'd already squandered the last several months on circular histrionics, my tortuous family dramas, and it was only fair that I set ego aside for one weekend and be present.

She knew I despised my ex-girlfriend, her castles in the air and knee-jerk lies, but how could Emma be expected to feel the succubine pull Sofia had exercised over me, in apparently enduring form?

I shuddered. My wife had indulged the annals of erratic reactions to my novel's failure to sell. She'd entertained my muddled history with addiction, my obsessive fits of suicidal fancy and inability to cope with disappointment. As far as she was concerned, she'd done her diligence. But it wasn't her life. She'd never know the intricate caprices of my terror world. There was enough pressure on her reentering the workforce in the wake of suppressed, appalling events I hadn't managed to wrap my head around. And Emma and I hadn't even determined how her job would impact our day-to-day, where we lived, or anything else. Would I be returning to Rhode Island or joining her in the city? Would she be working hybrid, or in-office, or remotely? The last thing she needed was the weight of new extraneous uncertainties. But that was all I could offer. Orotund illusions, pitiless waves. They were my very makeup. The succor and fulcrum of my ungodly architecture among the roar of surf-tormented shores and dreams within dreams.

Something felt off about the deal with Sofia besides. Did she really believe my Gatsby angle could sell? I couldn't put my finger on it.

With my free hand, I thumbed through the wrung paperback. I took a photo of its thirty-fourth page, cropped so all that remained were three short paragraphs of dialogue:

> "I almost made a mistake, too," she declared vigorously. "I almost married a little kike who'd been after me for years. I knew he was below me. Everybody kept saying to me: 'Lucille, that man's 'way below you!' But if I hadn't met Chester, he'd of got me sure."
> "Yes, but listen," said Myrtle Wilson, nodding her head up and down, "at least you didn't marry him."
> "I know I didn't."

And in the lower right corner of my phone's screen, I pressed a blue plus sign button and posted the picture to Twitter, appending a caption, which said simply, *daisy-chained*.

I found Turmeric stalking a case of art books. I pulled her up by the scruff of the neck and swung her off the back patio.

—You're not welcome here, I gnashed.

Emma looked up from the hammered glass table, looked back down. She'd changed into a string bikini, and her skin glowed under a fine sheen of lotion. Neat rows of jellybeans arrayed the tabletop. My wife picked at them, appraising burnish and speckles, while across the lawn, Houdini squatted. His neck contorting, head arched back, vulnerable and anxious.

A sturdy log plunked. He stomped his back paws and sprinted in widening gyres. Emma rose with a newspaper leaf and picked up the excretion.

—Hey, I said, trotting over. —I can get rid of that for you.

My wife studied the paper, then glanced in my direction. I held out open arms.

—Allow me, I slipped into my Cockney accent.

Houdini came over and jumped at our knees.

—Sit, I said.

He tilted his head to Emma and started to pant. I took the newspaper to the garage, dropped it in a trash can. I returned to the patio and sat at the foot of my wife's chaise lounge.

—Thanks, she muttered.

—Oh, my pleasure. I have no aversion to handling errant fecal matter.

Emma didn't look as impressed as I'd hoped.

—So, she said. —Where were you last night?

I watched my hands. I wished I was wearing sunglasses too.

—I got sand in my ear at the beach yesterday. I didn't want to make a big scene, but it's been bothering me a lot.

I shook my head, stuck my pinky in to prove it. I made a fragile face.

—And then with the party . . . and all the people you know, I just felt . . . overwhelmed. I wanted a drink. I was embarrassed. So I walked to the Talkhouse. But then I wanted one more, so I kept walking around and I lost track of time, and by the time I got home, everyone was in bed.

I did my best to meet where I figured Emma's gaze landed. She exhaled.

—Why didn't you say something?

—I don't know.

—Or text me. Or reply to any of my texts or calls?

—I turned my phone off, I said. —It was in the house the entire night. It was, like, a distraction. If I'd brought it with me, I never would've cleared my head. I was all out of sorts.

—You should've had your phone with you. What if there'd been an emergency?

—I hate my phone, I said. —I hate the way it ties you to everything . . . Or, not you. I hate how it fixes everything. Convenience makes for boring plot. I like the freedom of solitude.

—But you're not solitary, Jacob. You're not a hermit. There are people counting on you.

I rubbed my face. I wanted her to know how I felt. Even if it wasn't the way things had happened, what I was saying was still true, to me. It was my truth. I wanted her to agree with it.

—I don't know why it has to be like that.

—Like what?

—Like why do you have to be a victim? Why do you have to prove you weren't wrong?

—Listen. Emma. I can tell you how I was feeling, or I can just say I'm sorry.

—An apology would be nice.

—Well, I am sorry.

But why didn't she want to know how I was feeling? Did that matter? I couldn't be sure.

—You missed the cake, my wife sulked. —And handing out gifts.

—Was the cake gluten-free?

—No, she said. —But it wasn't your birthday, was it?

—And how should I have known about gifts? How many parties are there this weekend?

—If you didn't know there were supposed to be gifts, why did you get my dad something? And why did I have to wrap it and give it to him last minute?

—What, I frowned.

—The plaque you got him. The office thing? I told him it was from both of us. But why didn't you tell me about it? Why did I find it knotted up in our sheets?

A tremor ran through me. My stomach turned. I could feel the wandering lump reemerge and somersault against some organs. The sand yowled in my skull.

—I . . . I'm sorry, I stammered. —I didn't realize we were supposed to give gifts last night.

—It's fine, she said, waving her hand. —Anyway, he loved it. He hung it in his studio this morning. You should take a look. He wanted to thank you.

She popped a jellybean in her mouth.

—Well . . . I'll make up for it. Or something . . . Somehow . . . I raised my hands in surrender. My wife nodded.

—Hug?

She nodded again, and we embraced in the afternoon sun.

—So, I let the word fall. —What're you up to for the rest of the day?

—Well, my dad is off playing golf. He should be gone until three or four. And my mom's swimming laps at the club. We've got the house to ourselves, if you wanted some privacy . . .

My brow furrowed. Emma's short, filed nails skated over my thigh.

—My ear really does hurt, I complained. —Are you planning on going to the beach?

—I was thinking about it, she said. —I guess I'll walk over in a bit . . . Will you join me?

—I need to do something about this sand. It's fucking killing me. I hardly slept.

—Take a hot shower and lie on your side. I'm sure it will maneuver itself out.

—It feels very bad, I said.

—You're just tense. You just need to relax.

—I felt relaxed when we were coming down here.

—I thought you were stressed.

—I thought *you* were.

—I'm going to the beach, my wife said, standing up. —Take a shower and lie down. Meditate or something. I don't know. And leave your phone on in case I need to get in touch with you.

She bent over, her breasts brushing my forearm, and my blood moved. Emma kissed me, opening my lips with hers, and when I opened my eyes, she was disappearing around a corner.

—And look after Houdini!

The dog shot up, but she'd already latched the gate to the backyard, and all he could do was sprain on two legs scratching it.

I stood in the shower with the water on scalding. I kept popping my ears and smacking the side of my head, but nothing gave. The sand had become a part of me.

And I sobbed, mashing my eye sockets with my fists in the middle of one of the ambiguous spaces tucked into my wife's parents' home. It wasn't large, but the cottage was divided in weblike segments, and I remained its alien.

As a child, I'd fantasized about getting lost in a house. The allure of equivocal doors. Underground passageways. False walls and hidden tunnels. Stuff like this didn't exist. My fixations did though. The world was not designed for mystery. Yet mystery designed the world.

Upstairs, I found myself ducking at a slanted eave outside Michael's studio. I bowed in and was accosted by radiant gold. I squinted. The MY OFFICE plaque hung tantalizingly over my father-in-law's desk. Beneath it was a high-contrast glossy black-and-white photo of the family's Greenwich Village town house, stark brick with white stone steps.

The apartment on Tenth Street was fashioned with tireless maximalism. Michael had cut skylights in the third floor's paisley ceiling. High shelves lined with Penguin Classics and homemade penguin figurines. Rooftop apiary boxes teemed with ivy-fed honey. Jane's forte was glass and ceramics, candlesticks, floral arrangements. And something as subtle as a folding table covered with Christmas ornaments in early February exuded poignant humanity.

Naturally I'd assumed my in-laws were affluent. Until forbearance proved they were truly post-rich. Enough to sustain dignified mystique, but it didn't take long to deduce the best years of that well-spent money were a thing of the past.

I had a good idea before I proposed to their daughter anyway. Maybe they thought I was disappointed, but it had been obvious that Emma and I would be married from the moment we met, and ludicrous to suppose I'd ever been in a position that made social mobility appropriate.

The photo reminded me of a puddle. I wanted to keel into it. Had I, a Gateway computer monitor dappled with sticky notes would've broken my fall. The keyboard was nowhere in sight. In its place: piles of colored pencils, charcoal, crayons, fresh and crusted-up brushes, palettes, and sundry pens, quills, and nibs.

Diverse projects in varied states of completion accumulated on top of one another. Paintings of grids, silos, fences. Drawings of Chuckles candies and waves. A watercolor of a mauve, half-full bottle next to three cryptic orbs, inscribed *HEAVEN'S HIGHWAY*. And most recently an assemblage of different media portraying clusters of dewy trompe-l'œil grapes.

I unearthed yellowing front pages of the *New York Times*: Twin Towers smoldering, Jeremy Lin's hot streak with the Knicks in the spring of 2012. Disposable coffee cups scarred with half-and-half films. Chocolate stains and decomposing fruit peels. A Don Quixote and Rocinante marionette strung from the lintel. Blue bromide paper. One ivory piano key trapped in lucite. A note, which said, *Found a preposterous jug! –Jane*

There were popped-open SLR cameras, expired COVID tests. A broomstick slouched in the corner adorned with Citarella bags. Brooks Brothers boxers were torn into strips. A slab of corrugated metal was nailed to a piece of Masonite, nailed to a pine board, all slathered in lacquer and gesso with construction paper grape cutouts on top, and outlined in a border of skinny, corroding pastels.

I turned in a circle. The MY OFFICE plaque sparkled anew. I closed my eyes. I was woozy, and when I opened them, they fell on a metallic plastic bag of weed gummies. I shoved three in my mouth, chomped them to plasma, and backed out of the room.

With the flimsy Fitzgerald wedged under my armpit, I flung myself across a daybed. I repositioned my body with my feet until half of it was hanging off, tip of my cranium just touching the floorboards, arms tangled below, clasping the book upside down, inverted, like the condition in which I'd discovered Michael upon our arrival thirty-nine hours earlier.

So unlike my own father, Michael was a man without foibles or awkwardness. He was pure glazed wrinkly smiles, only to perceive upon sneezing that he'd lost a front tooth. And, faced with this, he'd shrug off any riddle of how or why it might have disappeared, cruise down to one of his dentists, and return with a replacement the same afternoon.

Emma's father floated through the days, from his mostly defunct art consulting firm in the Upper East Side to the shores of the island, forgetting iPads on park benches, passports on city buses, and driver's licenses in foreign rental cars along the way. He took life's pernicious inconveniences in stride with fazeless aplomb. The closest he ever came to rattling was when he got hungry, which happened often enough, but was more quickly assuaged. Hence, he effused powerful confidence, though this may have been genuine disengagement with the here and now.

Michael had been diagnosed with stage four pancreatic cancer before I'd met his daughter. He'd been given three months. And these six years later, the disease went strictly unmentioned, and my father-in-law enjoyed his red wine and gin, in addition to the weed edibles, cigars, and Danishes.

Initially, I'd been under the impression that his lackadaisical attitude toward mortality and the disruptive crises of each day had something to do with his upbringing amid mammoth wealth. Hints were dropped of a great real estate mogul in the ancestral lineage. Anecdotes that as a boy, growing up in the Carlyle Hotel, to which some family member held the deed, and where Ludwig Bemelmans had immortalized his cherubic smirk among the iconic bar's decor, Michael had believed cabs were an organic amenity of New York and, because the doormen of miscellaneous origins and destinations always paid his fare, ergo free of charge.

The more I got to know him, the more I believed my father-in-law would've adopted that same temperament had he been raised destitute in a shanty buried in the Deep South. The man was indeed aberrant, steeped within a private world of baroque inner beauty and outlandishness.

Rumor had it, he'd been poised for success as the next painting cynosure. I'd seen photos of him cavorting with the likes of Gerhard Richter, Claes Oldenburg, and Julian Schnabel. He'd been kicked out of prep school by the father of our onetime attorney general for improper grooming. He'd gone on to teach at universities in Santiago and Rome. He was an expert witness in a high-profile forgery case in the nineties, as well as one in marble and wallpaper and landscaping, and had designed a few celebrities' homes.

But something implicit must have prevented his eminence, because Michael didn't have a Wikipedia page, and none of my peers recognized him by name. Like many seniors who become embroiled in televised far-off conflicts, he was being relegated to irrelevance by time. And while his lauding contemporaries steadily aged out or perished, I related to that. He was the thread running between Emma's curious love for me and her devotion to this endangered Waspy stripe.

I felt guilty for not making more of an effort with Michael on his birthday. It was probably a big deal to him. Yet I felt guiltier still ruminating on how much more I admired this man than my own flesh-and-blood parents, and I'd all but resolved to stop wondering if we'd ever have the chance to plainly sit and talk again.

It had been too much. I didn't want to think. I could barely hear out of my ear now. All it detected was inflammation. I whipped the *Gatsby* paperback out of view and cradled my face.

It took a few minutes to locate the book, jammed fast in a transfer grille under a Chippendale secretary.

I reread the first page, and by the time I'd validated my analysis that Nick Carraway's exordium did not solely establish him as an unprejudiced, unreliable narrator, but withal differentiated his broadminded tolerance from the insidious antisemitism of the ensuing Anglo bourgeois cast, the garage door engaged, and Michael's Fiat choked off.

I was abruptly very stoned. I tried to look casual, but alternatively I fell off the daybed as my father-in-law dragged his golf bag into the chamber and leaned it against a wall.

—Jacob, he rasped.

I pushed myself upright and extended my hand. He mooned at it, shook it once.

—Happy birthday, I said. —How were the links?

—Luxury, man, Michael answered. —Your ear doing okay?

I blushed. Emma must have warned him. It was an ordinary impulse on her part, a natural trouble on mine, absolutely nothing to feel ashamed of, yet I did. I presumed everyone privately believed I was oversensitive, vainly weak, perpetually on the brink of another breakdown.

—I've just been taking it easy.

I wagged my book.

—Fan-tas-tic. Emma tells me you've been writing?

—Not exactly.

—Plugging away on a singular tract of criticism. Nose to the grindstone and whatnot.

—Oh . . . Well. I'm still in the brainstorming phase.

But Michael was looking away.

—Have you seen my navy-blue blazer?

—I think it's in Emma's closet, I feigned dubiety. —Let me grab it for you.

The jacket was covered in pinpoint blemishes left by the haze from my midnight stroll. I brushed it, smearing them. And when I returned, garment over my arm, Michael was gone.

I heard him whistling something militaristic through the television snow in my ear. Then a splash and sputtering of water.

—Oh hell, Michael yelled.

—I'm ho-ome, my mother-in-law called.
—Janey, can you hear me, from behind the bathroom door.
—I fell in the toilet again!

I slung the jacket over the golf bag and waddled back to Emma's room. I lay on a tousled coverlet, trying to decide where I should count backward from and by what integer. Beneath me Houdini made puckers in the box spring. After a while, I heard voices. The jingle of a shaken cocktail.

Then Emma was peeling off her bikini. Her body ripe, glimmered with salt. I couldn't help noting it had been extra luminous the past few weeks. The bed soughed under her naked physique.

—How are you feeling?

—Pretty bad, I replied too hastily. —I think I need to see a doctor.

She pressed her lips to my forehead.

—Will you be okay for one night?

I screwed my eyes up, opened them.

—Just one night, my wife implored. —It would mean so much. I know it's not easy. I know you're probably . . . triggered . . . And you have every right to be. Your parents . . .

—Okay, I interrupted. —It's all right. I'll be fine.

—I know where my dad keeps weed edibles, Emma intoned from a distance, the swishing sound of her towel. —Do you want some? To help with the pain?

She passed me two more gummies, and I ate one and gestured. She shook her head.

—Keep it. In case you need a refresher.

I saluted, and Emma bumped around, dog at her heels, smelling of oceanwater and bonbons, and as the fourth weed edible took root, the twinge in my ear dwindled, and I joined my family on the back patio and gladly downed an espresso.

Spirits rose. The drone of crickets and frogs. And at seven, we all frittered away, eagerly dressing. I hadn't worn my suit since our wedding. It didn't fit any differently, but something wasn't right. It felt mired, gauzy on my thighs. Almost as if it were decaying. I observed myself in the mirror, and Emma appeared in the glass, just about painted into a black Versace knit dress. She put her arms around me, then seemed to have the same inexplicable reaction to the suit that I'd had and let go.

—You look sexy, I said.

She dropped a hand to her hip, then went back to making adjustments. I took out my phone. Sofia had emailed me a Google Calendar event: *Invitation: Meeting at the A. Martha Philips, Ltd. Office @ Fri July 14, 2023 2pm - 3pm (EDT)*. I opened the link. My thumb hung over the *No* button. I pressed *Maybe* and deleted the email.

—Everyone ready, Jane chirped.

I ran my tongue over itself.

—Try to have fun, I said, but no one noticed.

And as we climbed in the BMW, I slipped the fifth weed gummy into my mouth.

The country club parking lot was already full. A Rolls-Royce had its hood open and two frosty cavaliers were falling into it, golf cleats pointed to the sky like park bench anti-homeless spikes.

Michael emerged from the M3 and threw back his head. He was wearing a shellacked straw hat, the navy-blue blazer with a Drake's pocket square, Nantucket red chinos embroidered with little yachts, Italian loafers, and loud Paul Smith socks. Then, arms akimbo, he bent at the knees, both of which had been replaced with titanium counterparts the preceding fall.

—How are your springs holding up, my mother-in-law inquired.

She was wearing another Marimekko sundress and a wide-brimmed crochet hat.

—Exquisitely, Michael said.

A couple of natty dotards were stationed against a stone wall, brandishing cigars. They waved Michael over, and my father-in-law bounded across the lot.

—Careful, Jane shouted.

—Happy birthday, Dad, Emma hailed.

I blinked, seeing spots. The sky a dome of pink. The tide trickling out with terns cutting swaths through the wan combustion, their wings black blades, winnowing.

Jane greeted guests, each progressively older and richer than the last. My feet were heavy, ankles loose. I had to concentrate on every step. Doormen clad in white twinkled at the corner of my vision. A cannon blasted, and Emma grabbed my arm to keep me from collapsing.

Everyone had turned toward the four beating flags, their right hands over their hearts. The Red, White, and Blue was unsnapped from its halyard and some teens in maritime garb folded it up. I felt weak blood jumping behind my ribs. And suddenly the ritual was done.

We skimmed into the clubhouse. Hands clapped on my back, foisted drinks, which I snuffled, and Emma moved them away, plucking miniature spring rolls and bacon-wrapped dates off silver trays, abiding overwrought compliments, abbreviated introductions, pushing palms into meaty, jeweled fingers, half-curtsying to our recipients' glee.

A guy with a rockabilly haircut led a drowned-out swing band. Waitstaff darted, gagged by pointy bowties. Sweating bottles clattered in and out of buckets. Candles melted chartreuse tears three feet down. Pats of butter were pressed into the shape of seashells. A piping plover ice sculpture chipped apart. And we found our seating assignments on a dais overlooking it all.

—How are you feeling, Emma asked.

—Baked, I said.

Which worked out fine, because the gluten-free options for dinner included a buffet of lobster tails, oysters, prime rib, striped bass, cremini mushrooms, asparagus, and caprese salad with Cherokee purple tomatoes and buffalo mozzarella, and I ate until my jowls were cramped.

Emma had finished. I saw her perched on the knee of a man whose eyes looked closed by the assortment of moles on his cheeks and brow, as several tiered cakes were carted out.

I burped my way to the bathroom. Every color vivid. Beads of sink water dotted my face, and I believed I must vomit, but in the stall I just sudated and retched.

Back in the hall, someone was clinking a fork against crystal. Then more people joined in, and I had an awful premonition something was going to shatter, so I shielded my eyes.

—All right, Michael pretended to demur. —Okay. Just a second. Thank you everyone.

A cordless microphone was conferred from body to body until it found itself in his clutches. He tapped it. Feedback whined through the speakers.

—Woof, Michael barked.

The feedback ceased.

—Old army trick.

I scanned the room for Emma. She wore a look of bamboozled revulsion. Michael was holding his arms out, flapping, wangling the party down, then back up, then down again.

—Okay, he croaked. —Thank you. It really is an honor. An honor to have even, his voice caught, the throng hushed. —Even made it to tonight. For a minute I was sure I'd be late . . .

Expressions of merriment. A rim shot from the drummer.

—I'm not one for speeches, he carried on. —I'd just like to say thank you. I love you all. For the past seventy years, you've been a part of my world. A part of my family. And family . . .

He pursed his lips. Eyes misting his glasses. He took them off, clumsily cleaned the lenses. Jane wiped tears with her napkin. He nodded to Emma, and then me, hugged his free arm around his wife's shoulder.

—Family, Michael repeated. —Is everything!

Applause broke. The man of the hour dropped the microphone. The band maybe started going, but I couldn't hear over the popping of corks, and I felt relieved. A champagne flute was thrust into my grasp. Emma pinched my butt cheek. I pointed at the drink and she showed effulgent teeth.

—Go ahead, one can't hurt.

My eyes widened. I tipped my forehead to hers. Then tipped it back and allowed a drib of Piper-Heidsieck to fizzle across my tongue. I swallowed and gasped, and Emma kissed my neck. Michael pulled her into an embrace. He wrapped me in a bear hug.

—*Mazel tov*, I said.

—That's rich, Jacob. Rich!

And he howled, trotting wolfishly to the mob.

I reeled to the edge of the banquet hall and tugged a claret curtain. The sun had set. The sky was a bruise that wished to go black. A waning gibbous refracted the atmosphere. I let it fall.

The party was settling into that flatline whir it always does. I watched a flushed Emma make her way through the swarm.

The champagne was the first trace of alcohol that had passed my blood-brain barrier in five years. It left me tranquil, vibrating, robust.

—Hey, my wife said.

Her pelvis poked at her dress. I stroked it.

—What's up?

—Do you want to meet Mr. Minnowitter?

Emma signaled without raising her hand. The man with moles all over his face beckoned.

—Oh, I said.

—He drives me crazy, she whispered. —But he's, you know? I can't escape? Protect me?

—That's what the binding document we signed guaranteed.

Emma laced her fingers in mine and towed me over the carpet.

—Emmeline, the man gurgled.

I thought I saw one of his skin tags fall in his old-fashioned.

—Mr. Minnowitter! This is my husband, Jacob. I don't believe you've had the pleasure.

—It's Danny, Emmeline. Danny. How many times do I have to tell you?

He gulped at his orange rind, then turned, eyebrows knocking me off balance.

—So you're the one who ran off with Amagansett's best gal.

—Yes, I confirmed.

—Mr. Minnowitter, Emma exclaimed. —You have a wife.

—It's true. And I had one before her. And I'll suffer ten more to win your hand.

Minnowitter stood a head above me, two heads above Emma. He extracted a noxious green glove from his back trouser pocket and playfully slapped the air.

—No thank you, I said.

—Then she's mine, fair and square!

He imitated ravishing my wife.

—Danny, someone affected disgust. —How could you?

—I couldn't resist. Have you seen this peach flesh?

—Marabelle, this is my husband, Jacob.

I took her hand.

—Enchanté.

The plastic surgery–smoothed lady batted her lashes.

—So my wife gets a Christian introduction, Minnowitter burbled. —And I'm stuck with the third degree?

—It's a ladies' thing, Marabelle assured.

—Are my parents bothering you, Emma, a new voice interjected.

—Yes, she answered, astonished.

In his linen jacket and brogans, the figure was no less than humbling. Instead of moles, he had a prudent mottle of freckles and a forty-tooth grin. He and my wife lingered, kindling in the candlelight.

—Oh, Dan. This is Jacob . . . my husband.

I stuck out my hand.

—Husband, he acted shocked. —Since when?

He hadn't seemed to look at me. I wadded my fist in my pocket.

—We were married last September, Emma beamed. —In New Hampshire.

—You don't say, he swiveled to take me in, patted my arm, then squeezed a bicep too freely. —I'm sure Emma has told you all about me.

—Uh, I hesitated. —I can't really remember.

—Daniel Minnowitter the Third, he articulated.

—Esquire?
—So she did!
—Oh, I said, and looked at my shoes, then up again. He was as tall as his father and knew it.
—You're a lawyer?
—Natch! I've known Emma since she was yea high, he did something with his hand. —We used to play doctor.
—Dan! Stop!
My wife's flush had drawn deeper.
—They were two peas in a pod, Mr. Minnowitter butted in. —You couldn't pull these two apart. Sandcastles and slumber parties.
—There wasn't much slumbering done, Dan said.
Emma coughed.
—So you're married, huh Em?
—Why shouldn't I be?
—No reason, he mused. —What was your name again?
—Jacob, I said.
—That's right. Jacob wrestled an angel. Daniel in the lion's den. But what's more noble, some spat with a make-believe seraph, or conquering a living, breathing beast? Don't answer that. What line of work are you in?
—Well, I paused. —Right now I'm in between jobs. Things have been kind of hectic in my . . .
—Times are tough, the elder Minnowitter vociferated. —Have to pull yourself up by the bootstraps.
—You'd be amazed how much trouble I've had closing on your neighbor's chalet, Marabelle imparted.
—And they aren't getting any easier, Dan weighed in.
—Jacob is actually a brilliant writer, Emma said. —He nearly published a book.

—Nothing beats a good history, Minnowitter huffed. —What's your field of expertise?

—I, um, wrote a novel. A few years ago. But it's not going to be published.

—A novel, the man bayed. —What about?

—It was more, like, I stumbled. —A mixture of memoir, and like, social commentary. Anyway, it's just a thing I did. I used to work in production.

—How vague, Dan pulled a signature cocktail off a passing waitress's tray. —What kind of production?

—Fashion photography, Emma answered for me.

—Isn't that a little . . .

Minnowitter held out his hand, wavered it side to side.

—Frou-frou, his wife said as a question.

—I think it's foo-foo, Dan exhaled.

A stick of a woman had scuttled up to our circle. I could smell her before she appeared.

—Alice, Dan cried.

He kissed her gnarled fingers.

—Alice, old gal, Minnowitter resounded.

—Oh Alice, Marabelle extolled.

A lifeless gentleman in a drab three-piece suit propped the hag up like a coat rack. She respired between khaki teeth. I estimated this was her way of smiling.

—Good evening, Alice, Emma said.

—My dear, the dowager shrilled. —What a party! Have you met Dr. Masterson?

Her consort toyed with his tie clasp, and I did a double take, realizing this was the same golden-ager who'd been cracking wise in the backyard the evening prior. And yet he seemed transformed, drained and pasty, with none of the dapper frisk he'd displayed in the company of his tweaker paramour. My wife relinquished her hand, which he sniffed more than pecked, not letting on, unless he legitimately didn't remember, he'd tried to cop a feel up her sleeve only a few hours past.

—Dr. Masterson is my date this evening. His missus couldn't be bothered. So, my luck and her loss. What a marvelous soiree. I cannot believe your father is scarcely seventy years young.

—Thank you, Alice, Emma said. —I was just introducing Jacob to the Minnowitters.

—You know Jacob did *not* go to Harvard. Don't let his apparel deceive you.

The group ogled me.

—It's just my dad's hat.

—Please pay our devoirs to Mrs. Masterson, Marabelle warbled. —I understand she's been quite put out with a case of Lyme?

—At least it's not alpha-gal, Minnowitter bemoaned. —I got bit on Juneteenth. The doc says I may never eat mutton again.

—A pity, Alice stated. —What have you all been discussing?

—Emma's husband here was just going to tell us about the novel he's written.

—No, no, I said.

—What's your surname, Dan pried.

—Why?

—I want to know if I've ever come across your work!

—Garlicker, I said.

Masterson looked askance. He teetered, parting his lips, as though in eerie recognition, endeavoring to force language, but none issued. Rather, a tinny squeal of gas from his larynx.

—What kind of a name is Galgalatz?

—It's Garlicker, I monotoned.

—Same difference, Dan laughed.

I searched for Emma's hand, but my wife had been cornered by Marabelle, who was haranguing her about realty.

—You'll never believe these developers. Last year we brokered a shack with three whole stories of basement. Do you think your parents would be opposed to felling some of their oaks?

Her son prodded my chest.

—So why *haven't* I seen you in the book review supplement?

—Bad timing, I said. —I don't know.

—Anything in the works?

—Right now, I sighed. —I'm taking notes for a piece on *The Great Gatsby*.

—Oh, because that hasn't been scrutinized to death.

—Actually, I had an epiphany rereading it over the pandemic. And when I looked into my findings, I discovered that very little, basically nothing, has been published in support of it. And . . . I don't know. I think it could make for a, like, compelling bit of scholarship.

—And what exactly did this, Dan selected his words. —Revelation amount to?

—That Jay Gatsby is Jewish.

—Ridiculous!

—I mean, it's all in there. You just have to have the inductive skills to look for it. Feel free to refer to my Twitter on the subject, *gatsbyjewish*, one word, no underscore.

—But I'm highly familiar. I wrote my undergrad thesis on the lead-up to the 1929 crash and referred to the literature of the era a number of times. As far as I'm concerned, Tom Buchanan is too often reduced to a villain. In reality, he represented the landed gentry, striving to negotiate the old order's allegiance to market capitalism during the Progressive Era. His greatest objective is to rein in his promiscuities, repair his relationship with Daisy, and enact the role of reliable, prosperous family man.

—Tom is a bigot, waxing paranoiac on the end of white civilization. He keeps returning to society *throwing everything overboard* in favor of interracial marriage.

—It's a dated viewpoint for sure. But it's true to the time it was written. And I'm not really certain how Tom's social conservatism supports your quixotic theory.

—That quote comes from the same bit of dialogue about sitting back and letting *Mr. Nobody from Nowhere make love to your wife*. I don't see how that could be anything other than a direct reference to Gatsby, drawing a through line about him not being rightfully white.

Dan grabbed my collar and cackled.

—Now who's waxing paranoiac?

—When the novel was published, in 1925, it's safe to say that Jews were *not* considered fully white. Its working title was *Trimalchio in West Egg*, a classical reference to a garish freed slave, a stand-in for the eponymous antihero. And who were the first historically notable freed slaves . . . Anyway, the story itself is set in 1922. Europe was reeling post-World War. Germany was broke, in turmoil, looking for a scapegoat. National Socialism was founded on eugenicist principles exported by Ivy League elites like Lothrop Stoddard. Hitler took over in '21, and the narrative's only clear-cut antagonist is a hideous Jewish mob boss named Wolfshcim. The first edition spelled it Wolfshiem, but I prefer the *ei* orthography. Anyway, he wears human molars for cufflinks and just *happens* to have taken that ambiguous *nobody* Jimmy *Gatz* under his wing and built him up to wealth and infamy. The innuendo is everywhere. *His tragic nose.* Wolfsheim's office behind a door marked *The Swastika Holding Company*. The

Nazi Party adopted the swastika as their official emblem in 1920. Fitzgerald was living in the French Riviera. He would've been deeply engaged in this stuff.

—Shiem, sheim, Dan said. —Bit of a Garlicky ring to it, no?

I was stunned beyond retort.

—But seriously, he softened. —It is a charming take. Have you heard of Slingshot Press?

—Yeah, I nodded.

—Now I don't go in for much *heady* stuff. Perhaps I'm too literal-minded. But my dear friend is Slingshot's editor in chief. She's ballsy. Radical. Publishes what the mainstream won't go near for fear of reprisal. I could put you in touch. My word goes a long way.

—Isn't she related to the Bushes?

—Why yes, as a matter of fact. We lived in the same dorm freshman year at New Haven.

And instantly, just as they'd all known to pause for the flag, everyone in our horrific clique save myself grabbed a signature cocktail off a passing tray. My mouth watered. My ear ached. My wife was drifting, and I was not stoned enough anymore. I wanted to evaporate.

—Where did *you* attend college?

—*Not* Harvard, Alice seethed.

—Oho, Dan baited. —He's an Oggsford man, then?

I tried to make eye contact with Masterson. Surely he'd come to my aid. He was the only one not actively assailing me. He had jaunt, got on with commonplace townies, but Alice's companion seemed drugged. Stupefied. Stoic in a condemned way. What had happened to the gent? He'd been the life of the patio. Now Alice hewed to his arm like an axe lodged in a stump.

—Perhaps we got off on the wrong foot, I said. —It's my father's hat you're alluding to. He went to Harvard. For grad school. I went to NYU.

I turned from Dan back to Alice, who glared down at me somehow, though the crown of her blow-dried wisps barely came to my chin. She wore a platinum gown affixed with pearl polka dots and a string around her neck that looked dense enough to upend her. Something crept from her nostrils. A fetid, invisible fog. Dr. Masterson wheezed. My eyes burned.

—And what about this father of yours, Alice asked. —What does he do?

—He was a salesman for a chromatography instruments company. Before that he was a scientist.

—Very noble.

—He was . . . He's just a person.

—And is he proud to have his very own out-of-work, unpublished novelist for a son? A graduate of New York University?

—It's the number one dream school, I said.

I glanced over my shoulder. Marabelle had Emma at bay, leaning into her face, peppering it with signature cocktail spittle. Danny Minnowitter was petting the bare skin of my wife's back.

—And where are your parents tonight anyhow, dear?

Alice's tone had changed. It was cold, a hateful question, delivered with heinous, saccharine distortion no one but those privy to my ricocheting echo chamber could ascertain.

—Yeah, Dan needled. —Where *are* your folks, old sport?

—I don't know, I murmured.

Dan scowled. Dr. Masterson trembled and slurped. Hot tears welled in my eyes. Overhead, a bell started to toll.

—What's that, Alice sneered.

—I don't know where they are, I roared.

# IN A NIGHTMARE

Shortly before Emma and I were married, my parents took us on a trip to Alaska.

We'd been planning a visit ourselves. My friend Alexander was supposed to be there all summer picking through sought-after outerwear in hippie climbing communities for his and his wife's vintage store, but he'd claimed to have been mistreated by the locals and had returned to New York before we could arrange flights.

Whenever I reminded my mother of this, she pretended not to hear, so I dropped it, remaining as gracious and taciturn as I could over the course of our sojourn.

It was a time of inflation and abashment. The fact of the matter was my fiancée and I could hardly have afforded a vacation. We made some dilatory attempts at budgeting, with the hope that an influx of cash awaited us at our nuptials.

For three months, we'd been living out of a tent on a plot of nine rocky acres we'd subleased for the wedding near the New Hampshire coast. At eight hundred dollars a month, this proved a better bargain than renting a venue for one single weekend, and granted us some reprieve from bouncing between parents' houses, which was, after two years, getting old.

When our drawn-out unemployment and stimulus benefits had finally expired the previous fall, we'd purported to try to get jobs. What we hadn't predicted was everyone else returning to the workforce while there was still welfare to mooch. We'd been betting on the world ending, and it hadn't, and the only positions immediately available had been at a food co-op in Warwick, where we'd started at three days a week, slowly paring our hours down until the schedule didn't include our names.

The wedding was taking up most of my bride-to-be's attention anyway. And cooking over a fire on a cast-iron skillet, evening romps with Houdini down to the truncated shore, scaring dead field mice from Turmeric's jaws, and all piling into my patched-up REI tent to listen for katydids and coyotes left her plenty of time to work out the particulars.

Two months before the big day, we had just shy of fifteen hundred dollars between us. Emma's parents assumed the burden of matrimonial expenses. My parents invited us to tag along on a cross-frontier tour of the forty-ninth state.

Given the circumstances, we allowed my mother to lead. We allowed my father to pay. We did not ask questions or direct activities. We *ooh*ed at appropriate times. We spotted sea otters and moose. We bushwhacked through tundra. We summited glaciers. I pointed out a pygmy owl. We boarded ferries and buses and planes.

On our final night, I drove the rental Chevy Suburban into Anchorage. We followed my parents through a grid of avenues to a many-starred restaurant, which touted indigenous and North Asian cuisine.

I ordered jerk halibut and stabbed the exquisite filet. Emma ordered Mongolian-style ribs. Both my parents had been born in New London, Connecticut, and ordered dishes served in wide shallow bowls, and everyone complimented one another and the food.

## DON'T STEP INTO MY OFFICE

—You know, my father said for the fifth or sixth time that week, as his mantra devolved into inside joke. —Only one out of three people who visit Denali actually even get to see it.

The reason for this statistic, as we four knew by now, was atmospheric. Likewise, the atmosphere in the restaurant had become one of denouement. A diffuse downhill descent, taken sideways to mitigate impact on the joints, those pressure sufferers, which were always the first to go. And right on cue, all our phones vibrated simultaneously. We underwent the motions of checking into our flight, a red-eye set to depart in twenty-four hours, before our dessert of fluorescent macarons arrived, and we settled on our haunches and suspired.

A silence wormed in. We'd been jabbering for almost two weeks. Mass shootings kept blending together. Fires blazed across various states. A new plague with the word monkey in its name was failing to capture the public's imagination. It seemed like we'd run out of things to say.

—I need to be near the ocean, someone professed then, I don't remember who. —Wherever I go, I have to smell salt air.

The whole table agreed.

—What do you think they'll serve for dinner on the airplane?

I don't remember who said that either.

Nor who responded, —They don't serve meals on planes anymore.

At this point any one of us could be interchanged for another. We'd invested significant stakes in the family unit. Three years earlier, a trip like this could never have happened, but I'd stopped hazarding expectations. I was even attempting to get a job in financial marketing. There was an email chain going, and though it would promptly fall through after the wedding, this was undeniable evidence that middle age was no longer a faint hue. It had become a cresting wave.

—The last time I flew, I got cheese and crackers, I said. —Now we were on the plane for seven hours, and they only did drink service once.

—It was more like eight hours, my mother corrected.

—When I went to CDMX they did drink service twice. And that was only three hours.

—Flights to Mexico City, Emma hesitated. —Are five hours from New York.

—They say the airlines are suffering, my mother said. —They say because of the virus they can't mess with our food.

—But we know it's not foodborne.

—They're short-staffed, Emma said. —Think about how much collaboration and prep goes into the, um, to make all those meals. And dietary restrictions. Nobody wants to do that.

—Commissary, my father chimed in.

His voice had started to sound the same to me as my own. And despite the pre-roll Emma and I had shared on the walk to the restaurant, I was irritable still.

—COVID is bullshit, I said —Flights cost more than ever. Why can't they give us food?

—Shareholders demand profits, Emma griped. —They can get rid of a bunch of employees and outlays in provisions and quality control if they don't do the, um.

—Commissary, my father said.

—Right. And then they can blame the staff. That they're short-staffed.

—And make the consumer pay more in tip, my mother added. —I got an email from the rehearsal dinner woman that they no longer accept eighteen-percent gratuity and require a guaranteed twenty before signing the contracts, because they say their staff is underpaid.

—That's unrelated, I said.

—Why not just raise their wages?

Another silence insinuated itself among our quartet. It was clear we were losing steam.

—I remember our flight to Vienna, my father advanced whimsically a minute or so later.

One hundred pounds separated me and my old man. I was at least two stones underweight. He was more like four over. A hat was about the only attire we could share.

—Vienna is nowhere near the ocean, I said. —When I studied abroad in Palermo they served three kinds of cheese. And bucatini. And pancetta. And I got hammered on the flight.

My elbow twitched toward my glass of bitters and soda. I felt out of control, not wanting my father to speak. Tics about Turmeric and Houdini and getting the Camry's oil changed sparked in the depths of my consciousness. I glanced at Emma. She was looking at my drink.

—I'd like champagne at our wedding, I'd said a couple weeks prior. —Just a glass.

Emma had nodded and smiled, her lips tight.

—I can't even drink beer, I'd asserted. —How can I backslide without beer?

After four years of gluten-oriented amendments, I was still defeated all the time.

My fiancée's phone lit up and went dark in her lap. I downed my tincture sulkily.

—They had the most wonderful pear liqueur, my father went on.

He was caught in an eddy of reminiscing and would not be stopped, I realized, no matter how many rejoinders I threw his way.

—Not this story again, my mother stiffened.

—Pear schnapps, I said. —That neon green stuff.

—Not schnapps, my father continued. —This one was pale yellow. More like limoncello.

—It's called *crème de poire*, my mother said, craning over the dust of our conversation at the swinging doors to the kitchen. —I wonder where those macarons could be.

—*Crème de poire*, my father said, in a dream. —It was the Christmas of 2013. And every time she came by after dinner, which was chicken in a white wine sauce by the way, the stewardess would ask if I wanted another thimble of *poire*...

He pronounced it with put-on inflection and chuckled.

—And I would say, *oui oui oui*! *Ja ja ja*! And she'd place another bottle on my tray. A little alp of *poire* bottles. I got a kid with his music class kicked off his school trip.

—Oh stop, my mother admonished.

And just then the doors swung open. Our server sashayed, balancing a plate of macarons.

—Thank goodness, she said, feigning clapping her hands.
—Beautiful!

There were four meringue cookies. One blue, one green, one orange, one pink.

—Made fresh this morning, the server cajoled. —And all corn- and gluten-free.

I couldn't tell whether his subsequent wink was directed at my father or me, and we cracked open the confections with gigantic forks. The blue was flavored with huckleberry, the green a cool tangy pine, the orange with cloudberry, and the pink botanical fireweed.

—These are divine, my mother said.

We chewed.

—Wait, Emma laughed. —What do you mean you got a kid kicked off his school trip?

My mother looked in her purse. My father's mouth spilled bright orange crumbs.

—Just what I told you, he crowed.

The man had been born for an audience. He'd turned his Harvard PhD into a short-lived professorship, wherein he had abandoned us each summer to research and lecture at a Catholic university in the heartland. There, he'd gone toe-to-toe with administration on student access to abortion and published an open letter in the daily tribune about the local KKK chapter, which put on a beloved annual carnival, and we received death threat letters all the way to Massachusetts. Soon, my father had developed chronic migraines that he attributed to the region's heavily sprayed cornfields, but we suspected had more sinister origins. In any case, these corn-induced headaches persisted to this day, long after he'd given up higher education in favor of selling the biotech equipment he'd once put to use.

—I liked to talk too much, he'd justify in hindsight. —Talk more than write, mull more than plot, dish more than build a network or coalition. Sales is a better fit for my personality.

But I thought teaching would've been good for it too. Anyway, that evening in Alaska, he hemmed and hawed, knowing he had a rapt assembly on the hook.

—We had tickets to the symphony, he explained. —Every year the Vienna Philharmonic puts on a tremendous New Year's concert of Strauss family arrangements, and I'd managed to secure a pair through their lottery system. This is very competitive, mind you. I'd been applying for over a decade, before you could do it online and you had to mail in a request with a self-addressed stamped envelope. I had no expectation we'd ever get to go, and by the time we were notified of our good fortune, I'd had to scramble to book flights. Of course, no decent seats were available, and we'd ended up in coach, flying out the weekend before Christmas.

My father dipped a napkin corner in his glass of water. He dabbed his forehead and chin.

—Come on, Emma goaded. —Tell us the story.

—Well, you know what coach is like. We were in one of those double-decker jumbo jets with the row in the center of the aisle. Far from a window or bathroom or any relief. And we were squeezed in with our knees knocking up against the seatbacks . . .

—Speak for yourself, my mother said.

—I am. I was like a tinned fish. And there in front of us and behind us and sharing half the middle row were a bunch of high school seniors packed in for some big AP music class function. They were going to the concert too.

—How did you know that?

—I asked one of the chaperones.

—Naturally, my mother said.

My father's inclination for striking up repartee with strangers was no secret.

—It was a boisterous, choppy long flight. We were hubbing in Frankfurt, so there was no real break, no chance to stretch your legs or move the blood around. And it would have been absolute hell if not for that sweet Bavarian stewardess and her bottles of *poire*.

—Let me guess, I said. —You asked where she was from.

—Correct! She grew up on the Danube in the city of Ulm. I had a colleague from there when I was a postdoc, and we bonded over some Einsteinian anecdotes. It doesn't hurt to be kind to our service workers. Her generosity with that liqueur is your proof.

—But how did you get one of the students kicked off the trip?

—By exactly the same qualities I admired in my buxom little cabin attendant. Largesse can be a double-edged sword.

—He gave the kid sitting next to us booze, my mother said.

I strangled, laughing.

—He was eighteen!

—I'm sure you inquired.

—Yes, I did, my father affirmed.

Our server reappeared, and my father ordered an espresso.

—But why would you give a total stranger, a minor, alcohol, Emma asked.

—Well I've told you already. The stewardess kept bringing bottles. I was getting soaked to the gills, and I wasn't thinking too hard. This kid looked bored out of his wits, so I just, you know, gave him a nudge and offered him and his friend a couple nips. I was very discreet.

—But he was only a kid.

—He was eighteen, my father repeated.

—That's still below the drinking age.

—As far as I was concerned, we were over international waters, on our way to Europe, where it's legal to drink at sixteen in most countries. It was the middle of the night. I figured they'd just have a sip and fall asleep.

I turned to my mother. She was examining her fingernails.

—And what were you doing during all of this?

—Don't look at me. I told him it was a bad idea. You know your father. When he gets a notion . . .

—But he was a total stranger, Emma urged.

—I put myself in his shoes, my father prevailed. —I imagined myself at his age, off on an adventure. On my way to Austria, free and full of vitality. Champing at the bit of fine art.

—You would've wanted some weird guy to offer you schnapps?

—It was *crème de poire*. Hardly enough to get drunk off.

—That's what you thought, my mother said.

—Well, he must've pilfered my stash. I only gave up a few.

—What happened to the friend, Emma asked.

—I guess the friend knew better. Or knew how to hold his sauce.

—You would've wanted some random older man to offer you pear liqueur, I said.

—In the seventies? Sure, why not? When I was eighteen, the drinking age *was* eighteen. Before that, you could just hang out in a parking lot and link up with whoever looked hip. Back then people did each other favors. People were more connected, more humane. We hitchhiked from Groton to Key West without giving it a second thought.

—I'm serious, though. Like, what were you thinking? Bothering a teenager on an airplane? Did you think he'd think you were cool?

—I thought he would think it was cool to cut loose. He was on vacation. And I was glad to provide a catalyzing agent.

—This is messed up on so many levels.

—That's your opinion.

—Why haven't I ever heard this story before?

I tried to meet my mother's eyes, but they seemed permanently averted.

—I think the boy was appreciative. He told me about his interests in composition and violin-making. He showed me a nice, illustrated edition on the history of lutherie in Vienna.

—I don't understand, I said. —So they kicked him off the trip?

—When it came time to debark in Frankfurt, he was a tad over-enthused. Another hour, and he probably would've sobered up. But when he vomited in a trash can, some of those little glass shooters rolled out of his pocket, and we could see him being pulled off to the side.

—Jesus.

—That's awful, Emma said.

—I felt pretty rotten about it myself.

My father's espresso arrived. He stirred in two sugar cubes.

—So what did you do, Emma asked.

—Well, your mother was pretty disappointed with me.

I looked at her. Her expression was shadowed, cabalistic in tawny light.

—Pretty soon our hub was taxiing in, and the kid was still nowhere to be found. Students were gossiping. I went up to the chaperone I'd been chatting with earlier and asked what was going on. She said the boy was being sent on a flight back to JFK. Apparently, he'd been warned about something like this. He had some kind of track record. No room for mercy or grace.

—You're insane, I said. —You caused that.

—I felt terrible.

—You ruined his Christmas so you could feel cool.

—I wasn't trying to feel cool, my father said. —I just wasn't thinking. We all screw up.

—Why did you let him do that, I asked my mother.

—I didn't let him do anything. Your father is a grown man. We've been married forty-six years, and he doesn't need my permission to make mistakes. But that's all it was. A mistake. And you've made enough mockery of him. I think we should drop the whole thing.

She stood up and marched to the bathroom.

My back hurt. The lump in my stomach turned. Everything was altered and strained.

—I'm sorry, I said.

My father nursed his espresso.

—Oh, it's nothing to apologize for. It doesn't bother me much. Your mom is just sensitive because, at the time, we couldn't let it go.

—What do you mean, Emma said.

—I mean, my old man started, glancing at the bathroom. —I mean, I was set on finding out where they'd taken the boy, and did everything in my power to get him back on our flight.

—You took responsibility?

—I told them my story. Just as I've laid it out now. No one to blame but myself. The kid was a kid. A high-schooler. I was the one who'd messed up. It was my poor judgment. Don't take it out on the student. It's not his place to be punished for the improprieties of an adult.

He looked toward the bathroom again.

—So . . .

—So the administrators said he was eighteen. He wasn't a child anymore, and he'd have to take accountability for his actions. They had it out for him. He was a known entity. He looked all right to me, but what did I know? Did I know his history? If they didn't follow through with some kind of discipline, they said the boy would never learn. He was going to graduate in a few months. It was time he acknowledged that when you slip up, you have to face the music.

—That's absurd, Emma said.

—That's what I thought. But I wasn't going to let it ruin my vacation. I've suffered and atoned for my share of miscalculations. I know life isn't fair. I know shit hits the fan, and I was ready to forget it. If he was a courteous kid in general, not a troublemaker, I expect they would've exercised some leeway. It really wasn't my business how his life panned out.

—So that was it, huh?

My father rose up an inch, paunch bulging into the table, then sat down and leaned close.

—No, he lowered his voice. —That wasn't it. Your mother was very annoyed with me at that point, very upset. She's too empathetic, you know. I think she saw *you* in that boy. She didn't like to feel responsible for his losing out on a once-in-a-lifetime experience. And she thought they intended not to just bounce him from the class trip, but to expel him from the school altogether. This was a very prestigious prep school we were dealing with. That much had become clear.

—What did she think she could do, Emma whispered.

—She thought we could advocate on his behalf. Your mother, my father turned to me. —Insisted we accompany the boy on his flight home and appeal to the school's headmaster. Get everything straightened out so they understood it was not the student's fault he'd ended up intoxicated, but because of *my* indiscretion.

—You did not fly all the way back to New York, I said.

—We flew all the way back, my father averred. —Out of pocket. With that crocked crazy kid squeezed between us, hysterical and humiliated, bellyaching about how his mother was going to eviscerate him.

His eyes were darting back and forth between the bathroom door and my fiancée and me.

—So what happened, Emma pressed.

—Well, as you can imagine, what with Christmas at hand, and having made no plans, no hotel, our car buried in long-term parking, and the prep school shut down for the holidays, we put the boy in a cab and proceeded to do what we could to get in touch with the headmaster.

I cocked my head in anticipation. My bride-to-be held her breath.

—Were you able to reach him?

—Eventually, my father said. —Yes.

The bathroom door released, and my mother emerged. She appeared renewed and relaxed. Her brown eyes glistened. She began to glide between the tables toward our own.

—What happened, I hissed.

—We hashed it out. Life went on.

—Did you make it back to Vienna in time for the symphony?

—We did not, my father grinned.

My mother sat down beside him and smoothed her palms along the front of her slacks.

—I am stuffed.

On the walk to our hotel, my father and Emma broke off, sauntering along the waterside, mooning at far-flung fjords. My mother and I fell behind. She held me by some remote muscle where my neck and shoulder joined, intuitive reflex from her profession, though she'd retired years before.

—I hope you weren't too hard on your dad, she belatedly spoke. —He's very sensitive.

—Oh, I said. —It doesn't seem like it.

—You know him. He's really quite embarrassed about what happened on that trip.

—I'm sorry, I muttered. —I didn't know.

But I felt confused. My old man hadn't seemed the least bit ruffled. Still, I took her at her word. We'd always been closer. As mother and son, we'd invariably left my father out. If she said he was self-conscious, it must have been worse than I'd surmised. The man was practically without shame.

A month and a half later, we conducted three box trucks full of sailcloth canopy and catering accessories over the spongy New Hampshire pasture.

—I used to unload trucks for a living, I said.

—Cool, the rental guy replied.

Jane painted place cards. My mother moved folding tables. My father and Michael spent an afternoon constructing and varnishing a chuppah, which they erected at the peak of a knoll.

—I will be honest and confident in our marriage, I said. —Our collaborations, our struggles and successes and realizations. Because I have faith in you and the foundation we've built together. Because I have faith in the family we've united and in the one we're still in the process of building. Because I have faith in everywhere life moves us, and because our love is vigorous and singular and rare. It can deliver us wherever we want to go.

Emma was crying.

—I love you, she sputtered. —I didn't have time to write anything down.

Before we kissed, I stepped on a wineglass. And when it came time to dance, Houdini joined us on the parquet floor pads, and everyone applauded and we prowled off to our tent, where we discovered Turmeric stuck in a tree, and I scaled the tree and tossed Emma the cat and we smoked weed and took MDMA.

Two barmy gray uncles or cousins or friends of friends reclined at a table passing a bottle of slivovitz among themselves.

—It's all about chemistry, one of them said in a fossilized Yiddish accent. —It doesn't matter how they look. It's got to be in the blood.

He beat a fist on his heart.

—Well, well, cawed the other, pronouncing *well* with a V. —I've got to be attracted to someone. I'm not getting into bed every night with any old jokester. She's got to have the goods!

—Aha, the first wiggled a bony bruised finger. —But that, my friend, is part of chemistry.

—You don't understand. I need to be able to lean in and smell her.

The second geezer threw his arms to his sides, squeezing handfuls of air, and dropped his nose to the linens sniffing virulently.

—And I still say, cried the first. —Smell *is* chemistry!

Michael gave his weepy thanks into a microphone from Guitar Center. My father made a speech.

—I'd like to leave our young couple with a message I discovered years ago. The best advice I've received on the subject. It's guided my and my wife's marriage ever since, and we've been wed almost forty-seven years. It came through an unexpected

Cupid, a chance encounter while working out at the gym. Yes, you may not be able to tell, but I did used to work out . . .

He paused for laughter.

—It was a Valentine's weekend, and above the ellipticals on the big screen TV I was watching Ina Garten. That's right, the Barefoot Contessa. And she was preparing a scrumptious strawberry shortcake for her doting husband Jeffrey, and in the course of gently folding sugar and berries, she looked into the camera and noted the reason, a rule if you will, for their long and storied marriage, and it was this: a lifetime of love and commitment is truly quite easy. For if you get up every morning and do one nice thing for your special person, it doesn't have to be big or planned, just one simple, earnest act, it makes a difference. It reminds each other why you're together. It shows you care. It's that easy. One nice thing every day. Are you up to the task?

My father turned to me and Emma.

—What do you think, I asked my wife.

—That sounds fine, she said.

—And with that, I raise a glass with our hearts to Emma and Jacob, and wish them a long and joyous life together. *Mazel tov!*

My mother and I danced. The song went too long, and I didn't know the steps. She kept catching her breath.

—Are you happy, she asked me. —Are you ready?

—Sure, I said.

Emma had stopped drawing her eyebrows on during the pandemic. Her hair was pulled in a bun. She smelled like vetiver.

The sun set. We were rolling. Alexander and Miriam DJed, and the groans of struts from cars driving over the uneven terrain trickled among a clement clash of unseen waves.

I sat with my parents, sipping seltzer with lime. All at once, it was as if I'd never known them. We'd missed out on so many respective intimacies. Our relationship was too well-defined, and in the wake of this ceremony, the lines had faded like a freckle on the palm of my hand.

I wanted to meet them all over again. I wanted to spend decades reliving our lives, recontextualizing what each human provides to the others they touch. But I was also jittery from the drugs, and I hugged them and hugged them and saw Emma with one of her friends and went off to pursue other diversions.

My parents waited for "Hava Nagila," but our DJs were taking too long, and they left.

—I love you, son, my father choked.

—We'll see you soon, my mother said.

She smoothed the front of her dress. And when Emma was hoisted up in a chair, and I a second later, waving a napkin between us as our revelers cheered, and Miriam hollered in Hebrew, and the horah crescendoed, I watched my parents' Chrysler Pacifica grunt away.

That was the last time I saw them. They weren't around for the casual brunch of gluten-free pancakes and sausage links we cooked on the leftover catering stove the following afternoon. They didn't show the next day when the trucks came and piled everything off and left us with only dents in the turf. They weren't there when we filled the Camry with presents and checks and drove up into the mountains and tried to have sex in a hot tub, which didn't work, and Emma got her period, and I lapped at the thick, fragrant blood.

We didn't receive any calls from them, or texts. And when we pulled up to their door in Rhode Island, no one was there. Their car was in the garage. Their clothes were neat in their dressers. They'd left no note or indication of having departed.

We spent the night in the guest room, and the day after that sprawled on the wall-to-wall carpet of the upstairs loft. We stored our gifts in the basement, and drove to Long Island, and I called my mother and left messages, and she didn't respond.

When we returned on the ferry over the sound yet again to my parents' condominium, it was exactly as we'd left it the week before. I discovered my mother's phone in her bedside table drawer. And when I saw how many missed calls had accumulated, I ran to the bathroom and hurled.

The cops went over the condo with flashlights and black lights and combs. My mother had kept the place so tidy there was hardly a point.

They looked for evidence of foul play. They sifted through notebooks and phone logs and interrogated neighbors but came back with nothing of use.

They set a watch with the Coast Guard. They dredged a nearby salt marsh. They tested their bathtub for acid used to liquefy bones and flesh and found only traces of Preparation H.

My nerves overflowed into madness. I stopped sleeping. Guilt ravaged my stomach. The firm, wandering lump swelled to the size of a fist in my groin, and I lost ten more pounds that I couldn't afford.

I circled the neighborhood, trudged through ivy, woods, parking lots, dumpsters, and dunes. I called their names to futility. Like waking up a dead star before its nova could appear in the cosmos. I bit pillows apart. I howled into my knuckles, crusted with eczema and dried blood.

Emma didn't know what to do. She traveled to New York. She went somewhere on a boat. When she came back to Rhode Island, she found me unconscious on the floor. Days later, she woke to me prying shingles off the roof.

Eventually, the detectives assigned to the case explained they'd have to take a step back. Something bigger was going on, inconsistent with typical missing persons protocol.

—Do you think they're dead, I implored.

—We don't know, they repeated.

I was granted power of attorney over their estate. I was given every assurance the authorities were doing everything they could.

Nonetheless, other law enforcement priorities were creeping in. Someone had vandalized a Halloween display at the local Starbucks with Day-Glo swastikas. Yuletide was coming. Turkeys were being slaughtered by the millions across the Western Hemisphere, and my entreaty fell on deaf ears.

That Christmas Eve, in the apartment on Tenth Street, we prayed. I don't recall ever getting on my knees before a dinner table, and it left me feeling lousy. The ham tasted like metal. I went to bed at eight o'clock.

—Are we going to be okay, I said.

—I don't know, Emma answered. —I want to be. Do you?

—Yes.

And I felt honest and confident, and we made a pact to not talk about my parents' disappearance for the first month of the new year, and revisit how we wanted to deal with it after that.

—I got asked to curate a show at a new gallery in Chinatown, my wife said. —Should I do it?

I thought about the savings in my parents' bank account, which I controlled. I thought about them showing up at the door of their condo, haggard and contused five years later, to find it had been sold by their only child. I didn't want to touch anything. I didn't want to move until there was a body recovered, in whatever form. I wanted a drink, but I was too weak to swallow. I was too weak to be reckless anymore.

—Sure, I said. —If you think it would make you happy.

—I think it would take my mind off things.

—We could use the money.

My wife nodded, and Santa brought Houdini many glorious dog biscuits.

I drove back to Rhode Island with the *New York Times* Super Mega Puzzle Mania crossword and fed Turmeric and ingested a cache of Michael's weed gummies and OxyContin until it was New Year's Eve, and at some point Emma had shown up, and I was moaning, I couldn't cry, holding my stomach, and I hadn't started the crossword, and Ryan Seacrest was on television, and Houdini's nose issued a single wet drop on my cheek, and Turmeric jumped on his shoulders, and I saw everyone's eyes, my family's.

Emma held my hand.

—We won't talk about it anymore, I said.

—Just one month, my wife soothed. —To get you out of this loop. Try to see something different. Try to be present, relax.

Ryan Seacrest began counting back from ten.

—If you don't look, you won't see.

I don't remember who said that.

# SUNDAY

The bell tolled twelve times through the country club.
 I was sweating. Everyone was looking away from me. I turned in a circle. I couldn't reach Emma's eyes. My mouth filled with salt water. I sucked in air without engaging my nostrils. Then I lurched from our horrific clique, barreling into a man who might've been packed with sawdust.
 —What're you drinking, I growled.
 —The club's signature cocktail.
 —What's it called, I demanded.
 —It's the name of the club.
 I scattered across the room to the bar.
 —I'll have one Maidenhead, please.
 The bartender stared at me.
 —Oop, I said. —Wrong name, wrong name. I'm sorry. What is it? Oh yeah.
 I said the name of the club. He fixed me my drink.
 —Do you make those double?
 He looked over his shoulder at nothing, swirled my glass, and poured in another finger of gin. I guzzled it, sidling about the banquet hall, too sheepish to return for a refill straightaway.
 Instead, I kicked up my heels, snatching half-finished drinks off half-empty tables, downed them carelessly, and

moved to the next in the image of a robotic vacuum. My shoes scuffed. My suit an envelope of grease, with me, the shaved meat, spilling out.

—You know, I remarked, elbowing an old toad, drool running down her chin and into wheelchair spokes, splashing her with the contents of some backwashed digestif. —Anyone who insists there are geniuses toiling in obscurity, turning over great truths only they may exhume, is just trying to protect their own vanity. Tongue lashed to brain by a bungie cord. Those of us unlucky enough to have been on the receiving end can tell you . . . Now let's fucking air this out . . .

I trailed off. The wheelchair smelled like pee. I glared in many directions. Emma was showing Dan Minnowitter something on her phone. Jane was limboing under a butterfly net. Alice was guiding her increasingly catatonic escort past a wall of many mirrors, reflecting the nefarious bile she wore so well again and again.

They slipped out a partition, and darkness exploded around them. It was plaid. The night was plaid cement. Michael's pants had asps and daggers embroidered on them. And the door breathed closed against the din.

I danced over to my blushing bride and hip-checked her companion.

—What the fuck, Dan recoiled.

A swatch of port had begun crawling over his sleeve.

—I am *so* sorry, I said. —Such a clutzawitz. How embarrassing.

He was batting at the stain like it was an autumn leaf in need of punishment.

—I was just showing Dan the artist's Instagram for the exhibition I'm taking over.

—Oh wow, I said. —Well, what do you think, Dan?

—It's . . . pretty interesting.

—Gets your gears going, huh?

—He was offering to help me with the press release, Emma said.

—Oh, I widened my eyes. —Fascinated by the intersection of art and technology, are we?

—I'll be right back, Dan motioned to his jacket.

—You should carry a Tide pen, I called after him.

—Are you drunk, Emma hissed.

—What would give you that idea?

—Jesus, Jacob. I can smell it on you.

—That's just my natural *parfum*.

Emma folded her arms and shivered. The party was dying down.

—Are you trying to humiliate me?

—Are you flirting with that lawyer guy?

—I've known him since I was a kid.

I scoffed. Emma scoffed back.

—He was just asking about my new job. And I was trying to be polite. After all the shit we've been through, I was just trying to have a pleasant night with my family.

—Must be nice.

—Okay, my wife rebuffed. —Maybe you should go for a walk or something.

—I think I need to go to the bathroom, I puled.

But Emma wasn't reacting. She was striding away, ass cheeks cradling each other behind tight black knit.

The facilities were steamed up. All the faucets were running. All the stall doors were closed. I tried to push a couple open, but they wouldn't budge. I sunk to my knees looking for brogans.

—Hey, I yelled.

But I didn't see anything. Just my hands on the floor of the country club bathroom. My voice bounded down the corridor. The insides of my lips raw, as though I'd been biting them.

—Dan!

Yet it seemed I was alone. The candles lining the row of sinks flickered.

—Fuck you!

My vision crinkled and bobbed. I supposed I'd become unaccustomed to alcohol. Still, it had the power of maternal warmth. It covered me. This was the skin I'd been missing. My phantom pelt. I leaned over a sink, wiped a reflecting hole through the fog. It was me all right. Dripping with perspiration. Claw marks at my collar. Yellow sclerae. Jaw locked.

I started to grab for my phone to take a picture. I slapped myself around. Then my other hand went for it, and it grabbed the device and held it chortling under a streaming faucet for I don't know how long.

I tried to wipe the screen off. My phone was saturated and sort of fizzing and shocking me through my pocket as I swung by the bar for another signature round.

—Sock it to me, I monotoned.

The bartender didn't appear to recognize me, though, so I ordered two drinks and sipped at both until I was able to combine them in a single glass.

I was dragging my feet, scudding through a deserted chamber and thinking it was probably time to find Emma and apologize and check in with her parents about getting home.

But that sounded like work. And if there was one thing I'd never gained any pride from . . .

I passed a case of sailing trophies. Shuffleboard cues and crew oars and old polo shirts hung on the wall. A list of names in gold foil. I scanned for my in-laws' and found them and yawned and ground my teeth and tears seeped from my ducts.

And then I was somewhere else. I could barely make out the thrum of music. I picked my ear, transiently forgetting why it was bothering me, and saw red and gray and went blind for a second. Crumbs came back on my finger. A spoiled aroma. Perhaps I was disintegrating. Good fodder for a novel, I thought. *The Man Who Was, in Fact, Sand* by Jacob Galgalatz, Esquire.

I padded along a tiled hallway to a door, which said, IN CASE OF EMERGENCY ALARM WILL SOUND. All the same, I took my chances, and the alarm did not, and soon I was hovering over the beach behind the establishment flanked by tick-addled grass under a stifled lunar blob.

The ocean wept. That's all it knew how to do. The coast unrolled to the east and the west, but it knew it ended too, and I knew that was its purpose. Oceans were made to weep. Coasts to end. Garlickers to wend and vanish.

I punted the line where the bank and concrete united, my arms punching air, drawing momentum for more acute calcitration until my socks filled with detritus. I finished my drink, sloshed much down my muzzle to collect clavicleward. I threw the glass at the ground, which swallowed it whole, then caved to gravity's force.

I tried to picture my parents observing me from a cloud. Their brows furrowed, disapproving, so I imagined myself with a salary, but they still seemed concerned, mouthing clammy character judgments, folding hands over each other's in solemn misgiving gestures.

I sat that way as the shadow of the moon skated sideways along the horizon.

It took me a while to realize I was hearing something.

A guttural sound. A ravenous slavering, which caused my instincts to whip with arcane anamnesis. My innards curdled, like a windmill in distress, swatting mud where there used to be a runnel, and I was transported by vague collateral dread.

I turned my ear to the noise. But the sand in it clogged the waves of vibration. I flung my head on my neck, flailing, trying to sense from which direction the sound emanated.

Air gushed.

The sound said, —*Flunphb* . . .

I pulled my earlobe. More granules of pus came away. The depth and density of sonic resonance were struggling to make themselves known. I smacked my skull and saw stars, but I couldn't tell if they were the chimeric kind or the genuine article.

—*Flunphb, fluhgghr. FLLALALLLLLLLLLLW!*

The sound sirened. And suddenly, I was up. Two sand-laden shoes flopping beneath me. I smelled low tide and seaweed. I heard whistling through my teeth. The gaps in my gray matter telling me one story, sensory impulses thrusting me onward in spite of my limited ability to analyze meaning.

I was one step behind the sound's origin. I was one blink behind caring why I sought it. I made out footsteps swishing into a separate distance. Not sprinting, like mine, but off in the parking lot. Tip-tapping away at a leisurely escape, and the sound of an engine catching.

Cars were leaving the party, and I raced to the shore. My feet sodden below a slow, ebbing break. Green slaking over them, foam slaking over green.

The sound said, —*Floraizipojuengggggghhhh* . . .

Then everything fell away. And I could see it. The shape of a body being drawn under the water. The dead water. A dead body. Again.

But this time it was recognizably human. The figure not beaten beyond identification. It was green like the water. Black like the sky. White as the blood stopped pumping and leaked in rivulets from the critical fissures we call life. It was covered in vomit. Much more slime than the outsides of bodies endorse. A kind of disgorging that only happens once. When this much falls out, it's for good. A sheet of mucosa. Preserving fluid with nothing left to preserve.

I should've known better than to keep looking. I wasn't thinking. That part of me had gone with the booze, the results of which I didn't notice trickling down my leg and into my ruined footwear. The empirical part of my mind, however, kept doing its thing, interpreting the image and automatically, subliminally comparing it against billions of other data inputs I'd exposed it to over the ages, trying to match it with some concept and name:

Dr. Masterson, I registered, would not look askance or toy with his tie clasp or teeter or disport or frolic with a woman or joke about the Global South again. He was locked in his ultimate womb of puke and eruption. The shell left behind after one sheds its mortal husk and goes on to psychedelic infinity or whatever.

It all felt so different. I wasn't bent to my knees. I wasn't pleading with the body, berating it with impossible questions.

Yet it was exactly the same. The sea purled, licked our suits. I ran my hand over the sick, spewy film of the old man's ambient self. Masterson's eyes had rolled back, showing cold ghostly whites. His mouth a hole of gore, with dentures dislodged, regurgitating in dull bursts, as the death throes heralded some new height. The spontaneous flex of his expired corpse . . . Or was he just dying then? Could a deceased body pulsate and seize?

And witnessing these convulsions, crisp intel cascaded: if he was moving, he wasn't dead. And if he wasn't dead: I had a responsibility.

—Hang on, I screamed.

I bobbled my phone. Thunder crashed, and I picked it up, and I dropped it again, and when I retrieved it that time, brushing it over my waterlogged sleeve, pounding and shaking it, little beads of precipitation appeared on its screen.

It was raining, and tributaries of chunder surged from Masterson's maw. He was lost, and I knew it, and my phone was already wet from my recent bathroom lunacy, and I rattled it in the wind and the torrent and the flash of my parents up in their cloud rolling their eyes.

Then, in an instant, I saw the screen brighten. A silhouette of an apple. Sharp strings of pigmentation. I couldn't remember my passcode, and I didn't need to. In the oncoming storm, as Dr. Masterson's wincing agony grew less fierce, I pressed *Emergency* and punched in nine-one-one.

The phone was hopping, throbbing, jolting against my palm, and I was wailing, and a staticky voice was telling me to, —Calm down, sir. Sir? Can you hear me? Calm down. Where are you? Can you tell me what's going on?

—I don't know! At the club! I don't know! Masterson! He's a! By the water! Doctor! I'm! Can't remember!

The next thing I remember was a wash of red and blue. The onslaught of vehicles and uniforms and machinery and being strapped to a gurney and lifted away from the surf. My phone still whining in my hand. My heart rebounding in my shirt. The stickiness of encroaching hangover. My wife's look of repugnance, and the back of an ambulance, which I lay in for what couldn't have been more than a half hour, because when they unstrapped me, I heard someone chuckle.

—He's fine. His vitals, everything. Just an excited little prick. No surprise after what he's been into . . .

Because when they carried my body, limp, unresisting, and deposited it in the back of a squad car, I saw the radio dial, and I saw the clock, which merely said, *1:01*.

I came to in a gray folding chair in a gray windowless room. A surveillance camera perched at the highest corner, and I glowered up to it.

—Can anyone hear me, I asked. —Can I have a change of clothes? Or a glass of water? I don't feel so good.

I had a headache and an auricular organ swollen to about the size of a Kafka contemplation. A bare bulb dangled from the ceiling. And another folding chair was folded against a wall. There was a door with no handle and a fob chip embedded in its frame, and I wasn't wearing my shoes.

I considered this situation. I made an effort to parse how I'd gotten there. I put my hands in my pockets, tottered on the chair, close as I could to the camera. My reflection wagged back.

—Plus I'm innocent, I exhaled.

After a while a cop came in. He peered at me, squeezing through the door sideways out of necessity, then carefully replaced it in its jamb.

His hair was red. His face was red. The buttons of his striped shirt stood at attention, ready to shoot off the moment things got out of hand. His gun was holstered and shiny and black.

He grabbed the chair leaning against the wall and unfolded it in a loud, practiced snap. Then he snapped at me a few times, though I couldn't have been more vigilant. He banged the chair in front of where I slumped and sat on it backward, his roll of girth and suffocating genitals on full view through the aperture in the metal. He withdrew an iPad and went about scrolling and padding with plump nubby fingers.

Minutes passed. Finally, he dropped the tablet face down on his lap.

—What kind of a name is Garlicker?

—Why do cops always want to know that?

—So you've had run-ins with the law before?

I hunched lower in my chair.

—Mr. Garlicker, let's start over, the cop put out a hand. —My name is Sergeant Lenihan.

I tried to decide what to do, but my limb decided for me, consumed in Lenihan's grasp.

—Do you care to tell me what exactly went down on that beach?

—Am I being charged with something?

—Not yet. Should you be?

I looked at my hand. It was pulsing, purple.

—Should I ask to speak with a lawyer, I said.

—That depends, Lenihan pawed at the iPad, spun it over his massive quads. —Usually it's people with something to hide that seek legal counsel without a formal charge . . . Do you?

I wanted a clock to be ticking, but all I could hear was the wheezy incessance of the cop's constrained lungs.

—I don't think so, I managed.

—We just want a few questions answered.

—Who's we?

—My associates haven't arrived yet. You know, Saturday night.

—It's my father-in-law's birthday, I said. —I was just . . . I went for a walk on the beach.

—That much we've gathered. Care to elaborate?

—I called you guys as soon as I came across the . . .

My throat caught. I wrestled a breath.

—Start from the beginning, Lenihan said.

So I told him about the party, and got into every detail of what I had experienced after the stroke of midnight, down to the faucets in the bathroom, the footsteps in the parking lot, Dr. Masterson's retching yawp. But a lot of it didn't make sense said aloud.

Lenihan typed on his iPad.

—So, you heard footsteps behind you before discovering the body? Have I got that right?

—I heard something. But I also sustained an ear injury a couple days ago, and it's been . . . excruciating . . . And creating a lot of confusion.

—How convenient, the cop said.

—I'd say it's actually *in*convenient, given the circumstances. Is my wife here? I've told you everything.

—Hold on now. So if you heard footsteps near the body, why didn't you try to find out where they came from? Why didn't you call out when you found Dr. Masterson?

—I did call out. Or at least I think I did. The whole thing happened so fast. I couldn't put it all together. And why should I have assumed those footsteps meant anything? There were people around. All types of movement. It was a party. It was late, and I'd been drinking . . .

—You'd been drinking, Lenihan interrupted. —You hadn't mentioned that aspect.

—Everyone had been drinking. It was a *party*. I wasn't any drunker than the next guest.

—That's not what we heard. We heard you were rather intoxicated by the end of the night. Daniel Minnowitter informed us that you'd become erratic and aggressive. Something about throwing a drink on him while he was engaged in friendly small talk with your . . .

—I didn't throw a drink at him. God. That guy. He's . . .

—Mr. Minnowitter has been nothing less than an apostle to you. He even offered his attorney privileges.

I shook my head.

—Forget it. Besides, you just said I'm not being charged.

—I said you hadn't been charged.

—Jesus Christ, I bawled. —You know, I went looking for Dan right after I *accidentally* bumped into him. I thought he'd gone to the bathroom, but he was nowhere to be found . . .

—There's no reason to take the lord's name in vain, son. That's twice.

—And there was all this steam on the mirrors, and . . . and so fucking Dan disappears right before Masterson is killed, and I'm the one interrogated? Has anyone tried finding, like, old Alice whatever. Wasn't she the guy's date? Wasn't she the last one seen with him alive?

—On the contrary, Mr. Garlicker, *you* are the witness who best fits that description. The coroner pronounced the time of death as ten minutes *after* the police reported to the scene.

—I saw the two of them sneaking off together right before everything went haywire. Don't you think Dr. Masterson's wife would want to know about *that*?

—We've spoken with the matron's secretary, the cop said, regarding his iPad. —She arrived home at a quarter past twelve and went straight to bed. Old Alice, as you call her, is a valued member of our community. She is well-known to both Mrs. Masterson and myself. And I can assure you, she'll cooperate readily once she's had a chance to rest and been briefed on this horrible crime. In point of fact, everyone we've spoken with tonight is a reputable, trustworthy figure in our little village. Almost everyone, that is.

—Give me a fucking break, I ejected. —I'm married to the toast of the town's only child.

—Quite recently married, if I'm not mistaken.

I wanted to refute this, but couldn't think how, and was prevented by a knock at the door.

—Ah, the cop smiled. —That must be my backup . . .

The two additional cops were wearing Yankees caps and blue windbreakers and in the middle of a debate as Lenihan labored to his boots and unlocked the door with a fob.

—All I'm saying's fried okra is the superior po'boy. The shrimp are too puny at that spot.

—Shrimps are supposed to be little, the other said.

—Not that little, the first cop said under his breath.

The room somersaulted. Bits of inner ear atomized. It took a second for my vertigo to abate, as though pulled by tired magnets, and grimly I apprehended why this scene seemed so familiar.

—Remember us, Detective Powell stuck out his mitt.

I couldn't move my arms. Detective Winston lifted his phone-holding hand.

—A pleasure, Mr. Garlic, the cop said.

I sat tight-lipped, nauseated. The lump in my abdomen seethed. The trapped sand fell another inch toward my gullet, making a dank thud only I could ascertain.

—What's wrong, Winston asked, shining a flashlight in my eye. —Pupils delayed. You on something? Or is this just how you treat old friends?

I gathered my knees in the chair, trying to make myself smaller, dissolve, like my parents.

—What? You don't remember?

I faltered.

—Let me remind you, Powell said. —We were introduced several years ago. There was a murder in your neighborhood. Coney Island. Kings County. Ever heard of it?

I nodded.

—Traded up since then, huh? Big man. Welcome to the husband club. You still getting it on the reg? Mighty nicer beach to find a dead body on, I'll give you that.

I opened my mouth. It hurt with dryness. I let it sag.

—They never did find the perp, did they?

—What've they got on you this time?

—I didn't do anything, I groaned.

—Says here you have an outstanding parking ticket. Enough to hold him on, Sarge?

Lenihan shrugged. He'd somehow edged to a corner, though he almost filled up the room.

—What? That was from yesterday! How could I have paid it? This is all a huge misunderstanding! I can't believe they brought you guys in all the way from . . .

—There's that memory, Winston gibed. —I was beginning to think I was forgettable.

—And you can still work that tongue, Powell laughed.

—Underrated cut, if you ask me.

—Care if I bring you two up to speed, Lenihan said. —Out of the kid's earshot, that is?

They all got stuck in the doorway trying to get out at once. Then the lock clicked behind them.

I wondered what time it was. I wondered if I'd be getting a divorce. I briefly wondered if I'd killed Dr. Masterson, but it felt too incriminating for even my internal monologue. I'd read about gang stalking and EMF mind-reading technology that was probably not totally real but pointed in the direction of a reality too uncanny to ever be disclosed.

I figured if I did anything, it would be used against me. I figured they were watching me, or would be reviewing the footage as soon as I left. But I also figured doing nothing would make me seem too slick. So I got up and paced, then sat, looked at the camera, and mouthed, —Water.

I thought about Houdini. I thought about Turmeric. I thought about my wife, my novel, and about how Gatsby was Jewish. Maybe Sofia could drum up a book deal if I was convicted to life behind bars. That sentence had historically proven a jumpstart to many great authors' careers.

—Voice of my generation, I said unwittingly.

Then I remembered I couldn't eat bread. Would the prison system recognize my dietary restrictions?

—What's that, Powell asked plowing through the door.

—What, I startled.

—What were you saying, Mr. Garlicker?

—I've been, I paused, panicking. —I was asking for water.

—Looks like you've had your share, Winston gagged.

# DON'T STEP INTO MY OFFICE

He wafted the air. I was still in my wedding suit, drenched to the bones.

—I'm, I said. —I'm ready to talk or whatever. I'll tell you exactly what I told Officer Lenihan.

—That's *Sergeant* Lenihan.

—Right. I'm sorry. I'll cooperate. There's been a whole weird conspiracy or something. Or maybe not even. But I'm not the one to blame. I don't know what's going on. I promise I didn't kill anyone.

—Whoa, whoa, Powell hooted. —Who said anything about kill?

—I . . . I'm just . . . I feel sick and . . . and not well . . . Have you considered how traumatic this has been on my end?

—We're very sorry for your trauma, Winston said.

—I stumbled upon a dead body, I yelled. —If I'd killed Masterson, why would I have immediately called the cops?

—Guilt, Powell said as a question.

—Guilt, Winston stated.

—And you hardly called immediately, Lenihan added. —Coroner says the poison had been working for hours within the victim's system before he succumbed to its fatal effects.

—Poison, I screeched.

—Pretty serious stuff, too. You don't come by tetrodotoxin every day.

—Tretro . . . what? I don't know what you're talking about.

—Tetrodotoxin, Powell repeated. —Comes from the gonads of the illustrious puffer fish.

—It takes some serious balls to get your hands on that crank, Winston said. —Pun intended.

—I . . . I don't have access . . . to pufferfish . . .

—And yet you live by the beach here, Winston said.

—And used to live by the beach down in Brooklyn, Powell said.

—And spend an awful lot of time hobnobbing around the beach in Rhode Island, Winston crooned. —Now that's an interesting story, isn't it?

—How do you . . .

—You spend a lot of time fishing by your long-lost parents' abode, Mr. Garlic?

—I . . . don't fish, I stammered. —I . . . What do my parents have to do with this?

—Awful lot of coincidences surrounding your profile, Powell said.

—We know all about their regrettable disappearance, Winston winked.

—That investigation has been going for almost a year, I coughed.

I didn't want to start crying. I didn't know what to do.

—No breaks in it yet, Winston said.

—You'd think they would've found something, Powell looked at his phone.

—This is insane, I cried out.

—You should know, Winston sniffed. —All that therapy you went through. Got your noggin straight yet? Or are you still drunk-driving trucks over our fine city's parkway medians?

—I'm . . . You're coming down on me on the most . . . I had a hard time. I'm *still* having a hard time.

—Tell that to Lauren Smith.

—Who?

—Your neighbor!

—I really didn't know her.

—You didn't follow the story after we stopped by your apartment, Powell asked.

—I mean, I kind of just wanted it to go away. And when I never heard from you guys again . . . Well, so I forgot her name. I was preoccupied . . . I was all messed up!

—In our business, we call it a nervous breakdown.

—Okay, I sobbed. —Okay! Call it whatever you want! I still don't have anything to do with my parents' disappearance! I don't have anything to do with Dr. Masterson being poisoned! And I don't have anything to do with my neighbor being killed, *seven years ago*. As far as I'm concerned, I'm a victim too. I don't know why you can't see things from my . . .

—Says in our file you're linked with multiple deaths in the years following Ms. Smith's murder.

—*Excuse* me?

—One Matthew Poole . . . and a . . . Jal Darwish Bin Bilal? That's a mouthful.

My jaw was locked, my teeth gritted.

—Those were my friends. They ODed. It was . . . totally unrelated . . . We . . . I mean they were . . . burnouts . . . I don't know what you want me to say.

Winston grabbed Lenihan's iPad and gave it a twirl.

—Says they both overdosed within two months of each other. Both from the same drug.

—It was 2018! Fentanyl was all over the streets! They were putting it in everything!

—Some victim, Winston snorted. —And some friends. What I want to know is how you made it out unscathed. You slip your buddies a couple hot bags? Got your jollies? For the thrill?

I stood up.

—This is ridiculous! Why would I have done something like that? How could . . .

—Can't you understand how it looks from our side, Powell loomed overhead. —With your name tied up in so *many* violent crimes?

—Oh my god, I collapsed. —I assume it looks bad. But I'm telling the truth.

Tears tore from my orifices. Snot writhed down my lips.

—What's going to happen?

I smeared my face on the floor.

—Hey, listen, Winston put a hand to my shoulder.

I cowered and hiccupped.

—We believe you, he said.

I buried my nose in my armpit.

—Mr. Garlic . . .

—We know you didn't kill anyone, Powell spoke over him. —We even told as much to the Sarge.

I sat up a bit.

—Just figured you might need a friendly reminder. You're not the only victim in town.

Winston grinned.

—I mean, I figured you didn't have the ways and means to get your hands on a neurotoxin, Lenihan relented. —You're not exactly the most connected guy in Amagansett.

—You . . . you what, I whimpered.

Powell heaved me up by a soaking lapel and shoved a glass of water into my hands.

—Death sort of follows you, huh, Winston said.

—Doesn't it follow everyone?

—So why'd you do it?

I dropped the glass.

—Am I under suspicion or not?

—You know, we haven't totally decided, Powell looked at his phone. —Why don't you not leave the state in the meantime?

—I'm . . . I have nowhere to go . . .

—You'll testify at the inquest, of course, Lenihan said.

—When . . . is that?

—We'll let you know. You'll be easy to get in touch with, won't you?

I studied the three of them. Their faces matte boards of obfuscation.

—Stop freaking out, Winston said.

Gradually, I acquiesced.

—Get some rest, Lenihan picked up his iPad and doddered away.

Winston and Powell adjusted their belts.

—What time is it, I asked.

—You don't want to know, Powell said.

A woman at the front desk wearing a vintage US Open T-shirt so threadbare you could catch a case just by noticing it had me fill out a pile of discharge paperwork.

I poured coffee in a styrofoam cup from a Moccamaster simmering on a Duncan Phyfe lowboy, and through the tinted windows of the police station lobby, I could see daylight. What's more, it had ceased to rain. Like the whole horror hadn't happened, and my hangover, my ear, and my feeble vestige of an ego were duking it out for which would have the honor of laying me to waste.

I returned the forms to the attendant. She handed me a paper bag of clean, dry clothes.

—Your wife dropped these off for you.

I wiped my eyes with my putrescent sleeve.

—Thank you, I mewled.

—You can change in a holding cell.

Emma had brought Club Monaco khakis and a soft L.L.Bean button-down, Brooks Brothers boxers, argyle socks, and Top-Siders, creased and blunted with age, indubitably dug out from the to-donate bin in the closet. And on top of it all, my bucket hat with the letter H.

So my wife hadn't disowned me. She didn't hate me. Not enough to leave me bedraggled and destitute in my basest hour at least.

Or perhaps she was only covering for herself. Her family honor. Not risking any further dirt to throw on their name.

Did you see what that homicidal Hebrew was wearing when he escaped from the jail?

Reluctantly, I balled my suit in the bag. So maybe Emma did hate me. Too many factors to deny or confirm. She certainly wasn't waiting teary-eyed and pearl-clutching, waving a white Hermès handkerchief to greet me when I slunk out the doors into the beating sun.

I had to shield my brow. Disoriented and stricken. I had no clue where I was. No sense of direction. Little notion of the island's street names or cardinal points or how to order a car.

My phone had been in the pocket of the khakis, but it was malfunctioning vainly, and I put it to sleep. The boat shoes didn't fit right. My feet were too narrow. I got down on one knee, tightened the laces. And I kept my hand like a visor, a whacked mariner searching for shore, overcome with a desire to go and live in a lighthouse. And not one at the end of a promontory, or an island either, but truly at sea, without foundation or anchor, like the one I'd seen from the ferry, free-floating, brittle autonomy lost to the tides.

I was crouched in the parking lot, dreaming of this void, when a car horn intervened. I stared up as a Dodge Charger approached and a figure leaned out, flipped sunglass lenses.

—Need a lift, Winston jeered.

The engine revved. Powell drummed nibbled-down fleshy nails over the steering wheel.

—Hop in, Mr. Garlicker, he said.

I didn't ask questions. I was locked in as soon as the door closed behind me. The car was unmarked, but it still did the trick. I jiggled the handle.

—Cut that out, Powell said. —This is my personal ride.

I folded my arms. Winston looked back over his seat.

—When's your novel coming out?

I leaned my head on the window and tried to think about nothing.

—Aaron Judge should write a book.

—He'll write one, Powell said.

—When, Winston asked.

—When he's ready, that's when.

We weaved through centuries-old lindens, London planes, sycamores, birches. The hedgerows grew taller, more severe and forbidding. And as we turned onto Further Lane, I knew we weren't headed to Emma's parents' place.

—Wait, where are we going?

—There's someone who wants to see you, Winston said.

—Special request. Thought we'd do you the favor of chauffeuring. Make sure you get there in one piece.

We pulled up to a driveway. I couldn't see its terminus, so walled in with verdure, but it began with a long row of concrete rounded slats. Ubiquitous in the billionaire parts of the island, these were designed to thwart the local deer population, should any be so audacious as to breach private land. If they were crippled in the process, that's just what nature intended. The Dodge rattled over the grating. Then it stopped at a gate another twenty yards on. An intercom crackled.

Powell rolled down the window, announced, —We've got Jacob Garlicker.

The speaker emitted a whine, and a lock disengaged. The gate slowly swung backward. After what felt like five minutes, we arrived at the estate. The Charger wrenched to a halt before ten white columns, six chimneys, balconies and bay windows. The ocean was audible. A gauze of salt spray coated the windshield. Powell jabbed Winston, who churlishly extracted himself and opened my door.

—This is where you get off.

I unbuckled my seat belt.

—Aren't you guys coming with me?

—Just you, Powell said.

My heart started thrumming.

—But how will I get home?

—I'm sure she'll've arranged something.

—But who is *she*? What am I supposed to be doing here?

—Why not go to the door like a good little boy and find out?

Winston grabbed at my forearm, but I shook him off and stepped from the car. The sea breeze chilled my nerves.

—Goodbye, the cop pushed my ass with a boot, half his body already restored to the passenger seat, slammed the door.

I watched them back out of the twisting lane of crushed oyster shells. Drops of sweat dried at my temples, and I crept to the mansion's wraparound porch.

The front double doors' knocker was forged in the shape of a fox. Before I could reach it, the entryway broke apart. Some kind of maid ogled me.

—Mr. Garlicker, she said.

It wasn't clear as a question or accusation.

—*Ándale*, she directed, and I mounted marble steps, followed her through a basilica-like foyer, up a grand staircase, down incredible halls lit by candelabra and many low-key eminent paintings, to a library, dim and high-ceilinged and cold as a morgue.

—*Sombrero*, the maid hissed.

I touched my head and took it off. The walls around us were adorned with priceless volumes without names on their spines. A couple choice numbers were displayed under glass, and velvet curtains drew over the windows so as to prevent any marveling at the briny deep.

A tall, padded cathedra was nested in a corner under an Arco floor lamp. A sophisticated machine of snaking tubes and attachments reposed on wheeled legs. Two lines ran concealed behind the throne, and when I turned to the maid, I found she'd already left. I pondered my shoelaces on the hypnotic mauve carpet, which depicted scenes from Genesis.

—Are you going to stand there all day, a voice asked.

—No, I said. —Should I . . . come to you?

—I believe that's what you've been working toward.

—I'm sorry, I called out too loudly.

It echoed, and I wrung my hat. A bony white hand, like so many others on the island, rested on the chair's arm. I forced my legs to keep walking until I'd performed a full orbit and beheld the paltry woman as a whole. She was wearing some kind of frock, with a tartan wool afghan draped on her lap. Her feet were bare and did not reach the ground. Her kneecaps, knotty and tumescent, protruded from what looked like painful angles. Her cheeks were sunken and pocked, sooty under the eyes. Frizzy twigs sprouted across her oversized gourd, sequestered by patches of dark red bald spots. The IV lines were attached to her wrist and inner elbow, the tubes bloated with black cherry blood.

In front of her was a stool I hadn't seen from the entrance. She slanted to it with her incannulated hand, and I plopped. She opened her mouth and attempted to smile, which must be harder to achieve with just gums.

I thought perhaps she'd dozed off. But eventually she fell into a long, wet hawking fit.

—My apologies, Jacob. You don't mind if I address you by your Christian name, do you?

I shrugged, and she rubbed at her chest.

—I suppose you're wondering who I am. Why you're here, and the rest.

I nodded.

—No need to be stuffy, boy.

—I'm sorry, I said.

—Well, I'm Gladys Masterson, she enunciated. —I've no doubt you've made my husband's acquaintance.

—Oh god, my physique turned to jelly. —Mrs. Masterson, I'm . . . I don't know what to say . . . I'm so, so, so sorry. I'm . . .

—Enough, she waved at the pervading nothingness my existence had adopted. —It was a long time coming, and there's no love lost on my part. You could say he was a good husband. Once. Perhaps to his second wife. But I settled that score long ago. I'm not interested in your or anyone else's condolences. I've already sent instructions to the crematorium. Miss Lopez will strew his remains to the Atlantic. Or the pool for all I care.

She tittered. I shivered.

—Whatever you think is best.

—Indeed, Gladys said. —That's the spirit. And I apologize for the chill. It helps my inflammation. I've caught the worst case of Lyme this summer, and my joints just can't take it. This plasmapheresis hardly does anything. I'm all migraines and neckaches and being carted around by señoritas. I know they've got reefer, and I think it would help a great deal, but they pretend not to understand when I ask. For god's sake, the stuff's legal. They think I want them dismissed. It's so difficult to communicate with anyone lately. I don't care if they were raised in Wainscott, everyone's incoherent. And speaking of spirit, terribly rude, can I offer you a drink?

—I...

—I can't make it myself, of course, and I wouldn't dare trust any of the help with the top shelf, but the cellarette's over there, if you don't mind mixing...

My forehead still split, but at the mention of libation, I was salivating too.

—Well... if you insist.

I left my hat on the stool and selected a bottle of Watenshi, pouring it over an immense cube of ice, which I tonged from a refrigerated drawer of the converted bookshelf-cum-liquor cabinet.

I sipped silently, then my throat opened of its own accord and the gin flowed forth to cloak my stomach in a blanket of love. I poured myself another generous dram and wobbled back to my stool, hung my hat on my knee, smirking dumb. Gladys clapped her hands once.

—Now we get down to business. I must ask, did you have much of a chance to confer with my husband before his hapless end?

I bowed, lost in juniper reverie. My eyes swam. I glanced up.

—Not really, I murmured. —I saw him once before, but we didn't meet till last night at the club . . . And he really didn't say much. He seemed highly . . . laconic . . . Almost, like, stoned.

—That would be the effects of the tetrodotoxin setting in, to be sure. So you didn't have a chance to know him at all? His occupation, his history? Any of his quintessential anecdotes?

—I heard he went to Madagascar. But he was stuck on the arm of that woman, um, Alice, I gulped. —She said he was her date for the night, and . . .

—I know all about Alice. Spare me the ghastly details.

—But, like, yeah . . . No . . . Nothing exceptional . . . I'm . . . My wife . . . I'm recently married to the daughter of Michael, um, who the party was for, and . . .

—Right, right.

—And, um. Like, everything's so confusing. I've been out here a bunch of times. But it was always the pandemic, and everyone was nice and gave each other space. It wasn't like this at all in my previous experience. Things have seemed more . . . contentious . . . Super . . .

I swallowed.

—Cilious . . . I mean at the party, and . . . Sorry. I don't know. What was your question?

—You've answered it splendidly, Gladys looked smug. —So you really don't know a thing about my late husband?

—I know he was a doctor, I intoned and gestured my highball.

—Oh yes, Gladys said. —He was a doctor all right. A doctor of education. He was the headmaster of Livingston Prep, coming on forty years.

My hostess waited.

—Does that ring any bells?

I shook my head and my drink, drank my drink, shook my head.

—No, I said. —I . . . didn't grow up in the city. I went to public school in Massachusetts.

—Boston Latin, she beamed.

—Just . . . near Worcester. Just the local assigned district.

—But you went on to great things.

Her eyes burned on my hat.

—Oh, I choked. —No. This. No. My dad went to Harvard for grad school. He was fairly proud of himself and owned . . . owns a lot of paraphernalia. I didn't realize how misleading it would be for me to wear it around here. Most people think the H stands for hockey.

—And what is your line of work, Jacob?

I finished my drink.

—I'm actually between jobs right now. I've been dealing with some estate stuff. I'm . . . my parents' executor . . . or attorney-in-fact . . . I'm overseeing their . . . It's very complicated.

—I would imagine it is.

Gladys tapped her nose. Her bloodshot eyes twinkled.

—It's been a big ordeal, yes. But, um . . . no, I've never heard of that school . . . I went to NYU. I met Emma five years ago, and now we're married, and I'm . . . hanging in there.

—Good on you, Gladys said. —Well, well. It's nigh time for my *siesta*, and I do look forward to it all morning, so I'll just spit it out. Livingston Prep was a very prestigious academy. One of the first and best in the country, and my husband drove it straight into the ground. No surprise you're unversed, come to think of it. With upstarts like the Ethical Spectacle Cultural Cult making waves. In any case, he was mostly emeritus by now. His slinky shrew Sybil Parker handling the day-to-day. That is, when she wasn't fellating him, or watching him be fellated withal. Whatever they got up to in their little bordello behind the institute's gates. I'm digressing, aren't I? Or am I, Jacob? That's another question. Why did I ask you here today?

Two beats happened.

—Oh, I'm sorry, I said. —I thought that was rhetorical.

—Perhaps it was. Unless you have an answer?

—It doesn't seem . . . that I do.

—Not yet, no. But perhaps, if you needled a bit . . . Perhaps if you went on a visit to inspect Livingston for yourself . . . perhaps you'd be lucky enough to encounter Ms. Parker, and perhaps she would fill you in.

—Fill me in on what?

—If I told you outright, wouldn't that ruin the fun?

—It doesn't sound like much fun.

—I suppose you're misunderstanding.

Gladys fiddled with her IV, then fixed her gaze on me intently.

—I don't need any answers. As you can see, I'm not long for these seashores, irrespective of whether I recover from my pesky infection. But I do like revenge. And I know for a fact we've got a common interest, and an enemy moreover.

—What exactly are you implying?

—They never did find your parents, did they, dear?

I tensed up. My whole body chafed. It seemed I would lose permanent hearing in my ear.

—I don't mean to upset. Not being found has advantages. No dead bodies, for instance. Then perhaps they persist. Nothing's absolute. All I know is your and my husband's affairs *have* intermingled. You were the last to see him alive for a reason, even if only the lord can attest.

—Can't you be less, I suppressed a belch, which fed my wandering lump. —Obtuse?

—You're not obliged to me, you know. I'm quite confident you've nothing to do with Masterson's murder.

—Then who did? Do you know? Was it . . . was it Alice, I gasped.

—Oh my, Gladys sighed and looked off. —How could you suggest such a thing? Why would someone like her? Even older, frailer than I? What would her motive be? No, I would never pin Alice . . .

—Then what's with all the insinuating?

—I've no idea what you mean.

I sprung to my feet, glass in hand, ice cube clanging like a bullet in a funhouse hall of mirrors. My hat fell to the floor.

—What's with all the surreptitiousness and hints? Why did you even call me here? Had those cops bring me in like some kind of wretch? You know I didn't do it! You say Alice didn't either! If you know who did, why not tell Officer Lenihan yourself? I don't want any part of this!

—Forget him, Gladys spat. —I'm trying to tell *you* something. This concerns *you*. I'd hardly get myself involved in a criminal inquiry. That is just not polite or respectable. And had I known you couldn't hold your liquor, I would have never offered you a refreshment.

—I . . . I'm sorry, I said, sitting back down.

I left my hat on the floor.

—I should say so, my hostess scolded.

I wilted in the cold air. Then Gladys rang a bell.

—I've imparted all I desire to bestow. You may take it or leave it. As I told you, you're under no obligation. No charges will be filed with regard to my husband's untimely passage. These things happen. He probably tried to prepare that pufferfish himself. Sent away for it from some catalog. And Livingston will press on in his absence without missing a beat. In fact, Ms. Parker will be nothing less than ecstatic. I do apologize for the abominable incident you bore witness to. I don't expect you deserved it, though I hope you will heed its call. Because . . .

And Gladys Masterson tapped her nose again, and this time she winked blatantly, sticking out her chin and parting the side of her dried-up little mouth so I could make no mistake.

—This *was* a call, Jacob. You might even call it a warning. And there's much to be learned when you care to go looking.

I squinted at her.

—*Hola*, Lopez!

The maid was standing in the doorway.

—Now it's time for my respite. You can see yourself out.

—You know, I whispered. —I can get you weed if you want.

Gladys tittered and presented her hand, and I kissed it, unbelievably, like I'd known the routine from the start.

I hated to admit it, but the cops were right. A driver had been arranged to usher me off. The dark green Bentley idled outside the converted stable garage. I slipped in and savored a glass of Roederer as I was conveyed to my in-laws'.

I smelled the fish market first. My head rushed, and the turbocharged automobile feathered to a stop. The driver looked over his shoulder.

In my Cockney accent, I implored, —Once more around the block?

He, however, was silent. I peeled myself off the upholstery. The car pulled out of view.

The cottage looked ominous. My Camry slouched on pine needles, and a Porsche Taycan hatchback with California plates was parked in the neighboring driveway. A couple tawny influencer types in athleisure were walking around the abandoned A-frame, poking its trim with Chelsea boots.

I didn't know what to expect. To be received with embraces of relief or served with dissolution of marriage papers. The fact it was Sunday was working in my favor. Harder to obtain legal documents.

But inside the house, it was quiet. No skittering Houdini. No greedy repine from my cat. I peeked out the sliding glass door, the back patio desolate, and opened the fridge to discover a half-full bottle of rosé. I uncorked it and chugged until it was as hollow as my echo chamber, and I lobbed it at a trash can, because Suffolk County maintained no recycling infrastructure.

These island denizens knew better than to pretend there was any saving the world. They were stockpiling our planet's wealth so future generations could colonize Mars. Maseratis on asteroids. Montauk Ganymede Outpost. Or something worse. Provoke a hot war with Russia and China, wipe out enough global population to reduce carbon emissions and curb climate change.

The wine steadied me, though. Enough to face the stairs. And I plodded up to the shower, where the drain was dry, and I couldn't distinguish the high-pressure deluge from my tears.

I washed away the sleepless hours. The sand and vomit and salt and already-rickety recollections of the past half-day's hysteria. I dug at my ear. The pain was unbearable. Thick, oozing suppuration spurted over my finger.

I swaddled myself in a towel, lolling under bafflement and fatigue. I tumbled into my wife's bedroom and down across the lumpy mattress.

—Ow, it cried. —What the fuck!

Houdini growled and scuttled from under the box spring and jumped onto me barking. We fell off, the dog's paws on my chest, snarling and popping his jowls, ropes of spume like a pendulum.

—Help, I squealed.

—Houdini, Emma yelled. —Stop.

The beast withdrew and retreated, sneering, ready to attack should his master give the word.

—God, my wife flared. —I was trying to get some sleep.

—I'm . . . I'm . . .

I started to blubber.

—Don't, she said.

—I'm sorry, I composed myself.

She leaned over the bed, prone, leering at my nude body. The towel had come undone. Splayed out like that, I imagined I looked a bit like Christ.

—I'm sorry, I said again.

—I'll bet.

—It was . . . a major accident.

—What was? Getting drunk, or getting yourself implicated in a fucking killing? Or humiliating me and my parents and everyone we've ever met at my father's seventieth birthday?

—All of those. But the killing thing the most. That was seriously not what I wanted.

—My parents are mortified.

—Have you considered how I feel?

—How . . .

My wife started but didn't finish. She rolled back over the bed so I couldn't see her. Still, the ire was palpable, and, I guess, justified. I didn't know. I was both patsy and perpetrator. A role I'd excelled in for most of my life. There was something frightfully typical about it all.

—I'm pathetic, I moaned.

—Somehow declaring it doesn't make it less abject.

I crawled up the bedframe and under the covers, quivering. Emma suckled a Jolly Rancher.

—Would you believe me if I told you I only had good intentions?

—It would take some convincing.

—But I'm well-intentioned all the time! Remember when I pointed out that pygmy owl! And I saved a seal pup in Maine!

—You're just naming animals.

—I love all animals, and people are animals.

—What does that have to do with anything?

—I never meant for stuff to get so out of hand. I've been feeling very, like, alienated. Ever since we got here. And all this shit. I feel literally cursed. I don't even know how to explain it. Every single interaction for the past three days has been hostile and catastrophic. I'm doomed! My parents are gone, and I'm, like. I'm all alone in the world, and I was accosted by the police, and I . . . I witnessed a, like, gruesome murder, and nobody seems to be concerned about . . .

—Why does it always have to be about you, Emma interrupted. —What about me? What about *my* parents? Their son-in-law getting wasted and insulting their oldest friends and the entire town getting wrapped up in this horrible situation! This weekend wasn't supposed to be about you. It wasn't supposed to be about how your parents are missing. I don't care how that sounds, but it's all we've been dealing with for almost a year. This was supposed to be about celebrating my father's life. And my last chance to enjoy a little downtime before I start this new job. Because we've been floundering. Stagnating. You're not going back to work. You're not applying for anything. And you're not writing. What do you expect? If you just loaf around that condo in your underwear all day that sooner or later your parents will show up at the door, like, hey hi, did you miss us, it's all over, everything's back to normal, carry on!

I rocked slightly, naked, taking what I had coming to me with nothing to counter it.

—I got sand in my ear, I sputtered. —It hurts so bad.

—Oh my god, Emma cried. —I just wanted to get some rest before my first day tomorrow. Do you have any idea how big a project this exhibition is? And how much strain I'm under? I can't deal with your problems right now. You think you're hurting?

—My ear does hurt, I said.

—You know, I really don't have time for this. I would appreciate it if you just gave me some space. We can talk tomorrow. I don't want to see you anymore today. I'm going to take Houdini for a walk, and I'm going to spend the night in the guest room. Please, do not bother me. Please, please. Hear me. I don't want to interact with you for the rest of the day.

I sniveled in assent.

—And figure out a way to apologize to my parents. I'm serious. I don't know how you feasibly could. They're at the club, doing their best to recuperate. But they're bewildered and ashamed and exhausted. How you can possibly make up for this? You figure it out.

—Emma . . .

—Do I smell fucking *wine*, she screamed.

—I just needed to take the edge off.

My eyes stayed closed the rest of the day.

No one brought me the crossword. All I was aware of were drawers opening, banging, zippers fastening, doors swung apart, crashed shut with fury, the metal clasp of Houdini's harness, the faint trickling alluvium loosed from my ear, and a roar of irresolution.

I had to think of some way to rectify things with my in-laws and wife. I had to think of anything but what I'd seen on the beach seven years ago, and last night. I had to, but actually I didn't have to do anything. I could be the first person to close his eyes as a lifelong protest. Perhaps Emma could work that into her next curation. Then who'd be the one not contributing?

I was straying. I didn't want anything. Or, that wasn't right. I wanted to recede and forget. And yet my colloquy with Gladys kept boomeranging through my conscience.

I needed a plan. A course of action. A flow, like yoga, like raking sand, letting everything out of my control fall away, taking my limited powers in stride to provide for what was left of my family, before I was left without one.

It would begin with sitting up, putting on clothes, pulling myself together, salvaging the frayed remnants of my scant life and beginning anew, acting with grace and discretion, mindfulness and gratitude.

Instead, I started counting, and no sooner was I in the arms of Morpheus, dead to the world.

# MONDAY

In a dream I was scaling a kind of bread that wouldn't allow you to come in contact with its glutenous nature. Wisps of dough glossed by semitransparence separating molecularly in midair. Sieving the grist for the mill, as it were, I wasn't sure, but something about gluten, and I held my stomach, and it was tepid, soft, and amenable.

Then a piece of gluten, a madman gluten particle with a spiteful little mustache came galloping in on a tower viewer, and it was all over for me, sitting at a café counter, trying to order a bitters and soda, but they kept bringing beer in low, wide, inch-tall glasses, and I told them I couldn't drink beer, and the gluten man was on the move, getting closer, except Matthew was sitting beside me, swiveling on a pleather cushion, speaking too quietly to communicate anything useful.

He was wearing the same apparel he'd found compelling in life. Raf Simons sneakers and Acne raw denim jeans and a white APC T-shirt, gold chain arraying his throat.

He took a baggie from somewhere, rapped a bump between thumb and index knuckle on the back of his hand. I leaned in, but now Matthew was Jal, and she twitched it away before I could blow.

*Whatever*, I said.
*For the record*, she sniffed, bent and spiraled.
*What's it like?*
*Nothing special.*
She lay across my lap. I cupped her breasts. They were Sofia's.
The hum of insects and appliances.

I opened my eyes. It was dark. My head was too heavy to lift, still I managed to do it. A globule of discharge issued out my ear and glistened on the pillowcase.

That was that, a thought sang. I was dead, and I bolted down the stairs, blindly stormed through the halls but was stopped by the neon glare of the stove's digital timepiece. *3:11*, it said.

I wormed to Michael's office. I strewed papers and paintings and pencils away. My ear pounded, squelched with purulence. I kicked a printer I hadn't noticed on the ground. Its tray table clattered open. A keyboard emerged acting coy, like, who me? I jostled it out, plugged it into the Gateway case. I held down its power button, and miraculously, the thing booted up, and I navigated to Firefox and proceeded to google *how to get ear stuck out of my sand full of rocks and pus pressure and salt help fastest and easiest way.*

I followed instructions. I funneled a pint of hydrogen peroxide into my external acoustic meatus. I did jumping jacks. I took three hot showers, filled the garbage with bloody Q-tips, slapping my jaw. And soon I found myself crouched with a toilet plunger suctioned to my skull. Bare ass on the tub floor, neck jarred in an L, striving to dislodge the muck.

I heated spoonfuls of olive oil over the gas range. I winced at the sizzle as I dippered them into my brain. This was supposed to break up compounded clumps and lubricate out the debris. But as I lay on my side on the bitter patio bricks, I knew it was too late. My ear woefully infected. All was lost.

I groped my way to the basement, where a chalky, moldering cabinet stooped next to the washing machine under the stairs. I jerked its weak padlock off and snatched a bottle of Blanton's Straight from the Barrel from its foamy case.

I broke the seal directly and let the whiskey burn down to my stomach. My lump bounced, accepting the gift. I even decanted a nip in my ear. Without delay, I felt easier.

—Who's stressed out, I croaked.

I nursed the bottle a minute. Then I skulked back to my wife's bedroom, the jug cradled in my arms like an infant. I slithered under the covers. I spooned the elixir, and it soothed my pain. No more dreams.

I awoke again to new aches.

I depressed my phone's home button. It flashed on a background of Emma and Houdini and Turmeric in New Hampshire, a sea of wildflowers behind them. It blinked off.

I tapped the button, but now the background was black. My phone said, *11:03*. It vibrated, and I was able to make out the beginning of an incoming text from Sofia: *Are you okkk??? I just heard*, before it died. I plugged it into a charger.

My ear was sticky and dribbling, exuding a harsh, cloying scent of liquor and something else. Rotting tissue? The bottle was three-quarters empty. I rolled it under the bed. I tiptoed to the guest room, but the linens were laid and smelled fresh, and Emma's suitcase was gone. Houdini's claws lengthened and retracted beneath the four-poster.

In the kitchen, the Moccamaster was on. I poured a mug and tried to listen for movement around the cottage. Some clue for what to do next.

Something knocked from below. I shuffled to the basement door, cracked it, and was assaulted by a brown mass of fur, turned incomprehensibly sideways, legs thrust out in desperation, clambering up the musty corridor.

Then my eyes locked on Turmeric's, which were whirling, attempting to balance the dying bunny between three fangs and make her way to the door. I slammed it and heard the dull thud as wood collided with feline.

—What was that, Jane called out.

But before I could duck for cover, my mother-in-law was at my side.

—Oh, Jacob, she exclaimed.

—It was just Turmeric, I said. —I'm sorry. She knows she's supposed to stay outside, but she keeps sneaking in.

Jane gave me a look as though I were disfigured.

—We've been worried about you.

I shut my eyes, forcing a tight smile, hoping to disappear.

—It was just Turmeric, I repeated.

—But my god, are you ill? You look terrible. What's wrong with your ear?

I prodded the side of my face. The organ was scorching. It twinged at the slightest graze.

—What's wrong what, Michael rasped, coming in from the garage, palms oil-slicked.

—Jacob's ear. Michael, look. Oh, poor thing. What could've happened?

—I . . . I got sand in it, I wavered. —I . . . Oh god . . . I'm so sorry about your party, Michael. I'm so sorry, Jane. I'm so sorry. I didn't mean to . . . I didn't know . . . I promise I . . .

—What are you talking about, Michael said. —The party was great. Best night of my life! Can't wait for eighty!

—But the . . . Dr. Masterson, and the . . . and . . .

—Water under the bridge, Jane insisted. —It's not like *you* had anything to do with it.

—But . . . I . . . Are you really not mad?

—You think I'm gonna let a little mortality ruin my good time?

—But Emma said . . . Emma gave me the impression you guys were . . .

—Oh, you know her, Jane chuckled. —Always overreacting.

—We sincerely don't care.

—Her blood sugar gets low, and she snaps.

—At least the geezer had the decency to hold off until most guests had left, Michael yawned.

—Anyway, Jane squeezed my shoulder. —Your wife made it safely onto the LIRR at the crack of dawn. She just texted from the museum. All is well. She only needed to sleep her mood off.

I swayed on my feet, mystified. Jane patted my forehead.

—You're running a fever!

—No, no, I said. —I'm fine. I slept on my ear, and it was already bothering me, and . . .

—You need a doctor, Jane stood firm.

She craned her neck and peered into my festering orifice.

—This looks serious . . . Michael?

—I'll ring up old Schwartz. He owes me a favor. For robbing me blind every checkup.

My in-laws guffawed.

—You hold still now, Jane cooed. —What you're really in need of is some proper mothering, but . . . Well, for now let me get you a warm towel.

She carried herself with a muted kind of bereavement. Hoping to project joy on the loved ones around her. Hobbled by the burden of a sorrow no one of us could pacify or subdue.

At the height of the pandemic, Jane had lost two of her sisters, her mother, and her estranged cattle-ranching father. Emma had never even met said patriarch. And something lurked in that. A kind of Protestant repression or ethic I hadn't the wherewithal to broach. Each sweetness Jane put forth settled with a tinny, stale aftertaste. But what could I do? I studied her gaze. I shrugged into the involuntary gut gulp at the pit of every lilting chime and remark. My stomach hurt too.

The stories of her socially mobile, overeducated New Mexican upbringing included a recurrent anecdote about how my mother-in-law's family had been the first to befriend the new physician in town, a Hungarian-Jewish refugee, who treated all five of her siblings, and fixed pitchers of martinis with her parents, discussing literature and theater and Cold War developments in the evenings. Jane's mother had by chance witnessed the great glow of the atomic bomb test at Trinity on a long late-night drive across the desert, and it had changed her such that her entire progeny was required to appreciate the near whiteness of Oppenheimer, and the Semite at large. Their equal hardiness, hard-earned skepticism, and love for debate.

But now, with so much of Jane's stock dead and gone, the debate was over. Fate writ. Sometimes I felt a swell of pathos rocking behind those stolid silver eyes. And my heart screamed out to her. We had too much in common. It was better for us to smile and squint. I already had a mother, even if, at that moment, I didn't know where she was.

And still Jane guided me to the daybed, where she lay me down, groggy and littered.

—Hold it over your ear, but don't press down . . . not too hard!

Distantly, I heard Michael snicker, engaged with his phone. The stucco swarmed in whorls where there should've been a ceiling fan, and before long the celadon Fiat was bucking beneath us, as my father-in-law conducted me to the village's premier medical clinic.

A nurse took my blood pressure and had me stand on a scale. She looked concerned.

—I know, I said. —Pretty embarrassing.

—Have you tried lifting weights?

—About eight years ago, yeah. I pulled out my back.

—So what's brought you in today?

I pointed at my ear. The nurse cringed, brandishing an otoscope and shining it in the grotto.

—Let's get you into an exam room, she said.

There, I found a paper gown folded over a reclining table. I stripped and tied the garment above my haunches. I hopped on the table, listening as the flaccid tissue parchment tore. I scooted on my ass until I could lie back comfortably, and I tried to look at my phone, but I remembered I'd left it plugged in at the cottage. I hoped it still worked. Actually, I didn't care if it did. But then how would I get in touch with my wife?

Life complex, I thought. I had a life complex, like an Oedipal one, but for life in general. It was a complex concept, as I was a complex, eccentric person. I drummed my fingers on the tissue paper. I scanned the room. Sinks and boxes of latex gloves. A corkboard dotted with thumbtacks. A magazine rack filled with pamphlets about the latest breakthroughs in medicine.

—Medical Aid in Dying, I said. —I specifically asked for a housekeeper! But since you're here . . .

The relief of not being charged for Dr. Masterson's murder was still sinking in. I'd really have to get his widow some weed.

But where was Dr. Schwartz? I sure hoped his surname wasn't a put-on. I needed the real McCoyerwitzenstein. I was owed that much.

What else was there to look at? A poster of a caterpillar: NEVER STOP BELIEVING YOUR LIFE CAN TAKE ON WINGS. Ten cartoon faces on a spectrum of bliss to agony.

And then I glimpsed above the doorframe and was deflated to a renewed state of chagrin. There, held fast by two tiny nails, was a gilded nameplate, which said simply, MY OFFICE, and as the door started to open, it winked.

My awe scarcely had a chance to soak in. The doctor looked at my ear and broke into a cackle. He removed a long steel curette from a sanitary case and jammed it in the canal.

A deafening salvo spilled through me, followed by a high-frequency ring, which pitched out as the weight of an encyclopedia set lifted off my sinus and the pressure released.

—Better, the doctor asked.

I nodded. My eyes flooding with tears.

—Just a bit of backup, he teased. —By the way, why'd you get undressed?

—Force of habit . . . I've had a lot of doctor's appointments.

He snorted and showed me an instrument that looked like a hot glue gun and pulled a miniscule trigger, vacuuming the wreckage. My brow felt light and sunny. I saw more vibrant colors, borders defined with greater clarity. I took my first non-shallow breath in what felt like weeks. My neck was limber. The doctor turned me over, so my butt cheeks caught a gust of air-conditioning, and squirted a dropperful of liquid toward my cerebellum.

—Lie still for ten minutes.

—Thank you, I whispered.

—For this? It was nothing! I'll thank you when your insurance provider pays up!

—About that . . .

—Ah. We can resolve at another time. Perhaps it will get mixed in with your father-in-law's coverage.

—You're a mensch, I said.

He really was Dr. Schwartz. And I lay there imagining that the worst of my life was behind me. I couldn't hit much bottomer. I'd capsized and ascended from the abyssal zone.

—Hey, I said. —If you don't mind my asking . . . where did you get that, like, plaque thing? That thing that says your office. I mean *my* office. You know?

—Huh, my savior sounded distracted.

—The, like, little gold nameplate. It's hung over the door.

Dr. Schwartz paused. I felt paranoid. A sink ran. Water sloshed. The drain gurgled.

—Sorry, I said. —I didn't mean to . . .

—What? You have five more minutes. Please lie still. Let the medicine work.

—I'm sorry. I was just curious. I had one just like it. In my apartment. In Coney Island. A long time ago. And then the other day I found another buried in the sand at Two Mile Hollow.

—One of *those*?

—The, um, I rose an inch, stopped myself. —The little gold sign. It says my office, right?

—Yes, yes, of course, Dr. Schwartz was preoccupied.

—Where did you get it?

—But there's no way you could've found it on the beach. They only sell them one place. A stationery store near Times Square. Very old school. The last of its kind. It's where I make my secretary get all my pens and whatnot. I knew the proprietor. We grew up together in the Bronx.

—Wow, I said. —I gave the one I found on the beach to my father-in-law for his birthday.

—Wonderful shindig. Great spread.

—And I was hoping . . .

—The shrimp dip. *Azoy geshmak*! Don't tell my wife!

—I won't. But I was, like . . . I don't know. It's odd. That plaque thing keeps showing up at the weirdest times. And I'd love to meet the guy who makes them . . . I'd love to get one for myself. Again. I never should've thrown it out.

—Pah, the doctor said.

—No really. I'm like . . . into old-school crap . . . I'd love to check out his shop.

—Sit, Schwartz asserted.

I did. He was getting nebbishier by the second. He clapped me on the back. The paper gown was grainy and already coming apart on my skin. He scribbled on a prescription pad, ripped off a sheet, and handed it to me.

—What's this?

—It's the address of Geshaltn Stationers, what do you think?

—Thanks, I said, impressed by the stereotype. —Gestalt Stationers?

—Ges*haltn*, he reproved.

—How do you spell that?

The doctor looked flabbergasted.

—It's on the prescription!

—Can you spell it out loud?

Schwartz tore the sheet from my clutches, wrote *G-E-S-H-A-L-T-N* in unmistakable block letters.

—What does it mean?

—What does it mean, he puffed. —It's a name! I thought you wanted your ear fixed. It's done! Now! Goodbye! I'm a busy man!

—I'm sorry, I smiled bashfully. —Is there anything else I, like, need to do?

—It's fixed, Schwartz adjured.

—Any, like, stuff I need to get at the pharmacy or anything?

—Swish your mouth out with warm salt water twice a day.

—So . . . I don't need antibiotics?

—I drowned the whole organ. You want more of you killed? You're done. Cured!

He turned away, folding his arms. I didn't want to push the man toward further caricature, so I promptly dressed, crumpled the prescription page in my pocket, and found Michael waiting in the Fiat, smoking a butt of cigar that smelled conspicuously of schwag.

—I really can't thank you enough, I said. —I feel so much better.

—Hey. Someone's gotta give this old bird a lap around the block. Engine's been wanting to shit out on me for years.

—Well, I really appreciate it.

—Consider it my one nice thing, his eyes glittered as he shifted into gear. —What's your plan for the rest of the day?

—Oh, I don't know. I guess I was going to try to check in with Emma and . . . Do you think she's going to spend the night in the city?

—I'd expect so, Michael said. —Two and a half hours is a ruthless commute.

I slid my hand in my pocket, fondled the slip of paper.

—Well, maybe I'll take a ride in and see her. You don't mind if I stop by Tenth Street?

—You'd be doing me a favor, Michael veered, narrowly evading two fawns limping across the highway. —Flush the toilets. Make sure the pipes are clear.

I watched the island streak by through the window.

—And remember to put down the seat!

I looked at the floorboard.

—No problem.

—You need a key?

—Yeah, I guess.

He pried one off a carabiner still attached to the ignition lock cylinder, tossed the waxen brass, and it caromed off my forehead. I folded it in the prescription receipt.

Michael swerved into the driveway. I threw the Blanton's bottle, *The Great Gatsby*, my phone, and a change of clothes in a backpack, received an unmerited hug and kiss from Jane, and was aboard the off-peak Penn Station–bound LIRR line in a matter of minutes.

Riding the train, staring at Fitzgerald's words but not reading them, I saw the century stretched out between us, and how little had changed. I brooded on over the solemn dumping ground. Foul ponds. Discarded concrete and ties. The wraiths of scrubbed-at graffiti.

I touched the paper and key in my pocket. It was as though I were being pulled. I felt pointlessly driven, out of control. What should have been a friendly family weekend had reverted to a series of ongoing enigmas I didn't want any part in. Or did I?

No, I thought. I just wanted a life of leisure and predictability. I wanted to go back in time, or fast-forward until I was rich and respected. I wanted to be a novelist without writing more than I had in my twenties. I wanted to be coddled. I wanted esteem, validation, and status. I wanted my marriage to transform me. I wanted my wife to be fulfilled. I wanted to eat bread.

The visit with Mrs. Masterson had set something off. Or the horrific experience on the beach had. Or seeing those cops again after so many years. Or running into my junior agent. Or encountering the *MY OFFICE* plaques. Or maybe Turmeric's incessant troublemaking was behind my waning faculties. No matter how casual my in-laws played things, it all made me look bad.

Really though, I should've been excused. I was still in mourning, right? Excusably? Emma had wanted us to move on and try to find the good in what remained of our lives. Accept what you can't change or whatever. AA nonsense. It had worked for a few months.

The problem with grief is, without closure, one can hardly be expected to acknowledge his or her or their loss. I was stuck in a cycle of denial, anger, bargaining, and depression. I was waiting for a breakthrough that was not going to come. I was off the wagon, confronting things without direction, grasping at straws, and I was open to any lead I could conjure.

I'd been triggered by the mention of college and parents. Professional failure, creative angst. The vacant Ocean State condo. Questions so long unanswered I didn't seek any verdicts.

But that's exactly what I was doing. Wasn't it? Would my story be resurrected? Would everyone I'd watched die arise through my passion to walk the earth while I decomposed suspended? I was scattered. I could be no one's first choice for a protagonist.

Still, Gladys had wanted something from me, and it wasn't just weed. Or did I want something from her? Nothing made sense. I readjusted my bucket hat, unconvinced I'd emerged from that morning's dream. I unzipped my backpack and furtively took a pull of whiskey.

I texted Emma, *how's your first day?*

My phone vibrated.

Sofia had sent a picture of a dressing room mirror. She was wearing a Michael Kors pencil skirt suit generously slit down the thigh, unbuttoned, with no shirt underneath.

*What do you think of this fit for a lunch date? eXXXcessive??*

*why are you asking me*, I replied.

*I thought we were friends*

She texted a photo of her pouting face. Lip set out, practically drooling. I shook my head.

*idk*, I responded and tilted the bottle back.

I'd planned to drop my backpack at my wife's parents' town house, grab a coffee, maybe check out the Strand. But I was overcome with impulsion. I hopped off at Jamaica and transferred to the E Train. I rode to 50th Street, jogged up flights of stairs into beating humidity under a sharp overcast.

Gridlock shimmered from every vantage. Dining huts, 5G poles, defunct USB kiosks, miry Citi Bike docks, all these daft excess surfaces mere opportunities to cloak the metropolis in a lamina of pee. I could count on one hand how many times I'd passed through since absconding, and the thought of living here again was unconscionable. It had been my dream to move to New York. Fifteen years later, it felt like anyplace else. Not enough, and too much.

At some point I'd realized I didn't want to be anywhere. Despite that, I'd moored myself to beings who needed me around. Who would feed Houdini, I thought. Who would pick up the dog's poop? Was he, that panting fuzzball, my rightful son?

Office buildings were voided behind their black glass facades, reflecting gaunt homeless faces the cops hadn't managed to sweep off or lock up. Cardboard signs said, COMPSCI PHD FORMER APPLE WEB MANAGER I ALSO KNOW HOW TO BARTEND, and, MY PARENTS IN YEMEN. Leashes clogged the sidewalks. Feces seared in the sun. Electric scooters sped silently up curbs, keeling over granny carts. Handmade posters of missing executives were pasted on top of ephebophilic ads for an EP by someone called Le Dork. Knockoff Disney characters sold Poland Spring bottles for five dollars. AI bots scrolled out headlines on LED ticker tape: PENTAGON ACCOUNTING ERROR FREES UP $9 BILLION MORE FOR WAR EFFORT.

But there were weed bodegas everywhere. At least some conveniences accompanied the end times. I ducked in one and departed with a mouthful gnashing gummies.

And after several vertiginous minutes leaning into my phone's flickering maps app, I beheld Geshaltn Stationers. The bell overhead didn't tinkle, and the store was warmer than outdoors.

Buzzed from the bourbon, I regretted not buying an overpriced water or relieving myself on one of the alfresco sheds. Shelves overflowed with cheap pens, binder clips, rubber stamps. I let my eyes blur, willing nameplates to appear. I could almost taste the mildewed postcards and envelope glue on my tongue, and recalling an episode of *Seinfeld*, madly sneezed, upending a rack of paper swatches, rub-on decals. They fluttered like moths trying to escape a gas chamber, and I waded through this clutter to a counter in the back, where a chrome call bell sat. I pressed down, but like its friend above the door, no sound emanated.

—Hello, I called.

—Joseph's dreamcoat, a voice rebounded. —I'm coming as quick as I can.

The proprietor seemed to arrive from multiple alcoves.

—Yesh, he inquired in a strained Yiddish accent.

—Hi, my name is . . .

But it dawned on me that my name was irrelevant here. That was the purpose of the city, and I cut straight to the point.

—Do you know a Dr. Schwartz? In Long Island?

—Yesh, the man said again.

I hadn't expected such straight repartee.

—Oh, well, I stuttered. —He has a, like . . . plaque thing in his office. It says . . .

—Which office, he asked, pronouncing *which* with a V.

—Dr. Schwartz's, I said.

—Which Dr. Schwartz do you mean?

—The . . . one from Long Island . . . You just said . . .

—Which one from Long Island? You ask if I know a Dr. Schwartz on Long Island, I say yesh. You didn't tell me which one!

—I don't understand. How many Dr. Schwartzes in Long Island are you acquainted with?

The man scowled at me through half-moon lenses.

—I'm sor, I started.

—Six, he said.

I grinned.

—What is funny?

—It's just nice to be around, um, *segulah* again.

—You are not chosen, he said.

—No, I faltered. —No. I am.

—Where is your *kippah*?

I touched my head. I was still wearing the bucket hat. The proprietor tapped his skull cap.

—Do you give *tzedakah*?

—Who should I be giving it to?

—To whom. And *tikkun olam*. To support your brethren in *Eretz Yisrael*!

—I condemn the colonialist apartheid occupation of Palestine.

—Oho, and so what would you do with them?

—What do you mean?

—Where would you have these . . .

He grunted, waved peremptorily.

—The platitude comes to mind that no one is truly free so long as others remain oppressed. Thus, only by recognizing and upholding Palestinian sovereignty can we hope to ever unburden ourselves, and civilization as a whole, from the shame of the Holocaust. This goes for all nations under siege, of course.

—You're just one of those fakes.

—I'm . . . I just want to know about the Dr. Schwartz in Amagansett. Or East Hampton. I can never tell where one begins and the other ends.

—Feh, the man sissed.

—He said you knew each other as kids. And he has this, like, plaque hanging in one of his exam rooms. It says my office in all caps, engraved on gold leaf or something. Like this big . . .

I made a shape with my hands.

—I don't know him.

—Oh come on. He told me he gets all his office supplies here.

—Then why haven't I heard from him in sheven years, huh? All the pens stay full of ink?

—So you do know him.

—Feh!

—Listen, I'm not here to stir up old grudges. I was just curious if I could see one of those nameplates. He said you're the only one who sells them.

—Sold, the old man cried.

—What?

—Is Schwartz still eating shrimp?

—I don't know, I sighed.

I figured I should just drop it. What good would having another MY OFFICE thing do anyway? I wasn't getting closer to answering questions. But I was already there.

—I'm really into this . . . stationery stuff, I said. —I'm a collector . . . and it would mean a lot if I could take a look at your handiwork. I'm . . . I used to have one . . . a long time ago.

—You have a picture?

I took out my phone, but its screen had gone dead.

—No, I said. —But do you know what I'm talking about? I'm . . .

I tried to think of what he might want to hear.

—Prepared to compensate you for your troubles?

That seemed smart. The proprietor, however, was incensed.

—You know nothing of my troubles, *boychik*! Of course I know what you're talking about! And you're ten years too slow! A fine schnook like yourself ran off with my stencil, my materials, my press back in . . . what? 2014? I do the boy's mother a favor. I give him a decent wage. High school dropout. Drug head. *Narkoman*. Sad story. But he seems mayhap a nice kid. Deep down. Sensitive, so they say. And how does he repay me? Of course no one will admit it, his mother so rich and snooty, she covers for him and I get nothing. He loses his job, big deal, he's set. He can make infinite little signs and nameplates. How many offices without a handsome gilt? So who's the schnook, then? Is me? My troubles could keep a *nafkeh*'s analyst busy.

—Uh, I said. —So . . . what?

—So no signs! Does that answer your question, he pronounced *question* with a Kv.

—I mean . . . I suppose . . . But . . .

Pointlessly pulled, pointlessly pushed. I wondered with what treasures the liquor cabinet on Tenth Street was stocked.

—Did he take other stuff? Like . . . valuables, or money, or . . . just this one thing I'm asking about? I guess I don't understand.

—Why are there ants living in my kitchen sponge? No, nothing else. You're not the only one not understanding.

The man seemed to be fading. The room thick with hot breath. I was becoming stoned again.

—If you don't mind my asking, what was the, uh . . . your employee's name?

—You expect I remember? Now? How many years later? You come into my business?

—Do you keep any records? Anything I could . . .

I didn't know why I was digging. Sweat shivered from my pores. I should've fled.

—Bend my arm? You want to give an old man a coronary? I have a computer. If you promise to leave and cease pestering, I'll see what it can do. The *boychik*'s name? Moses's ashes.

## DON'T STEP INTO MY OFFICE

In retrospect, I don't believe he looked anything up. He'd known the whole time. He must've stood in his office, MY OFFICE-plaque-less and all, trying to make up his mind. Because when he came back and slammed the business card on the counter, he appeared even older, harried and, oddly enough, scared, and on the front of the card was the Livingston Prep insignia, its registrar fax and phone numbers, and on the back a name in nervy print: *Philip Springer.*

—Thanks, I said.

But the proprietor had already withdrawn. Outside, all the pigeons were acting drunk, so I slipped in a pub plastered with construction paper shamrocks and made like a pigeon on the rocks.

By the time I stumbled back out, the sun had fallen behind buildings. It was dusk, spotty, jaundiced. I couldn't see clearly, but I felt very good.

I rode the subway to Union Square and avoided the skateboarders. Social media had turned these fledgling urchins into discrete satellite surveillance states. They glided, lost balance. Their hoodies looked suffocating, and they filmed life in full.

The big digital clock over Best Buy counted down the planet's race to one and a half degrees Celsius of global warming. Someone was getting dragged out of Whole Foods by his or her or their ankles, and I felt like goose-stepping, so I did, and no one noticed, and I marched down Fifth Avenue until things got eerily subdued.

At the corner of Eleventh Street, I could see an old supper club in which the production company I'd worked for used to shoot fashion campaigns. The many hours wasted idling my box truck in a no-standing zone, waiting for the models to get too tired to be sexy. I could see the First Presbyterian Church, where Emma, Jane, Michael, and I had attended midnight mass on Christmas Eve, only months before the city's freezer cars filled with bodies. I could see my freshman dorm, seed strewn across its walls and commercial grade carpets, wet-dreaming, fidgety.

Like the best forms of technology, I was a pliant vessel for memories. I peered at the site where the Weather Underground had once ignited themselves. And one block south, I stuck my key in the lock, but the door just pushed open and the cool stillness of Tenth Street sopped me up.

The stairs were lined with a green moth-eaten runner. Many nails had pulled away, and each step required that I carefully lift my borrowed Top-Siders or risk plummeting to the foyer's unclaimed mail pile below. I was a petal, drifting, and the door to the second-floor entrance was ajar. It groaned as I leaned in, trying to remember the fastest route to the liquor cabinet.

I slid through the kitchen. The house was dark. The few windows were discolored by smoke. Tenth Street was devoid of traffic and, since the pandemic, half-deserted, between the eviction of long-standing, no-longer-rent-stabilized tenants, and the pashas in Saint-Tropez waiting for their gut renovations to be complete.

Even my wife's parents weren't safe. It was my understanding they didn't own the place outright, and from what I'd gleaned, venal parties were closing in. Rumors of legal action from some Satanic sibling, all so that the property could be broken into units and wielded as a hedge fund asset.

Warped orange parking tickets and court summonses were sprinkled about the apartment. Water stains intersected in rings on the wood. Springs coiled out of timeworn furniture. The threat of dispossession was getting less discriminating. One of these days, we'd receive the text message announcing my in-laws' expropriation too.

But booze mostly got better with age.

I crept up the servant staircase to the third floor. In the dining room, under a Daum glassware case, a mini cooler held a liter of Plymouth gin.

Breaking the seal gave me goosebumps. My nostrils flared. Still swimming from the edibles and additional drinks at the pub, I tried to steady my trembling hands. I cracked a cube from the ice tray, swirled my highball clearer than water, and took a vast enduring swig.

It must have reminded me to honor Michael's request, because abruptly I wanted to flush all the toilets. But as my stream egressed, a clack shattered the tranquility. Sallow pee doused the jungle-themed bathroom wallpaper, and I reeled, almost dropping my glass.

In the doorway, Emma was holding a squat, double-action revolver. Her mouth twisted to one side, one eye closed, focusing. She dropped her stabilizing grip, then the gun to her hip, and uncocked it, the barrel aimed at the tiles.

—Hi, I said.

We sat on a fat leather couch in front of a Sony flat-screen, which had been state-of-the-art sometime before 9/11, and upon which, after being pulled out of school and witnessing the Twin Towers' live dustification, Emma had absorbed the perpetual reruns of terror through the eyes of a girl four days shy of eight.

And I smiled, placing an arm around my wife's shoulder, stroking her hair to an episode of *Survivor: Blood vs. Water* we'd already seen twice before. The Ruger .357 Magnum lounged on the coffee table, pointing away from us. I still hadn't asked if it was loaded.

—I thought you were an intruder, Emma mumbled for a third time.

—It's okay, baby, I said. —I totally understand. In that case, though, I recommend you lock the front door in the future. But you still haven't told me, how was your first day of work?

Softly, my wife shrugged my arm off. She extracted the glass from my hand and sampled its contents. She gagged, shook her head.

—What are you doing? I thought you couldn't even stand the smell of hard liquor anymore.

—I don't know, I stared at nothing. —I'm not really smelling it. I guess I'm a bit stressed.

—*You're* stressed?

—You could've killed me, I said.

—You . . . Don't talk about killing.

I took the glass back and tried to gnaw the ice, but the cube was too big. I spit it out.

—Okay, I said. —I hear you . . . I *love* you . . .

I waited.

—How was your first day?

—Honestly?

I nodded.

—It was horrible! I didn't get any sleep. Houdini was up and down all night, and I was going to bring him into the city, but I was running late, and when I made it to the museum, the gallery was in total disarray. The show's opening in three weeks, and they're still putting up drywall. And the art handlers were, like, strung out. They couldn't remember my name, and one of them kept asking how old I was and if I wanted to meet him later at this quote-unquote *indie sleaze dive Clandestini's*, and the AV team said the projectors aren't coming till next week, and everybody's just dropping the ball. I mean, that must be why they hired me, but I'm not even making what I was before COVID!

—I'm . . .

—And then, Emma interrupted. —I started feeling really sick at, like, eleven a.m., and I went to the bathroom and I threw up, and I couldn't stop puking, I ended up going back two or three times, so now they probably think I'm bulimic, and I was trying to rehydrate, so then I had to go pee a bunch, and at three o'clock, I just felt so awful, they said I could work remote for the rest of the day, so I came back here.

—You're sick, I said, making a face.

—It's not like that! I don't know what happened!

—I don't want to get sick.

—I'm not sick, my wife moaned. —I feel fine now. It must've been food poisoning or anxiety or . . .

—Don't say stress!

Emma scoffed.

—Well, I'm glad they let you work from home at least . . . Did you have a chance to, like, ask if you'd be able to . . . do that regularly?

—No, Jacob. I did not have an opportunity to discuss my hybrid work options.

—Hm. Well I was walking around today . . . The city sucks. We really cannot move back.

—And you're really not in a position to make that call.

—The kids are all dressed like goblins, I said.

—That reminds me, Emma sat up straighter. —Your stupid fucking ex-girlfriend followed me on Instagram.

I met her eyes. They were vibrating in their sockets. I looked away.

—About that . . . She, um. Sofia wants to meet up later this week. She thinks, I swallowed. —There may be a better chance for me to publish something of consequence now.

—Like what?

—Well, she brought up my novel. But I told her I'd rather focus on Jewish Gatsby stuff.

I tried to look innocent.

—Why now, Emma snarled.

—I don't know. Maybe I've got a nice angle. Or maybe the zeitgeist's finally caught up with me.

—Because of the red-pilled downtown free-speech advocates?

—I guess so.

My wife laughed mockingly.

—I think, I said. —She was probably just trying to be nice . . . That's probably why she followed you, I mean. She knows we're married.

—So you've been chatting it up with that pathological bitch?

—We sort of ran into each other. In Long Island. She was at the beach, and . . .

—Oh my god, Emma said.

—What?

—Nothing, she cooled suddenly. —That's fine. I . . . I'm sorry. I just hope she's not fucking around. Publishing would be good for you. You need . . . something . . .

I pursed my lips.

—So what's your plan?

—My plan, I said.

—What are you doing here?

—Oh, I giggled. —I don't know. It's kind of crazy. I went to the doctor today. Your dad's doctor. He got the sand out of my ear, and then . . .

But in the milliseconds leading up to an attempt to vocalize my reasoning, the futility became overwhelming. After all we'd been through, the last thing Emma needed was more paranoia and pursuit of vain mysteries.

—I just wanted to see you, I said. —I felt horrible about last night. I didn't mean to get drunk. I'm not even drunk anymore. I feel fine.

Emma nuzzled into me.

—I threw up, she whimpered.

I put my arms around her torso and squeezed.

—I'm so sorry, my love. That's not right. Someone's gotta pay. Plus you're probably getting hungry now, huh?

—Mmph, my wife said.

—Should we order takeout?

—Mmph.

—Tacos? Thai?

—I want ice cream, Emma stated.

—No. You *need* ice cream. Please let me get you some. Let me be your humble varlet.

When I returned, my wife wrested the Häagen-Dazs pint from my grasp and started in. She could not have been more than ninety-five pounds. Most stuff isn't worth trying to understand.

—Are you sure you don't want a taco?

Emma's spoon waddled between her lips. And we watched reality TV stars exploit themselves for, well, I was never sure what, while the night settled gray through the skylights.

I folded my aluminum takeout tray into a neat little triangle, picked up the Ruger, and popped open its cylinder. All the chambers were empty.

—Where did you get this anyway?

—It's my dad's, Emma said. —He's an anti-Vietnam hippie, in case you hadn't heard.

—Violence sucks, I agreed.

I placed the gun on the coffee table and spun it.

—So . . .

I turned to my wife. We sat taut, between motives, between undeniable chemistry, consciousnesses bulging into each other. I dropped my hand between her thighs. Emma brushed it away.

—Thursday, she said. —Remember?

I nodded. I hadn't.

—What are you doing tomorrow?

—Me, I asked. —I . . . don't know.

The Livingston Prep insignia flashed in my mind.

—Do you want to get dinner or something? I could meet you at the museum after work.

—I have plans with Dan, she said curtly.

—That fucking! Minnowinter guy? He couldn't even pretend to say my name right!

—Minnowitter, Emma corrected. —You guys are actually really similar. If you gave him a chance . . . Anyway, it's just drinks. He wants to talk about the exhibition. I should be back by nine or ten.

—I guess I'll . . . make other plans.

—Why don't you meet up with your friends? When's the last time you saw Miriam?

—Uh, I said. —At the wedding?

—I like Miriam.

There was ice cream on my wife's chin. And she bent over the coffee table, elbowing the revolver, and set to rolling a joint.

—Maybe...

—Or better yet, go get Houdini. I miss that bugger.

—He's a right fluff, I modified into my Cockney accent, but my heart wasn't in it.

Emma sparked up and took a pull.

—I'm tired, she said, holding it in.

—So am I.

We passed the joint back and forth until it was crumbles of ash, and then we held hands and walked to the stairs, and Emma caressed my back, and I lifted her, and I dropped her in the bed, and she was glowing, glowing, and soon breathing hard, snoring, and I was stoned, but more wired, holding on to the drunks of nights past, and I was neurotic, twitching, and counted to five hundred and something, and then I got up and flushed all the toilets, and plugged in my phone, and its screen kept doing weird stuff, and then I was asleep on the couch, my echo chamber buffeted with delusory plinking sounds, the crank of gears, the depressions and whines of metal folding on metal, pressing letters in gold, like a sign, or a target, or a plaque.

# TUESDAY

I awoke in a fetal position on the floor in front of the couch. By degrees, I unfolded my body, detecting a faint rumble of construction on the buildings to either side of my in-laws' town house.

Emma had left a note on the kitchen counter:

*There's no coffee ☹ but plenty of tea in the cupboard. I know the past few days have been <u>BULLOCKS</u>! Let's be kind to each other. My one nice thing? I didn't shoot you when I saw you on the floor. And I forgive you. I hope to keep you in my bed tonight.*

*♡♡ Emma*

The digital clock on the microwave was blinking zeros. The notepaper smelled like vetiver. My phone had charged to forty-one percent and said it was after ten o'clock, and as two Tetley Classic bags steeped, I typed *Philip Springer* into the browser search bar and pressed *go*.

I didn't think the kid who'd stolen Geshaltn Stationers' nameplate press was the ninety-seven-year-old composer of "Santa Baby," and I wasn't prepared to dig much further.

I sipped my tea. It tasted like grass. I spilled a glug of Plymouth in. Better, but still bad.

The sun shone through the skylights. I poured another dram of gin and tea and jumped in the shower on cold. There, I stood on one foot, then the other. I pulled my bad earlobe. Gingerly, I explored the canal's opening with my pinky. It was as though nothing had happened.

And when I turned off the faucet, any aches from my sleeping posture had departed too. Freezing lucid, I pranced into boxers, trousers, and shirt. I regarded myself in the mirror, then went to my wife's parents' room and donned one of Michael's lightweight beige sport coats. I looked at my bucket hat on the dining room table. I tucked it under my arm, then thought better. It could only hold me back. I borrowed thick Gucci socks and double-knotted the boat shoes.

The business card had curled in my pocket. I studied its Upper East Side address, then googled directions. My phone's battery had already plunged to the twenties, so I put it in airplane mode. The Ruger glimmered on the coffee table. It seemed to be facing a different direction than we'd left it, and from that angle its appearance was of a mouth, simpering.

I opened it again. This time a single round was chambered. I tipped the cylinder, and the bullet landed in my palm.

Icy, trifling. Had I missed it the night before? I didn't think so. And I didn't think Emma would have even known how to load it, but that was stupid. All you did was insert a cartridge.

I gawked involuntarily, then forced my lips together. I stashed the bullet in the front flap of my backpack, and I wrapped the gun in my bath towel and secured it in the main compartment. I zipped everything up and stowed the bag out of sight under the liquor cabinet. I lifted the toilet seat with the toe of a Top-Sider and peed until I was vacated, then waited a minute as my bladder refilled. I peed more and put down the seat like a genius.

As I left, I was sure to lock every door behind me. The sidewalk felt spongy underfoot.

Once upon a time, the Q train had flowed all the way from the elitist blocks in Manhattan to my modest home by the beach. But now my home was wayward, and as I shambled uptown, I was working out how many more days I'd have to fill if I wanted to die without eliciting imputations of premature quietus.

The sum came to about fourteen thousand. And I hadn't lived through twelve yet. There was so much time left, and so little to do. Now I understood why people got jobs with benefits and kept them for decades. It erased the prehension of life's inertial aptitude.

Over the course of six months, seven years prior, I'd written a novel. In another six months, I could maybe write something else. If I produced one manuscript every seven years, I'd still have to complete at least five before I could turn in to the psychic beyond.

All my cells had regenerated. Ostensibly, there were things on which I might reflect. How, though, could I hope to communicate the horrors since incurred? Fiction demanded authenticity. Even to myself I was unreal. When had the world become the terror world? And why was I bent on self-expression when I apprehended nothing, except how a fictional antihero from a hundred-year-old book might have Ashkenazic origins?

I walked into a trash can at full tilt. I didn't need to apprehend that the wind was knocked out of me. I unrolled the business card and compared its insignia to the gothic architecture at my side, where gargoyles and lanterns loomed out towering from stony heights.

Upon entering Livingston Preparatory Academy, I was accosted by the many faces of the late Dr. Masterson. Wrinkled and boyish in military and religious regalia. Smiling and frowning and severely bored in academic robes. Photos with Henry Kissinger and Obama. A black-and-white poster of someone who might've been him playing what might've been water polo.

Trophies and ribbons and various honors were displayed in the lobby, and more were being sifted through on long folding tables, as two young administrators in short kilts teetered on separate ladders, working to pin up a banner, which said, IN MEMORIUM, and I caught a flash of pubic tuft before I looked away, hangdog, then back, hopeful and guilty, but she was descending the ladder, bluntly scrutinizing my presence.

It occurred to me that I hadn't concocted any questions, or a lead with which to approach the Livingston staff. Gladys Masterson had wanted me to come here for reasons she wouldn't explain. That was unconnected with Schwartz, and the proprietor of the stationery store could not possibly have known my role in the headmaster's final throes between life and death.

The first administrator's heels clicked down a hallway. The second was still twenty or more feet from me, squinting.

—Can I help you, she called.

The ceiling crawled to the top of the building, an atrium devised in the image of a gorge.

—Things are a bit chaotic right now. Do you have an appointment?

I cleared my throat, shuffled over, and put out my hand. She put hers out too, and I took it, but it flopped like she didn't know the maneuver.

—Hi, I said. —I'm . . . I was hoping I could speak with . . . Um. Sybil Parker?

The words fell off my tongue like someone else had put them there.

—Headmistress Parker?

—Um . . . Yes, I . . . It's kind of complicated, but I'm . . . a friend of the family's, and . . .

—Of whose family?

—The Mastersons.

The admin convulsed, then recomposed herself. She turned, looking over her shoulder, and signaled I follow while she made herself comfortable behind a reception desk.

—I, um . . . I won't be in the, like . . . system . . . I don't have an appointment . . . It's kind of a long story. Kind of hard to explain, but if I could just see Ms. Parker . . .

—As I'm sure you know, the admin said. —We've suffered a, a precipitous, profound . . .

Her voice caught. She typed viciously at the terminal.

—Loss, she croaked, tears welling.

—Yes, I'm . . . I know.

—And the headmistress. She was just inducted yesterday. And with the funeral on Long Island coming, and all the arrangements. She's very busy. Even if you did have a scheduled . . .

—I get it, I said. —But I was kind of, like . . . sent . . . by Mrs. Masterson . . . and . . .

The woman's eyes surveyed me at that bureaucratic slant they take behind desks.

—Well, if she can't see me, maybe you can answer a question? The admin's eyes shifted.

—I was wondering if you could tell me about a student that used to go here. It would've been a while back. I think he dropped out in 2014? His name was Philip Springer.

She made an angry little face, poked at the keyboard, and scrolled. I tried to check out the results, but the admin perked up and adjusted the monitor's slope.

—It's . . . But that's not that important to me, I said. —I'd just really appreciate if . . .

—What did you say your name was?

—I didn't, I said. —Jacob Garlicker. But that won't mean much. I only need to . . .

—Just a moment, she rose, her kilt flitting, as she swiveled down a passage out of view.

I rested my elbows and spine on the edge of the reception desk under a desiccating blow of A/C. I arced my neck and stared at the huge, oblique ceiling and unfocused my eyes until, like an autostereogram, tiny three-dimensional swastikas materialized, gamboling through its depths.

I could already imagine someone defending the symbols on Twitter. Explaining succinctly that Hitler's reverence for Eastern religion was a kind of nuance liberals could never hope to discern. I didn't hear as the four pumps drew up.

—Mr. Garlicker?

The two admins stood with their arms crossed.

—Right this way, follow me, the one I hadn't spoken with earlier said.

She turned on a stiletto, conducting us down a hall and a half-landing to an elevator bay.

—I really appreciate this.

I tried to smile. She looked away. She was wearing a Royal Trux T-shirt under her cardigan.

—Great band, I nodded. —I like them because they don't really sound like music.

She made a face.

—Juicy, Juicy, Juice?

—I don't know what you're talking about, she said.

The elevator dinged open, and we wound through a corridor lined with portraits of white men. I recognized Dr. Masterson's ruddy countenance, and for an instant I flinched at his black, bloody gape in the moonlit tide pool. A door was cracked at the end of the aisle. Through its cleft, blinding flashbulbs exploded every few seconds amid the whir and snap of a lens shutter.

—Sulk, someone called. —*Sulk*! Now glower!

The admin opened the door. A woman, mid-forties probably, and still fit, posed in a tweed Chanel suit behind a softbox lighting kit and between two flags, American and Livingston-insigniaed, one jackboot in front of the other, arms akimbo.

—Now teeth, the photographer seethed.

The black-haired, black-eyed subject accomplished a flehmen response.

—*Ja*! *Ja*, the photographer wailed, the roll exhausting as he popped out the film. —*Das ist es*!

—How did I do, the woman asked.

—*Wunderbar*, the photographer said.

The admin leaned in farther.

—Headmistress?

She glanced up.

—Mr. Garlicker is here to see you.

—Ah, Sybil Parker said. —So he is.

Livingston Prep's new chieftain dismissed the underling. Her office was clearly in transition. She rearranged folders on her desk as the photographer packed up equipment.

—My apologies, Parker muttered, not making eye contact. —PR has to get that portrait off as soon as possible. And then there's the memorial banquet tomorrow evening, before I head out east. I hope Gladys will have some accommodation lined up. I do hate trying to book a hotel.

—*Auf Wiedersehen,* the photographer waved.

—Thank you, Hans.

Parker latched the door behind him. She returned to her desk in long strides, showing off lithe legs clad in hose. She ran her hands down the back of her thighs and gestured to a wooden chair designed to chastise scoliosis cases.

—Now, she said. —Isn't this something.

A beat happened.

—Were you . . . expecting me, I asked.

—Not really, Parker appeared distracted. —But following the events of last weekend . . .

I reddened.

—I'm really sorry to have . . .

I couldn't tell where I was going with that. I stared around, landing on Parker's cleavage.

—I'm so sorry about your institution's loss, I said.

—Well, it had to come to an end eventually.

She put at a pen in her mouth, and I nodded, mesmerized, then shook my head.

—Not like that.

—No, Parker shrugged. —Perhaps not. And yet, does it make a difference? He'd been grooming me for this post since I was fourteen years old. I've been ready for at least a decade. I suppose I should be more upset, but I'm . . . just in my element.

—Understandable, I said, though it wasn't, not to me.

—So . . . You can see we're quite busy here. I've made an exception to a strict no-appointment, no-Sybil policy. What is it you wanted to see me about?

—About that, I grinned warily. —Don't take this the wrong way, but I feel like I was . . . compelled to come here?

The headmistress glared.

—Would you believe it if I told you I don't know the reason why? Not exactly?

—As a matter of fact, I don't believe that for a second. And I don't have time for games. I should think you'd have more shame than to play it in this manner.

I was stumped.

—But Mrs. Masterson said . . .

—Gladys knows very little of what goes on behind the walls of Livingston Prep. As far as she's concerned we're some cabal plotting geopolitical coups. In reality, we're a school. My position required constant vigilance and maintenance well before her husband's unfortunate end.

—Why does no one seem very surprised that . . . that the headmaster was . . . poisoned?

—Because when you play with the inferno, you're bound to end up in hell. Do you know for whom Dante's eighth circle was reserved?

—No.

—Frauds, she snorted. —And I know precisely in which ditch my forerunner is interred.

I looked over my shoulder at nothing before meeting Sybil Parker's gaze.

—What can you tell me about a student who used to go here? Philip Springer.

—That's what I thought, Parker laughed.

—He dropped out in 2014, right? I heard he'd gotten into drugs or something and went on to work at a, like, stationery store near Times Square?

—Mostly correct. But he didn't drop out. That's why you're here, isn't it? He was expelled, of course.

A chill ran from my sacrum down my butt cheeks and legs.

—What for, I asked.

—Well, Parker looked at her phone, placed it face down on the desk. —He'd had plenty of chances. We did what we could. We tried to work things out, for his mother's reputation more than anything. He simply wasn't fit for an academy of this caliber. Even his psychiatrist agreed. After he was caught smoking in a bathroom stall in ninth grade, we put him on watch. But that didn't seem to help at all. Some boys are just troubled. Then it was dealing marijuana out of his locker. Then the incident with the pills. He started seizing and vomiting in his sleep, passed out at his desk in third period. And . . . well, he was never up to the standards set for him. Perhaps it's because he didn't have a proper father figure, though he was surely given everything he needed to flourish. The whole bourgeoisie is slipping . . . But he did show some promise. In music. If not composition or performance, at least in affectation. He had a fine ear, and he was actually quite talented in woodworking, if only we had some outlet or avenue for that. But the incident in the girls' junior high locker room . . . His mother could only cover so much up. And then that trip to Vienna, with just one semester left of his senior year. You know, we almost got him to graduate. We probably could have pulled some strings and even snuck the boy into Berklee . . .

—Wait, I interrupted. —You mean. Did he get kicked off the trip for drinking on a plane?

—Why are you asking like you don't already know?

—I . . . I don't know, I choked, my mouth dry, my eyes dizzy. —This is . . . I'm sorry, it just reminded me of something. I'm confused. He was on a trip to Vienna? This was in . . .

—Christmas break, Parker mused. —2013. That was why he was so interested in the Philharmonic. He didn't want to go to college, forget how that made his parents feel. He wanted to train in Vienna as a violin fabricator. A luthier.

—Jesus Christ!

—I don't have time for histrionics.

—But . . . I thought it got sorted out . . . You really expelled him for getting drunk on a class trip? Kids do that shit all the time!

—It wasn't *just* for one instance of inebriation. The boy was categorically mad. Untrustworthy, erratic. He had fits. Caused no end of ordeal with anyone he came in contact. Take your mother, upended in but a handful of hours. I can hardly blame her for not saving him, though I admired her efforts.

—Excuse me, I stammered.

—You are Jacob Garlicker? I assumed that's what you wanted to talk about.

—I don't understand.

—Not that she was any Our Lady of Guadalupe herself. She was nearly seduced! You can ask Dr. Masterson. Or, you could've. Didn't you?

She sighed and looked into the distance. I was freaking out.

—Are you telling me, I tremored, clenching my hand in my hand, trying to guide words together. —That Philip Springer . . . this . . . student . . . is the one my parents canceled their trip to Austria for? To make sure he *didn't* get into more trouble?

—There are a couple ways of looking at that, Parker said. —Your mother did make an attempt on his behalf. Of course, there was no way for her to have known his full history. Had she, I expect she never would've bothered. It's also true that she *could* have done more. It would've been dearly out of character for Dr.

Masterson to pass up an opportunity at . . . exculpation. But she wouldn't abide his proposal. In the end, only Philip came out worse for the wear.

—What do you mean?

—I don't mince words.

—But I'm confused! I . . . I didn't know any of this! Please! Can you please elaborate?

—It seems you knew something.

—I . . . Gladys told me to come out and find you. The Springer thing was something . . . totally different . . . and . . . What do you mean she wouldn't abide his proposal?

—Some people, Parker pondered. —Are just very sensitive. She told Dr. Masterson that she worked with children with disabilities in a public school system. She said she empathized with Philip. He was obviously in need of extra attention. She couldn't bear to be responsible for the child's expulsion. She said he reminded her of her own son. She'd do anything to stopper the guilt, and . . . well, as I said, when Dr. Masterson sees, or saw, an opportunity to flex his . . . clout. The man could hardly control himself around me after thirty-odd years. He was in no position to forgo a convenient tête-à-tête.

—What are you suggesting?

My voice was rising in violence. I gripped the desk, but Parker was unmoved.

—Oh, don't be so naive, she smirked. —He asked your mother to fuck him. In exchange for the boy's pardon.

—I don't believe this, I said.

—It's not as though she went through with it. Though I'm not sure she wasn't tempted. Dr. Masterson was a bona fide ladykiller. Don't let the stuffy decor or mortarboards fool you.

—Give me a fucking break! My father was there! He never would've stood for that!

—Your father is a grown man. He knows how these things work. He said it was her decision.

—Bullshit, I screamed.

—And then he and I went down to Café Sabarsky and had a nice *einspänner* and chat while they hashed out the details. And by the time we returned, your mother was all tears and defeated, and they were free to go enjoy their holiday, a couple of underachievers.

—And . . . and Philip Springer was expelled?

Parker snorted again.

—There are such things as final straws, you know. Dr. Masterson was an incorrigible flirt, but even if he had succeeded in persuading dear old mom, I suspect he still wouldn't have been able to sweep another one of Philip's infractions under the rug. If anything, she was spared. You should be proud of her prudence.

—Then are you aware, I stood up. —That my parents have been missing for the past ten months! They dropped off the face of the earth! And now Masterson's dead, and, and . . .

—I hadn't heard, Parker remarked. —Though I'm not sure how it's germane.

—What happened to Springer, I cried.

—He went to work at a stationery store. You informed me of that. I didn't bother to keep up with his future engagements myself. Do you know how many students we have to look after? The moment he was disenrolled, he was no longer my responsibility, and not a moment too soon.

I was quaking, ticking. I collapsed in the chair and let out a sorrowful groan.

—Why are you even concerned with Philip? What does his fate have to do with you?

—I'm not, I yelled. —I don't know!

—Will that be all?

I put my face in my hands and proceeded to sob.

—Mr. Garlicker? I'm sorry you aren't sure where your parents are. But I'm beginning to see why your mother identified you with that boy.

—He . . . My . . . Masterson . . .

I burped.

—Yes. Now is there anything else I can do for you? I've got a busy afternoon.

My phone said it was half past one.

I needed to forget. I wanted a drink. I could not be alone.

I texted Miriam, *are you in the city? i've got to see someone please*

I texted her, *are you there? hello??*

I texted, *please please please please!!!!!!!!!*

I bought a twenty-four-ounce can of Angry Orchard from a bodega and drank it with a straw from a brown paper bag, all thirty-four grams of NATURALLY GLUTEN FREE sugar, and rode the subway seventy blocks south. By the time I debarked, I could feel a dribble of pee spasming at my glans.

I ran to Tenth Street, past freshman orientation pods strung with purple lanyards, past the twenty-dollar juice bars, past the people in hard hats, to my in-laws' town house, and threw myself against the front door, which was unlocked, and I didn't understand.

I bounded upstairs into the apartment and desperately ejected a hot, thick surge of urine. It was not until I was pouring myself a fresh glass of gin that I realized the toilet seat had been up when I'd entered.

I slunk back to the bathroom. My waste was still bubbling. I knew I had put the seat down before I'd left that morning. I'd taken special gentlemanly note of it. The door had been unlocked. Something was wrong. I slurped smooth, climate-controlled liquor.

—Emma, I hollered.

All was silent.

—Emma, I said.

I moved through time and space. I ran my hand along bookcases. I pulled a deteriorating Swedish crime novel off the shelf. It said, *Cop Killer*, and smelled musty and calm, and I was transported to bleary insomniac summers in a central Massachusetts library reading room. Where tinted windows bent the afternoon light suggestively red. With my mother. In her lap.

I dropped the book. I groveled around, whispering, —Emma, every five or ten seconds.

At three o'clock I was in my wife's childhood bed. I had the curtains drawn and a little gray TV on mute with the brightness turned all the way down.

My head hurt, because my body wanted caffeine, real caffeine, not black tea, but I didn't want to be awake, and I couldn't stand up. I was thirsty. The lymph nodes on my neck had swelled. My stomach was writhing from the hard cider sugar. My eyes hurt when they opened or closed. I touched the window with my foot. It was wet. I hugged my knees to my chest. Above me, the fridge made a noise, and I looked at my phone, but Miriam hadn't responded to any of my dozen texts, and I threw it in veritable anger, which quickly incorporated itself into a much larger embarrassment. What would Turmeric think of me now?

I turned off the TV, put the blankets over my head and participated in a coughing episode. I rolled over, took my shirt off and flung it in a ball, but it only traveled a few inches.

I climbed the stairs and served myself another finger of gin, but I didn't feel any better. I went back down and got my shirt, then found the rest of my clothes and my phone. I plugged it in, but its battery continued to decrease. I started counting down from one thousand by sevens.

—Six hundred ninety-two, I said. —Six hundred eighty-five.

I was so happy in my dream.

It was nothing like being alive. As soon as something surprised me, it didn't have consequences. I smiled at people. I sat among a row of chairs. Something was being presented. I was talking to a friend of a friend.

There were suggestions of sex. There were suggestions of going away forever. A parallel dimension. I handled my own feces. I cried, and awoke, and I looked at my phone, and I fell back asleep.

I've never dreamed I could fly, which is fine, because I've never wanted to. I've wanted to feel close to people without obligation. I've wanted to remain impertinent and guilt-free.

And when I looked at my phone for real, it said, *6:07*, and I had two missed calls from Alexander, as well as a text message: *You okay bish? M says you in town. Come by the store if you want*

I fixed myself another drink and dabbed up flecks of loose weed with my pinky, deposited them in a saucer, and heated the tips of two steak knives on the gas range. When their blades glowed red, I pinched the weed morsels between them and sucked the smoke that issued forth with my bodega straw, moving it haphazardly through the narrow kitchen until I'd inhaled every wisp.

Alexander had dropped out of high school and gotten his GED online and moved to Williamsburg when he was seventeen. He'd applied to NYU to study painting. He'd been a sophomore when I was a freshman, and before the year was through he'd dropped out yet again.

Sometime before that, we'd met in the library lobby to trade self-published, stapled-together poetry chapbooks. We'd first encountered each other via the comments section of a then-popular satirical blog run pseudonymously by a mutual acquaintance. Steadily, over the following several years, we'd developed into something. The type of ineluctable male association known as friendship.

Alexander had acquired blue-chip gallery representation and published a slim, stylish erotic novel before he was twenty-five. Then he'd been canceled for saying rude things about women on the internet. He'd been expunged from that gallery's roster and lost his professional contacts and gotten married to a fashion shoot art director, who helped me get a job at the production company, but it was never clear on what terms they stood.

For too long, Alexander didn't do anything except drink beer and smoke crack and look at Reddit. And he was always texting and hanging out with Miriam, whom he'd met through me and was seven years younger than him. Then, during the pandemic, his wife had found a deal on a retail space in the Lower East Side, and they'd turned it into a prosperous vintage store, with features in *Vogue*, *New York Magazine*, and the like.

They drove across the eastern seaboard and flew to Argentina and Japan, hunting designer watches and fine stoneware and band T-shirts, which they sold hand over fist. Not much in the store was appraised at less than three hundred dollars. And we didn't talk a lot these days, but I appreciated Alexander. We had enough history between us. It didn't make a difference.

*sup*, I texted.

It turned out our mutual friend was in town. Sam, who'd passed the apartment by the beach on to me after he'd impregnated his second wife, and who'd run the aforementioned blog, was crashing in the back office of Alexander's shop while said spouse filled his inbox with accusations of infidelity. Alexander had closed early, and they were making their way through a half-gallon of Knob Creek if I wanted to join.

I made sure my backpack was wedged safely under the liquor cabinet. I stared at the toilet seat before locking all the doors.

I bought an iced coffee, no ice, for seven dollars from a café, which was merely a window surrounded by darkness cut from a brick wall, and watched a Ferrari skid and flip along Sixth Avenue. It rolled three rotations before settling back on its tires, then pulled a sharp U-turn.

I rambled twenty minutes southeast to Alexander's store. A sandwich board had fallen over. The exposed half said, WHAT'S YOUR SALARY?, and the front door was locked. I rapped on the glass, and could see Alexander heave himself from the floor, hobbling batty and droopy-eyed. He held a children's book about penguins and kept turning it, examining the pictures on the front and back covers upside down.

—Sup, I said.

—Did you know penguins . . .

Alexander trailed off. He leaned on the door with one hand, pitching forward.

—Do I know penguins . . . what?

—What, he said. —This is . . . belongs to Sam's son. Sam's son is four. His daughter is three. His other one is . . . six. It's pretty decent.

He handed me the book.

—They're birds, I said.

Alexander had long, tawny hair, at one time matted and patchy, but now tamed, pulled back in a ponytail, held every inch or so with knocker ball ties. He took the book from my grasp, took my coffee cup, tipped it, but it was empty, and an androgynous twerp with an X adhered to each cheek made from electrical tape tried to worm in the store past us. Their dress dragging on the sidewalk. Cellophane wrappers clung to the hem. Alexander held out a hand, like, stop, careful not to make contact with the patron's actual flesh.

—Are you open?

—Yes, Alexander shook his head. —I mean no.

He hiccupped.

—I'm sorry, he pretended to say as an aside. —I'm a bit tight.

—Nice, I said. —But I thought you quit.

—I did . . . And then . . . I started up again. You?

—Yeah.

—Sam . . .

—Yeah . . .

—Do you want a drink?

—Definitely.

Inside, Sam was on the ground, legs extended, halfway concealed by a dressing-room curtain.

In its prime, his blog had garnered around a hundred thousand daily hits. For years, even after he'd stopped posting and moved upstate, he'd managed to live solely off the ad revenue. I didn't know how he made money otherwise. He was nine years older than Alexander, and eleven years older than me, but Sam looked boyish and acted without guile. He had short buzzed blond hair, a few days' growth of beard, a couple ironic stick-and-poke face tattoos.

—I didn't cheat, he moaned.

He tried to get up but was lost in the curtain. I drew it apart and sat cross-legged beside him. I helped my friend lift the heavy bottle of bourbon to his lips.

—I believe you, I said.

But I also knew Sam and his wife had met online, when they'd both had other spouses, so I could understand her misgivings.

—I just gotta look at a little porno sometimes.

—You said it, brother, Alexander swiped the bottle before I could drink.

—Sometimes I just gotta email the porn star and ask her about herself. I'm *inquisitive*.

—You're a cultural critic, I said. —You have to stay on the ball.

—I gotta know what makes people *tick*, Sam insisted. —But I didn't cheat. I got three babies at home.

—Did you maybe cheat a little, Alexander asked.

—I just sent some *pictures*, Sam whined. —I didn't even get any back.

I took the bottle and swished whiskey around. It was the next thing to brushing my teeth.

—Why do men cheat, Sam sighed.

—Do they cheat?

—Do you cheat, Jake, Alexander said.

My phone vibrated in my pocket. Sofia had texted. I didn't open the message.

—I love my wife, I swallowed. —What would I cheat for? Sex? I don't really think about it anymore. I mean, I *think* about it, but it isn't the same.

I took another short swig.

—It's not worth stuff. And it's not as though it's that different from one time to another. One memory of one woman to the . . . whatever. In the scheme of things, it's not really my priority. Not that I could tell you what is. I just want to while away. Nothing's that special.

—It's that special, Sam said. —You're not doing it right.

—Crack is better, Alexander said.

—Sex is cheaper.

—Not by much.

We let that sink in.

—I never think about what my life would be like if I weren't married, I said.

—Getting married is zen. It's about accepting suffering.

—L-O-L, Alexander monotoned.

For some minutes it was just the sound of breathing and gulping and the half-gallon shifting across the concrete floor. I lay down and mooned at a sweatshirt featuring an airbrushed portrait of Fred Hampton hanging on the wall.

—How much does that cost, I asked Alexander.

—For you? You can't afford it. Don't ask.

—Emma would love it.

—Where's your wife, Al?

—At home prob. Or something else.

Alexander's wife was kind, soft-spoken. She oozed tacit wisdom. But the steady women in our lives seemed reliably absent.

—What about Miriam?

—Oh shit, Alexander sat up. —We were supposed to meet her at 169 Bar.

—I don't want to go there, Sam slurred.

—Me either. Why were you so tweaked out at Miriam anyway, Jake? She said you texted her like twenty times.

I tried to imagine explaining what had been going on, and I couldn't rightly imagine it, so I looked at my phone.

Sofia's text said, *So excited for our meeting!! Only 3 days away!* <3

The screen was smudged from the inside. Rainbow smears of water damage licked the keyboard, and bits of pixels had gone permanently dead at the margins. The battery had dropped to single digits. It didn't seem like it had charged the whole time I was asleep.

I texted Emma, *i miss you. how are drinks with d\*n?*

—Do you have somewhere I could plug this in?

Alexander took my phone and slid it into a steel clothing rack with steel scorpions welded into it.

—Die another way, he said.

—Like a hot shot?

—Should be so lucky.

—Like Matthew? Like Jal?

—Like everyone.

—I get so jealous of my dead friends for never having to see how stuff turned out.

Alexander touched my shoulder.

—You'll get there.

—Being a father, Sam belched. —Is amazing.

—You irresponsibly bringing life into this shithole, Alexander asked, looking at me.

Five years earlier, smoking DMT in my apartment, we'd made a pact to never procreate. But five years earlier was a place we'd never get back to. Two guys saying things to each other. It had no lasting impact. In many ways it hadn't happened at all.

—No choice, I said. —You were at the wedding. It doesn't matter what I do. I don't have health insurance, Emma still wants a baby. I'm broke, she goes and gets a job.

—Kids are *a-ma-zing*, Sam garbled. —They teach you. You think you're teach them . . .

—Okay, Alexander said.

—You gotta do it, Jake.

—It's going to happen, I said. —Whether I want it to or not. One way or another. Or it won't. I don't know. In any case, it's out of my control.

—Family is everything, Sam gushed.

—What about you, I asked Alexander.

—I'll do whatever, he said. —I'll do literally whatever anyone wants me to. That's how you know you're a man. You stop having convictions, goals. Stop putting the stuff you need first. You have to solve other people's mysteries for them. You go to sleep every night to get up and deal with problems. At the end you're granted the luxury of losing consciousness for a few hours again. You do that every day until your body breaks down. Then you do it in your head for a bit.

—Tha's beautiful, Sam said.

We passed the bottle. We couldn't have spoken this way without alcohol, and we wouldn't have wanted to. And pretty soon we got drunker beyond wanting to as well.

—1-6-9 Bar, Alexander recited, lazily clapping his hands.

—1-6-9 Bar, 1-6-9 Bar . . .

—1-6-9 Bar, Sam chimed in.

And then we were all chanting, gathering ourselves, thumping our chests, patting pockets for phones, wallets, keys, and

Alexander was locking the door behind us as we staggered down the sidewalk, obnoxious and haggard, and for a moment I was actually happy.

We didn't end up at 169 Bar, though, but a cramped little dive with non-dive prices, and Miriam and a bunch of her friends were already taking up two tables, and she slung her arms around Alexander and hung chattering in his ear until he shoved her away laughing, and then we hugged perfunctorily, and she asked me what was going on, and I did a brushing-off gesture and swayed at the bar and was finally acknowledged and ordered a Negroni for some reason.

I was very drunk, and I made myself relatively scarce, standing around with my hands in my pockets, lolling to cadences of jokes or references I didn't entirely get. I believe at one point there was a heated debate going on about who was the worst artist under thirty to sell a painting for more than two hundred thousand dollars that quarter. Then something about movies or music. I tried to make out what was playing over the speakers. It sounded like a fire, and I in its lure.

—*The Brown Bunny*, Alexander said. —The original Cannes cut.

—I think the first one, Miriam said. —No, no, no, no, she interrupted herself. —It wasn't the one where they had the mask things without the, the, spirit of um, *cómo se dice . . . feygele*!

I excused myself and went to the bathroom. Emma hadn't responded to my text. My phone said, *10:09*, and I tried to take a picture to send her, but my face looked too craven and barbaric.

When I returned, someone was laying out bills on the table.

—Jacob, they put an arm around me. —*L'soirée s'améliore* upstairs!

Miriam and Alexander were standing in front of a cage elevator in the corner, pushing each other. Eventually Alexander pushed Miriam to the floor, where she sprawled, guffawing, and he placed a filthy sneaker on her chest.

—Come on, the person chirped, so I did.

The elevator opened into a converted warehouse apartment's kitchen, and Alexander followed Miriam, who was being whispered to by the person, whom I assumed was her friend. The cage submitted to a floating arc of gravity. I stopped it, stepped inside. An alarm clock on the counter said, *3:47*. My phone said, *10:13*.

—Who are you?

I turned to a woman in a bathrobe. She was Miriam's age, late twenties. Her hair in inky clumps, soaking wet, and she pulled it back and wrung it out on the tiles.

—I know Miriam, I said.

—Miriam's novel is being published by Random House, the woman replied.

I winced. She hadn't apprised me. I didn't even know she'd written one.

—So awesome, I said.

—So, who are you?

—Jacob.

I put out my hand.

—I'm Morgan's cousin, she said, wiping hers on her robe, holding it up to her nose. —Too pruned, she went on and rotated, displaying a palm of ulcerating blisters and sores.

The woman smiled tightly and looked into a fridge. Her head kept going deeper in, and I took the opportunity to squirm past.

People were dispersed throughout the suite's living room. I recognized Alexander. He lay supine with his Common Projects sneakers on a tremendous daybed, champagne flute dangling off the side. Next to him, a broad, serious-looking man with a beard seemed in the midst of a story:

—Most centers were, like, so fixated on therapy and liturgy. But this place was all about hobbies. They had a theory that drug use, or, like, addiction in general, was the product of an idle mind. They said it's a lack of stimulation. Doesn't matter if you're a junkie on the street or some Wall Street mom boss, the role of drugs or gambling or whatever is to fill a physiological void. Some of us require more stimuli. Not neurological or genetic or anything, it's just numbers. Drugs become an obsession, but so does sculpting for great sculptors, or, like, bocce for some ultra elite league of bocce players, and no one's throwing those jerks into lockups. So, like, what they wanted was for us to practice transference. To relocate our stimuli-seeking apparatuses and attach that to a hobby. We did a lot of workshops. Cars, furniture, gardening, et cetera. So one day this lady comes in with a ton of old equipment to give us a demo of CB systems. And she's this, like, goth CB tech specialist. You wouldn't fucking believe. I've got a picture, man, hold on . . .

He riffled through his pockets.

—A CB specialist, Morgan's cousin said.

She'd slipped in from the kitchen and was twirling a celery stalk around a tub of sour cream. Her robe had loosened. I could make out the subtle hue-change of an areola.

—Sure, the guy said.

—That's crazy, a different guy said.

This one was dressed up in a silk Burberry shirt, leather pants, alligator skin boots. He sat on a windowsill smoking. Two or three women, also on the daybed, wriggled around the broad guy, who continued going through his pockets. And a lone body, blending into an anonymous love seat's fibers, supped from a liter of Beefeater. I realized it was Sam only after we'd exchanged nods.

—I mean, it's good, the dressed-up guy said. —Just a little . . .

—What's crazy about it?

—Well, like. I don't want to say too much before you find that pic, but like, when I first came to the city, I was supposed to live with this old friend of mine. He said he had a room he wasn't using, and I was broke, like, working at this video store for months to save up, and whenever I'd check in with him, he'd be like, dude, it's fine, don't worry about it, until finally, like, when I finally got all my shit together, like, like a week before I was supposed to arrive, he backed out. Said his girlfriend needed the space for a film she was working on. That was it. And I'd already bought all this crap for the apartment, quit my job, let go of my spot back in Hull. So I was desperate. I didn't know anyone. I didn't have the credit to get a place of my own. And couldn't afford one anyway. So I took out an ad in the *Village Voice*, that's how long ago we're talking, and I moved in with the first person who replied. She was a CBT master. And to be fair, she did warn me she used the apartment for work. That it was part of the deal or whatever, and that she'd give me a break on rent and be really respectful, but . . .

Alexander had come up behind me with a baggie. Inside were shards of brown and gray and pink crystals. I licked my finger, did a little scooping motion, licked it again. Alexander moved away, and someone touched the back of my neck. The guy remained talking.

—Like, so at first it was just noises and stuff from her bedroom. It didn't seem that crazy. I'd known my share of people involved in the industry, but I'd never been so close. Then, after a month or so, she started getting more comfortable. The noises got louder. Screams and crying and apologies and stuff. She had these guys in and out, walking around our living room in blindfolds and harnesses. She called them *slaves*, and she'd, like, lay out on the sofa while they were tied up by their gnads in, like, bondage. I'd come home, and they'd be, like, mopping our floors, tethered to bridles she'd be yanking, suffocating them, cutting them. It was, like, totally . . .

—That's not what I'm talking about.

—What? You said CBT.

—Cognitive behavioral therapy?

—No, no. It stands for cock and ball torture.

—Citizens band, the broad guy said. —I'm talking about a radio technician.

He tilted his phone so the dressed-up guy could see.

—So did you get into it? Did the goth radio chick help you clean up?

—Nah, the guy said. —That place sucked. Relapsed the day I got out.

Someone was massaging my neck. I moved the hand away. It squeezed my palm.

—Do you want to go to your place?

It was the person who'd invited me to the elevator.

—No, I said. —Isn't this . . . your place?

—Yes, they laughed. —Did you read that new psychological thriller set in the Hamptons?

—I only read *The Great Gatsby*.

—How is it?

—Check my Twitter. At *gatsbyjewish*. That's one word, no underscore

—It's not a thriller, someone interrupted. —She fucks Larry Gagosian and he asks her to leave. That's the whole thing.

—Didn't Bret Easton Ellis obtain the distribution rights?

—Of what?

—Isn't *Tender Is the Night* antisemitic?

—Just racist.

—F. Scott Fitzgerald had a notoriously small cock.

I took the Livingston Prep business card out of my pocket and flattened it on my thigh.

—What's that, Miriam interjected, snatching it away. —Hey Megan, didn't you go here?

Morgan's cousin drifted over. She was wearing clothes now. Distressed Diesel jeans and a baby tee that said *Cocaine* in the Champion logo font.

—Where?

—Livingston Prep, Miriam growled.

—That's mine, I said.

Morgan's cousin Megan studied the card and handed it back to me.

—You went there, I asked.

She nodded, distracted.

—What . . . what year did you graduate?

—What year did I graduate high school?

—Yes, I hissed. —It's important.

—Uh, she said. —2015?

Alexander thrust the bottle of Beefeater into my hand.

—You need this more than Sam.

I looked behind me. Our now-defunct blogger was asleep with his mouth open. People were recording videos sticking their fingers in, then pulling back. I suckled the gin. Megan was walking away. I stumbled and grabbed her by the elbow. She turned, exasperated.

—I'm sorry, I said. —I'm . . . Did you know . . . was there a kid in your, or the year before you's class, who like . . . got expelled for, like . . . His name was Philip . . . Philip Springer?

—Phil, she said.

It was like I'd activated something. I could cry. I shook my head and tried to keep my balance. Megan was talking, but I couldn't parse the language.

—Hold on, I said. —Hold on . . .

—But I'm leaving, she murmured. —I'm going home.

—But I . . . I've got to ask you . . .

—Ask my cousin.

—What?

—Ask *Morgan*, she said. —They were in rehab together. He knows him better than me.

—But . . . no, but . . .

I twisted. The broad, serious-looking man was nudging Sam with a Birkenstock.

—But you must have, like . . . Do you have a . . . do you know where he lives? Or a picture of him or something? Anything? Any info I can use to get in contact with him? His Instagram?

—It's been nine years, she rolled her eyes. —I don't know his handle. I haven't talked to him in . . .

—What about a student registry? Or a yearbook!

She paused, considering something.

—Do you have a yearbook, I asked. —From when you guys were there together?

—Well, yeah, Megan faltered. —I was in the graphic design program. We were required to work on the yearbooks. I have PDFs of them somewhere.

—On your computer?
—Probably . . . or an external hard drive.
—Can I look at those? Please!
—Can't I just email you in the morning?
—I . . . Please, can I just come take a peek? I wouldn't impose if it wasn't . . . urgent. I . . . I just really need your help.
—Okay, come on. I didn't want to take the train home alone anyway.

I kept fading in and out. The moon was waning, dimming into a crescent, and Megan and I were talking, about what I could hardly fathom.

We went north several blocks. I remember looking at a building I'd lived in twelve years before. I'd kept a small room on the fifth floor with a two-burner stove and a window that wouldn't open all the way, to prevent me from jumping out of it, I presumed. Next door had been a place homeless people lined up outside to eat lentils. Later it became a surfboard boutique.

I tried to text Emma, but I couldn't get my messages app to open. Megan was droning about the class she taught remotely at RISD, and we walked past the bar that was a historical landmark, where they put sawdust on the floor. It was closed.

And then Megan was helping me down the stairs to the subway, and I was mumbling that I was okay, and I was asking her about Springer, and she said I should really ask her cousin, and then she was trying to hold my hand with her unblistered one, but its muscles were too drunk to answer, and she was tittering, talking about herself, blurring, and I was blacking out, thinking this is pretty much it isn't it, and Megan was flapping my wrist, she was prying at something, cracking up, whooping, and then the train shimmied, rocking wildly, and I didn't know what train we were on, and she was pulling my wrist, enunciating, striving to make eye contact, so I forced mine to meet hers, and I nodded, listening very closely to what she was entreating.

—What *is* it, she urged.

Then I got it.

—Oh, I said. —My wedding band.

# WEDNESDAY

I scrunched against the arm of a love seat, my father-in-law's boat shoes kicked up on the opposite end in front of me, tangled in sweaty, crumpled clothes amid an apartment I'd no memory of entering.

Pigeons made nasty sounds. An elevated subway train rattled across my field of vision. I sat up and watched a silhouette lurk through the room. The body stopped, turned fast, and peered into me, backlit glare obscuring its features, then skated to the door and weaved out.

My phone was dead. From a corner, the kitchen faucet dripped. I limped to it, lapped its trickle, and pawed my way to the bathroom, where I stared at a framed Garfield strip above the toilet. He splayed over Jon Arbuckle's counter cradling a distended gut. NO MORE LASAGNA, the cat said. Followed by, OKAY... MAYBE A LITTLE MORE.

Relatable, I thought, and I braved my gastric burden, working to piece together the final events of the night before. I couldn't get there, though.

There was a sliver of soap on the edge of the sink basin. I washed my hands until it disappeared, perseverating over microscopic gluten crumbs I may have touched in my insensible state, and when I reemerged, Megan was draped in a knee-length

T-shirt, brewing matcha on the stove, one forearm and all the way down to her fingertips wrapped in thick white bandages. She glanced over her shoulder, then went back to whisking.

—Hi, I said.

—Good morning, she intoned.

I sat in a chair that felt made of cork. My face was hot and my extremities cold. I slouched my forehead to a matching table.

—Did something bad happen last night?

—That depends, Megan stated. —Do you think imposing on someone, insisting on following them home, and exploiting their goodwill when you have nothing to offer in return is bad?

I stiffened. It didn't seem that bad, but I didn't want to gamble.

—What happened to your hand?

—None of your business.

She poured the pan of green froth into two mugs and dropped one in front of me.

—Do you have any coffee, I asked.

She shook her head.

—What about, um. Advil? What was in that baggie last night?

—I don't know what you're referring to. And I don't believe in Western medicine. If you don't want the tea . . .

—No, I wheezed. —I want it.

Megan's eyes sunk in her skull. She appeared both older and younger than I remembered. But I didn't really remember her, or why I was there, and I didn't think she was going to give any clues.

—Do you have a phone charger I could borrow?

She sighed, beckoning me to a blazing white bedroom. The walls were bare, with one window shut to the outdoors and no fan or air conditioner, a twin size mattress on the floor, and a desk fashioned from two rusty sawhorses.

When I saw the Apple Pro Display XDR upon it, our conversation, if you could call it one, came flooding back. Megan handed me a cord and I plugged in my phone. She sat on a stack of two milk crates before the computer.

—So, you have, I choked. —Photos of Philip Springer?

—All I have are digital copies of the yearbook. If he got his picture taken, it should be saved on here.

—Can I see?

—Hold on, Megan said. —I've got to check my email.

My phone's screen lit up. Emma had texted, *Where are you?* and *Is everything okay?* and *This pattern is getting kind of tired.*

*i'm so sorry*, I replied. *i went over to alexander's and things got kind of out of hand. i guess i blacked out. i think i'm in bushwick*

Megan was typing something. I felt uptight and restless. I wanted coffee or liquor or weed or an upper hand. I drummed my fingers on the wall.

—Jesus, okay, Megan griped. —Why do you want to see Phil so bad?

—It's a long story.

—Care to fill me in?

—I really don't, I said. —And I'll get out of your hair as soon as I can get a good look. Or if you can answer some questions for me?

I doubt it.

Megan clicked around the terminal.

—Here, she said, opening a file. —This is the 2014 yearbook. That would've been his senior year, right?

I leaned over her. She smelled like chips.

—Where is he?

—Just a minute.

She scrolled through the PDF.

—Search his name, I said, itching my leg.

I pulled my trouser and was accosted by a cavalcade of tiny schizomids scaling my shin. I sucked in air, my eyes focused, and there was nothing.

—Control-F, I exhorted. —Search Springer!

—Just let me find it, she snapped.

But Megan searched *springer*, then *philip springer*, then *philip*, then *phil* without success.

—I don't know. Maybe because he was expelled . . .

—Can you check the 2013 edition?

—I've got work in . . . Shit! I've got to get out of here. I need to shower. Why don't you just ask Morgan? He should be at the garden on Moffat Street. He volunteers there Wednesdays.

—What day is it?

—Wednesday!

—Right, I said. —And where's the garden?

—On Moffat Street!

I smiled.

—Can we just look at the 2013 yearbook?

—Here, Megan flung the wireless keyboard. —You look. I'm going to shower. And if you'd be so kind as to be gone by the time I'm done . . .

—Noted, I said.

She started to take off her T-shirt, reevaluated, and stomped out, slamming the door.

The yearbook's front page was covered in Photoshopped overlays of the Livingston Prep insignia, stretched and distorted and adorned with anime characters, Nicktoons, rare Pepes, and Drake.

I skimmed the file. Dr. Masterson nestled between two teenaged, bikinied beach volleyball players, his arms around them. One hand rested low on a clavicle, the other groping the waistline of her partner, pinching glossy pubescent skin.

I searched *springer* and was immediately delivered to a group photo of THE CLASSICAL MUSIC APPRECIATION CLUB. A row of six students, two boys and four girls, stood as though in police lineup, their names captioned below.

One boy was gangly and grinning and swarthy, the other waxy and shorter, but not shorter than the girls, scowling, and quite juvenile-looking. The picture was grainy, black-and-white. It divulged nothing I didn't already know.

I pressed *return*, and the file sprung to a page farther down, a narrow portrait among the rest of the junior class. And there he was: Philip Springer. The blond, sulky child, scowling identically as in the previous photo. I scrutinized his features, searching for some indication, some hint or evidence or suggestion of how he fit into my world.

This guy, I thought. This is the kid my father tried to befriend on a red-eye. And that my mother took pity on, and got her virtue and integrity wrapped up in perplexing smut. He looked so young. Young and familiar, from another lifetime. Something impossible. And for an instant, I flashed on the visage. Out of context. The background streaming by, ghostly dark.

I'd seen him before. I knew this face. Over the course of a blink, I knew everything, then it dissolved, and I forgot.

Or more likely I'd never known. I was trying to put together pieces from separate puzzles. What had this adolescent's lame, ill-thought-out impulses to do with the crisis at hand? The picture was a decade old. My parents' disappearance could have nothing in common with his transgressions. And yet, why did it feel like I'd shared space with Springer? What was so intimate about his ominous frown? It didn't make sense.

I pressed *return* again, but it just brought me back to the group photo above. I squinted into the monitor, racking my brain. Ten years accumulated into ten million associative branches. We simply weren't connected. And I was hopeless, lost, getting nowhere, and propelled still more inanely from the scant family onto which I should be trying to hold.

A sound stopped. It took me a moment to realize it was the shower. I heard the scrape of a curtain pulling back on its rod. Megan hadn't said what would happen if I wasn't gone by the time she was out, but I didn't want to wager against my hostess's generosity.

I checked my phone. It said, *9:11*, and had charged to seventeen percent. I unplugged it, took a picture of the screen, zooming in on Springer's grimace, capturing an odd bend of light and pixels, then did the same with the formal portrait. I padded for my wallet, grabbed my crotch to make sure it was intact, and scooted out of the apartment, short of breath.

I'd never heard of Moffat Street. It was kind of hard to imagine, and I misspelled it several times, my phone's battery dipping to twelve percent, before landing on the desired result, nine blocks away.

I shouldered into a bodega, chugged a water bottle, filled a plastic cup with ice and simmering coffee, and bought a pack of off-brand ibuprofen. I leaned outside against the brick facade. Then I went back in and bought two Fireball shooters and a fat pre-roll, which the cashier repeatedly assured me wasn't K2, and by the time I made it to the chain-link fence enclosing a sandy patch of mulch in an alley, I was ready to roll.

The maple leaf sign was scarred with graffiti. It said, DUSTHEAD, and stuff in maybe Korean. The broad, serious-looking man teetered against a high stucco wall, bicep raised to his brow, urinating on a flower. I waited for him to shake and zip up before I approached.

—Hi, I said loudly.

Morgan looked confused. He grabbed my arm, pulled me in for a bear hug, then patted my chest and legs down and shoved me back several inches.

—Hi, I repeated. —I, um . . . We didn't exactly meet, but I . . . know your cousin, and I was at the, um, apartment last night, and . . .

He folded his arms.

—I was wondering if I could ask you a few questions.

Morgan spit on the ground between our feet.

—You a cop?

I laughed automatically.

—I detest cops, I said. —My name's Jacob.

I stuck out my hand, but he didn't engage.

—You're Morgan, right?

—Man, he trailed off.

—Megan told me where to find you. I need your help.

He shook his head.

—But it's just . . . It won't require anything of you. I think you knew a, um . . . friend of mine . . . Well, not exactly a friend, but . . .

Morgan stooped to his knees and started digging in the sand with a spade. Some wiry roots fractured. A lot of little bits of glass and a beer can came back too.

—What are you growing, I asked.

—Zucchini, the man answered.

He stabbed the chalky earth.

—My mom used to make zucchini bread, I said.

—Fucking wildfires.

Morgan spit in the hole he'd ruptured. He pushed the powder around with a Birkenstock.

—Remember those orange skies?

—I saw them online, I said.

—That was HAARP. They're killing whales.

I nodded, and Morgan scanned me up and down like he was considering how much of an effort it would be to throw me over the fence.

—What do you want? I don't have all day.

—Cool, I swallowed. —I, um. So the story you told last night about rehab. Megan said you were in there with this guy Philip Springer. I'm trying to find out what's going on with him.

—That was, like, Morgan yawned. —Seven years ago.

I twitched.

—What's there to tell?

—Just, like . . . what was his deal? Why was he there? Where did he end up?

—Jesus. Phil. I don't know. Most of us had got into Percs. Or Oxys or whatever. There were kids in for weed. It was a bad vibe. Phil was okay, though.

—What was his drug of choice?

—All of them . . . Except that didn't seem like why he was there. Not really. He was just into trouble. He'd gotten thrown out of school, got caught stealing. It wasn't his first stint. It wasn't any of ours. And it wasn't the hobby place I was talking about either. This one was strict. For repeat offenders. But he was rich. That was the kicker.

—I heard his mom, like . . . looked out for him?

—Well, sure. She paid people off is why he never ended up in jail. He had the typical daddy issues. I guess his biological one ate shit before he was old enough to know. And his mom married some guy he hated, and Phil couldn't live up to the guy's expectations. Like he was always fucking up and getting caught messing around with girls, and a lot of times the girls were a lot younger, and his stepdad was this really loaded, I don't know. He worked in media or something. Something rich. And he was getting tired of Phil's mom constantly bailing him out.

—What did his mom do?

—I don't know. But they were rolling in it. Pretentious snobs. Phil was resentful about it all. Mad aloof. I remember him saying how fucked up of her it was to marry a guy with the last name Philips, so he was the only one with a different name, 'cause he wasn't gonna be Philip Philips, which, you know, I couldn't argue with. I guess he was lashing out against that too. His mom did seem to love him, though. Do anything for him, the way he made it sound. No one else talked about their mom like that.

—So how long were you guys in there?

—Like two, three months.

The broad man seemed to withdraw then, lost behind his eyes, in private trance.

—Phil might've fared better in the hobby house. He was always talking about how when he got his shit together, he was going to Europe to be a violinist or something. He just needed to prove he was stable. He had a serious temper, but he'd play these symphonies off a Walkman. That chilled his ass out. Holding it to his ear, volume real low.

—You guys were friends then?

—I don't know, man.

—Did you like him?

—Like I said, he was okay. He was just trying to blow time, figure out how to be clean without going insane, like the rest of us.

—But he didn't seem, like . . . cruel . . . or mean?

—He's like anyone. Anyone can get violent when they need a fix. Or they're not in their right head. He was trying, though. He had all these little signs. He said he was going to make chips, like tokens for sobriety, two weeks, two months, whatever. But he hadn't figured out how to work the machine without using a stencil.

—Signs?

—Yeah, little like metal signs.

—Did they say my office?

—Hey, Morgan said. —If you know it already, why are you bothering me?

—I don't know it all. I need to . . . know everything.

—Why?

—It's personal.

—I'm not telling you shit. You're acting like a fucking cop.

He tightened his stance.

—Believe me, I said. —I'm not a cop. If anything, I'm more likely to end up arrested.

—Then why do you want to know about Phil? I haven't seen him since right after we got out. I don't know where he ended up. I'm just trying to bank community service hours.

—He manipulated my mother. He crossed a line. He took advantage of her altruism, and when she went to bat for him, she got sucked into a disgusting indecent proposal, and . . .

—Whoa, Morgan took a step back. —Don't speak on your mother like that.

—I wouldn't.

—That's fucked.

—I agree, I said. —And now my parents are missing. I'm just trying to fill in the blanks.

—Jesus . . . He really couldn't get out of his own way. Everyone he encountered, it was like he couldn't help himself. Just sort of wreaked havoc wherever he went.

—Did anything strange happen while you guys were in rehab?

—Nah, Morgan coughed. —But he had stories. I assumed he was going through shit he'd grow out of. He wasn't like the rest of us. He could afford better. Or his mom's husband could.

—What about when you got out?

—When he left, Phil was, like, optimistic. He had a job lined up at this woodshop. And he ended up getting married pretty much as soon as he was released. I went out for drinks with them. His wife was a dime. Last we chatted he was in a good place.

—When was that?

—Couple months after my discharge.

—What's his wife's name?

—Man . . . you know I don't remember that.

—What about the woodshop?

—It was some place around here. Like, an artist workspace.

—Seems like you can't remember a lot of specifics.

—Man . . .

—You were using again the last time you saw him?

—So what?

—No judgment. I recently fell off the wagon myself.

—Congrats.

—Anything else you remember?

—No.
—What about the bar?
—What about it?
—Where you met up with Springer and his wife, I said. —Do you remember where that was?
—Sure. Um. Well not the name. Or the cross streets.

Morgan looked amused. It might've been the first time in his life.

—But it's not far. That place that serves honey wine or whatever.
—You mean mead?
—If you say so.
—I think I know the spot.

I left him with a Fireball shooter, kneading his forehead over the puny hole he'd carved. I downed the other and smoked the bodega joint. According to my phone, the bar where I'd met Emma five and a half years prior was the only one in the neighborhood that served mead.

It was a fifty-three-minute walk or a seventeen-minute subway ride. I opted for exercise. My stomach twinged. I hadn't eaten a proper meal since the tacos Monday night. That morning's bowel movement had left something to be desired, and Emma still hadn't replied to my texts.

*how are you*, I sent.

My phone's battery was waning.

*i love you*, I texted.

And when I got to the bar, it was obviously not open for business. I cupped my hands on a window. Shiny vats and dark stools, a jukebox, a popcorn popper, some booths.

In the corner, I could see the scene of my and my wife's first convergence. Emma had told me a joke. And Springer had been here with his wife, too. When? Morgan wasn't the most credible witness. Was it before or after? Had the kid known what he was unleashing on my mother? Why couldn't he have just held his liquor? Held himself together another hour? Why had my father, full of pride, egged him on? What was time?

I bumped the pane with my forehead. I knocked a little beat with my knuckles, not knowing how rhythm worked. Not knowing anything. And I saw movement. The contour of a body slumping behind the warped bar, and I pounded my fists on the glass.

The outline by no means rushed to my aid. It drew a glass of something from a soda gun and froze, disappearing in umbras of reflection, taking in my harried attempts to attract its attention.

I looked at my phone. It was almost noon. The screen was flickering with water damage again.

Finally, the phantom caved and sauntered over. He looked my age, unshaven, kind of emaciated, kind of flabby, wan and apathetic.

—What, he called. —We're not open for another five hours.

—I need to ask you a question!

—We throw away debit cards people forget. Circle back later. I'm going to bed.

—I come bearing gifts!

He studied me.

—Like what?

—I was lying, I yelled. —Can you please let me in! I promise it won't take long! I love this place! I met my wife here!

I heard a bolt sliding slowly. Another clattered. The bartender cracked the door.

—Is this about love, he whispered.
—It's what makes the world go round.
He perked up.
—Do you have any coffee, I asked.

We sat at the bar sipping Sanka, which did nothing, and mead, which helped a bit. I kept trying to unlock my phone, but its touchscreen was messed up and my passcode wouldn't enter.

—Philip Springer, I said. —He worked at a woodshop near here. Do you know Morgan?

The bartender rumpled his mouth, swirled a lock of hair through his fingers, and regarded his nails by holding the back of his hand out in front of him.

—Never mind. But this guy, Springer, he and his wife would come here. Or they came here once at least, and . . . Do you know what I'm talking about?

The guy poured more mead in his glass.

—When did you start working here?

—Um, he grunted. —God. I don't want to think about that?

—A while?

—2015? 2016?

He scratched his five o'clock shadow. I mashed my fingertips at my phone, and it opened.

—Yes, I howled.

The battery was at two percent. I navigated to the pictures I'd taken.

—This is who I was talking about, I said, zooming in.
—Philip Springer. He would've been . . . I don't know, a few years younger than us.

—How old do you think I am?

I flinched.

—My age?
—How old are you?
—Thirty-three in December.

The guy snorted.

—Look, I pressed. —Do you recognize him?

The bartender took my phone and stared at it indignantly. He pushed it back.

—*That* guy, he said.

—You recognize him?

—You want to know about *that* guy? What the fuck, are you his friend or something?

He stood up, hands clasped on the bartop. He was suddenly fuming, tendons and hairs jumping. A vein cropped out from his forehead.

—I'm not his friend, I stammered. —I'm . . . I've never met him. But I'm afraid he's enmeshed in some not okay stuff. He has a kind of semicriminal history, and he . . .

—*Semi*? *Semi*criminal!

—He was never arrested, but . . .

—That fucking *prick*. God, I'd totally forgotten his . . . I tried to wipe him from my memory. That guy was ba-ad fucking news. An actual psychotic. You didn't want to be around him.

—I . . . got that sense, I said.

But I was dazed. It was hardly the reaction I'd expected. Until now, people had more or less treated the delinquent triflingly. This was the first genuine emotion his mention had elicited.

—Do you know what this little prick did, the guy asked.

—Did he come here sometimes? He had a wife? At least that's what Morgan said, and . . .

—Well I didn't know his wife. But I do know he kept company with a close friend of mine. We went to Sarah Lawrence together. She worked down the street as a framer, and she was a stunning, gifted artist. She had the most adorable secluded studio where she made these precious bobbin-turned wands. Like this . . .

The guy hoisted himself over the bar and squatted. He ascended holding a spindly stick with round orbs whittled every half-inch or so. He extended it, and I turned it over a few times. It was nice. She'd perfectly molded the timber. I handed it back.

The bartender ran it through his palms wistfully, then replaced it under the bar.

—And you know what he did?

Without warning, abruptly, I didn't want to. I wanted to leave. I wanted to go back to Tenth Street, grab my wife, take the train to Long Island, and hide for the rest of the summer, the rest of my life. I didn't want to know about Philip Springer. Knowing wouldn't solve anything. It wouldn't bring my mother back. I nodded.

—He fucking killed her.

My stomach sank.

—And you know what?

I shook my head.

—He got away with it.

Every muscle in my intestinal tract convulsed and tensed.

—He beat her into the ground until she was unrecognizable. I was at the funeral. I know it was him. She'd tell me she was hanging out with this guy. He was like younger, but *so sophisticated*, the bartender did air quotes. —He was into classical music. *Okay.* He was going to take her away to Vienna. *Okay.* Promises. They met at the woodshop. I don't know how he got hired. He was clearly, like, rich. Clearly someone was pulling strings, because the guy was seriously out to lunch. He was so messed up on drugs, when he'd come in here he wouldn't even drink. He'd just ask for water and maybe a cocktail for his girl and go to the bathroom and nod. I don't know how he kept the job without losing his fingers, but she probably vouched for him, helped him out. She was like that. When she fell, honey fell hard, and then she found out he was married. Yeah, she came in here crying because he was married, and I told her. Cut. It. Off. End it with him straight up. And she was frantic, you know, she was like, she'd been trying to end things, but she couldn't just stop *seeing* him. They worked together.

The guy put his face in his hands.

—But, I started. —But . . . He *killed* her? Doesn't that seem a little extreme? Are you sure?

—She was murdered, okay? That much wasn't up for debate. There was a whole police investigation. And if you'd heard the way she talked about that prick. If you'd seen the way he carried himself, the way they'd carried on. You wouldn't have disputed it for a second.

—But then . . . why didn't you tell this to the cops?

—Uh-uh. Come on. I was not going to get myself involved in that. You think the Blue Lives Matter Gestapo would've done anything? The kid was *flush*.

He rubbed his fingers together. I got it. Languidly, I bowed my head.

—He fucking killed her, the bartender sobbed.

I put my trembling hand on his shoulder, but that only made it worse.

—Did you ever see him again?

—Only once, the guy sniffled. —He was tottering around, wasted, yanking car door handles by the industrial park, like trying to find one unlocked. I don't know. He didn't recognize me, no matter how many times I'd served his junkie ass. He asked me what day it was.

—And?

—I knocked him out. Left him lying in his own spit. Don't think I can't.

—And you never saw him again?

—Well, he wasn't there when I closed up for the night anyway.

—Do you . . . know where I could find him now?

The bartender looked into nothingness.

—In hell, I hope.

—What . . . what do you think happened to him?

—From what I heard, he got what was coming to him. At least I'm pretty sure. Word was he ODed on fent less than a year after he . . . he ki . . .

His throat caught.

—Where, I stuttered. —Where was the woodshop?

But I already knew.

—Behind that gallery, he gestured limply. —The one down the block. On Knickerbocker.

The one run by Miriam's friend.

—And the girl . . .

I hesitated.

—Your friend . . . What was her name?

I mouthed the words along with him:

—Lauren Smith.

I slipped out with the bartender still weeping. There was nothing I could do for him. I couldn't tell him my story. He might have misunderstood. He might have pummeled my ass or ate his words and called Winston and Powell or Mengele's boys from Brazil.

I almost jogged to the gallery. It was closed. CLOSED-4-GOOD, a sign said. But the gate was open, and a concrete slab edifice emanated from where some of the dumbest art in Kings County had once been on view.

An old factory door separated me from the building's innards. Next to a buzzer, a piece of paper covered in clear packing tape said, EXPONENT FRAMING #2. The buzzer was affixed with three buttons. I held down 2 for ten seconds. I waited, feeling crushed and hungry and pointless. I thumbed all three buzzer buttons in a sequence of jabs. I pressed down for several seconds. I pushed the door with all my weight. I stepped back a foot and vaulted into it. I kicked and kicked, and I pressed the buzzer some more.

—Hello, I called out. —Help, please, I need help, I need you to help me please!

I stood back.

—Oh god help, I screamed. —Oh fucking god! Please! He's going to kill me! Just stop! No! Don't kill me!

All was silent. I kicked the door.

—Help, I wailed.

And then, something. I noticed the peephole. A tiny shutter sound issued. Light flashed into the lens. I wobbled in its sightline. I tried to look harassed and scared, and it wasn't too hard.

—Help, I said.

I knocked on the door again. But no one answered. I loitered for what must have been thirty minutes, then I left.

My phone said, *2:23*. Emma still hadn't responded to my texts. I was about to send one more forlorn attempt at rapprochement when it died.

I wended to a subway station. A train was idling and, upon my entry, took off without delay. I accidentally punted a half-full malt liquor can across the aisle. I looked around. No one was with anyone else. They took out their phones, watched acrid music videos like they were alone in their bathrooms, retied their shoelaces, and disappeared into a mist of globalism.

I got off at the next stop. I ran around the terminal to another train, which hadn't arrived. A man in Hare Krishna attire deserted a bench, leaving a newspaper behind. I sat beside it and read the headline: *KOMODO DRAGONS IN ROCKAWAY?* The train came and I hopped on, resting my head against the plasticky window.

The train bucked. It felt like it bounced off the track. Then it went aboveground, and at the following stop, a fox boarded.

It walked up the aisle and sat like a good dog. I rose and stared at the platform. I turned my neck until it hurt. The doors closed. I watched the fox move to the end of the car, lift its leg, pee. It trotted back, tongue wavering. Its tail wagged. It sat before me. Bushy appendage thumping over the salt-stained linoleum.

—What's up, I said.

I wanted to pet its head, but not actually. I experienced a pang of regret and desire for Houdini, my son. Turmeric, her name was yellow, and she was my partner in crime. A couple stops later, though, I'd lost interest. And then the creature was gone.

I rode to the end of the line.

Cabs queued up outside the station, and no one was getting into them. Walls on buildings peeled. Parts of things went in the wind. A bus angled on the sidewalk. Potholes collecting filmy paper. Sand and melting. Blotches of exhaust daubed across swathes of tar.

A group had barricaded themselves in imitation-down sleeping bags alongside boarded-up windows. An extension cord ran up a utility pole, and a person was propped against a wall, phone charging, watching an archived episode of *The O'Reilly Factor* on YouTube.

I needed to be more drunk. And though I'd been better off to other people, my wife, my parents, whomever, when I'd abstained, I also understood that once I'd started drinking, on any given day or juncture, there was no use in trying to stop until I reached a dead halt. I needed to reach that dead halt. I didn't know what I meant.

I saw a sign glowing before me. It said, GARGIULO'S. Below that it said, RESTAURANT. Below that it said, PARKING. And below all that was a fenced-in lot, stretching a block in each direction.

A guy in a fluorescent vest paced up and down the asphalt. I waited for him to finish tagging a hubcap, and I hawked, gathering a knot of phlegm in my mouth too precarious to eject.

—Is the restaurant open, I asked, gulping.

—Yeah, he said and looked at his phone.

I made for the door.

—Uh, he huffed.

I turned around.

—You don't have a car?

—I'm sorry. It's in Long Island.

—You know, he said —A bad driver is always safe until he meets another bad driver.

—What are you, some kind of modernist scholar?

He shrugged. I figured he wanted a tip.
—Sorry.
—What?
But I hadn't meant to apologize twice, so I said, —I didn't say anything.

I'd never been inside the restaurant. It was the only one in Coney Island that was supposed to be expensive. I wiped Michael's Top-Siders on the welcome mat and stared at a Christmas tree.

Wreaths and lights and tinsel and chandeliers swarmed the ceiling. Garish crimson drapes adorned the dining room. Ascotted ancients scaled a perimeter, attending to the few customers. And every window was interior. You couldn't see through them if you wanted to. I sneezed. I fondled my lymph nodes.

—How can I help you this evening, a hostess asked.

Was it evening? I touched my phone through my pocket.

—Yes, I said. —I mean hi. How are you?

—I'm doing fine, she replied. —And yourself?

I don't know why I'd expected the floor to be carpeted. Instead, it sparkled a little, as if I might get sick.

—Do you have a reservation?

—Oh, I said. —No. I was actually hoping I could just get a drink.

—Well of course.

After a moment, I realized the bar was in the lobby, where I was standing.

—Can I take your coat?

—Yes, I said without taking it off.

I'd been wearing it for two days, and I couldn't afford to lose anything else. I kept my eyes on the floor until I couldn't stand it.

—Where's the bathroom?

I felt better after throwing up. I washed my face and picked my nose, cleared out everything I could. The wandering lump had returned. It was spinning, so I pushed it around until I wasn't sure where it was, went back to the lobby, and collapsed on a barstool.

—I'll have an extra dry Botanist martini.

—Tanqueray okay?

—Sure.

—Olive or twist?

—Olive please.

Reflexively, I came up against a passive apprehension about money. Then I recollected some things. I almost grinned.

—*L'chaim*, the bartender said.

—Thanks, I answered. Then, —You wouldn't happen to serve food, would you . . . Like, bar food?

—What were you thinking?

I hadn't been.

—Gluten-free French fries?

He shook his head.

—What about . . . You probably don't have chicken wings either.

—Nope.

I drank my drink. I wanted to get drunker, and I did. How many people were getting what they wanted right now, I wondered.

—It's not Christmas, I said.

The guy was older. A gentleman. I might never catch up to him.

—Not yet, he confirmed.

—What about . . .

—How's some bread sound?

—It sounds great. Thank you. Oh my god . . . But alas, I can't.

—Why not?

—No time to explain.

I balked.

—I can pay for all of it too.

He held his eyes on me. I couldn't tell if he was being nice.

—Well, but I can, I said. —I have full jurisdiction over my parents' effects.

—Right, he said.

—Can you charge my phone?

He spirited it away and returned with a cup of potato salad to take my phone's place. He set me up. I became yuletide cheer. He turned on the TV, and we were joking around. We were watching a rerun of the previous night's All-Star game.

—I haven't seen it, the bartender said.

—I haven't seen it, I echoed.

—Fucking Yankees, he said. —Sooner or later . . .

—Aaron Judge, I said. —Fucking . . .

—Trump, the bartender said.

—Oh yeah?

—I'll give him a second chance.

There was a lull, and we watched the game. I didn't like sports at all. But I didn't think they were that bad, because I didn't care about anything anymore. But I did care about something. I had to, I figured. Based on . . . evidence?

—You have a problem with Trump, he asked.

—I have problems, I said.

—Right.

—I'll tell you what.

He waited.

—I like everyone, I relented. —All the people in this world haven't had the advantages that I've had.

That was the trick. He gave me another drink, so I liked him. I'd give him a second chance.

—Be right back.

I went to the bathroom, and, what the hell, I gave the urinal a second chance! And when I came out, I saw the hostess in her street clothes. She was wearing a basketball jersey that said SLAY above the number twenty-three. That's correct, I thought. Prime numbers slay.

—Hi, she said.

—Oh, I paused. —Do I have to leave?

—I'm just going to have a drink, she smiled.

We were sitting there, the three of us, being ourselves even. Then I said, —Listen, I need to ask you a question.

Neither of them replied. I finished my drink and chomped the ice. This was the type of place they put ice in martinis. Had I been drinking a martini? In any case, not half bad.

The hostess said, —Who do you need to ask a question to?

—Well, um . . . actually, I don't know. It's weird. Were either of you working the other night? Like, um, I mean, like, a December night? A Tuesday. About six and a half years ago?

—Which one, the guy said.

—December twentieth.

—I work Tuesdays, the hostess said. —I might've been here. Why?

—Yeah, why, the guy repeated.

—I just . . . Did anything weird happen?

—Like what?

—Like any weird people, weird vibes near the beach?

They looked at each other.

—Like did anyone come in acting morbid, or unruly, or was there an altercation or anything, or like . . . um . . . anything?

—Not that I remember.

—Um, I said. —There was this guy. I think he's tied up in some pretty formidable stuff, and . . . Wait, I have a picture of him, give me back my phone!

The bartender got it, but it hadn't turned on. I handed it back to him.

—There was slavering.

—What's that mean?

—A ravenous, slavering figure, I said.

—Davey?

—No, his name was Philip Springer.

They cracked up.

—What's so funny?

—We know a Philip. He's a puss.

—Is he blond, I beseeched. —Kind of young? Rich and evil and has these little gold plaques and . . . slavering?

—No, the hostess laughed. —He's a little bitch.

—Did he kill anyone?

They fell into hysterics.

—Never mind, I said.

—What?

—Forget it. He's probably dead.

I stopped being in love with them. It was bound to happen. It happened when the bartender gave me my phone back for a second time, and it still hadn't turned on, and I said, —Hey, what gives, and he said he was tired and turned off the TV and proceeded to do uncool stuff. Stuff like with the cash register and not giving me drinks. And I didn't say goodbye. Why should I have? So long for goodbyes. All affection from me had been wrung.

I was sulky, booting stuff in the street, maybe letting out suffering moans, trying to get music on my phone, but I couldn't think of a song I wanted to hear, and my phone was broken besides, and, as it was, I wasn't particularly fond of music.

A crash crashed. I looked at the beach. Steam was coming off the sand. Dozens of seagulls stood in a dense clump, all facing the same direction, away from the bay. Waves were droopy. Something was burning.

The crash crashed eleven more times, and the roller coasters blinked flashing lights they hadn't had when I'd lived here.

Skyscrapers were being erected in the flood zone. A plane sparked overhead. And at the final crash, fireworks started to explode, suffusing the horizon.

# AT SEA

I dreamed I'd signed a lease on the late Joan Didion's apartment, which was a Victorian mansion uptown. I only ended up exploring one room in my new home, but it was enormous and clean and filled with furniture, which I resolved to sell as a means to make the rent.

Some men wearing back support belts took apart a white couch. It extended the length of the chamber. The rest of the room was white too. The walls were mirrored. The mirrors were removed, and I took my repose in a corner on a rollaway bed.

Then a doctor notified me that I had three weeks to live. I plucked at the lump in my lower abdomen. A week passed. My mother showed up, and I explained what fate had dealt her sole heir. And for some reason we argued, and I shut her out of the mansion. I spoke to someone in charge. Nurses and attendees set a white table with craft services. I watched from my bedside but didn't get up to eat. I propped pillows behind me. I now had two weeks to live, and I felt acceptance and peace. The unknown would be delivered. I wanted to be open to it.

All the same, I remained skeptical. I wasn't depreciating fast enough. Probably the doctor had told me three weeks, but realistically expected six, so that when I lived for three weeks longer, people could condemn me to a state of heroism.

I took out my phone. I wanted to tell my wife about this happy suspicion. But Emma was already there, nodding, saying nothing. She ushered my phone outside, and I watched from the high window as she lip-synced into it then got in a limo. Houdini's ears blew from the driver's seat.

Turmeric wheedled through a hole in the locked door to the basement gnawing a vagina. I rolled my eyes, and when I awoke, I'd missed my stop by five subway stations.

I bought a pint of Cutty Sark from an all-night liquor store, which was a bulletproof sheet of plastic with a sliding box apparatus for exchanging money and bottles. I thanked the guy in a language we both knew, one of woe, and reeled to Tenth Street.

It was deep night, but at least the doors were locked. I silently let myself in and peeked into my wife's room, wanting to give her a kiss before I finished my drink. The bed was made, though, and without her in it.

—Emma, I called in a half-voice, slinking up to the third floor.

Her note was resting on the counter, almost two days old. *Let's be kind to each other . . .*

—Baby, I sang.

The gin in the cooler was verging on empty. I held the pint of Scotch in one hand, the liter of Plymouth in the other. I put them down and padded blindly under the cabinet. I wrenched my backpack free, grabbed at the double-action revolver swaddled in the bath towel. In the front flap, the single round. I resecured them and lunged to my in-laws' bedroom, dug through Michael's sock drawer, ferreted out two lint-covered weed gummies, and swallowed them whole.

—My love, I hollered at full volume.

I was keyed up, prickly and suspicious, more desultory than ever. I wanted to crawl back in my dream and lie on the interminable couch and be pitied and cosseted. I raced to the bookshelves, dislodged a *Hamlet* folio, and lay on a faded woven rug, gaping at skylights, wanting to see stars and seeing the opaquest glaze. I flipped around. None of the words were as I recalled. I spread the book over my eyes. My nose held it up, and I flung it into a fireplace.

—Emma, I said.

I went back to her room. Her suitcase was gone. The only clothes in her closet were wool and velvet, heavy and wrong. Tags emblazoned with occult, mystic names: agnès b, Maryam Nassir Zadeh, Jacquemus. Her phone and laptop chargers were nowhere to be found. I dug through a kitchen drawer for a USB cord and plugged my phone in a port and lay prone at its side. I held down buttons. The screen did not react. The digital clock on the microwave blinked zeros. I didn't know what time it was, didn't know when the trains to Long Island stopped or resumed service.

I paced, counting, but the numbers wouldn't accumulate. They seemed discrete, superfluous. The toilet seat was up, and my echo chamber kept expanding, stuck in meaningless, sorry loops until the skylights weakly brightened.

I stuffed my bucket hat with the letter H on it next to *The Great Gatsby* in my backpack and was rocking on heels in Grand Central Terminal when the big clock hands pointed to twelve and six.

The train to Montauk wouldn't be leaving for another eighty-three minutes. Meanwhile, an announcement said the six-nineteen to New Haven was now boarding. I beelined to the platform, plopped in a sticky red Metro-North seat, closed my eyes.

Two hours later, I transferred to the Shore Line East. Pressing my face to the glass, I watched cattails and beach grass and beetle-eaten pines.

In New London, I hobbled along the waterfront. I found a quarter on the ground and stuck it in a tower viewer. I stared out at the free-floating red brick lighthouse. Ashy shapes zigzagged behind its white-framed windows.

It had barely been a week since I'd beheld it, but the structure seemed crooked. It bobbed mockingly in the surf. It mocked my lack of buoyancy. My lack of worth. Why had my family forsaken me? As ferries keened in the sound, I waited on a corner to board a bus to Rhode Island.

I debarked a stop early when the carousel came into sight. Children were riding in circles, pulling rings from a dispenser at the end of the gyre. If you got the gold one, you got another ride free. In my salad days, I'd gotten it more times than I could count.

Horses rocked. Sandlots offered parking for twenty-five dollars an hour. At the Ocean House, guests were dressed in all white, batting croquet balls across a newly turfed neon lawn.

When my parents and I had come down on the weekends, driving an hour and change from central Massachusetts, the resort's roof was caved in. The clam chowder watered-down. Hot dogs came in two sizes, and to eat off the kids' menu you paid what you weighed in cents.

In the distance, I could make out the many chimneys and gables of High Watch on its bluff. Waves burst against the seawall. An American flag flailed at half-staff. This view of the sprawling colonial-style estate made up my earliest memories, and somewhere inside it Taylor Swift had consummated the great late-capitalist decline under the lustful paws of a Kennedy.

Our fair littoral community had been sold off to the lowest common denominator. Vague forces of financial speculation had usurped my deadbeat, beachcomber heritage. Everything I knew was eroding, and they continued building on top of it, and I was further lame, unemployed, uninspired, timeworn, and orphaned.

I trudged away from the sea, along the highway to my parents' condominium.

It had been nearly three years since the State of Rhode Island had dropped *and Providence Plantations* from its official title. Still, the domain in which my parents, and about a hundred other geriatrics, hung their hats was proudly named after one: Sliver Orchard.

Across twenty-nine acres of rolling hills, babbling brooks, luscious gardens, and faithfully manicured grounds, the complex boasted more than seventy varietals of specimen flora. The hemlocks and ginkgos, golden cypresses, Kanzan cherries, and dogwoods made succor for cottontail rabbits, painted turtles, coyotes, snowy egrets, green herons, and so forth. And because most residents were too old to amble, it often felt as though one were alone in this hydrangea-lined utopia.

When my folks had moved in, I'd been disturbed. I'd thought they were giving up. They weren't yet at retirement age, and all their neighbors were clawing death's door.

My mother had originally planned on finding work, but no one wanted to hire a sixty-year-old physical therapist, and instead she joined the condo association's landscaping committee. My father had commuted into Cambridge right up until his disappearance, demoing and installing chromatography systems throughout the region's many research institutions. During COVID, he'd set up a drop screen in their unfinished basement and sold via Zoom.

—Hey, he would say. —I like to talk.

In the late afternoons, he'd hitch a kayak to his Chrysler Pacifica and paddle around the salt marshes, shucking oysters over his crotch.

Once, in the years I'd dallied around the loft, my mother had asked to read my novel. I'd even printed it out for her, but then I'd sealed it in an envelope I never told her about.

Since her departure to destinations unknown, Sliver Orchard's trimmings had gone to seed. Weeds and burned-out grass and ant colonies dominated its winding one-lane arteries. I crept in the back entrance, through a wrought iron fence closed to car traffic. Venetian blinds shivered in divers shapes amid my lonely perambulation, and the front door to my parents' unit squealed in its jamb.

Inside, all was the same as Emma and Houdini and Turmeric and I had left it. I plugged my phone into a built-in charging dock. Nothing happened. The magnetic timer on the fridge said, *11:11*. I made a wish. I opened the fridge. A bottle of rosé was chilling on its side.

I remembered my father ruminating, —It's so rare to find a rosé in a Gamay.

Okay, old man, I thought. My parents were getting hazier. Pretty soon I'd have to give credence to their destinies. And where the hell had my wife gotten to?

In a cupboard I found a corkscrew, cut the foil, and listened to air escape the bottle. I gave myself a generous pour. The meniscus of the wine sparkled. And I toasted to my progenitors' souls. I hoped they were resting easy, not being mutilated or dissembled part by part.

—*Salud*, I said.

And then I was crying, fitful and fitly, conjuring elementary, inconsequential innocences: twinkles of grandparents, waterfronts, sunsets, synagogue plafonds, tissue-thin pages of Tanakhs and Library of America editions.

I opened the freezer. I removed a well-concealed plastic baggie containing a strip of blotter paper. With shaking hands, I cut two tabs of LSD. I placed them on my tongue. I stood on the back patio and watched an osprey drift in circles. It didn't care about lines, probably didn't know about them. It had stuff in its beak. Not for itself, for someone else, and I ducked away.

I flopped on the wall-to-wall carpet of the upstairs loft space, waiting for the acid to kick in. I sipped pale wine. I emptied my mind and let it fill with all the bits of information I'd uncovered.

At Christmastime 2013, my parents had traveled almost to Vienna. They were on the same flight as a Livingston Prep class trip to the Philharmonic New Year's concert, and Philip Springer was seated next to them.

Philip Springer's father had passed away when he was young. His mother had remarried a man with the surname Philips. He'd worked in media, maybe. He was rich, and Springer had resented him. He'd become a troublemaker, a drug addict. His stepfather had resented him back.

Philip Springer was reprimanded for drinking on the flight. My father had supplied the ammunition, and my mother had shown compassion for him. Sybil Parker said she'd said he'd reminded her of me. Dr. Masterson had tendered an indecent proposal, the only deal he'd oblige for the student's pardon. But she'd rebuffed his vulgar advances, and Springer was expelled.

Roughly eight years later, my parents had vanished without a warning or trace, shortly after my and Emma's wedding. And where was Emma now? I batted the thought from my consciousness.

In the meantime, Springer's mother had gotten him a job at Geshaltn Stationers. The proprietor had done her a favor, and her son had stolen a nameplate press, a stencil, and materials to produce MY OFFICE plaques. Since then, I'd come across one on the beach in Coney Island, one on the beach in Suffolk County, and seen a third hanging in Dr. Schwartz's exam room.

His mother had protected him from paying legal retribution for the theft and subjected Springer to a succession of rehab clinics, which, at one, he'd talked enthusiastically about getting his act together and moving to Europe to become a luthier. He'd left the center full of hope, gotten married, as well as a job at a woodshop behind the gallery where I'd first set eyes on Emma.

There, Springer had become embroiled in an affair with his coworker Lauren Smith, who, coincidentally, maintained an art studio in the same apartment building on the peninsula where I lived. When she discovered he was married, she'd tried to break things off. Had Springer killed her? It seemed plausible. The mead bartender had claimed he was psychotic. And to the best of that man's knowledge, Springer had died sometime after his mistress, from a fentanyl overdose.

In photos, he looked oddly familiar, but Philip Springer was impossible to pin down. We hadn't met. On the other hand, I had borne witness to Lauren Smith's murder. The wielder of the blunt or sharp object gone so rapidly. Refracted by light. Slavering. And I'd been demoralized and lied to by my ex-girlfriend-cum-agent. My novel had failed to sell. My friends had died. I'd gone through therapy, quit drinking, and accompanied my wife to her father's seventieth birthday party. I'd fallen off the wagon and happened upon Dr. Masterson giving way to a poison several hours in the making, such that no one could ascertain how, where, or why he'd ingested it.

Gladys Masterson knew more than she let on. Old Alice had it in for me, and was the last person, besides myself, seen with Masterson before his demise. Emma had a new job. She'd gone for drinks with Dan Minnowitter, whose mother was having trouble selling the A-frame abutting her parents' Amagansett cottage. Now she was AWOL too, and I had no way to reach my wife.

What else? What was missing? Everything, I thought. Nothing was holding these strained perplexities together. The grisly, tangled strands all seemed to be linked, but the chain was broken. And soon, I was tripping. Hard.

I was watching the lines glow and curl and trail off my pen nib. I was writing:

> *It's good to let go! But good to hold on, also.*
> *The people we touch . . . runnels of affinity, love . . .*
> *Your love belongs to me.*
> *At night when you're asleep*
> *We put so much emphasis on actions*
> ***BUT*** *passive thoughts, memories and dreams . . .*
> *that is most of what life is . . . almost all of it . . .*

My legs were jimmying. So Philip Springer was a psychotic. The difference between a psychotic and a neurotic is a psychotic doesn't really mind they're one. But a neurotic, by default, loathes his or her or their state. And is all the more aware of it to loathe.

But what is a neurotic, I wondered. *Neuro-* meant nerve, and *-otic* must be ear-related. I heard my wife rustle a candy wrapper. I turned around. A spider descended a string of silk.

I was paranoid. And *para-* meant beside. While *-noia* referred to thought. So paranoia was adjacent to actually thinking. A dimension parallel to the mind. Likewise, a man and a maniac were separated only by three letters, which indicated affliction with disease.

I was a neurotic, paranoid maniac. An ear-hurting, side-thinking man suffering from the disease of being one. I was making my life up as I went along. I rolled on the carpet. I finished the wine. I prowled through the condo with my eyes closed and my hands out in front of me.

—Emma, I cried.

I opened every drawer. I sought out every enemy. I turned on the radio.

It said, —God is a particle.

I turned it off.

I looked at my father's doctoral diploma. VE RI TAS. True, I thought, and ran up to the loft. I got down on my knees. Something was under my bed. I reached and trawled out a T-shirt. It was mine. I had worn it from the time I was sixteen until I was twenty-nine, and it said, WELCOME TO NEW YORK, arcing over a pistol, then, DUCK! MOTHER FUCKER, so I hit the deck.

I ripped open my backpack, slid the bullet in a chamber, spun the cylinder, and rammed the Ruger's muzzle against my temple.

I cocked the hammer, pulled the trigger. It clicked, and the cylinder turned.

—Fuck, I screamed.

I spun it again, felt the depression of the front sight cutting into my skin. I twisted it, mangling myself, membranous, erratic.

—*Fgrrreheeuuuuuhhh*!

I squeezed the trigger, and it clicked again. Nothing. I opened the cylinder with spastic haste. I considered the bullet. It was lined up with the barrel.

I laughed berserkly and wound the gun in the towel and buried them under filthy clothes and the paperback in my bag.

When I looked back to the T-shirt, I saw its myriad holes mushrooming. Frayed neck, crumbled cotton, loose threads, chasm yawns. It was disintegrating in my hands.

Like everything else, like everyone I'd known or ever loved, like I would one day too, regardless of whether I impelled the action or not, it had succumbed to time.

I sat at my mother's desk. In the extra bedroom upstairs. In case she'd elected to have another child at the age of sixty-seven. Or, I grasped, in case I had. I could hear her spectral tone:

—I've got all these puzzles leftover from work. For honing cognition and fine motor skills.

I shrugged it off. My parents still kept a paper Rolodex, and it was opened to the letter B. Michael and Jane's Long Island and Manhattan addresses were neatly printed in my mother's hand. She must have been planning to send them a thank-you note after the wedding, when . . .

I fanned through cards, catching names familiar from childhood, admiring my mother's penmanship, its recognizable strokes and flourishes. One by one, I watched her writing, and the lives it recorded, fall away. There were no entries for X, Y, or Z.

I gathered the two-inch stack's weight on my thumb and folded the pile back to the beginning. I hadn't realized some of the notes were out of order. My mother had prided herself in meticulousness. But here, the As started with first names: Aaron Gacy, Adrian Ramirez, Alexia Stano. And then my hand stopped and the lump in my abdomen jolted up to my esophagus. The card said:

*A. Martha Philips*
*A. Martha Philips, Ltd.*
*martha@amphilips.com*

*Office*                          *Home*

*433 Lafayette St. #5C*           *13 Heller Ln*
*New York, NY 10003*              *East Hampton, NY 11937*

But why did my mother have Sofia's boss's contact info, the namesake of the once-prestigious literary agency, which had stripped its staff down to two personnel?

His stepfather worked in media . . . His parents were pretentious snobs . . .

Why hadn't I thought of it before? Could it be? The same . . . *Philips* . . .

The desktop computer was in sleep mode. It hadn't been properly turned off since my parents' disappearance. Screens always look spurious on acid, and this one bent and buckled, emitting a prismatic band of colors, and I had to close one eye to peruse it directly.

My mother's account was still signed in on the browser. Her inbox filled with spam and promos, family birthday alerts, act-now sales, reminders for appointments that would never be kept. I entered *martha@amphilips.com* into her email search bar, and a heap of results cascaded.

I sat there, blinking under the pulsing hues, scrolling through my mother's correspondences with Martha Philips, growing wearier and more agitated by the second, as the gruesome details, and the devil within them, came into focus.

Then I became dizzy. My jaw fell agog. I was awestruck, overwhelmed and confounded and appalled, and I had to concentrate on breathing to keep from swallowing my tongue.

What I discovered wasn't at all what I'd imagined. Not in my most deranged dreams. It was worse.

Night fell. I slouched against a wall trying to decide my next move. Every ten or so minutes I checked the fridge for wine, but there kept not being any more.

I went back to the computer. My vision had stopped trailing. I thought maybe I'd made a mistake. But the emails were all there, flagrantly grinning. Nothing could erase what I'd seen.

And where was Emma? I needed to talk to her. If only I'd memorized my wife's number when I'd had the chance. But even if I had, my parents' landline was disconnected years earlier, and the cops were still holding their phones as part of the supposedly ongoing investigation.

I thought about emailing from my mother's account, but I was afraid. My wife hadn't answered my texts. Why were all her clothes and chargers gone? And who'd been in her parents' apartment? Who'd put up the toilet seat? Who'd loaded the gun while I slept?

I tried to check my own email. A prompt said, *To help keep your account safe, Google wants to make sure it's really you trying to sign in.* It told me to, *Open the Gmail app on Jacob Garlicker's iPhone.* I closed the window.

Downstairs, I pushed through the screen door out to the back patio. I felt dust on the soles of my feet, stretching my toes, spraining moss that cropped between them. Frogs were peeping. Insects played the same song with their legs. I stepped into the grass, wet with dew, and examined a petrified piece of dog excrement. Had we really all been here together just seven days before? Had I really been relaxed? Had I really thought we could move forward?

With what I knew now, it seemed incomprehensible. Yet I was the same person. My cells may have regenerated, but they were trapped in my context, and I knew what I had to do. I went back inside, grabbed a plastic bag from under the sink, and picked up Houdini's poop.

The days were growing shorter, but the morning came on fast, like a clock running on a small cold-fusion nuclear reactor-powered battery made possible by extraterrestrial intervention.

I couldn't tell if I'd slept, but at sunrise, I grabbed my backpack and left Sliver Orchard for the first bus to New London. I traveled the reverse line of trains I'd ridden only hours past.

My meeting with Sofia was scheduled for two o'clock. I arrived in Grand Central at a quarter after one. Somehow I was still latently holding onto a hope that my writing career could be rekindled, in spite of everything I had learned, and what I'd inevitably have to confront. Narcissism springs eternal. And it was the middle of summer, the fourteenth of July.

In 2017, Sofia and I had collaborated on the only complete manuscript I'd ever produced. My life had filled with promise.

But by the end of that year, she'd discarded me and my story. 2017 was a prime number. 2023, surprisingly, was not.

So there was still a chance. My agent didn't have to be wrapped up in the rest of the horror. One thing could hold true. And if it wasn't fiction, then what else? What other tools even existed for extracting reality from the impenetrable mythos of the terror world?

Didion said nobody wants to hear about someone else's dream, good or bad. Or to walk around with it. But she was dead, and I'd leased her mansion in a dream of my own. So what was genuine? Only the stories.

I walked south on Park Avenue until it changed appellations. In Astor Place, the cube was gone. The Barnes & Noble had been replaced fifteen years over by gyms, drug stores, vegan restaurants. Outside 433 Lafayette Street, I scanned the office directory for A. Martha Philips, Ltd. My thumb was hovering over the buzzer when an all-too-familiar voice called my name.

—Jacob! I'm sorry!

I thought Sofia would unlock the door and escort me inside, but she just lingered there, glistening with sudor in the leaden light. I recognized the Michael Kors skirt suit from the selfie she'd sent earlier that week. This time, however, my agent had graced it with a blouse, only the top three buttons undone. She stood erect, smiling, running her pink tongue over her teeth.

—I'm sorry, she repeated. —But Martha can't join us today. You know, with Dr. Masterson's funeral? She wasn't able to make it into the city.

The lump in my stomach dropped. I craned my neck behind me. No one was there.

—We could've rescheduled.

—Oh no, the agent gasped. —This is too important.

She smoothed her skirt, rubbed her palm inside her shirt, feeling herself up in a manner only Sofia could get away with.
—It's not that important, I said.
—You're my client, she stressed. —*Mine.* I want to see this through. I've been . . . in touch with that indie publisher.
She took out her phone, typed, slipped it back in her jacket.
—And?
—Huh, Sofia seemed caught off guard.
—The publisher . . .
—Right, she said. —Martha can't join us, so I can't exactly . . . God, it's hot. I'm sweating like a . . . Ugh. Do you want to get a quick drink? I know you're not boozing it up anymore, but . . .
—Yes, I said.
—Oh?
—I'm back on the horse.
She eyed me.
—I mean bottle. But don't you have one in the office? Where there's air-conditioning?
—It's . . . broken, she stammered. —It would be terribly stuffy up there.
I folded my arms, still clad in Michael's beige sport coat. Its fibers were beginning to wilt.
—You don't want to go to the office?
—No. Let's get a drink at a bar. Somewhere dark. Where no one can see us.
—Why didn't we just meet in Long Island then?
—Because this is more professional! You can't get any real work done by the beach. You of all people should know.
—Then why not go up to the office?
I peered at my agent's eyes. They were shooting about. I couldn't get them to meet mine.

—Be*cause*, Jacob. I want to go to a bar. Someplace where we have to focus. I'm afraid . . .

And then those eyes seemed to whir behind her cognizance, desperately searching for an excuse that made sense.

—If we went up to the office, we might give in to temptation . . . I know you're happily married. And, well, I'm trying to repair my own . . . relationship . . . If it means anything to you.

I searched the bowels of my heart. It didn't. Sofia gulped. She was evading something. She was a compulsive, pathological liar, and she was in her element.

—Whatever, she was getting annoyed. —Just come on. I know a place that's quiet, and you'll like it. I know you like it. You used to take me there.

I'd thought the doors to the bar that was a historical landmark, where they put sawdust on the floor and Abraham Lincoln had allegedly gotten drunk at, had been permanently shuttered, but I supposed even I could be wrong.

And Sofia was right. It was quiet. And dark. But they only served beer in pairs of two mugs at a time, and my agent returned from the counter running the frosty side of one over her forehead, drawing beads of condensation from fingertips, tracing them over her décolletage and the back of her neck.

—God, she said. —So much better.

And she took a deep drink, barm and bubbles streaming from the corners of her lips, frothing over her chin. She dropped a soda in front of me.

—What am I supposed to do with this?

—You think I don't come prepared? For *my* client?

She opened her purse to reveal a hillock of Bombay Sapphire shooters. My mouth watered. I took two, broke their seals under the table and hardened up my beverage.

—But, I started. —How did you know I was drinking again?

Sofia leaned over and slurped the foam off her second mug of beer. So I saluted, and we cheersed and sat sipping in silence for a minute until the liquor took hold.

What I'd discovered the previous night was more critical than ever, but it was fogging, and I was feeling relaxed. Perhaps everything I'd unveiled was just delusional desire, vainly summoned connections between gaps that weren't there. I started to enjoy the bar's tranquility, and I started to enjoy my agent's company for the first time in close to a decade.

The drink helped. And it helped me remember why I'd found her so alluring in the first place. I could almost imagine touching Sofia's thigh. Just a contact, a graze. Then nonchalant stroking. Higher. A bit higher . . . She readjusted her legs, and her skirt opened for a fraction of infinity. I stuck my fist in her purse and dug around for another shooter. Sofia spoke first.

—How did we end up here, she sighed.

Then I remembered why she annoyed me so much.

—We walked from the office, I monotoned.

—Jacob, she effused, cheek in hand. —Do you remember the last time we came here?

—I might need a few more to get back in the spirit.

—I really did like your novel. It was honest. Even if it was kind of jejune.

—There's a word you don't hear every day.

—But you *should*, Sofia slurred.

Another vessel of bones, supple where it mattered, and nowhere else. It was as though she and Emma were inverted doubles. One dark, one light. Two sides of an inestimable coin. Loyal and self-serving. Blonde and brunette. Family and interloper. Divinity and devilment.

I lowered my face to the chipped varnished table. I observed Sofia through the warps of my glassful of gin.

—You said *you work for me*, she mused. —That was so . . . sexy . . .

—Sofia, I grumbled. —This is exactly what you said you wanted to avoid.

She mooned back, looking moist.

—We're both married.

She frowned, swigged her beer.

—Why do people get married?

—I love my wife, I said.

—Sure, Sofia intoned. —But you loved me once too.

I didn't deny it. I didn't say anything.

—I'll tell you why I got married, she said.

—Why?

Sofia smirked.

—Fear.

The mugs at the bar held no more than ten ounces. And though much of Sofia's second beer sat untouched, she was a lightweight, and loosed to that place for which all souls most yearn: oblivion.

—You know I'm not really a triplet, she burbled. —I'm not even a twin!

I must have nodded. It wasn't a surprise, and I could not have been less interested.

—I saw that Joy Williams essay you were reading, and I just . . . I just really wanted to piss you off . . . I wanted to get a rise out of you.

—You told me you were a twin before I read it, though. We've been through this, Sofia.

She hiccupped into her beer, and it fizzed. She glanced up.

—Do you know why I lie? Why I just . . . irresistibly make shit up and run with it?

—Why?

—I don't know, Sofia giggled. —I've been doing it my whole life. It feels good. It gives me a sense of control, stability. I don't even have siblings. I'm an only child!

—Join the club, I said.

—But do you know what it's like? To be invisible? To live a life of complete anonymity?

I started to answer, but Sofia spoke over me.

—You're from the East Coast. It's irrelevant how much money your family had. You grew up among elites. The educated, the artistic, the privileged. Plus you're Jewish. You'll always have kin. Your people understand solidarity. You control the media, you drive culture. The entire global political machine.

—That's an awful stereotype.

—I meant it as a compliment. Did you know I'd never seen the ocean until I moved to Long Island for college?

—No. You told me you used to go up to Kennebunkport with your cousins.

—And you believed me! Can't you see how it gave me a leg up? It helped define my perspective and personality.

—But not, like, actually.

—Yes actually, Sofia insisted. —I manifested my history. I turned a youth squandered among Indiana soybean fields into a chronicle of highbrow Americana entitlement and experience.

—But it isn't real. Just fantasizing and divulging illusions to everyone doesn't make that stuff real. It doesn't change who you are.

—You're wrong, she said. —It really works. I never would've gotten the job with Martha, for instance, if I hadn't embellished a bit. Do you think anyone would've hired me if they'd known where I went to college?

—I don't know, I said. —It didn't help me much, going to NYU.

—You're so full of shit! The number one dream school. It opened every door. Everyone you met, every job you got, every publication opportunity was because you were a part of that.

—In the Hamptons, they seem to view it as an embarrassment.

—That's exactly my point! In Indiana you'd be a king. From Massachusetts you were going off to get a charming education. But on Long Island, you're a hick. Everything's relative. Nothing is solid or righteous or authentic.

I couldn't help noticing the way Sofia had said *on*. *On* Long Island. It came so naturally to her. And out east, they were still none the wiser that she was anything less than the rest of them. Perhaps my agent had a point.

—When I first arrived here, I knew no one. And I didn't leave a single friend behind. They all thought I was a snoot. They thought I couldn't stand the sight of them, that I was ashamed of where I was from, and who I'd become if I didn't abandon it. And they were right. I used to take the train to Manhattan and let the energy wash over me. Possibility and genius and light. I wanted to be a part of it. I started interning anywhere I could get my foot in the door. I'd say I'd worked here or there with so-and-so, and people believed me. And a month before I graduated, I had the junior agent position lined up with Martha.

You know she thought I was six years older than I was. I had to tell her I was on assignment abroad so I could finish my finals. I didn't even attend commencement. I was already at work, just down the block . . .

Sofia stuck a thumb over her shoulder, buzzing with adrenaline, inscrutable intentions.

—You probably don't even know how old I really am.

—Uh, I said. —I thought you were a year older than me?

Sofia's leaned back and laughed.

—Right. Because that's what I told Martha. I guess I was keeping up the facade. I mean, I *had* to. Be honest: would you have truly entrusted a twenty-one-year-old with your manuscript?

I thought about it. I considered her artifice, her guile, her perfidy and fraud, the repeated, protracted mendacities with which this woman had operated on me, and apparently everyone else. For almost a year we'd shared a bed. I knew Sofia could be unreliable, but I'd never imagined it going this far. And still it paled in comparison to the task at hand. How would I ever be able to get my agent back on track with my concerns? How could I prevail her to defer to my sorrows, and the sinister significance of what I'd unearthed in my mother's emails with her boss?

—I guess not, I shrugged. —But it doesn't make any difference now. It's all behind us.

—But it's still going, Sofia hissed.

—It doesn't have to. Listen, it's okay. You don't have to lie. You can trust me. There's other stuff that's more important.

—The only person I ever thought I could trust treated me like shit. He double-crossed me, denounced me, laughed in the face of our love.

—You're talking about your husband?

—Who else? He was the only one I told my real age to, my real background. And he accepted me. Or he led on that he did. If I ever met someone better at treachery than myself . . .

Sofia was on the verge of tears.

—Oh, Jacob, I loved him. I gave him everything. He was so full of life. Pure aura. Almost throbbing with power. He'd been victimized too. His upbringing had been bullshit. Nothing he wanted was acknowledged, nothing that was of value to him meant anything to his family. He was so bright, he had a future, and literally within a month of meeting him, we were engaged. And married a month after that. I know you probably think it's absurd, but it was more profound than anything I'd ever known. It was true love. We were soulmates. I was . . . scared . . .

She choked. Sofia put her hand to her forehead.

—He was so . . . authoritative . . . So persuasive and robust and inspired. It activated something in anyone who came near him. It activated . . . me! And I was afraid . . . I was so afraid if . . . that if I didn't say yes . . . if I didn't go ahead and marry him, he'd move on to someone more interesting, and I'd lose him forever. I knew it was stupid, outrageous. I never even told my parents. They still don't know I'm married. But he knew my truth. He knew I was nothing, and he made me feel so loved, so seen . . . If he picked up and left, my whole world would disappear with him . . . And I guess he . . . he could sense it . . . I guess he took advantage of that.

—But with me, even when you admitted you were married, you acted like it was trivial.

I was sweltering. People were getting off their summer Friday half-days and trickling into the bar. Ambient sounds gathered, and the dull draft of the A/C couldn't keep up. Abstractedly, I reached into Sofia's purse and cracked another shooter into my cup of melting ice.

—Or at least, I continued. —You didn't seem head over heels.

—Well that's the thing. As soon as we'd, like, tied the knot, everything changed. First he got really depressed and withdrawn. He was constantly agitated, like guilt weighed on him. He said he'd done something crazy, and he might go to jail. I asked what he meant, but he wouldn't confess. Then he started complaining that he was having a hard time at work, and he needed to stay there late every night. And then he was coming home so fucked up and claiming it was just alcohol, but I knew better. I knew junkies from where I grew up. Plus I could smell the other girl on him. And I called him out on it. I said I knew all the tricks of lying, and I knew when he was, and after all the honesty and rapport and intimacy we'd shared, he could be real with me, and we could figure it out. He just denied it. This happened over and over. And then he got violent. He would, like, throw stuff around the apartment. He would tackle me and put his hands on my throat, and I would black out. And . . . and . . . sometimes, like, I'd wake up. And I could *feel* that he'd been . . . inside of me. After throttling me unconscious . . . he would . . . It was disgusting . . . It was *humiliating* . . . I hated myself, and I hated him. I don't know who I hated more. But I had no one to turn to. The only positive thing in my life was my job. And Martha . . . She seemed to earnestly like me . . . She, like, held me in esteem. She was so impressed I'd gone to Swarthmore, and . . . it was a *good* job . . .

Sofia broke off.

—That's crazy, I said, not knowing what to say. —I hate working.

—See? You are privileged.

—Well, there's two schools of thought on that, I started, then, noting the look on her face, thought better. —But . . . I mean, if she liked you so much, why couldn't you turn to . . . your boss?

My agent looked at me. She dabbed the corner of her eyes with a napkin. Her lips curled.

—Because then I came across your manuscript. And . . . I don't know. I liked it. I believed it. I believed *you*. It was a welcome distraction from my life at home. I hated going home. I just wanted to be at the office all the time. And then we met for coffee, and what can I say? I really fell for you. I know I was in love with my husband, but I also hated him, and you seemed so safe in comparison . . . I recognized you had problems. God, I'd read your self-punishing autofiction more times than probably anyone. And I loved you too. I fell in love with you on the page, and . . . Finally, that night, I thought he was going to kill me. He had a . . . hammer . . . He was swinging it around, smashing things, saying his life wasn't fair, how he'd been destined for greatness and it had been taken from him and it wasn't his fault and he didn't deserve it . . . Somehow I managed to escape. And I fled . . . I remember running down the street, people gawking as I passed, and then I was getting on the subway, and I just rode to the end of the line. Without a plan, without thinking . . . and . . . it was like a revelation. It was fate. The way I ended up . . . Like I was drawn to you . . . I realized I was already in your neighborhood . . . on your street . . . And . . . and you know the rest . . . And when I left you . . . all those months later. On our birthday, remember? You were turning twenty-seven, I was turning twenty-two . . . It was because . . .

She was staring far away into the table now.

—I got a text that he was in the ICU. In a coma. Apparently he'd tried to kill himself.

Sofia was shivering, rocking in her chair, very distraught, overwrought, and her face had grown puffy and red. People were giving us cursory, concerned looks from the side. I put my hand on the back of my agent's suit jacket. It was soaked through with perspiration.

—I'm so sorry, Sofia, I said. —I didn't know . . . But I know other things now . . . I know . . .

—No one knew, she straightened her shoulders and pushed my hand off. —I had to suffer that alone. And I made it through. I kept my job. You thought you were the one going through hell, but you lived in your own little world. I never let on about my troubles.

I kind of couldn't believe it. If I'd been aware at the time . . . But the thought ended. I don't know what I would've done. And my struggle, my urgent discovery, my own hauntings suddenly felt trite and diminished next to Sofia's hardship. I exhaled.

—You're telling me *this* is the guy you're trying to reconcile with? Sofia, he sounds . . .

—Don't judge me, she sobbed. —You don't understand.

Yet again, she was correct. And I didn't have anything else to say on the matter, except:

—I'm sorry.

—It's okay, she said. —It's not your life. It's really not your concern. It's been . . . years. And you're my client, remember? I work for you. I'm not your responsibility. You've got your own wife, your own family . . .

And it all came roaring back. Life was too long, too abstruse and vague. By the time you got through one dilemma, you were shouldered with manifold more. I'd never catch up with the enigmas and questions and misfortunes and qualms. There would be no catharsis. No relief.

Sofia shook her hair, and I looked up. She was dazzling and steady and genial again.

—So, I said. —I'm assuming the, uh, Gatsby essay . . . that wasn't ever going to happen.

—Don't be silly. I wouldn't have called you all the way into the city for . . . I just needed to get that shit off my chest if we're seriously going to restore a business relationship. It isn't going to be easy. But it's worth it. I feel so much more at ease now that we're on the same page.

Sofia looked at her phone.

—Do you want to go to the beach?

I don't know why I agreed. I couldn't remember the last time I'd had a decent night's sleep, and Sofia's admissions had wrung the last vestiges of zeal from me. Ego sap all dried up.

My agent settled the bill, leaning over and flirting with the hoary barkeep. He had a wart about the size of a baby's nose on the end of his, and he scratched it, adoring her, bowled over by her coquettish adulation, as so many before him had been.

Then she skipped to the door, skirt aquiver, and arrested me with a smitten, full-body embrace. I held her for maybe a second longer than I intended. But there seemed to be no harm in it. After what she'd laid out, there was little chance of romancing between us anymore. Things felt professional, or rather, like unaffected accord. I wondered how I'd explain it to Emma.

And again, it slammed into me. My heart beat in my gut, disbelieving and fearful. Where was my wife now? Would I ever see her again?

—Come on, Sofia tugged my forearm, and I hunched my backpack up higher on my shoulders. —We've got to stop by the office so I can grab my car keys.

—But which beach are we going to?

—Our beach, she cooed. —Where it all started. Coney Island. I want to watch the sun set from the boardwalk with you.

—But aren't you tired, I asked. —I'm exhausted. Can't we just hang out some other time? In Long Island? If we're not even going to talk about my writing . . .

She seemed confused.

—That's exactly *what* we're going to do. You're not deserting me now. Right after I bared my soul to you? We need some levity, baby. We need to get back to work.

I sighed and nodded. Sofia laughed, and she dragged me through the East Village to the A. Martha Philips, Ltd. office.

At the buzzer, she punched in a key code. She elbowed the door open and let it fall back on its weight. I held it.

—Can I come up?

—Sure, why not?

It was hot in the elevator, as Sofia had alluded. It seemed like the A/C in the entire building had surrendered, and I was drunk and frazzled, depleted, melancholic, and it was eerily hushed on that Friday afternoon, when most New Yorkers were wallowing in parks or at the riverside, packing rental cars for getaways to the Catskills, or their duffels for the LIRR.

—You know, I said. —I don't think I've ever actually been in the agency office. You and I always met . . . elsewhere.

—Then you're in for a treat, my agent said sarcastically.

The door to the suite was unlocked, and Sofia slipped in, lost to view, and started knocking stuff around.

—Okay, she called from a closet. —So give me a better sense of this Gatsby slant!

I shuffled my shoes on the commercial grade carpet. The office lacked artwork. Piles of manuscript paper, newsprint, and books lined the floors.

—Well like . . . I've been thinking of it as a foil to our current political climate. You've got Tom as this white supremacist defender of society. Essentially he's alt-right. At one point Nick describes him as *flushed with impassioned gibberish, standing alone on the last barrier of civilization* . . .

—Do you want another drink?

—I don't know, I said.

—I've got your *favorite*! Botanist!

Sofia's hand shot out from the closet and swayed the bottle back and forth.

—Let me fix you a quick dry martini.

—Whatever. So Tom is like, he's ready to pounce on any excuse to fear the unknown. He's convinced of imminent apocalypse. Like he's read somewhere that the sun is getting hotter and the earth's going to fall into it. And then a second later he's like, *wait, it's the opposite, the sun's getting colder.* And when he has his freak-out about interracial marriage, Jordan Baker is like, *We're all white here*, and everyone ignores her, and I think that's a big tip-off that Gatsby, who's been tacitly misrepresenting himself as German, is actually something more menacing . . .

A framed photo on a desk caught my eye. And I sauntered over to look at it, but before I could, Sofia poked me in the rib.

—Hey, I said.

—Drink up!

She handed me a room-temperature glass of clear liquor. I sniffed it, too remote to care if it were mixed correctly, too jaded to guess at what Sofia surely had in mind. After all my years of distrusting her, after all she'd disclosed, didn't I owe her the benefit of the doubt? I took a sip.

—Wait!

The agent reached into the closet, and I cowered, shielding my gaze with my arm, but still looking, I couldn't force my eyes away. Sofia's fingers seemed to be digging around, slashing for something in that black vault. And then two emerged, pinching a single green olive.

—The cherry on top!

She dropped it into my glass, and the gin swallowed it without a sound.

—Thanks, I said. —Now where was I? I think I told you about how the book is full of obsessive references to noses. At one point, Gatsby and Nick are driving into the city, and it's *rising up in white heaps all built with a wish out of non-olfactory money*. Like, New York's grandeur as unrelated to its scent, its source, the origin of that capital, which we're expected to understand as fundamentally vile. But there's another way of reading it. Where the city's prosperity, basically the glory of America itself, is specifically in contrast with the tragic nose. And then a few pages later, they're talking about his Jewish mentor Wolfsheim and how *he just saw the opportunity* to get ahead by deceptive means, but that's the only way he *could* compete with the old guard. A lot of those newly rich people were bootleggers because they couldn't go about stuff through legitimate, respectable channels. It's like how the only way for Jews to earn a living in medieval Europe was to become usurers, because moneylending was against Christian doctrine, but it was still in demand, and then we were scapegoated for doing what we had to to survive, and the entire identity of the Jew gets ensnared in deception, just like

Gatsby's, and when he's found dead, chapter eight ends: *the holocaust was complete*, and I know that's not pertinent to, like, the *actual* Holocaust, but I've always thought it was uncannily prophetic, and that *obscene word* scrawled on Gatsby's *white* steps, I have to imagine was some kind of antisemitic . . .

I realized Sofia wasn't listening. She was typing on her phone.

I drank my drink and chewed my olive. I looked around. It was an office. This was where my career had been built up and laid to waste. Blank walls. Arcanum. Namelessness. Then something shimmered in the corner of my eye, and I turned grimly, panting.

There on the wall above the door to the closet hung a gold MY OFFICE plaque.

My eyes bulged, and I took a step back, losing balance. I nearly dropped my glass. I held it in two hands, tipped it up to my lips, but it was already empty.

—Where the fuck did you get that, I whispered.

—What?

I pointed, and Sofia made a face. Then she looked where I was indicating.

—Oh god. Do you want one? We used to give them away. I have more than I know what to do with.

—Don't you remember? I . . . I used to have one . . . in my apartment? In Coney?

—Now that you mention it . . . not really.

I was getting woozier, almost giddy. And then it was turning to groggy. Like vertigo. Like falling.

—Are you all right, Sofia asked. —Do you need another drink?

—I'm just . . . I . . .

—I'm sorry I don't remember your sign. I've seen more of those nameplates than I need to for a lifetime. Just look . . .

She stepped around the desk and flung open the bottom drawer. A mass of MY OFFICE plaques spilled out, and she rolled her eyes and sneered.

—You look distressed, Jacob, she said from a far way off. —You seem fatigued. Do you want to sit down?

My vision was cutting out, blurring dim at the corners. My stomach turned, and I tried to yawn, but I couldn't complete the maneuver, my jaw just dangled, and my head felt very heavy, and I clenched the edge of the desk.

—Are you ready for the beach, Sofia said.

The words sounded as though they were immersed in water. I was bobbing, flickering, sinking, coiling down through a wriggly void.

I readjusted my feet, but they were toppling under each other, under me, and before I lost consciousness I looked pleadingly to my agent. She was beaming.

I gaped at the nameplate behind me, the mountain of plaques at my feet, and all at once, all together, they winked.

# BEACHED

I came to under the crashing swell of breakers, seeing stars below an all black screen of night. The ground was giving beneath me. I tried to hold on, but it kept collapsing, twisting out of my grasp.

After several desperate seconds, I comprehended that I was sprawled across sand. I sat up. My vision fuzzed and pulsed to sharpness, yet all it could detect was the dark, and it fogged away again.

My forehead hurt. My brow felt strange. Something was weighing on my head. I pawed at my skull and came away with a handful of bucket hat. The letter H mutely nodded back. My mouth filled with salt water. I bent and retched. My back spasmed. A ropy cord of mucus writhed from my lips.

—Sofia, I called.

Just the sound of waves cresting and surging, gushing over each other. A peal of thunder in the distance.

—Emma?

Clouds moved, and a shred of moon, almost gone, flashed overhead. My hands gnarled damp canvas. I groaned, threw the hat to the strand.

—What's wrong, a wicked voice chimed from the gloom.
—You don't like it anymore?

—Alice?

—Don't call her that, Sofia warned, slithering out of the murk.

She loomed over my spread-eagle slump.

—Only Martha's dearest friends use her Christian name.

I scrambled for my backpack. It was down the beach, ruptured open, dirty clothes and pulpy pages scattered about. I tried to stand, but my legs were jelly, and I fell back on my ass.

—Alice, I repeated.

I searched for Sofia. Her body was skimming about.

—What did you do to me?

—I, she paused. —I was just . . .

—My daughter-in-law, the ancient hag glissaded into frame. —Was only abiding my instructions.

The world spun, and then everything clicked into place.

—What did you do, I screamed. —Where am I? Am I poisoned? Am I going to die? Someone help! Please! Help me!

A streak of lightning flashed, illuming the turbulent ocean and its vehement oncoming tide, blotting out the faint stars from the sky.

—Calm down, Alice clucked. —It was only Rohypnol. You're perfectly fine. You're in East Hampton. Just past Heller Lane. No one can hear you. No one is coming to your aid. And yes, you are going to die.

I may have passed out. Thunder boomed me back to life. Lightning struck in a skeletal zigzag. A shingle-sided windmill lit up, chopping madly. Great raindrops began to patter the sand.

—Where's Emma, I cried.

My heart was pounding. My extremities gone numb. I attempted once more to stand and floundered and plunged to the thickening shore.

—She's quite safe, Alice bared yellow teeth. —We look after our own in this community.

—What did you do with her? Why are you doing this?

The rain intensified to a spray.

—Do with her? I expect your wife is snug in bed. I just saw her parents at Dr. Masterson's funeral, and they didn't seem the least bit concerned.

—She wasn't at the apartment. Someone took all her stuff, and . . . and . . .

—Lovely service. It's really too bad you couldn't be there. Sergeant Lenihan asked after you. As did Powell and Winston.

—You killed him, I wailed. —You killed Masterson! You kidnapped and murdered my parents!

—Don't be silly, Alice snickered. —How could a dainty woman like myself do something like that?

—I know everything! I saw your emails with my mother! I know who you are! I know who your son is! You won't get away with it!

—I'm sure I don't know what you're talking about.

—Sofia, I called.

Through the sheet of rain, I saw my agent crouched trembling with her head in her hands.

—Sofia! It all makes sense now! When Philip said he'd done something crazy that might put him in jail, it was the instruments at the Met, wasn't it? He'd smashed them with his hammer!

—Naturally the boy was upset, the crone answered. —He'd been begging for money to move to Europe, and he was in absolutely no shape. He'd barely gotten out of rehab and had already latched on to my latest hire, my loyal confidante apprentice, and that seemed like enough excitement. I told him no, simple as. He'd have to prove himself. So he went off and cracked up the museum collection. I had a hell of a time getting that settled with the board of directors.

—He killed Lauren Smith!

—Ah, well that was another story. She was fouling things up terribly at the agency. Sofia could hardly focus on her work. I gave my opinion that he break things off with his mistress. Of course, Philip had a penchant for taking things a tad too far . . .

—He raped Sofia!

—Ridiculous. He could do nothing of the sort. She's legally his, they're man and wife.

—Goddamn it! You'll pay for this! Where are my parents? Why are you protecting him? He's a violent, perverted killer!

—He's my child, Alice said.

She towered over me, barefoot. She was wearing a white-on-white seersucker robe and a sun hat with a subtle Prada logo in the corner. The rain kept rushing down.

—He should be put away, I hollered. —He should be locked up! He's not fit for society!

—Philip had a hard time of it. I won't disagree with you on that. His father. His *biological* father, that is, wasn't there for him. It would've made all the difference. That smarmy slick Semite with an ideology all his own . . . He lived in Cuba for a spell, wrote a couple tight postmodernish dramas, played bass in a jazz trio, but mostly he was good with his hands. Oh yes.

—Alice, I howled.

—You have to understand, I'd been alone a long time. I'd watched my sisters go off and get married. I'd lived with my parents in that big house on Heller until they expired. I was labeled a spinster. An old maid. I attracted no one's fancy. It was assumed I'd shrivel up and drown in the bracken. And then I met Lucien Springer. Out here on vacation. Strolling along Two

Mile Hollow. He swept me off my feet. For the first time in my life, I experienced rapture. True euphoria. After that summer, I'd go out to his apartment on Perry Street and we'd play house for days on end . . .

She tittered.

—I was fifty-three. There was no reason for precaution. Never in my wildest dreams did I believe I'd bear offspring. Philip was our little miracle. The Isaac to my Sarah. I'd do anything for him. And Lucien loved him. He gave him his name and promptly had a massive coronary.

—But why . . .

—I'm getting to it, Alice hemmed, shooing me away. —You said you know, but you don't. Not everything.

My limbs were still useless. Between the shock and the sedative, I was half-paralyzed. Lightning moved over the water. Simultaneously, thunder pummeled the atmosphere.

—Help, I moaned.

—Yes, yes, the witch laughed. —Help is on the way. If only someone had bothered to help my Philip. I couldn't do it all on my own. And yet Lucien had changed me. Forthwith, I meant something different to men. Even in my middle years, I'd glowed with child. I'd earned deference. And Donald Philips had been paying heed. He was Lucien's friend, his onetime editor. In the golden age of publishing, when you were toddling around a public kindergarten, Donald's empire was just taking wing. I could tell he'd noticed me even before his dear confrere passed on. Shrewd squeezes. Footsie under the table. Philip's father and I never had a chance to be wed. It had all happened too fast, and he wasn't divorced yet besides. When he died, who was there for me? Donald. Who made me an honest woman, set me up with a business to support myself, piped in an assemblage of accomplished clientele? Who forged my influence and independence? It was Donald. Together we turned A. Martha Philips, Limited into one of the most prestigious and sought-after agencies in the literary world.

—Sofia, I cried. —*This* is your mother-in-law? Your precious Martha? You drugged and abducted me all the way out here for *her*?

—I . . .

—She's got no one else, Alice cut my agent off. —She *needs* me. I plucked that silly green girl out of obscurity and made her into a proficient, professional lady of the industry. Do you know who she represents?

—I don't care! She betrayed me! She delivered me to be murdered by . . . by the bloodthirsty mother of a lunatic!

—Philip wasn't always that way, the beldam brooded. —He was . . . well, probably to one end of the spectrum . . . A little like your mother described you. He wouldn't sleep through the night as an infant. He didn't sleep well at all. He indubitably could tell the difference between Lucien and Donald, though Donald doted on his stepson. He encouraged the child, gave him every opportunity and advantage. I suppose he grew disappointed when Philip wasn't the verbal virtuoso he'd envisioned. The boy preferred tinkering with LEGOs and clanging on xylophones. Philip just wanted his stepfather's approval, but after a while, they both recognized the divide. They were not one bit the same. And so Donald pulled back. He still lavished the boy with allowances, but specifically catered to a classic scholasticism. He wanted my son to be someone he wasn't. Philip's intelligence was aberrant to Donald's conception of worth. And as his affection for the child waned, as may be expected, Philip began acting out. First it was innocent transgressions. Tracking dirt across the carpet, breaking delicate antiques. Donald scolded him. Gave him a few decent, firm smacks. And as my son put it together that ill behavior translated to attention, he upped the ante. He started capturing and torturing small animals in the park. He picked on girls in the playground. Children years younger. He'd pin them down and steal their intimates right out from their jumpers. Oh, when Donald found the cache under his bed. Philip shrieking with fright, Donald wrapping the belt around his knuckles for a better grip.

—I get it, I yelled. —He had a tough upbringing. I've heard all about it. It doesn't change what he's done.

—But doesn't it? By the time he was a preadolescent, it was clear something was wrong. He'd developed dyslexia, ADHD, he'd raise hell in class, interrupt and sass his teachers, throw punches in the locker room. We had to change schools several times before I found a place for him at Livingston Prep. Fortunately, I knew Gladys Masterson. She vouched for my child. They gave him a chance. But now they were telling me instead of petty outbursts, he was increasingly indulging in alcohol and narcotics. Well, it took me some time to come around to that. Donald wanted to put him in boarding school or a military academy. But I was afraid . . . I was afraid it would only make things worse. He had his fair share of trouble, but we also got him a counselor, helped set him up with the music club. He was enrolled in furniture-building and woodworking extracurriculars. He wanted to move to Vienna to train as a luthier, specializing in violins, and for a while it seemed like a veritable prospect. Until that mother of yours came along.

—My mother, I bawled. —Is a kind, compassionate woman. Your son preyed on her goodwill! And I know you were in touch with her right up to my parents' disappearance! You emailed her two days before they vanished. You said you needed to talk with them face-to-face. You took them hostage! Why did you do it? What have you done?

—As I said before, I don't quite follow your line of reasoning. If they're being held hostage, what's the ransom? And how exactly could a puny octogenarian fuddy-duddy carry off two full-grown adults twenty years her junior? Of course the police read this so-called nefarious email as well. They contacted me, and I explained I'd caught cold and never had a chance to follow through on our rendezvous. That satisfied them.

—You're sick, I mashed my fists in my eyes. —I don't know how you did it. All I know is you did!

—Perhaps they merely got what was coming to them.

—I don't understand, I cried.

—Your parents had my child expelled from the only reputable institution that ever accepted him. The only place left that could've helped get him anywhere.

—Dr. Masterson expelled him! My mother tried to keep him from getting in trouble!

—Preposterous, Alice hissed. —If she'd just opened her legs none of this would have happened. If she'd just borne her responsibility. If your father hadn't gotten him drunk . . .

—My dad needs to be liked!

—If they hadn't traveled all the way to New York and told their story, Donald and I could've attended to the nastiness ourselves. We could've run damage control and got it sorted out. But once it was on record. Once that hussy Sybil Parker knew, Masterson had no choice.

—You can't possibly think it's my parents' fault that . . .

—No, no. Nothing is so simple as to lay the blame on them alone. Masterson's doom was many years in the making. I had to maintain a friendly facade for civility's sake. But not a second passed without my plotting revenge. I knew I'd have my chance. After all my years of suffering, I've come to learn patience. It's a quality you'd do well to try. I bided, I waited, and when the favorable circumstances came along to frame a nice little mark, I worked with swift action.

—You did poison him!

—Perchance an oversight on my part. It took some time to convince Sergeant Lenihan how you might've got your hands on tetrodotoxin. But after you left the state when you'd been specifically advised not to. After you missed the inquest and were impossible to get in touch with. After they were tipped off to look into your history of ordering drugs on the dark web . . .

—I haven't done that in ages!

—It's a good thing internet histories are permanent. If you have the right connections, anything can be exhumed.

—But that doesn't explain everything else, I shouted. —When I talk to the detectives. When I tell them what I've discovered!

—Then you understand my position, Alice seethed. —There's no reason I can allow you to live.

The rain streamed down. I was hyperventilating. Trying to piece together all the loose ends. I'd uncovered the truth. I only needed to escape. I needed to tell someone.

My arms and legs felt almost stable. I had to choose my moment carefully. This old biddy couldn't kill me. I just had to get to my backpack. It was folding and rippling under the storm.

—You know it's not my parents' fault, I wept. —They didn't make your son deranged. Your husband beat him . . . He had . . . sociopathic tendencies . . . Everything you've described . . .

—Donald hit the boy, positively. A little corporal punishment never turned anyone mad. My generation took our lumps, and we made out fine. Your mother's despicable selfishness, her vanity, denying Masterson, full well knowing she was sealing my son's annihilation . . . Donald never forgave Philip. He was disgusted. He said there was something wrong at the boy's core. My husband wanted nothing to do with my marvelous offspring any longer. So I was compelled to fix things myself. I got Philip a job at a shop my doctor recommended. I thought it would inspire him. He could walk to work. He could make trinkets with his hands. I told him he could still move to Vienna if he proved he was committed to getting his life in order. I'd even put up the money. I just needed him to show some initiative. But what did he do? He used his wages to procure soporifics. He drowsed off on the job. He thieved from his employer. At that point, Donald said turn him into the police, let them decide what's best, let them prosecute, give him a sense of real consequences. But I couldn't bear the thought of him rotting in a cell. We agreed to enroll him in a rehabilitation facility for a few months.

—And, I said. —Did that make a difference?

—Well, it took some trial and error to find a suitable place. After a couple years he came back clean. At first. And he was very optimistic. I'd hired Sofia in the meantime, and he took an immediate liking to her, as you know. In any case, after his stepfather's mysterious passing . . .

—Mysterious passing, I screeched. —Do you mean he . . . he *killed* your husband?

—Donald was a decade older than myself. You must understand, a sudden shock, a sudden fall. Men can be very feeble in their senescence.

—Jesus Christ. Sofia! Sofia, please! Help me! It doesn't need to be like this! We can still get away from her! We can still get even for all this horror!

My agent sagged in the sand. She wouldn't remove her face from her hands.

—Don't talk to her, Alice snapped. —You don't know her. You don't belong here.

—Emma, I cried.

—Emma's not your wife anymore. My son could not be saved, and neither will you. After Donald departed, after he and Sofia were married, you'd think it would be enough. Philip had everything he'd desired . . . Well, at least more than ever before. Yet the boy was unfulfilled. When you're a manic-depressive, as I'm certain you, Jacob, are aware, every high is attached to an equal and opposite low. And just as often, the lows descend deeper. I think the weight of that crushed him. Yes, he defiled those instruments. That was a pity indeed. And started stepping out on Sofia, which, in a way, stood to reason. She can be a lot to handle. A bit of a bitch sometimes.

—She lied to you too! She went to Farmingdale State! She's five years younger than me!

—Than *I*, Jacob. I. And furthermore, you're mistaken. Sofia is a Swarthmore College alumna. She graduated with highest honors.

—Sofia, I whooped.

My agent did nothing.

—She said she'd love him no matter what. Nevertheless, after he'd sacrificed his stability, potentially his freedom, even after he got rid of his paramour, she forsook him. She was slipping away. She couldn't stomach his vagaries. And I would've come down on her harder, made sweet Sofia mind her obligations by force, until I realized what we had on our hands. It was you. The child of my adversaries! With a lurid dross of a novel to boot! By sheer kismet, I could give your parents a taste of their own medicine and keep my family intact without frivolous distractions. It was all too delicious. We'd set you up! That manuscript made you a glaring patsy already. Damningly impudent, disaffected, self-involved, and just misogynistic enough . . . You'd take the fall for your downstairs neighbor's demise. I clued in the authorities, but they wouldn't play ball. Said there wasn't ample evidence with which to charge you. I told them to keep an eye out. But it wasn't thought through. I hadn't been patient. My design failed, and Philip lost it again. Tried to take that hammer he'd used on the instruments to poor Sofia. And, of course, she ran to you. She jilted my son, just like everyone else. She wasn't very nice to him either. And he was inconsolable, three thousand sheets to the wind, wasting his life pumping opioids into his bloodstream. He'd gone virtually catatonic by the time the police began to suspect him. I don't know why. Forensics maybe. Or I'd gone too far pushing your name. His wife was living with his sworn enemy, and he didn't even know who you were. Wouldn't have recognized you on the street, the state he was in. And then, on the anniversary of his butcherous crime, he stuck fentanyl patches all over his chest, in a frenetic attempt at suicide.

 A lightning bolt lit up Alice's face. There were tears in her eyes. Or was it rain? Thunder followed. I looked to my backpack. It was hardly twenty feet from me. If I could just reach it . . . Would the Ruger still shoot? I'd have to hope the towel had kept it dry enough. I'd have to pray.

 —He was in a coma for three months, Alice said quietly.

She seemed tired. This was my chance. I sprang to the backpack, tore it apart, but the towel had been undone. I riffled through sodden fragments of *Gatsby* paperback. The gun was gone.

—Looking for something, Alice sighed.

I buckled under the downpour.

—As I was saying. I sat at his side every day, every hour, watching his eyes move under near-transparent lids. I wondered what he could be dreaming of. Sofia came too. She proved herself. Together, mother and wife, we tended to Philip. In nursing my boy, his miracle birth washed over me anew. He was my blessing. And if I just held out, if I just waited until things were perfect, I could still have vengeance on his nemeses . . . When he awoke from his stupor, it was not a joyous occasion. He'd been deprived of oxygen during the overdose. My Philip had suffered an anoxic brain injury. He spent the following year relearning to walk. He spent the year after that brushing up on hand-eye coordination. Basic motor function, simple typing, holding a pencil, proved markedly arduous. He'd sustained severe damage. He never regained verbal acuity. He was subjected to a dire state. The only thing he could enjoy was listening to music. And he would never, never be a luthier . . . And then, in the midst of all this, I had to find out that *you*, you of all demons in this sick, cruel universe, had taken up with Michael and Jane's precious daughter. It was too much! The girl I'd bounced on my knee. The young playmate of my scion. Before all his quandaries, Jane and I had quipped about Philip and Emma being one day united. And still, I had to be patient. I developed a plan. But before I could act, the pandemic came along and disrupted everything! I'm an at-risk individual, and you can imagine, with my son's condition . . . He couldn't rightly breathe. We had to take every precaution. So my reprisal was delayed yet again. And all the while, watching my baby deteriorate before my eyes. Working with his unfaithful, thankless, shifty wife. I just hoped Emma would see you for who you were, concede that you weren't quality, didn't belong in her orbit. I reached out to your mother, begged her to discourage the relationship. I vied to get her to look at things from my perspective, accept her culpability, her central role in prostrating my son, my sociality, myself. But she shrugged me off again and again. And then, much worse, I caught wind of the engagement. Your plan to *marry* Emmeline. And there I was, still condemned to quarantine. All my prior plans thwarted. I resolved once and for all to find a way to bring down your heinous lot in one fell swoop. Your parents had set all my anguish in motion. They'd ripped me from my child. They'd stolen our future, razed and ravaged my household. If I couldn't take you from them, then I'd take them from you! And after your little espousal, that's exactly what I did. And I only had to practice a hair more forbearance. I knew with Michael's seventieth on the horizon, you'd be making it to my neck of the woods in due course. With COVID cooling, I was able to solidify the operation. I even met you on the ferry to make sure. And now the time has arrived. At long last I'll be rid of you too!

The rain came down in blind torrents. My hands were in my backpack, still pawing helplessly for the gun.

—No wonder my novel didn't sell, I muttered.

—What's that?

—It wasn't fair with *you* as my agent. Despite the editors' praise. Now it all makes sense!

—Your manuscript served a purpose, Alice smirked.
—Though it actually wasn't all bad.

—You read it?

—Well not the whole thing.

—You tried to sabotage me!

—I hate to break it to you, but no one wanted it anyway. Your novel was unmarketable!

I rose to my feet and stared daggers at Alice.

—Where's my wife?

—As I said, at home in bed, I presume. It's nigh five in the morning.

I shook my head, advancing.

—Where are my parents?

—They're subterranean, of course. Dig all you want. You won't find a trace.

—What did you *do* to them?

—Why are you so obsessed with every tiny minutiae?

—That's the job of a fiction writer. To cull narrative from the entropy of existence. I need every detail.

—You can't really believe that, can you? Writers are as contrived as the diddlings they produce. People like me create them. I'm an arbiter of fate.

—But . . . but you said it yourself. How could you have coerced my parents to go *anywhere* with you? How could you possibly have held them hostage? Or transported, or killed them? You're so . . . decrepit. So elderly and weak.

—Let's just say I had some help . . .

Lightning struck in three directions. For an instant, it was pure radiance. And I saw all: the boiling sea, the driving precipitation, bits of hail mixed into the shower, Alice's gaunt physique, Sofia's groveling shame, and the shadowy figure, its contours sifting out of the mist and opacity, through the blazing witching hour, drawing nearer, lurching, and slavering.

—*Philip*, Alice sang.

I recognized him from the Livingston Prep yearbook pictures. But something was wrong. His eyes cocked in different directions. His respiration wheezed and sputtered. His mouth flapped half-open, a rivulet of drool threshed from his chin. He was angry-looking, blond. His hair caught in pluvial knots. He was wearing a suit, which seemed somewhat farcical and made him look young, like a kid warily dressed up for church.

He gnashed his teeth. His throat chattered, and he was throwing back his head, laughing, wrenching his neck around at the black, bitter ocean, the dark messes of beach, and each of us.

And that's when I realized where I'd seen him. All those years ago, on my rueful twenty-sixth birthnight. He'd been riding the train and I'd sat down across from him. He'd been frenzied, demented. I'd told him to chill, and he'd apologized. He'd said he was almost done. Before Lauren Smith's murder. Was that what he'd been almost done with?

This was Philip Springer. This was where we finally collided. Our moment of reckoning. And he was wielding Emma's father's double-action revolver. He was pointing it directly at me.

The boy, no longer a boy, seemed to be trying to say something. He hobbled around, gasping, swinging the Ruger haphazardly. His speech garbled, and he kept repeating the same muddled staticky notes.

It sounded like, *Meyer is, Meyer is* . . .

And he staggered closer yet, approaching at a pace of excruciating indolence.

Then I thought he was saying, *My office, my office* . . .

—It's . . . not me, I jabbered. —I'm not the one . . . responsible for your . . . suffering . . .

But Springer only careened forward. His carriage brutal, though stabilizing, his hand taking aim. And all of a sudden I understood what he was saying:

—Bye, Garlic . . .

Everything happened very quickly.

Sofia shot up.

—Philip, she shouted. —Don't!

She ran to him, but he sharply lifted the revolver and butted her to the sand. Blood trickled from a gash in my agent's forehead.

—*Good*, Alice fumed.

—No, I bayed, bolting up.

I clawed for her wrist, but old Alice swiveled, weaved away, and huddled behind her progeny.

A fulmination blasted, and in the brief eruption of light, I watched them, mother and son, bound together, harpy gandering over the gun-toting, amental Springer's shoulder, the pair cackling as one.

We were less than six feet apart. Then the rain ceased, and everything was eclipsed in umbrage. I could barely make out the rise and flex of Springer's arm. The balance of the barrel. The tautness of his strain. The whistle from his constricted breathing. His hanging jaw. Suspended violence. There wasn't space for life to flash before my eyes.

At the flame of the projectile, I heard a percussive bang, and was on the ground, rolling, dying, feeling for wounds, repentant for everything, forgiving us all, and gone, losing sensation.

When I opened my eyes, dawn was just creeping along the horizon's edge. No more than a few seconds could've elapsed, but the tenets of time held no meaning.

I felt no pain. And frantically, I reeled, inspecting my body for lacerations. After the din of gales and cloudburst, the scene had grown icily quiet. I arose, still patting myself, confused and unnerved. Some yards away pitched a pile of limbs, twitching, lapsing in throes.

Sofia kneeled in the wet sand. Thunder crashed from far off. Steam drifted sideways, and my agent was drenched, brow smeared with clotting claret, blouse torn and clinging to her ribs and areolae like a second skin.

And soon I heard her whimpers. She was crying softly, keening. She cradled Springer's head against her breast.

Gore spewed from his eye and jugular, where the shrapnel had penetrated and lodged. The molten remnants of the double-action revolver had exploded across his festering palm. Blood sluicing and spouting amid riven flesh, clumps of ruined tissue, outflow swollen, brown-red. His skin waxen and jaundiced and bloated. The grume collecting in Sofia's lap.

She ejected a deafening ululation. I reached for her shoulder. She recoiled and squirmed.

—Sofia, I said.

—Go, she yowled. —Just go! No one knows you're here! Let me deal with the police! Let me deal with . . .

She trailed off.

—I don't want you to get in trouble.

—Then leave! No one needs to know the rest. I can make up an explanation . . . I can take care of things. It's not your problem. He's my husband. It's my . . .

She hiccupped.

—Family.

—But . . .

But where was her mother-in-law? I thrashed in a circle, searching, scanning the beach. The old lady wasn't there. She'd evanesced. I abraded my temples. I squinted at the coast.

—Oh god, I called. —Alice!

I stepped to the churning, furious shoreline. The tempest had abated, but the swell was out of control. Waves broke from every vantage. No division between them, just whipping, flailing, flooding over my ankles, the riptide pulling from a distance of only a few inches out.

And beyond, I could see the harridan's white tresses spindling in the surf. She went over, under, over, flung sidelong into and across the raging waters. I could almost make out the anthem of her bones bending and twanging, resounding, wasted, withered, and snapping in the spume, rent asunder, cleaved and severed, just like music, into dreams, and out to sea.

I stood there until her body was gone. The combers were lashing, then calming. The morning star crawling out under the earth.

Sofia gaped at her phone. Her fingers hovered over buttons. Philip Springer had taken his last halting, strangled breath. His brainpan lay on her skirt like a moldering piece of fruit. I sidled over, put out my hand, moved it away. I opened my mouth, but I had nothing.

Sofia was making faint futile puling noises, and I left her there, seizing with lamentation.

As I stumbled over the dunes, through the sandplain and rockrose, to the asphalt and turned onto Further Lane, a family of deer blocked my path, and I had to stop for a minute and wait. There were three of them. A doe and two fawns, and they were not in a hurry. They rustled into the rhododendron and honeysuckle and poison ivy, covered in ticks.

I made my way to my in-laws' cottage. My clothes misshapen, wrinkled and blemished with oceanwater and sweat. My father-in-law's Top-Siders squelching with each step along the two-lane highway, alien returning again.

The sky gleamed pink and orange. Tufts of smoke mingled with fish market aromas. Michael and Jane's American flag swayed in the humid breeze, and as I limped into the driveway, I picked up the *New York Times*, glancing at the neighbor's house. Its wrought iron ornaments, its vacant secretive yawp. Then Turmeric slunk from a hole in the fence and galloped over on lissome paws.

—Oh my word, I crooned. —What've you been up to, m'sweet?

My cat unhinged her jowls and let out a forlorn mew. I grabbed and held them open. She was missing a second front tooth.

—Yellow, where's your fang? Have you been getting into trouble?

She made a sound like *prrrrrip!* and I ruffled her head. She darted off. I swung open the gate, latched it behind me, and ambled over the patio and through the sliding glass door.

There was no coffee in the Moccamaster. I dropped the paper on the kitchen table. The neon glare of the stove's digital timepiece said, *5:47.*

Everyone must have been asleep. But then I heard something. Like gagging and heaving. A toilet flushed. The spurt of water from a faucet.

The door creaked, and Houdini trotted out, tail wagging hesitantly, tongue lolling from the side of his mouth.

—Hey buddy.

I crouched, extending my hand. He sniffed it and turned around. Emma was leaning against the bathroom doorframe, wearing baggy linen pants and a hoodie that said *arf*, her arms folded.

—Hi, I said, standing up.

—Well look what the cat dragged in.

—You know Turmeric isn't allowed inside. Your mom's allergic. Have you seen her by the way? She lost another fang.

—Where have you been, Jacob?

—How about a hug?

I moved toward her, and my wife balked, almost flinched at my touch. But as I wrapped her in my arms, I felt her muscles loosen and relax. She nestled into my caress. We held each other. I kissed her neck. I smelled her, breathing in the love of my life, getting hot behind the eyes. Then Emma pushed me away.

—What the hell has been going on?

—It's kind of a long story.

—You missed our date.

—Yeah, I said. —Was that last night?

—Two nights ago.

I grinned.

—Do you maybe want to go outside? I think a discussion of this caliber deserves some . . . discretion . . .

I slid open the door. We sat down. I drummed my fingers across the hammered glass table. Emma raised her eyebrows.

—Okay, I said. —On my twenty-sixth birthday . . .

By the time I'd recounted my tale, the sun was high above the trees. Songbirds flitted. Orioles and tanagers, migrating farther north as the planet grew hotter, and Emma was squeezing my hand.

—And then I found Turmeric, and then I left the newspaper in the kitchen, and then I heard the toilet flush, and . . .

She let it go.

—I bet you'd like some coffee, my wife said.

—You'd win that bet.

We filed in. The click of Houdini's claws punctuating the delicate lull in the wake of my narration. The house was peaceful. It scarcely grieved under the hum of appliances at rest.

Emma spilled water in the coffee maker's reservoir, scooped whopping spoonfuls into a filter. The Moccamaster coughed to life, and the elixir brewed in drips.

—So where are your parents?

—I don't know, I itched my nose. —Where are yours?

—They must still be sleeping, Emma answered. —We had kind of a big day yesterday.

—Oh yeah? Masterson's funeral live up to the hype?

My wife giggled.

—Unfortunately, I had to miss that. I was hunched over the toilet all morning, and in the afternoon my mother took me to Dr. Schwartz's.

—That guy's a genius, I said. —You're still not felling well, my love?

—I haven't been feeling well all week.

—I'm so sorry. I'm sorry I wasn't there for you.

—It was weird . . . I didn't have any other symptoms. I'd feel fine, and then all at once I'd have to run to the bathroom. I spent my lunch break rushing home for some privacy, then rushing back. I couldn't even get through a glass of wine with Dan. After my third day of this, the museum told me to take the rest of the week off. They didn't want the whole staff infected. So I got a train and came back here. I was puking the entire trip.

—So that's why the toilet seat was up.

—What?

—Forget it.

—I tried to text you, Emma said. —After I got here Wednesday night. But it wouldn't send.

—My phone died. I ran it under the sink at your dad's birthday.

—Why?

—My ear hurt . . . I was feeling eccentric.

I shrugged. Emma looked away. The coffee finished percolating, and she poured me a cup. My stomach growled. It tasted golden. I closed my eyes and basked in it. I opened them.

—Baby, I murmured. —Aren't you having any tea?

My wife shook her head and smiled.

—I'm not supposed to have caffeine.

I met her eyes. I looked askance.

—Like I said, she simpered coyly. —Yesterday was kind of . . . well, let's call it a watershed moment.

—What are you trying to tell me?

But I already knew.

—I'm pregnant, Emma beamed.

—But . . . from last week? I don't think that's biologically possible.

—Six weeks ago, my wife slipped into her Cockney accent. —When we lattermost had it off.

—Damn, I said. —You have been eating a lot of candy lately.

—I always eat that much candy!

—Okay, okay, that's not what I meant . . . I'm just . . . Wow. Congratulations. Or, I guess . . . we did this together, huh?

Emma nodded.

—I suppose this calls for a celebration.

I took her in my arms, lips searching fiercely, tongues interlocking, glazing over our pain and devotion. It was interrupted by a splash. Houdini jerked around, panting.

—Janey, Michael rasped from behind the bathroom door.
—Emma? Jacob? Someone help! I fell in the toilet again!

That night we had a seafood cookout. Boiled lobster, steamed clams, oysters on the half-shell, mussels and scallops and corn on the cob. We toasted the future. We laughed at the past. Tears were shed, and promises made. I took a lengthy shower, and when I lay my head on the pillow, next to my glowing, fertile wife, I conked out immediately.

I dreamed of a dank velvet tunnel. Its walls were pliable and warm. They pulsed with luminosity, and I walked through it. I walked through it all, until I was awoken by the vibrations of Emma's phone.

She rolled over, snarled, —Who is it?

I lifted the screen, and a series of Instagram notifications issued forth. Sofia had DMed my wife five times:

*Emma i'm so sorry this is Sofia can you please get in touch with Jacob for me????*

*This is really important!!!!!*

*I tried to call his phone but it's dead and I really need to talk to him*

*Please you or Jacob call me when you have the chance*

The fifth message listed her number.

—What is it, Emma mumbled.

—I'll be right back, I said.

I rubbed the rheum from my eyes and waddled to the patio. I pressed the number my agent had sent. She picked up on the first ring.

—Jacob?

Sofia sounded wired, high-strung, out of breath. I cleared my throat.

—Jacob? Jacob, is that you?

—Hello? What's wrong? I thought you said you'd take care of everything.

—I *did*, Sofia stressed. —But something's happened. Something major. You're never going to believe this!

My stomach turned. I clutched the back of a chaise lounge to keep from keeling to the bricks.

—Sofia, I said. —What's going on?

—I can't tell you over the phone. Please just get over here ASAP. I'm not joking!

—What happened?

—I'm going to text you my address!

She hung up. Seconds later, Emma's phone vibrated, and a number and *Hither Lane* flashed across its screen. My wife strode outside, yawning.

—What's up, she asked.

—It's Sofia, I breathed, sucking in more air than I needed. —She DMed you. She said there's something I need to see. She wouldn't tell me over the phone. I'm going to drive over there. It's only a few minutes away.

—I'm coming with you.

—Emma, I said. —I don't even know what it's about. I don't want you wrapped up in this.

—I don't care. I don't care about that agent of yours or her sob story problems. You're the father of my child, and if you're in trouble, then I'm going to get you out of it. People know me around here. Just let me help.

She had a point. I was nodding automatically. I grabbed my keys from the Baccarat ashtray, still barefoot, clad only in a T-shirt and boxers. Emma slipped into her linen pants. Houdini followed and hopped in the Camry's back seat.

The drive was only four minutes, but we had to pull over twice so my wife could empty her stomach.

The car rattled, accosting a concrete anti-deer grate and skidded shells across the lawn. I parked at an angle, left the keys in the ignition, and fell out of the driver's side door. Sofia was standing at the salt-worn bungalow's entrance, waving hastily.

—What's wrong, I called. —What's going on?

—Come here, she spurred. —Inside! Now! Everyone quick!

I hurtled into the shack, my family swerving behind me, and we stood body-to-body under a vicious ceiling fan swirling over the kitchenette.

—What *is* it?

—Well, Sofia started. —But you're never going to believe me. I didn't *know*. I swear. I really thought Martha was serious about your writing career. I never would've agreed to play along if I'd known all the . . . if I'd known . . . You've got to believe me! Will you believe me?

Houdini grunted.

—Just spit it out, Emma said.

—Am I in trouble, I asked. —How did everything go yesterday? What did you tell the cops?

—Everything's *fine*, my agent attested. —I told them my husband tried to kill me. It's the truth, isn't it? The gun blew up because it was old, jammed, incorrectly loaded, and wet. I told them about Martha's confessions, and that she'd cast herself into the surf. They found her remains last night.

—So what's the problem?

—Just let me finish.

Sofia was breathless.

—All that is fine. You're not in trouble. They don't think you have anything to do with Masterson or anything else. But.

Okay, so when I got home last night . . . God. I didn't know what to do. After all that, all I wanted was to lay down and die. But I started thinking about, like . . . Martha had me move into this house after she bought it last fall . . . and . . . and . . . It's cute, right? But I told you, didn't I? It doesn't even have basement access. Which is weird. Because there's this door that's always locked. Like it doesn't even have a handle. It's just a lock. I didn't know. I asked Martha about it when I moved in, and she said not to be stupid. I tried to fit keys in it sometimes, but nothing worked. It was a false door or something, wiring or electric or . . . I didn't *know*! She said there's just a crawl space. There's no basement. And I'd been so dependent on her . . . I really thought she had my best interests at heart, regardless of everything with Philip . . . But when she said your parents were *subterranean*. I couldn't get it out of my head. When I got home from the police station, I saw that hammer . . . Philip's hammer . . . That he'd smashed the instruments with . . . That he'd threatened my *life* with. Maybe Martha had left it there as a warning. She told me to bring you out to her house. She'd said it was about that indie press fast-tracking your manuscript . . . And the roofie . . . I thought it was all a joke! I get so caught up in my own . . . Anyway, someone had left the hammer out, taunting me. And I . . . last night I had a dream. And when I woke up, I broke the lock off that false door. And when I got it open . . . it led to a flight of *stairs*. And at the bottom of the stairs there was another door. I broke the knob off it too. And . . . and on the other side of the unfinished basement. More stairs . . .

Sofia was sniveling, wiping tears from her bloodshot eyes.

—I went down three flights like that, and then there was still one more door. But this one didn't even have a lock. It was, like, made of steel . . . It didn't have . . . anything . . . but a . . . It looked like a peephole, but from the opposite side, so I couldn't see through . . . I didn't know what to think. I felt insane. There I was, three stories beneath my house. Thirty-some-odd feet under the place I've been living for almost a year. And as I was looking at this peephole, like . . . I thought I could hear movement behind the door . . . I thought I could hear voices . . . And then the light changed . . . It . . . it came out of the glass . . . And I called through the door. I yelled, *is anyone there*, and they said . . . I think they said their name was Garlicker. They said they were being held captive . . .

—Sofia, I said. —Where are the stairs?

She burst into tears and pointed, and I ran, clambering down, down into the nadir, past the bedrock, past the loam, through the dark, clammy silence, wife and dog at my heels, to that final door.

—Mother, I screamed. —Dad? Are you down here? Are you alive? It's me! It's Jacob!

I clobbered the steel.

It didn't budge. It barely echoed. Its hinge held solid.

And then I heard a muted scratching. An ache of hissing metal. I stepped back and looked at the peephole. Light flashed into the lens.

—Mom, I choked.

Tears stung and leaked from my ducts.

—Dad, I bellowed. —Are you in there?

—We're having a hell of a time hearing you, son, my father rejoined. —But if that's really you I'm beholding, maybe you can call a fireman. Your mom's been working on this door for months, and we're getting nowhere . . .

As the sirens whirred into the driveway, and uniformed workers blew past, I sat in the grass in my underwear cupping my chin in my hands.

My wife massaged my shoulders. My dog snuffled my boxers' gusset.

—The first decent shut-eye I've had in a week, I griped. —They could've at least let me sleep in.

Sofia detached herself from an emergency medical technician and squatted next to us.

—Oh my god, a voice came from deep underground.

—Give them air!

—Are you two all right?

—Mr. Garlicker? Mrs. Garlicker?

I shuddered and exhaled.

—Look on the bright side, my agent said. —It ought to make for a pretty good novel.

# IN VIENNA

A hazy, snowless New Year's Day, and I was sweating in my tuxedo, pacing through the lobby of the Wiener Musikverein.

It was our first landlocked vacation, made possible courtesy of the generous folks at the Rotary Club of East Hampton. Their way of saying, we're sorry for approving and upholding the construction of a complex, fully functional confinement chamber buried fathoms below the surface of a Hither Lane bungalow, which had covertly imprisoned your parents for ten long months at the mercy of a madwoman and her sociopathic, drug-addled, brain-damaged son.

Marabelle Minnowitter had led the campaign, and the Vienna Philharmonic was more than happy to lend a few choice box seats on behalf of these subjugated Jews and their family. Now it was almost time for the show, and I was anxious for it to be over. As of a quarter to eleven a.m., I was the only one of our party of six who'd arrived.

I took out my phone. A background of Emma and Houdini and Turmeric flashed in a definition so high it hurt to look. All the ways you were supposed to get it to do stuff were different from my old one. I'd yet to figure out the strokes. I couldn't get my messages app to open, so I shuffled to the bar and ordered a gin on ice. A brand I'd never heard of, called Monkey 47.

—A lot of ice, I said. —*Bitte schön*. Water it down, water it down. *Vielen Dank*.

I stood rapidly sipping the drink as concertgoers in tails and ballgowns flooded into the neoclassical atrium, red-faced, chortling. I'd heard it wasn't too hard to find hash in Austria, and I scrutinized the crowd, trying to ascertain which among these ticketholders was most likely to be holding.

There was a guy who looked perfectly alienated, unshaven, hair mussed and arguing with himself under his breath, who seemed like an okay candidate, but before I could approach, I was pulled into a bear hug I couldn't escape.

—Buddy boy, my father said, letting me go some seconds later.

—Hey Dad.

He was decked out in Brooks Brothers with a pointy black bowtie and ten-pleat broadcloth shirt. My mother waited beside him. She wore a plain navy dress she'd owned my whole life under an undyed alpaca wrap. I leaned in, held her shoulder, and gave her a kiss on the cheek.

—How are you?

—A bit jet-lagged, my mother winced. —But your father suffered the worst of it. He thinks there may have been cornstarch in the schnitzel he ate on the plane.

—All better now, my old man kneaded his forehead. —This is pretty incredible, huh?

He did a little flourish.

—You've got great taste, I said. —I just wish Houdini and Turmeric could've been here to enjoy it.

—Who did you end up finding to take care of them?

—They can look after each other.
—Very funny, my mother said. —How's your stomach?
—Not as good as my wife's.
—And where is Emma, my father asked.
—She and her parents were supposed to stop by the Kunsthistorisches Museum. Jane wanted to see Vermeer's *The Art of Painting*. She says the subject looks just like Emma when she was a girl.
—All that walking.
—It's good for her.
—How's the baby holding up?
—Fine, I think. We spent an hour in the Zuckerlwerkstatt last night, so mother and child should be set for the day.
—And how are you two?
—We're great!
—That first year of marriage can be a challenging one, my father said. —And you had a lot going on.
—What do you mean? I think everything went pretty smoothly.

I was looking beyond my parents, eyeing the door for my wife and her clan. More bodies pushed through, stoic and stodgy, determined to find their seats within the Great Hall.

—Lotta Nazis, my father whispered.
—We are all Nazis now, I said.
—Watch it, my mother hissed. —Though speaking of, I finished your manuscript this morning.
—What?

I shot her a look.

—And how exactly did you get your hands on that?
—It came in an email. With good tidings and Chanukah cheer from the desk of Sofia Cutler Inc.

—Jesus Christ. It's only a first draft! I did not give her permission to share it.

—Well I'm glad she did. It's nice, my mother paused. —Perhaps a bit overembellished.

—It's a novel, I said. —It's meant to entertain.

—I can appreciate that . . . But why did you have to put me in such an awkward position with the headmaster?

—To build suspense. To create more context for the rising angst and animus.

—I thought there was plenty enough already. And don't you think you went somewhat overboard describing his final moments? What if someone got the wrong idea? Death is so personal. If I'd ended up raped or poisoned or bludgeoned or killed, would you have portrayed it in as much detail?

—I would've never forgiven myself.

—I'm your mother after all.

—Mom, I said. —It's tongue-in-cheek.

—Well I'm just grateful nothing like that actually *did* happen. Nothing *could* happen, you know. You saw how old Dr. Masterson was. He was just fooling around. We drank tea.

—And I drank *einspänners* with his mistress, my father interjected. —Now she was a hot piece. You should've had us fool around! That's a rumor I wouldn't have minded circulating.

—You read it?

—Your mom filled me in on the particulars. You should include a summarization of our basement digs, by the way. That dungeon was pretty nice. Wish we could get Carrara marble tiles at Sliver Orchard.

A squall of brisk yuletide air drafted through the entryway. Emma leaned on her mother's arm. Her father held the door for them. I waved.

—Fam-i-ly, Michael called.

They waltzed over, and we all exchanged hugs and greetings. My father-in-law in his Thom Browne overcoat and a new blue-and-white Charvet tie dappled with Stars of David. In overlapping, tiny embroidered stitches it said, *SLAVA VSIM!*, dozens of times.

—I'm sorry we're late, Emma puffed. —I was on the phone with the insurance company.

—On New Year's Day?

—HR submitted my maternity leave paperwork wrong. They thought I gave birth last calendar year. And they still had our address listed as Tenth Street. They didn't know we'd moved upstate.

—Classic, I rolled my eyes. —I can't believe we have to trust a private bureaucracy with your health care.

—At least we have insurance. Imagine if I'd gotten pregnant before I'd interviewed at the museum. They never would've hired me. Do you think all the weed I smoked will give the baby cognitive impairment?

—No. I think it will hone creativity and antiauthoritarian fervor. Lead a new revolution.

—All right, calm down.

I placed my hand on Emma's stomach.

—I'm calm, I said.

My wife sighed.

—Emmeline, my father cooed. —How's the little one?

—Good, she chirped. —Do you want to feel? She's awfully fussy today.

—Wouldn't want to ruin my appetite, my father laughed.

The house lights dimmed, came back on.

—Does everyone have their tickets, Jane inquired.

She was wearing a Dries Van Noten hand-painted gown. I patted the breast of my jacket. My father straightened my tie. He pulled and snapped my lapels.

—Are you nervous?

—No.

—Do you think you're ready for the baby?

—Sure, I said. —Anyway, we've still got two months. Plenty of time to brush up on the literature.

—What are you going to say when you're berated for the very act of conception?

—What are you talking about?

—Don't you remember when you'd get upset? You'd blame us for bringing you into this evil, unforgiving cosmos?

—I'll simply explain that my only alternative would've been wasting away in solitude in Coney Island while the world burned. Would my child really have wanted that life for me?

—When I was in high school . . .

—In your younger and more vulnerable years.

—Right, my father agreed. —In sex-ed class, or hygiene, whatever they called it, they asked us what we were most afraid of, in terms of having a kid. All the guys said they didn't want their son to turn out gay. But if I had a son, I said I'd want him to be queer. My biggest fear was being usurped. And had Oedipus been a little, you know, he would've never married his mother.

—Or maybe he would've, Emma advanced. —Maybe he just wanted power.

—Everyone is gay, I said.

—Well don't worry, my wife rested her hands on her stomach. —This one's not going to do anything like that.

—Kids are allowed be themselves today, I said. —It's not like when we were growing up. Our baby will change gender with the tides.

—Usurp or not usurp, my father intoned. —That is the question.

The house lights dimmed again. The lobby was clearing out, and our parents followed suit. Mother and father and father and mother blathering about preschools and vaccination schedules and electronic basinets, bound together, opening and closing their legs, fading into history, and falling toward the future.

I lingered in the winter light.

—What I still don't understand is . . . there was a bullet in the gun . . .

—What gun, Emma asked.

—Your father's Ruger. I woke up that morning on Tenth Street . . . There hadn't been any bullets the night before. But someone had slipped one in a chamber. It saved my life. It killed Springer . . . I can't wrap my head around it. Who put it there?

Emma hesitated.

—I did, she said.

—What?

—I was watching you sleep before I went off to work. You were on the couch. You'd left me alone in my bed, you were drinking again, all that horrible shit had gone down . . . I figured if you wanted a way out, you could have it. Just let us off the hook. You'd always threatened as much. And if you didn't want to be with me. If you didn't want this life . . . That way, there would be no arguing. No pressure. No responsibility. You weren't trapped. I wanted to give you an opportunity . . . if that's what *you* wanted. Thank god it wasn't. Of course, I didn't know I was pregnant at the time . . .

A beat happened. We collapsed in laughter, holding each other by the forearms. I stroked my wife's stomach once more, and the baby kicked, and I shivered in ecstasy.

—Now come on!

—Just another second, I breathed. —Stuff like this . . . You never know . . .

—It's almost time!

But Emma was smiling, really smiling. She held her hand on mine.

—What's time to a pig, I said.

An eternity happened. Then it was normal again.

—We really should find our seats.

—Right, right, you go ahead.

—But you'll miss the opening overture!

—I've got my ticket, don't worry. I just need to use the bathroom. I don't even know how long this will last.

—Jacob!

—I'll see you in a second. Go on, baby. I won't be able to be present if I haven't had a chance to pee.

My wife gave me a look. Then she scurried to the concert hall, oversized Simone Rocha dress trailing under her Italian ballet flats.

I ordered a second Monkey 47 and left a rather un-European tip, nodded to the bartender, and sauntered to the water closet.

I was buzzing, feeling relaxed. I had the place to my lonesome. The floors sparkled. I wondered if they were Carrara and made myself at home in front of a urinal at the farthest corner of the swanky corridor and unzipped.

While I was relieving myself, I patted my jacket again, felt for the ticket neurotically, and when I was sure it was there, extracted another paltry, wrinkled card from my pocket and reread:

*Dear Jacob —*

*I cannot thank you enough for this glorious cannabis plant you and Emma bestowed upon me. It will surely be a green Christmas. Good luck to you three in the New Year!*

*Respectfully,*<br>*Gladys*

I finished and shook.

The booze seemed to be doing its job. Suddenly I was excited to see what a philharmonic was about. I'd only wanted a novel aesthetic experience. If people traveled across the globe for this one, I guessed it couldn't be too bad.

I took a step back, stretched, craned my neck. And there above the plumbing a gilded corner caught my eye. A plaque, about the size of an envelope, was nailed just over the toilet.

It said, MEIN AMT. I scanned the row. Each urinal was adorned with an identical one.

A stall door groaned behind me. I turned around. It hung ajar. There was a long, hard, muffled silence. Then the music began.